WD-B

# hap
# endings

## About the Author

Born in Southampton, England, in 1975, Jon Rance is the author of the bestselling romantic comedy novel, *This Thirtysomething Life*. He graduated with a degree in English Literature from Middlesex University, London, before going travelling and meeting his American wife in Australia. He drinks a lot of tea and spends far too much time gazing off into space.

Please visit his website at www.jonrance.com or connect with him on Twitter @JRance75.

## Also by Jon Rance

*This Twentysomething Life* (A sort-of Prequel Short Story)
*This Thirtysomething Life*

# happy endings

## jon rance

HODDER

First published in Great Britain in 2013 by Hodder & Stoughton
An Hachette UK company

1

Copyright © Jon Rance 2013

The right of Jon Rance to be identified as the Author of
the Work has been asserted by him in accordance with
the Copyright, Designs and Patents Act 1988.

A CIP catalogue record for this title is available from the British Library.

ISBN 978 1 444 77751 2

Typeset by Hewer Text UK Ltd, Edinburgh
Printed and bound by CPI (UK) Ltd, Croydon CR0 4YY

Hodder & Stoughton policy is to use papers that are natural, renewable
and recyclable products and made from wood grown in sustainable
forests. The logging and manufacturing processes are expected to
conform to the environmental regulations of the country of origin.

Hodder & Stoughton Ltd
338 Euston Road
London NW1 3BH

www.hodder.co.uk

To Mum and Dad, for everything

Happiness is the meaning and the purpose of life, the whole aim and end of human existence.

Aristotle

## KATE

'It's about doing something you love,' said Jack. 'Every single day waking up and doing the one thing you know makes you happy.'

'Are you talking about Emma?' said Ed with a pithy smirk.

'Of course,' Jack said with a smile. 'Nothing makes me happier than knowing I get to wake up next to the thing I also get to do.'

'I'm right here,' said Emma with mock indignation.

'That's a compliment,' said Jack.

Emma smiled, leaned across and gave him a kiss.

'I know,' she said. 'It makes me happy too. Sexy and convenient. I'm living the dream.'

We were at the pub around the corner from our little one-bedroom flat just off Balham High Road. The flat Ed and I had been in since university ended and we were thrust completely unprepared into the real world.

It was our weekly Sunday session, something that had just sort of happened. It began after Emma started dating Jack and now it was a part of our lives; intertwined to such a degree than none of us could imagine a Sunday without it. When we were kids it was the Sunday roast, but now, in our mid-twenties and all based in London, it was the pub. Lunch, newspapers and drinks, talking about everything and nothing.

'And what makes you happy?' said Emma, looking at Ed. 'Apart from Kate, obviously.'

I

'Thank you,' I replied with a courteous smile.

Ed sat and looked at us for a moment. This wasn't an easy question for him. Emma wasn't being that serious and she probably didn't care that much about the answer, but she didn't know Ed like I did. I knew it bothered him. Such a strange thing, to imagine that happiness could bother someone. Annoy them, actually. But when you're under as much pressure at work as Ed, happiness is the very last thing you can spend time thinking about. 'I'll let you know when I figure it out,' said Ed.

I reached down and squeezed his leg and he turned and gave me a smile. Just then Ed's phone beeped, as it did most weekends, and he looked down, read a quick email and then excused himself.

'Sorry, work,' said Ed, as though we didn't already know. It was Sunday and, while the rest of the office world was taking its two-day hiatus, Ed's maniac boss was still online and making sure Ed was too. Ed scurried outside.

'And what about you, Kate, what makes you happy?' said Jack.

Jack always started these sorts of conversations. He was a writer and always wanted to go deeper. Ed would talk about the price of stocks, football and work until the cows came home. Emma loved gossiping about which famous person she'd seen recently, what acting roles she was going for next and the latest on any reality show. I would talk about anything except work, but Jack always seemed to go back to the big questions. The meaning-of-life conversations you have when you're seventeen and stoned for the first time with your best friend.

'What makes me happy?' I mused. I took a sip of my white wine and fingered my packet of Marlboro Lights. What did make me happy? It wasn't a simple question. 'This makes me happy,' I said. 'Sitting here on a Sunday with my best friends, feeling like this, drinking, talking, eating and not wanting it to end.'

'Me too,' said Emma. 'I look forward to Sunday more than any other day. I dread Mondays.'

'Why do you dread Mondays?' said Ed, joining us again. 'It isn't like you have to go to work.'

'Oh very droll,' said Emma. 'That's exactly why I dread Mondays, actually, Ed: because it reminds me I don't have a job.'

'Yes you do,' said Jack, always the first one to support Emma and her dreams of being an actress. I suppose with him trying to be a writer, they shared the same pain. 'It's just that your job isn't nine-to-five, and you're constantly auditioning to get rehired.'

'And you'd be absolutely useless in a proper job,' I said, smiling.

'Oh, thanks,' said Emma.

'You're welcome. Now, whose round is it?' I said and we all looked at Ed.

'Just because I earn the most it's suddenly my round. Didn't I get the last one?'

'Stop being such a stingy git and get the drinks in,' I said and then leaned across and gave him a peck on the cheek. 'Love you,' I said with a smile.

'I'll give you a hand,' said Jack.

The boys went off to the bar, via the fruit machine, leaving Emma and I alone for the first time that day. Emma and Kate. Kate and Emma. Best friends since, well, forever. She looked at me with her gorgeous eyes and I knew what she was going to say before she even opened her mouth.

'Have you spoken to him about it?' she said.

'Not yet.'

3

'Oh, Kate, when are you going to do it?'

'I don't know. He's talking about buying a house, putting down roots, getting a promotion at work. I don't think he's going to be into it and we're still young. Plenty of time . . .'

'But, Kate, you've talked about going travelling since we were teenagers. Remember that week in Newquay? That night we sat on the beach looking up at the stars drinking Bacardi Breezers and smoking weed.'

'The badly rolled joint that fell to pieces just after you lit it, you mean?'

'And we had to ask those boys if they could help us skin up, but then you were so drunk you were sick all over that one boy's feet.'

'The one with the flip-flops!'

'Yeah, that one,' she said and we both laughed.

'That was the night I told you I was going to be an actress and the night you told me all about going travelling. You made it sound like something you *had* to do.'

'I do. It's just . . . Now isn't the right time.'

'And when's the right time going to be?'

'I don't know.'

A part of me knew she was right, but I couldn't let myself agree with her. I loved Ed so much and my job was still just about the right side of bearable. I was only twenty-five, part of the London hip-erati; there was plenty of time left to travel. Plus, in a couple of years we'd have more money and we could do it properly.

'I just want you to do what we dreamed about back then.'

'I will, Em, and you will too. I know your big break is just around the corner.'

Emma smiled at me as the boys sat back down again. Ed put our drinks down, while Jack tossed two packets of crisps in the middle of the table. It was a beautiful day outside and the pub was packed with people just like us.

'Jack's got another one,' said Ed, before his phone buzzed again.

'Go on,' said Emma.

Jack sat down next to her and Ed wandered off outside, phone to his ear.

'Where will you celebrate your thirtieth birthday?'

'That one's easy,' said Emma. 'With you lot, in the pub.'

'Kate?' said Jack, looking at me expectantly. 'What about you?'

I didn't know what to say. Four years was a long time.

'Who knows, right? You could be a successful writer. Emma could be a world-famous actress. Ed and I could be . . .' I stopped, not quite sure what to say next.

'Anything you want,' said Emma, finishing my sentence for me.

'Right,' I said. 'Anything we want.'

# four years later
## january

## KATE

'Love you,' said Ed, holding my hands gently in his.

'Love you too,' I said. A wash of salty tears, which I'd been trying my best to keep in check until I was at least on the plane, suddenly leaked out and slid down my face. I pitied the unlucky person who had to sit next to me, a blubbery backpacker bound for Bangkok, for twelve hours. 'I should probably get a move on. My flight leaves in forty minutes and I still have to go through security.'

We were at the departures gate at Heathrow: the final goodbye hurdle. People walked past, apprehensive-looking parents with children who clung tightly to their teddy bears, oblivious solo travellers playing with their iPhones, businessmen and flight crew, while Ed and I stood motionless, caught somewhere between the past and the future. It was why I loved airports, because they were neither a part of where you'd been or where you were going. They were a separate entity. A sort of purgatory between states of being that held the promise of adventure and freedom.

'I just . . .'

'What, Ed?'

'I just wish you weren't going, that's all.'

The past week had been the Olympic Games of emotional blackmail. Ed had been quiet, depressed, loud, obnoxious, loving and every other possible state in the hope something would break me down and stop me from leaving. Now he was being morose. His whole being was dripping with sullenness.

Ever since that blustery November evening when I'd sat him down and explained I had to go travelling otherwise I'd regret it for the rest of my life, he'd had the same strained expressions of annoyance and incredulity. He couldn't understand why I had to do it and, like a lot of men when placed in an uncomfortable emotional situation, he made it all about him.

'Is it something I've done?' were his first words.

'Is this about me?' were his second.

'How can I change your mind?' were his third.

I tried to explain it had nothing to do with him: I needed this for me. I conceived the idea after Nan died and left me some money; it wasn't much, but sufficient for a year away and just enough left over for my half of the mortgage. I'd realised that, at twenty-nine, if I didn't do something a bit impetuous right away, that would be it. My life would tumble headlong into middle-age and the usual suspects of marriage, kids and a fridge door full of mundane lists that would run my life forever. I needed time to breathe. When I was young I thought I was special and would do something amazing with my life, and then I grew up. I wanted that feeling back. I wanted to be amazing again.

The simple truth was I wasn't completely happy. It wasn't one thing in particular, but the combination of every aspect of my life not equating to a big, happy whole. My job in public relations was stressful and the initial excitement I'd felt when I started the job after university had been replaced with a depressing feeling of inevitability. I looked at the people higher up the corporate ladder and I didn't want to become them: crushed by the weight of a career that sustained a life I wasn't even sure I wanted. Every tiny facet of our lives seemed so depressingly settled in a way I hadn't ever intended. I needed to get away. I needed a break. And, of course, there was the tiny fact that I'd really thought Ed would come with me.

'I'll be back before you know it. It will fly by,' I said, trying my best to keep our last few moments together as civil and upbeat as possible. I wanted Ed to be happy for me. I wanted to see a spark of something in his eyes other than the lingering disappointment and bitterness that had kept me awake for the past week.

'It will for you. You're off travelling the world, while I'm going to be stuck here in depressing, miserable London, working like a dog for twelve hours a day just waiting for you to come back.'

'You could have come too,' I said, finally losing my patience as he made the same cloyingly annoying face he'd been making for the previous two months.

'You know why I can't come,' said Ed in that oh-so-patronising voice of his.

I hated it when I felt like I was talking to city banker Ed. I imagined him at work in his giant phallic office, shouting at other miserable-looking suits and telling people to buy this and sell that, while nervous-looking secretaries served up coffee and biscuits, terrified of being scolded because the FTSE was down against the Yen. It wasn't the Ed I knew and the Ed I loved.

'But don't you see. All the reasons why you're saying no are the same reasons why I have to leave. I know you love me – I love you too – but it isn't about that. I can't keep going along pretending everything's fine when it isn't. I don't want to wake up at forty and blame you for me not doing this. I want to be happy and this is going to make me happy.'

'So what you're saying is I don't make you happy anymore,' said Ed glibly.

'Don't be like that, Ed, please. I know this isn't what you had planned for us and you think it's a giant waste of time, but I don't. Look, I don't want to leave on an argument; can you please just be happy for me?'

'Promise me one thing,' he said, a sudden cloud of vulnerability descending upon his face. He reminded me of one of those children of the war, fleeing London during the blitz for the safety of the countryside. A sad little schoolboy standing by a steam engine while his parents cried and handed him a jam sandwich for the journey. All he needed was a raggedy old teddy bear under his arm and a pair of short grey trousers. 'Promise me you won't change.'

I suppose what he meant was, don't cheat on me and not come back. I had no intention of cheating on Ed though and even if I was I wouldn't have needed to go to such extreme measures. Plenty of men at work had shown enough interest in me and hinted that if I ever wanted to turn public relations into private relations, they would happily oblige. My trip wasn't about men. It wasn't about sex, Ed or having a quarter-life crisis, it was about me. It was something I had to do. For me. 'Of course I'm not going to change. It's just a six-month holiday, Ed, not six years in a kibbutz.'

'Good, you'd better not. I want to marry the girl you are right now,' said Ed, forcing a smile.

'Come here you two,' I said, turning to Jack and Emma, who had been standing dutifully behind Ed, waiting for their moment to say goodbye. We'd done everything with them over the last five years. They were our couple of choice: the two additional sides who made us a perfect square. They waded in and we had a group hug. Four late-twenty-somethings at Heathrow airport; it could have been a Richard

Curtis film – except for the distinctly un-romantic-comedy air wafting towards me from Ed.

Emma had been my best friend since primary school and the one person who when I said I wanted to go travelling didn't scoff or look disappointed, but supported it wholeheartedly. She encouraged me from day one because she knew what it meant. I would miss her and our chats terribly, Saturday mornings at Starbucks catching up on the week, bitching about the boys and gossiping about everything and nothing.

'I love you all,' I said, trying to stem the rising mass of tears that were forming a less-than-orderly queue behind my eyes.

'Just make sure you're back in time for my wedding,' said Emma, tears welling up in her eyes. 'You're a bridesmaid, remember?'

'I'll be back by then. Promise. And fingers crossed for the film.'

I gave Jack a quick peck on the cheek and Emma a long tearful hug before I took one last look at Ed. I was afraid I'd forget what he looked like, which was crazy because I'd seen him every day for the past eight years. But it felt like once I stepped onto the plane his face would be wiped from my memory forever. The thick, dark hair with the schoolboy haircut I publicly mocked, but secretly quite liked. The steely blue-grey eyes, the long, thin nose, the high cheek bones, the slightly narrow mouth and the chin dimple; the sort of face that would look good on a coin. His weekend-casual outfit, which wasn't actually that casual, as though he could never quite let go of his weekday self: navy blue V-neck jumper over white work shirt, khaki chinos, boat shoes and a long wool coat. Ed didn't really do casual. At weekends, while I would slouch around the house in pyjama bottoms and old T-shirts, Ed wouldn't go less than a pair of dark jeans and a freshly ironed polo shirt.

I filed a mental snapshot and gave Ed one last kiss before I turned around and walked away, too afraid to look back. Too afraid the life I was leaving behind was not only better than the one I was heading towards, but also that it wouldn't be there when I got home.

As the plane turned to begin its take-off, I looked out of the window. It was a typical drab winter's day at Heathrow. Sullen clouds drifted across the runway, making everything seem like a dream. England's green and pleasant land was hiding behind a smokescreen of cheerlessness. I kept thinking back to what Ed said in the airport about not changing. I promised I wouldn't, but I knew it was a promise I wouldn't be able to keep. As the plane took off, slowly gaining altitude above London, fighting through the dark, leaden clouds to the bluer skies above, I began to cry. For months all I had wanted was to be on that plane. I had been so excited to leave and begin my adventure, but finally, sitting alone, all I felt was a terrible sickness and a craving for what I was leaving behind. I had wanted the change. I had wanted to feel the ripple of its excitement touch me again and move me the way it used to. I had wanted to travel, but now I was terrified it was a decision I might regret for the rest of my life.

## ED

'Look on the bright side,' said Emma from the front seat of her Mini Cooper. 'It's only six months and in the big scheme of things that's nothing.'

I was crammed in the back like a piece of luggage: the price of having trendy friends with tiny cars. My legs were bent at a funny angle and my back twisted so I looked like I was skiing, but not in a cool way. Still, it was better than the journey there with Kate and her backpack squashing me against the window. Outside, the sun finally lost its battle with the gloomy, grey clouds and rain began to pelt against the window.

'She's right, mate,' joined in Jack in his diluted Australian accent. 'She'll be back before you know it.'

'Right,' I muttered back.

I was trying to work out why I felt so shit about Kate leaving. I mean, obviously, just her leaving was enough, but it was more than that. I was hurt and angry. Really fucking angry, actually. Why did she need to travel the world? I'd promised her on more than one occasion we'd eventually go to Thailand, Australia and Timbuktu, if that's what she wanted. I really thought she'd come to her senses and realise everything she needed was right here. I think that was why I was hurting. It wasn't that she was leaving, but that she was leaving me. I was rejected in favour of a needless holiday and it didn't make any sense.

'So,' said Emma, carrying on as though my girlfriend of nearly eight years, the girl I loved, lived with and hoped to one day marry, hadn't just hopped on a plane to Thailand. 'I have this meeting tonight, Ed, with the director for this new film – the next *Four Weddings* type of thing. Rhys Connelly's already signed on. The script's amazing.' She looked at me in the mirror and then crunched a gear into place. The Mini suddenly lurched forward as the engine roared and then we wobbled momentarily into the next lane. I hung on for dear life.

'Ed probably doesn't want to hear about the film, love,' interjected Jack, as always the thoughtful one, the mediator. Emma and Jack, the thespian and the wordsmith, our bohemian mates from west London and my support system in Kate's absence.

'Oh, shit, sorry, I . . .'

'No, no its fine, Em, really,' I said, smiling back. 'Honestly.'

It wasn't fine though, was it? My life felt like it had been torn into little pieces and then put back together with some crappy Sellotape in all the wrong places.

We were soon outside my house in Wandsworth. The rain had briefly let up and I was leaning on the open window next to Jack.

'Seriously, Ed, are you going to be OK? We can come in for a bit if you want,' said Emma. 'Have a cup of tea?'

'Of course he's going to be all right,' said Jack, with a brisk, manly grin. 'Aren't you, mate?'

'Yeah, course,' I said and smiled. 'Now you two bugger off. I'll see you soon.' I tapped the door and they drove off, the Union Jack on the roof disappearing through the leafy streets of my salubrious pocket of London.

I stood outside my house and sighed. The two-bedroom Victorian terrace with sash windows and a little blue door had cost us a fortune. It was minutes from the Thames and had stripped hardwood floors, original iron fire-places and a little garden – it was the house we'd made our perfect little home. The final piece of the jigsaw, or so I'd thought.

I took out my front door key and let myself in, popped the keys in the little tray on the sideboard and stood for a moment. It was terrifyingly quiet. The noise I was going to have to get used to for the next six months. I looked along the hallway and saw the flowers Kate bought last week. They hung down, limply grazing the top of the vase, pathetically drooping as if in a yoga pose. But they weren't, they were slowly dying and in a couple of days would be tossed in the bin and forgotten.

Waking up alone was strange. The bed had never felt so big and in a moment of fitful sleep, just before I properly woke up, I forgot she was gone. It came back to me in a horrifying flash when I reached across to cuddle her, but all I felt was a cold sheet. I looked across and there was her pillow, puffed up and untouched like something straight out of the Habitat catalogue. Kate was an active sleeper and usually by morning most of the sheet and duvet was pulled and stretched to her side of the bed and her pillow was often on the floor. Now, in its current state, it looked out of place. A sad reminder she was gone, and even though it annoyed me how she routinely turned our bed into a jumble sale pile, without it I felt empty.

Despite it being only six o'clock, I decided to head into work early. The tube was quieter than usual. I even got a seat to read my copy of the *Metro*, instead of having to try and grasp the headlines while being jostled and pushed against the rubbery rolls of a fellow commuter. By the time I got off at Bank station, I actually felt quite relaxed and a bit Zen. I grabbed a large cappuccino and a bacon roll – the breakfast of champions – and headed into work. Even my office floor was bereft of workers; a tired-looking cleaner was emptying the last few bins and then my immediate manager and the Director of Investments, Hugh Whitman, a balding man in his late fifties, strode past me towards his corner office.

'Early today, Hornsby, eh. Trouble with the missus?'

'Something like that, sir.'

He chortled and kept on walking, leather briefcase in hand and stomach jutting out like a Swiss mountain face. Hugh ran the office with the cut-throat ruthlessness of an army general. If you did well you were rewarded, but one mistake, one black mark against you and you were gone. Despite being a working-class speck in a sky of upper-middle-class employees, I'd stuck around for seven years, slowly easing my way up the banking ladder towards safety.

I turned on my PC and checked my email. As I drank my cappuccino and ate my bacon roll, I began working on the building blocks of an idea. In six months I could get a promotion. Without Kate and all the distractions of a relationship, I could work harder, longer and better. Maybe Kate pissing off across the globe could be a good thing after all. Kate had her dreams and I had mine. She wanted to ponce about in South East Asia with a bunch of drop-outs, hippies and graduates trying to find themselves, while I would stay behind and make sure everything she needed, we needed, was still in place and working better when she got back. It would also help keep my mind off what she was doing and with whom.

By ten o'clock the office was a tornado of energy: people were working hard, making and losing millions. It was like a beautiful symphony, every aspect working together to produce a capitalist masterpiece. Our floor was an open-plan football field of computers, telephones, fax machines and men in expensive suits shouting at each other for twelve hours a day. However, on that Monday morning at ten o'clock an office of fifty bankers all stopped working as a girl walked across the floor. She was beautiful: every man's dream in a grey business suit and high heels. All eyes, including mine, stopped scrolling through emails and watched her walk, slowly, gracefully, with Harriet from HR, until they stopped quite suddenly at my desk.

'Ed, this is Georgina Hays. She's new and going to be shadowing you for a few days. Make her feel at home and keep the vultures off her back, will you?' said Harriet with a motherly smile. Harriet was the office matriarch, head of human resources and feared and loved in equal measure by every employee. I suddenly felt like every pair of eyes in the office were on me and when I looked up I realised they were.

'Hi,' said Georgina, shaking my hand briskly and then sitting down next to me. 'Call me Georgie, please.' She had the poshest voice I'd ever heard, which was no mean feat considering I worked in an office packed to the rafters with Oxbridge alumni. She was stunning. She had long blonde hair – but not just regular blonde, it was pure, clean, almost ethereal – the biggest, bluest eyes and a small, perfectly formed nose with a spattering of freckles. Her face was symmetrical, balanced, refined and she had a flawless body to match.

'Ed, before we start, I just want to say thank you.'

'I haven't done anything yet. I could be awful.'

'I doubt you're awful,' said Georgie with a gorgeous little giggle. 'Uncle Hugh wouldn't have put me with someone awful.'

'Uncle Hugh?'

'Oh, yes, Hugh Whitman is my uncle, but that doesn't change anything. I want you to treat me like you would any other employee.'

'Right, will do,' I said, suddenly terrified of what this training session might lead to. 'Then you'd better get us both a big cup of coffee before we start,' I said with a smile, and she smiled back, probably the most perfect smile I'd ever seen.

The next hour was something of a blur. I learnt that Georgina Elizabeth Hays was twenty-two and grew up in Bath. She attended boarding school in some Hogwartian mansion in the home counties, took a gap year and helped underprivileged children in Peru, went to the University of Cambridge, represented England at youth-level netball, was currently single and trying her hand at the world of banking. When Harriet eventually came to rescue her for some mandatory paperwork, she thanked me with a warm smile and told me she would see me after lunch.

On my way out for a quick bite, I shared the lift with Hugh.

'If you don't mind me asking, sir, why did you put Georgina with me?'

'Because you're the only one I can trust not to bang her senseless, Hornsby. My niece, you see, but mum's the word, eh. Promised I wouldn't let anything happen to her. Take good care of her. No funny business.'

'Of course not, sir, no problem,' I said as we stepped out of the lift.

During the short walk to Pret thoughts of a BLT and images of Georgie in her netball kit clouded my mind. I didn't know if Hugh trusting me was a good thing or not. Was it a slap on the back? A hearty gesture of goodwill that would garner a mutual respect and eventual promotion, or did he just consider me an unattractive, spineless eunuch?

The afternoon wore on much like the morning had, with Georgie and me in close proximity, knees occasionally knocking together under the desk, while I tried to give her a rundown of what I did on a daily basis. It was a little after six when we started to pack away for the night.

'Thanks so much for today, Ed, you've been brill.'

'Oh, no worries, my pleasure.' A few co-workers walked by, loitered for a moment, pretending to fiddle with scarves, and then smiled at Georgie and gave me a cursory, 'Night, Ed' before they waltzed away. 'Does that annoy you?'

'What?'

'Men ogling you all day. Making lame excuses so they can try and peek down your top.'

'Oh that. You get used to it.'

'It must get a bit annoying though,' I said, grabbing my bag and scarf.

'Sometimes, but mostly they're harmless and it's flattering when people find me attractive.'

'As if they wouldn't,' I said without thinking. Georgie flashed me a smile. 'I . . . umm . . . didn't mean anything by that, sorry.'

'Of course, and bravo, I didn't see you peek down my top all day,' said Georgie with a cheeky smile. I suddenly and without warning went a deep shade of red, my face swelter-ing in embarrassment. 'Oh, Ed, I was only joking.'

'Right, well, see you tomorrow?' I said, wrapping my scarf quickly around my neck with Hugh's words ringing in my ears, 'no funny business'.

'Yes, yes, can't wait and honestly, thank you so much. I was so nervous this morning.' I smiled and started to walk away before Georgie stopped me. 'Actually, do you have any plans for tonight?'

I was caught off guard. I didn't know what to say. Did I have any plans? The answer was a definite no, unless plans involved getting a curry, a four pack of lager and watching television on my own, which I'm sure is the very definition of a sad twat.

'No plans.'

'Then, and just to say thank you, how about a quick drink?'

Had she actually said that? The gorgeous, ultra-posh new girl at work was asking me out for a drink? I stammered like a far less attractive cross between Colin Firth's King George and Hugh Grant at his upper-class bumbling best.

'I . . . I . . . err . . . umm . . .'

'I don't have many friends in London at the mo. All off doing the travelling thing or their MAs and you seem like a nice bloke and Hugh trusts you, so you can't be that dodgy.'

'You'd be surprised,' I said for no apparent reason and then I laughed like a bloody idiot.

'Then let's have a drink and you can show me how dodgy you are,' she said with a delicious wide-faced smile.

I thought about it for a second. It wasn't cheating or even technically wrong. I'd gone out for copious work drinks over the years and yes, admittedly, none of them had been only with women, but still, it wasn't like anything would happen. For a start, I would never cheat on Kate and, secondly, Georgie would never, in a million years, fancy someone like me. It was just a drink. Mates. Co-workers.

'Sure, why not.'

'Fab. I have to pop to the toilet, back in a jiff,' she said and then skipped off.

I watched her for a moment. Her perfectly formed little bottom was squeezed into a tight-fitting grey skirt above long, slender legs that curved towards a pair of black high-heeled shoes. A couple of men stopped to gaze at her on their way out and ran their salacious eyes over her pert, ripe little body. A knot of fear unexpectedly formed in my stomach and began to work its way towards my brain, making me feel nauseous: the terrifying fear that maybe I was just like all of those other men, and all it would take for me to lose everything would be a solitary word from her soft, beautiful lips and the promise of a glimpse at what lay beneath her glossy white blouse.

## JACK

'Ready?' said Emma, walking into the room, fiddling with a pair of earrings and looking flustered.

Emma always got nervous when she had business dinners. Of course, it wasn't me who was trying to get a part in a film that could change the course of my whole life. I was nervous too, but trying to keep it together for her. She had spent years treading the boards, getting small parts in small plays, a few lines on television and even a couple of call backs for lead roles, but nothing like this. This was huge. This would make her career and change our lives forever.

'Just finishing up, love,' I said, closing down my laptop.

'Do you think Ed's going to be all right?' said Emma, zipping herself into a little black dress she'd treated herself to from Reiss, and looking every inch the film star: cropped blonde hair, a beautiful face with Audrey Hepburn features, big green eyes, full, curvaceous lips and the most perfectly petite body.

'I hope so. He seemed a bit lost in the car.'

'He did, didn't he, poor thing. Although if I lost you for six months,' she said, looking across at me with a tender smile. 'I think I'd be depressed too.'

'You never have to worry about that. I'm not going anywhere.'

'You'd better not, or—' said Emma with a smile, making a scissor action with her fingers and nodding toward my groin.

Emma had been telling me to get ready for the last hour, but I was lost in thought over my book. I needed this novel to be The One because I'd already decided it would be my last attempt before I gave up and got a proper job.

I needed to prove to Emma, and more importantly to myself, that I could do something worthwhile. Ed told me frequently about jobs he could get me in the City, where I could earn four times the amount I made at To Bean or Not to Bean, the shitty Shakespearean-themed café I managed, serving ridiculously named coffees like The Taming of the Brew, the Caramel Macbeth and, my personal favourite, the Antony and Cappuccino.

I didn't want to work in a dreary, soulless office, but it would give us a life. At that moment we were living off hand-outs from Emma's parents and in the flat they owned. My life wasn't mine, or as Ed said in the pub last week: 'You're a man, Jack. You need to be a man. To provide. To have some-thing to measure your success against. Instead you're being emasculated by her in-laws and a job you hate. It's time to face reality, stop living a pipe dream and get a proper job.' I was finally coming to the conclusion that perhaps he was right.

'How do I look?' said Emma, bouncing across the room, a ball of nervous energy as she gave me a kiss on the cheek.

'Stunning,' I said, grabbing her around the waist.

As we headed out of the door, hand-in-hand, and towards an expensive restaurant in Soho, I looked at Emma and a terrifying thought suddenly popped into my head. Maybe after dinner, we wouldn't ever be like that again.

Matt Wallace was from Glasgow, had directed two very successful films already and was being touted, along with Rhys Connelly, as one of Britain's brightest young things.

He didn't look that bright or young though as he sat opposite us: he was bald, probably nearer to forty than thirty, with ashen skin and a pair of tatty blue jeans and a creased green shirt.

'It's yours,' he'd said as soon as he sat down.

'Excuse me?' said Emma, although we'd both heard him quite clearly.

'The role of Sarah. It's yours. If you want it, that is.'

Emma started squealing; she cried, hugged me, kissed me, kissed Matt and I fell to pieces. I was elated for her, but also suddenly petrified that our lives were about to change dramatically and that, as much as I wanted the change, I might get left behind in the scramble.

'Oh my God, I can't believe it, really?' she said about twenty times.

'Emma, you're going to be amazing. From the moment I saw you at auditions you were my first choice,' said Matt. 'I've asked Rhys to join us. He should be here any minute.'

My heart began to ache and suddenly I didn't want to be in that restaurant with Matt and Rhys Connelly. My chest tightened and I needed some fresh air. Before I had the chance to go, a hum of muttered voices reverberated around the room and when I looked up Rhys Connelly was striding confidently towards us. A flash of paparazzi cameras snapped through the restaurant window like small fireworks.

Matt made the introductions and Rhys sat opposite us. I reached across and put my hand on Emma's leg. Rhys Connelly got his big break in Matt's first film, *On Primrose Hill*, as the dashing lead in a syrupy romantic comedy. Then he traipsed across the Atlantic, starred in a huge American production and became a household name. Rhys was tall, ridiculously handsome and had the swagger and confidence you'd expect from a film star.

After some polite chit-chat, Emma excused herself to go to the toilet and so it was just Matt, Rhys and me.

'So, what do you do?' said Rhys, looking at me.

What did I do? I wanted to be a writer, but as much as I wanted to say it, I couldn't, because their first question would be the same question I always got. Oh, what have you had published? And the answer would be nothing. The difference between being a writer and a published writer was the same as between being Rhys Connelly now or Rhys Connelly two years ago, before the fame. I hated moments like these.

'I . . . umm . . . manage a coffee shop,' I said.

Both Rhys and Matt tried to look vaguely interested or impressed, probably not impressed, but I could see what they were thinking. Emma's getting married to a coffee shop manager? That isn't going to last.

'Which one? Maybe I know it,' said Matt.

'To Bean or Not to Bean?'

'That is the question,' said Rhys, laughing.

'It's just around the corner from the Globe,' I added quietly.

'Always packed with tourists,' said Matt. 'I prefer some-where a bit quieter.'

I nodded and smiled because I didn't know what else to say.

A waitress suddenly appeared, took our drinks order with a nervous smile, before returning quickly with a tray of drinks and a plate of starters. I took a quick sip of beer, picked up a small tart and shoved it in my mouth.

'You must be so proud of her,' said Matt.

'Of course, yeah, over the moon.'

'I'm really looking forward to working with her,' said Rhys in his sexy Welsh accent.

Everything about the man screamed sexy bastard: the perfect amount of stubble, the messy long hair that somehow didn't look too messy, the casual jeans, the piercing blue eyes and the impossibly square jaw.

'And you're OK with the nudity?' said Matt suddenly.

The nudity? Emma hadn't mentioned any nudity. The idea of millions of people seeing her naked made me sick to my stomach, but what could I say? I knew being an actress brought with it a whole smorgasbord of unappetising side dishes I had to pretend I liked, whether I did or not, but she'd never done nude before. I guess it was part of the deal and there was nothing I could do about it.

'No worries.'

'It can be a bit daunting for partners who aren't in the business,' said Matt.

'Sure,' I replied, taking another sip of my beer and grabbing another tart, needing something to settle my churning stomach.

'And I'll do my best to be professional with the sex scenes,' said Rhys, with a humble smile.

His best? Was that a good thing or a bad thing? Was his best his best or his worst? I smiled, but my stomach was turning and twisting with an uneasy jealousy. It wasn't a feeling or emotion I was used to. I wasn't the jealous sort, the typical over-bearing bloke who tried to control every single thing his girlfriend did in the hope she wouldn't leave me. It wasn't me and I didn't want those feelings drilling their way down into the bottom of my stomach and setting up camp. But this was Rhys Connelly, Britain's best-looking bloke – what else was I supposed to feel?

It reminded me of the time I went to the fairground with Dad when I was twelve. I'd asked him a dozen times if I could go on this one particular ride. It looked terrifying, but thrilling at the same time. Finally, just before we left, he said we could go on it. We sat together in the small metal pod and as the man buckled us in the adrenalin and anticipation pumped through my body. I really thought I wanted to go on that ride. But once it got started, spinning around and around, going faster and faster, I closed my eyes and just wanted it to be over. I held on to Dad's arm and cried until it stopped. It had seemed so exciting, but once it started, I couldn't wait to get off and put my feet back on solid ground again.

Emma came back and sat down. I looked at her and something inside of me felt numb. She had a twinkle in her eye. She'd finally found her place in the world. She was going to be a film star and there was nothing I could do about it. She'd do the film and fall in love with Rhys, while I'd be the bloke she used to go out with before she became famous. Every celebrity has one of us. A year from now I'd be doing interviews with Sunday tabloids to pay the rent on my studio flat in Hackney.

'Excuse me,' I said, wiping the corner of my mouth with my napkin before getting up and walking off towards the toilet.

As I crossed the room, zigzagging my way between the maze of tables full to the brim with successful, happy people, all laughing and enjoying themselves, I couldn't help but feel a deep sense of fear. I briefly looked back towards Emma and she was popping the cork of a champagne bottle. She squealed with delight as its frothy, expensive foam exploded and then slid down the sides of the bottle like lava and onto her hands. I looked away and kept on walking towards the toilet. Despite being in a room full of people in the centre of London, I'd never felt so completely and utterly alone.

## EMMA

Something was definitely wrong with Jack. Ever since our dinner in Soho, he'd been super quiet, wrapped up in his own thoughts and even more engrossed in his writing than usual. It's not hard to tell when something's on his mind because he shuts down – a typical bloody man I suppose. I asked him several times if he was all right and he gave the bog-standard reply with the mandatory furrowed brow, 'Fine, Em.' But he wasn't. He wasn't fine.

I would have been more concerned, but I just didn't have the time. Matt had sent over the full script for *The Hen Weekend* and I'd been at Starbucks ever since. God, it was so bloody brilliant. There I was, drinking my café lattes, cracking up and feeling for the first time in my life like a proper actress. I'm absolutely in love with it. It's funny, touching, thought-provoking and just a great romantic comedy. And I was going to be in it!

I also got to work with Matt and Rhys, who were both so generous with their time and ridiculously talented. It was surreal at first, calling Rhys with a question. Rhys Connelly, a world-famous film star, on the front pages of national newspapers, and I had his phone number. We were mates, sort of, and soon we'd be naked and kissing. I hadn't told Jack yet, for obvious reasons, and also because I wasn't sure how I felt about it myself. It was Rhys Connelly for God's sake! Britain's sexiest man and I was going to be canoodling with him. Millions of girls throughout the land would no doubt swap places with me in an instant, but it just made me uncomfortable and I felt awful for Jack. It was just another part of the job and it meant nothing, but it was hard to wedge into a conversation that, oh, by the way, in the middle of the film Rhys was going to be kissing my breasts and, shortly after that, most of the English-speaking world was going to see me completely naked, but it's nothing, really . . . more tea?

I was at Starbucks having another read through, but I couldn't focus. Outside, thick black clouds made everything gloomy and dark. I was annoyed Jack had to work like he did every bloody Saturday. It was better when Kate was here because we'd often go shopping, get a drink or just wander around London, but she was gone and I was at a loose end. I'd never thought of myself as a loose end sort of person before. I was the end people generally hung on to. So, with nothing better to do, I decided to pop in and see Jack at work. Perhaps we could have lunch and maybe, away from the confines of our cramped Notting Hill flat, he'd tell me why he was acting so un-Jack-like.

To Bean or Not to Bean was a shoddy place a few streets away from the Globe theatre. It was decorated like an old Shakespearean set and filled exclusively with tourists. When I walked in the café was in the middle of an influx of Japanese tourists, all shouting their orders in broken English and pointing at the menu. I looked around until I saw Jack, hastily trying to get his apron on and take orders. He looked tired, miserable and irate, but still bloody gorgeous: short blond hair, slightly sad blue eyes, cheek bones to die for and those arms, so big and safe. The sexiest thing about Jack though, and one of the things that had attracted me to him in the first place, was that he didn't know it.

I waited for the queue to die down before I found him behind the counter.

'Bit busy now, love,' he said as soon as he saw me.

'Time for a quick Taming of the Brew?'

I smiled. He looked annoyed.

'I'm rushed off my feet. We have two staff members out and we're expecting half of Texas any time soon.'

'Five minutes and I'll even buy you a coffee. What's the special of the day?'

'Our famous Bard Blend.'

'Famous where exactly?'

'I don't know. Five minutes,' he said tersely.

He poured us two cups of the Bard Blend and we sat outside. The streets were buzzing with people as we sat in the small area on the pavement where if you craned your neck and looked really hard you could just make out the top-left-hand corner of the Globe theatre. Inside, the horde of Japanese tourists were busy drinking their coffees, eating their traditional English scones and reading their Shakespearean literature diligently, while outside Jack was giving off a distinctly cold and unloving air.

'Are you going to tell me?'

'Tell you what?'

'What's on your mind and why you're acting like you hate me.'

'I don't hate you, Em.'

'Then why are you being all weird and quiet? Is this to do with the film?'

Jack did this thing when he was nervous. He would chew on his lip and his right eye would twitch ever so slightly.

'Of course not,' he said, but I could tell he was lying.

'Then what is it, Jack? I need something,' I said, reaching across and placing my hand over his.

'It's . . .' He looked at me for a moment and it seemed like he was going to say something, but then he stopped himself. 'It's nothing, love, just tired.'

I didn't know what to say. I didn't want to push him, but I knew something was wrong and it annoyed me that he couldn't tell me. It was the one thing about Jack that really pissed me off. I wouldn't have cared if it was about the film or whatever it was, I just couldn't handle the pent-up silence, the mawkish refusal to talk it out. To me feelings were like rubbish in a bin. If they weren't emptied routinely they would start to overflow and make an awful stench. Jack would keep stuffing them in, pushing them down deeper and deeper, never giving them the chance to clear out and start over fresh and clean.

I was deciding how far to push him, but before I could say anything else, a stream of loud, brash Americans flooded around the corner and swamped us. My moment had come and gone.

'I really need to get back,' he said, giving me a quick kiss before disappearing back inside.

I was left alone, still no wiser as to why Jack was behaving like a spoilt child and with half a cup of famous but foul-tasting coffee. I cursed Kate for being gone, but then my phone buzzed and when I looked down it was Matt.

I was four when I decided to become an actress. According to my mother, I ran into her bedroom dressed up in a wonderful jumble of costumes and said, 'Mummy, I'm putting on a play, five minutes please,' and then I acted for the first time. It probably wasn't very good. I was four and I had made the whole thing up, but after that day I was always playing dress-up and acting out scenes from television. I was quite a precocious child, probably very annoying, but I always knew what I wanted. I wanted to act, to perform, to have hundreds, thousands and, maybe one day, millions of pairs of eyes just on me.

As a child I just needed my mother, but as I got older and began acting in school plays, I craved it more and more. I studied drama at university in Bristol and when I left I thought it was only a matter of time before I got my big break. That's the thing about dreams, you think because you've wanted it for such a long time that it will just happen. It has to. You forget, of course, that a million other people are thinking exactly the same thing. I got a couple of jobs here and there, but eight years later I was still scratching around the dregs of the acting world.

When I was offered the lead role in *The Hen Weekend*, it was like every moment of my life, every second of doubt, regret and uncertainty, was justified. It all meant something. My biggest fear had always been that I was so focused on acting that if I didn't make it my whole life would have been a waste. However, getting that role vindicated every single thing I'd ever done.

So why when I was so deliriously happy about it was Jack so miserable? Was it something I did? Said? Didn't say? Could he be jealous that I'd finally achieved my dream and he hadn't? We met as struggling artists, both intent on making it in our chosen fields and somehow one of us achieving it broke the balance and sank the ship. Our joint failure had been the glue that kept us together, but maybe now it was tearing us apart.

'A whole week?'

'I do it for all my projects. It's fun. We stay at this incredibly old mansion in Berkshire. We get to bond as a group and start working on the connections between the characters. It's a good chance to have a few beers and relax before the hard slog really begins,' said Matt.

'I understand. It's just, Jack, I . . .'

'We need you there, Emma. We can't do it without you.'

'Of course I'll be there.'

'Great, fantastic. I'll email you the details and travel arrangements. We'll send a car to pick you up on the day. It's going to be wonderful. Trust me, yeah.'

'I do,' I said, and then we hung up.

A week away from Jack was going to be tough. Since we'd started dating five years ago, and moved in together a year later, we'd barely been apart. I was excited though. A week with the cast at a mansion in the Berkshire countryside, it was the stuff of dreams. A week to bond, drink, talk about acting and finally, after all the years of struggle, be an actress. A tear suddenly leaked out and down my face. It felt like my life was just starting and the first person I wanted to tell was also the person I was most afraid to. Jack would be fine though. He knew what it meant to me and what it could mean for us. He would come around. He had to.

## KATE

I always thought I'd go travelling much earlier. In my head I was about twenty-one, fresh out of university, the world at my feet, carefree, confident and unaffected by the rigours and strains of adulthood. Backpacking was meant to be the last bastion of my childhood before the reality of life outside of education began. I hadn't ever considered I'd be teetering on the edge of my twenties, timidly tip-toeing into the big beyond with a whole life behind me and more baggage than I could carry.

On the plane and once I'd stopped crying, watched my second film and tried my best to sleep, the realisation that I was totally on my own began to hit me. The enormity of what I was doing started to hammer away at me and it was then I really wished I was a happy-go-lucky twenty-one-year-old instead of a tightly wound, scared-shitless almost-thirty-year-old. I wished Ed was there too because despite his many faults one of his biggest strengths had always been to make me feel safe and secure.

After touching down in Bangkok and going through the roulette of baggage claim, I found myself standing outside the airport. I was tired, sweaty and had nowhere to stay. And it was really bloody hot. The sort of scorching heat I'd never felt before. Without even moving I was dripping in sweat. I'd been so caught up in leaving and dealing with Ed I hadn't had time to think about what I'd do when I actually arrived.

A mass of swarming local guides had already offered me numerous lifts, choices of hostels, tours and trips, but none of them seemed remotely trustworthy or part of a legitimate company. As it turned out that was just how things were in Thailand and I was being far too Western and English about it. Thankfully, just as I was beginning to feel the heavy pull of panic tug me towards tears, a voice came out of the blue.

'You OK?'

I turned around and there was a man, well, more of a boy really: early twenties, English, and wearing a pair of camouflage shorts and a white T-shirt with a picture of The Beatles on the front. He was tall and quite gorgeous actually, with long chestnut-brown hair and sparkling blue eyes, but that should have been the very last thing on my mind.

'Umm . . . well . . . no, not really.'

I almost started to cry, but somehow kept myself together. I didn't want the first memory of my trip to be me blubbing like a baby outside Bangkok airport. I also didn't want my first travelling friend to think I was a stereotypical girlie mess who couldn't handle life on the road.

'I'm Jez,' he said, offering me his hand. 'Jeremy really, but everyone calls me Jez.' His wrist was full of different coloured bands, which made me feel about a million years old. I used to wear the same friendship bracelets at sixth form and university before the corporate suits and expensive dresses filled up my wardrobe. 'You must be fresh off the plane and a first-time traveller if I'm not mistaken?'

'Is it so obvious?'

'People that white don't tend to have spent the last year somewhere warm,' said Jez and we both laughed. He was right. I was hideously pale while he was the colour of golden syrup. 'I just dropped a friend off, but I'm heading back to my hostel if you want to join me. I know how daunting the first day can be.'

'Thanks, I'd really love that.'

The next minute Jez and I were on the Skytrain heading into Bangkok. He took me to his hostel on the Khao San Road, helped me check in and luckily I managed to get a bed in his dorm, sharing with two Canadian girls, a Scottish couple from St Andrews who never seemed to be there and an Australian called Scott, who always was. From feeling the loneliest I'd ever felt and like I wanted to head straight back home, tail between my legs, I became happy, relaxed and, with Jez by my side, I toured Bangkok for the next week.

We went to the Chatuchak market, the biggest market in Thailand, which was a crazy maze with tiny bunnies dressed like burlesque dancers, fried maggots and cockroaches, and a myriad of other interesting and repugnant stuff. We visited temples, the reclining Buddha at the Wat Pho Temple, had incredible, if painful, Thai massages and spent time in Patpong, the red-light district. It certainly opened my eyes to a few things you don't see back in London.

However, the best part of the week wasn't the touristy stuff, but the evenings Jez and I would spend in bars, drinking, chatting, meeting other backpackers and generally not doing much. I was almost thirty and had spent the last eight years working hard, forging a career and growing up, but suddenly every day felt like Freshers' Week. Admittedly, I did feel a bit like the weird mature student I used to try and avoid, with the countless stories about her 'experience' in India, but, being around all these younger travellers, life felt fun again and as if anything was possible. It was during one of these nights that Jez first asked about Ed.

'And he didn't want to come?'

'Not really his thing.'

We were at a bar on the Khao San Road. It was late and we'd had quite a few already. Despite it being almost ten o'clock, the air was stifling hot, almost like a heavy mass that sat upon us. We were smoking one cheap cigarette after another, an old habit that had somehow come back to me rather easily, and drinking bottles of Singha lager. Jez had on a black Rolling Stones T-shirt and I was wearing a light green dress I'd bought in the market for next to nothing. We looked like all the other backpackers and I loved it. I loved that I felt like a small part of something so much bigger than myself. I was part of a community, a small band of laid-back people experiencing the world together. My stresses in London felt like something from a different lifetime altogether.

'I don't understand. Why would he not want to come travelling? It's the greatest thing in the world. We have our whole lives to make money, settle down and be as boring as our parents. This is the only time we have to really live, experience life.'

'Because Ed loves his job and thinks travelling is essentially a waste of time. Something graduates do to avoid work for another year.'

'And you're going to marry this man?'

I smiled, but inside I was confused and insecure. Even when I said it, I knew it sounded terrible. I was in love with a man who I felt loved his job more than he loved me. I loved a man who didn't want to travel, experience new things and was happier staying in London and being a weekend person forever.

'One day,' I said, but my voice lacked any real conviction.

'Is that like when you say one day I'm going to learn Spanish, or as in one day we're all going to die?'

'As in, one day soon,' I snapped, but more out of embarrassment than anger.

Maybe I should have defended our relationship more, but something inside of me knew I couldn't. Not at that moment and definitely not to Jez. Jez the free spirit who played a beat-up old guitar and wrote songs and who one day wanted to be a singer. Handsome Jez who made me feel like I did when I was twenty instead of almost thirty. Jez the musician who unfortunately made me think of my father.

'You know, Ed wasn't always so annoyingly pragmatic. After we met at uni, he used to love going on minibreaks. We probably hit every European capital during the first few years of our relationship.'

'Then what happened?'

'Then what happened' was a good question and one, if the truth be known, I didn't really know the answer to. I met Ed during the last term at university and he literally had me at hello. We went from strangers to dating, to living together in a rented flat within six months. Recently though, the magic had started to fade. During the previous year, as his job became more and more demanding, Ed seemed to stop wanting to do anything and our lives ground to a depressingly settled halt. He used to scoff at the obnoxious middle-aged bankers as much as me, but like everyone who starts making six figures before their thirtieth birthday, he changed. The Ed I loved definitely wasn't the Ed I'd fallen in love with.

'Life, I suppose.'

'And that's it? Life is boring and that's OK?'

'No, but it happens,' I said, before I added swiftly, and rather condescendingly, 'You'll understand one day.'

'What, so because I'm only twenty-two, I can't possibly understand?'

I hadn't meant to say that. I hated people who said things like that. Old people. Boring people. People who had long since accepted that life just became a bit of a slugging match and that's the way it was. Nothing to see here so go home, pop the kettle on and watch the telly.

'I didn't mean that, I'm sorry.'

A pang of anxious fear suddenly clamped itself to my chest, threatening to cause me untold pain until I surrendered. I could feel its razor-like teeth tearing into me. Luckily, before it had a chance to really grab hold, Jez smiled.

'It's OK, old lady, you're forgiven. And speaking of life, I have something to ask you,' Jez said before he looked away for a moment, his normally caramel-brown cheeks turning a bright shade of red.

'Sounds interesting.'

'Please say no if you want, but I'm heading down to the islands for a few weeks and I was hoping you'd come with me. I've been in Asia for nearly four months, Thailand for almost two and it's time to move on, but I fancy a few weeks in the sun first. It's incredible down there. We can scuba dive, snorkel, visit proper desert islands and I know this great little place. It's so chilled out. What do you say?'

Maybe I should have said no. Jez and I were getting too close. I could feel the thing that starts to happen when you spend every day with someone of the opposite sex – the inevitability of something sexual. Jez was handsome, fun to be around and I knew he sort of fancied me. I wasn't being arrogant, but it was fairly obvious. I should have said no, but I couldn't. Jez was my only friend in Thailand and I couldn't face being alone. I made the excuse that I'd planned on heading down there anyway, so I might as well go with Jez, but the truth was I was sort of excited about it. I wanted to spend more time with him and see where it went. It felt dangerous and for the first time in years life felt anything but inevitable.

'I'd love to,' I said, and with those three words we started planning the next two weeks. We drank, smoked and spoke about nothing but the present and the future. It felt like I had no past and had just begun to live in that moment with Jez. I'd been in Thailand for less than a week and yet my life back home felt like it no longer existed.

I did end up thinking about one moment from my past as Jez and I walked back to our hostel that night through the warren of market stalls, late-night food stands and neon lights. I thought about the day I asked Ed to come travelling with me.

I'd made us a special meal, bought a nice bottle of red and had everything ready for when he came home from work. He was obviously suspicious as soon as he walked in. It was, after all, a normal Tuesday evening. I was usually camped on the sofa in my pyjamas watching television, not propped up in the dining room, glass of wine in hand and looking creepily nervous.

'Shit, is it our anniversary or something?' he said as soon as he walked in.

'We aren't married, Ed, and we got together in May. No, it's something else. Here have a glass of wine.'

I handed him the wine and made him sit down.

'Are you . . . pregnant?' His face lit up and I could see he already had the next twenty years planned out in his head.

'I'm not pregnant. Listen . . . there's something I want to say and I want you to take it seriously.'

'OK,' said Ed, taking a sip of wine.

'I know we have a great life here, good jobs, a nice house and friends, but I'm not happy and haven't been for a while.'

'I don't understand, Kate. Are you breaking up with me?'

'I'm not breaking up with you, Ed, you idiot. I love you.' I took a deep breath and then a large mouthful of wine. 'I want us to take a gap year and go travelling.'

There, I'd said it. It was out there. My hopes and dreams were hanging tantalisingly by the merest of threads. I waited for his response, which came quickly and resolutely. I'd been thinking about travelling for years, but it took Ed only seconds to stoically squash my dreams.

'We can't. It's impossible.'

'Why?'

'Because it just is.'

'But I have that money from Nan. We could rent out the house for a year to cover the mortgage. Please, Ed, just think about it. We could go to Asia, Australia, South America, wherever we want. Just you and me having the time of our lives . . .'

'We can't.'

'That's not good enough, Ed. I need more than that. I want us to do something incredible and life changing and you don't. I need to know why.'

'Because I have my job. You think they'll just give me a year off? I've worked too hard and too long to give it up, Kate, and honestly I don't think travelling is that important. We're not teenagers anymore, we're almost thirty. It's time to put down roots.'

'And you think travelling is just for kids? Some immature rite of passage?'

'Honestly, yes. It's what young people do to avoid work, but we already have careers, a proper life, and we can't just throw that away because you've got itchy feet . . .'

'For fuck's sake, Ed. Young people, itchy feet, that's all you think this is? I've wanted to travel since I was a teenager and you said we would, remember?'

'Calm down, Kate, please. Look, if you want to do something we can go away for a few days over Christmas . . .'

'I don't want a fucking minibreak, Ed. I want to see the world.'

'But why do we have to take a year off to do it? Why do I have to give up my job?'

'Because it's turning you into a boring old fart, Ed, that's why and if we don't do this, I don't know if we'll make it.'

'Oh, here she goes with the emotional blackmail.'

'It's not emotional blackmail, Ed, it's the truth.'

'Well if I'm such a boring old fart, maybe you should go without me.'

'Maybe I will.'

'Good,' barked Ed.

And that was it. The year was whittled down to six months, but Ed still wouldn't come. He didn't see the point. I loved him dearly, but why couldn't he see it from my perspective? Why couldn't he realise he was becoming exactly the sort of boorish bloke he used to openly mock? Why couldn't he leave his shitty job for me? Why didn't he want to travel and see the world? I suppose what it all boiled down to was – why couldn't he be more like Jez?

**To: Emma Fogle**
**From: Kate Jones**
**Subject: I made it!**

Em,

I made it! I'm here! The first email from my trip. This is so strange. It reminds me of university when you were in Bristol and I was in London and we used to email each other all the time. Remember how far away that felt? Now I'm in Thailand and you're in London and it's even further. I hate being apart from you. I'm going to miss our weekly get-togethers, our chats on the phone, Starbucks on Saturday. Any chance you could pop on a plane and visit? I'm sure Jack wouldn't mind.

## Happy Endings

How did the film meeting go? Did you get the part? I have a feeling you did. Shit, Em, imagine if you did and then you became this super-famous film star? My best mate the film star. That would be so crazy. You deserve it though. Just make sure you take me on a few red carpets with you! Did you meet Rhys Connelly? Is he as sexy in real life? I bet he is.

I guess I should tell you something about Thailand. I suppose first I should tell you about Jez. There's a boy, of course. It isn't like that though. He rescued me from the airport when I was on the verge of a breakdown. He's good-looking, but far too young for any shenanigans. Anyway, as you know, I didn't come away for that sort of thing. I came away for me. And thank you by the way for pushing me and pushing me to do this. It's terrifying and scary and I've probably cried or almost cried more in the last few days than I ever have, but I'm glad I'm here. I just wish you were here too! I wish Ed, you and Jack were all here.

Thailand, well Bangkok I should say, is crazy. One moment it sort of feels like you're just in a big city and then you see an elephant walking down the street! It's so weird. It's really helped having Jez by my side. He seems to know what he's doing and he takes me off on crazy adventures every day. He's made the transition easier, especially because I had such a hard time on the plane after leaving you all at the airport and with Ed being, well, Ed. How was he after I left?

I'm still getting my bearings but every day it gets a bit easier. I'm a little homesick and suddenly six months feels like the longest time in the world. It's also really weird sleeping in a room full of strangers when I'm used to having a whole house, but I suppose I'd better get used to that.

I should probably get going. I'm at an Internet cafe and I have no idea how much this is costing and there's a little Thai man at the register who keeps giving me strange looks. I'm going to try and email you every week, but I can't promise anything. Jez and I are heading down to the islands in the south of Thailand next week. It feels a bit weird, travelling with a bloke, but he's the only person I know and we get on really well. Don't mention anything to Ed if you see him, I don't want him getting the wrong idea.

Miss you Em.

Love K x

## ED

The house always felt cramped with Kate there. Her bottles of lotion and moisturiser, hair straighteners and curling tongs forever took up most of the space in the bathroom. Our bedroom always had small piles of her clothes lying around, as if some ancient civilisation had put them there, carefully constructed at key points around the room. The lounge was usually cluttered with dog-eared celebrity magazines and the kitchen always contained at least one slightly coffee-stained mug she hadn't got around to cleaning. But now she was gone, it felt so large. The bathroom was mainly empty, the small piles in the bedroom were gone and the lounge and kitchen were clean and spotless. I hated it.

It was a week after she'd left and I was sitting in the lounge trying to watch television, but my mind kept drifting to Kate. I couldn't stop myself. Everything reminded me of her. Even things that seemed completely unconnected brought me back to her in some way. During the week I'd kept myself busy at work and I'd had drinks with Georgie, plus a quick wet lunch with Jack, but the weekend was biting and cold.

In the month before she left, Kate had hired out the basement of a pub in Islington for her leaving do. To be honest, I didn't see the point in a big leaving party. It was only six months, but Kate insisted on it. She wanted to get all of her friends, family and co-workers together so we could rejoice in her decision to leave us for six months and bugger off

47

around the world. I'd been dreading it ever since she told me. It felt like she was rubbing salt into an already gaping wound. People still didn't understand why I wasn't going and so I'd spend the entire night fielding questions about what this meant to us? Had we broken up? Was I fine with it? How was it going to work, exactly? And really, why wasn't I going? The truth was I didn't know how or if it was going to work. I'd been trying my best to avoid thinking about it and I was still holding out hope she would see sense and not leave.

A few days before the party, I found myself walking past a jewellery shop on Wandsworth High Street and suddenly a plan began to take shape. It was like a mini Big Bang and once it exploded I couldn't stop the ever-expanding universe of ideas, mapping out a perfect future in my head. I stopped and gazed through the window at all the rings and then I saw a man inside. He was around my age, dressed smartly in a bespoke suit and he was buying a ring. He looked so happy and a bit smug and it struck me straight away. Why didn't I ask Kate to marry me? I couldn't believe I hadn't thought of it before. It would solve everything. I was sure she'd say yes and then maybe she wouldn't leave or even if she did we'd be engaged instead of just dating and it would mean something. I stopped looking through the window and immediately went into the shop in search of the perfect ring.

By nine o'clock the basement of the pub was heaving. Admittedly, it wasn't a very big space, but there must have been at least fifty people crammed inside. A decent turnout and I was impressed. I definitely didn't know fifty people, or at least fifty people I'd actually want to invite to my leaving party. Kate was off dancing with Emma, while Jack and I loitered around the bar getting slowly hammered. I'd been drinking heavily, trying to settle my nerves. The ring box was snuggled inside my jacket pocket; I kept touching it to make sure it was still there. I was terrified, but not because I thought I'd lose the ring, but in case Kate said no. In my head she always said yes. Of course she'd say yes, but there was a tiny amount of doubt. The faintest hint of what if she said no. What then?

'How're you doing?' said Jack.

'I've been better.'

'I bet. So how's it going to work then?'

'Honestly, I have no idea.'

'Any plans to meet her somewhere for a holiday?'

'No,' I said. 'She mentioned that maybe I could meet her in Sydney, but it's her time to do what she needs. I don't want to get in the way.'

'Aren't you a bit worried though? I'd be terrified of letting Emma waltz off by herself around the world. You know what backpackers do all day?'

'Not really. Read books, watch crap TV and get pissed on cheap alcohol probably. Sort of like the first year of university without the lectures.'

'And what else did you do a lot of during your first year at university?'

I knew where he was going and, of course, I'd thought about it. I looked across at Kate and she looked more beautiful than ever. Her long dark hair was flowing out behind her as she moved effortlessly around the dance floor. She was wearing a red dress that hung low over her shoulders, perfectly accentuated her breasts and ended just above the knee, showing off her long, slim legs. She was gorgeous, but I trusted her and that was the key. I trusted that, no matter what, she'd do the right thing.

'Study?' I said with a wry grin.

The music suddenly changed from the Britpop classics the DJ had been playing for the last hour to something a bit

49

slower and romantic. Kate and Emma came stumbling over, giggling and looking for drinks.

'I'm knackered,' said Kate, falling into me and putting her arm around my neck.

'My round,' said Jack, trying to get the attention of the barman.

It was my time. My heart was beating nineteen to the dozen and I felt nauseous. It was my moment to ask her to be my wife, till death do us part, in sickness and in health and all the rest of it. I'd spent a great deal of time since I bought the ring working out how and where I should do it, but something about her leaving party resonated with me. It felt right. It wasn't going to be the perfect proposal, but at the end of the day, surely the gesture was the most important thing.

'Just give us a moment,' I said, standing up and grabbing Kate by the hand.

'What are you doing?' said Kate with an uncertain smile. She probably thought I had a surprise arranged for her, but when I walked her past the DJ and upstairs, she started to look confused. It was also January and quite chilly outside. 'What's going on?'

I'd rehearsed the speech in my head a hundred times, but standing there in front of her my mind went completely blank. I had nothing.

'Ed?'

'Yes.'

'Why did you drag me up here in the freezing bloody cold?'

People walked past, hugging themselves and each other. A few cars drove by in slow motion. I couldn't believe how afraid I was. I just had to do it. I took out the ring box, got down on one knee and looked up at Kate.

'Kate, I love you so much and this probably isn't how you thought I'd propose and maybe the timing isn't the best, but would you do me the honour of being my wife?'

I couldn't make out the expression on her face. She hadn't gushed with happiness and screamed 'Yes!', which was what I was hoping for, obviously, but she hadn't run away either. She stood there speechless. Had I made a huge mistake? The threatening cold had dissipated too and all that was left was Kate and me. The rest of the world seemed to evaporate, as if we'd been cut and pasted onto a blank piece of paper. After what seemed like an age, and just as my knees were really beginning to hurt, Kate said, 'Oh, Ed.'

'What?'

'Why are you doing this now? Of all nights, why tonight?'

I had to get up. The moment had come and gone. I'd thrown my heart into the ring and it had been returned slightly battered and a bit bruised.

'I thought it would be . . .'

'Romantic?'

'Yes, sort of.'

'Well it isn't, Ed, it's just . . . I can't believe you sometimes.'

'What? What have I done?'

I was completely flabbergasted. I was hoping to get engaged and in my head I imagined an emphatic 'yes!' or at the very least a 'maybe we should wait until I get back', but I definitely didn't anticipate anger. 'It's emotional blackmail. Get a ring on my finger and I won't be able to leave on my stupid trip. Was that your big plan?'

'No, Kate, of course not. I didn't want you to leave without knowing how I felt.'

'But why now and why here? It just doesn't make sense.'

It felt at that moment like nothing really made sense any more. The girl I loved was taking off for six months on a trip that didn't make any sense. We were standing outside in the freezing cold arguing over a marriage proposal that perhaps didn't make any sense. I was twenty-nine, almost thirty, and for the first time in as long as I could remember, my life didn't make any sense.

'I'm sorry, just forget it,' I said and I walked back inside.

## JACK

Dad died of a heart attack when I was fifteen. Up until that point in his life he'd been healthy, but one day, while Mum and I were out shopping, he had a massive heart attack and that was it. He was gone.

I loved and admired my father. He was a brilliant dad and an amazing man. In his younger days he had excelled at sport and played cricket for his state. In his twenties he started a thriving real estate business and we lived in a large house in Sydney and had everything we wanted. I idolised him. I wanted to be just like him and thought he'd always be there to set the example for me to follow. That was before his heart stopped, and after that I knew better. That's the trouble when you lose someone at such an early age, it destroys the notion that people are around forever. I'd barely touched adulthood and already I was one parent down. It didn't seem fair.

It crushed Mum and she returned with me to England soon after. She'd grown up there and only moved to Australia in her thirties when she met Dad. I loved living in Australia, it was my home and all I ever knew, but without Dad it was too much for her to handle. Every street corner held too many memories. Mum still had family in England and she thought a fresh start would be best for the both of us. At first I resisted and in some ways resented her. I didn't want to leave Sydney and especially for cold, wet England, but in time and once I realised the anger wasn't aimed at her, but really at Dad for dying, we made our peace.

Most Sunday mornings Emma and I would visit Mum. Sometimes it was a bit of a chore, but it was Mum. We were all she had.

'You can't make it?'

Emma was sitting at the kitchen table with a cup of coffee, going through the script. I was waiting for my toast to pop and for my tea to stew.

'I need to go through these new notes and I'm meeting Rhys for lunch.'

Mum adored Emma because I think she'd always wanted a daughter. My parents met later in life and Mum was in her late thirties when she had me. In those days having babies beyond that age just wasn't the done thing – I was their one shot at a proper family.

I was trying to be understanding about the film, but it was becoming harder and harder with every passing day. Emma and I already didn't see each other as often as we liked and so Sunday had always been the one day when we were always together. The day when everything else played second fiddle to us. If we weren't off to see Mum or to the pub with Ed and Kate, then we'd take a stroll, go shopping, pop to an art gallery or museum, or sometimes we'd just stay in, get under a blanket and watch films. But whatever we did, we always did it together.

'You can't come for a bit? Mum would love to see you.'

'I really need to do this,' she said, taking a sip of coffee and not even looking up from the script.

I'd been trying not to say anything, but suddenly anger rose up inside of me. I'd had enough of not saying anything, of hiding my feelings and not telling her what was on my mind. This always seemed to happen to me. I bottled things up and then unleashed them without warning. I suppose it didn't just happen. I didn't like talking about feelings, thoughts and issues – not because I was afraid of them, but afraid of what it would change. If I kept everything in, made it seem like I was fine, then Emma wouldn't have an excuse to leave me and I was more afraid of that than anything else. Just don't upset the apple cart.

'For fuck's sake, Em. Sunday's our one day together and you can't take a day off from the film for me? For Mum?'

Emma looked across at me, perplexed. She closed the script and stared at me coldly.

'So it is about the film.'

'What?'

'You being all angry and morose for the past week. You're annoyed about the film.'

'No, Em. I'm annoyed the film takes precedence over everything else.'

'But this is what I've been working towards my whole life, Jack. Surely, you of all people can understand that?'

'I can. You know I'm happy for you . . .'

'Do I?' she snapped.

'What's that supposed to mean?'

'Oh come on, Jack. Ever since I got the part you've been in a shitty mood about it. You can't stand the fact that I've finally made it, can you?'

'What?! Seriously?! That's what you think? It isn't about the film, Em. Maybe it's about the fact you're doing nude sex scenes with Rhys Connelly and didn't think to mention it to me. Maybe I'm pissed off about that.'

Emma looked at me for a moment with a sort of ashamed confusion. She'd been caught out and was trying to work out how I knew.

'You're jealous?'

'No, not jealous . . .'

'It sounds like jealousy.'

'I'm annoyed you didn't tell me and I had to find out from him.'

'I was just waiting for the right time.'

'And when was that? When Rhys had his dirty Welsh hands all over your tits or when he had his tongue down your throat?' As soon as I'd said it, I knew I'd crossed a line. I'd gone too far. Emma looked at me in disgust. I would have to apologise. She looked hurt, sad and angry, a whole cacophony of emotions – all I felt was overwhelming guilt. I was an idiot. 'I'm sorry, Em. I didn't mean that. You know I'm not that shallow.'

Emma looked at me for a moment and I couldn't make out her expression, but one thing was quite obvious, she did think I was that shallow. The truth wasn't that simple. I was over the moon for her and I wanted her to be successful and, honestly, I didn't mind about the nudity and sex because it came with the territory, but I was afraid she would fall in love with Rhys. I looked at her sitting there, so beautiful and wonderful, and I wanted to hug her, kiss her and hold her. She was enough for me. Suddenly, however, and maybe because of the film, I didn't feel like I was enough for her.

'Just go, Jack,' Emma said tersely, and so I walked away, my toast suddenly popping up to let me know it was done.

'Mum,' I said, walking in through the side gate of her house. She didn't hear me at first and continued on with the garden. 'Mum,' I said again a bit louder. Finally she looked up and a smile spread across her face.

'Oh, hello, Jack,' she said. 'Emma with you?'

'Not today. Tea?' I said and we headed indoors.

Mum got on with the tea while I settled myself into the living room. I liked coming home because it kept me in touch with my old self. In London, among the great unwashed masses and the hectic life that carried me along at its own pace, I felt lost at times. But there at Mum's house on the quiet tree-lined street with the back garden and my old bedroom, I felt completely at ease. It was like going back in time. Back to when I was a teenager, still full of hopes and dreams of being a published author. Back to when I knew I was definitely going to be a writer, before the rejection letters had piled up and my dreams felt impossible.

'Here you go,' said Mum, putting the tray down on the coffee table.

A tray with tea, biscuits and two slices of homemade fruit cake. Mum sat down opposite and I took a moment to really look at her. She was in her sixties now and her hair was full of grey. Her face, once so beautiful, was now full of wrinkles and her skin was like old leaves and sallow. Her body, which had always been full and plump, was skinnier because without me she lived on a diet of tea, biscuits and toast. She was starting to look old. In her fifties she still had that glow of beauty, but now it was hidden behind the weary lines of a life slowing down.

'Good cuppa, Mum.'

'Where's Emma then?' she said, ignoring my comment and getting straight into the cold, hard facts. Mum was never one to beat around the bush.

'She couldn't make it.'

'Did you have a fight?'

'Sort of.'

'Jack, dear, when it comes to relationships, there's no such thing as sort of. You may think it was sort of an argument, but I can guarantee if I asked Emma, she'd say you had a fight.'

'Fine, we had a fight.'

'And are you going to tell me what it was about?'

'It's stupid really.'

'Most arguments are.'

We settled into drinking our tea and eating biscuits and cake, and I explained how I felt about the film. How I was sure her success would mean the end of our relationship and Emma tucked up in bed with Rhys Connelly. Mum listened carefully without interrupting before she gave me her advice and, as usual, it was spot on.

'Jack, I love you, but I think you know you're in the wrong. You know it's foolish to try and hold her back and stop her from being what she's always wanted to be. Imagine if it was the other way around and it was you who'd achieved their dream first; how would you feel if she resented you for it?'

'But that's different because if I get published, I won't suddenly be recognised in the street. I'll be signing books at the Waterstones in Bracknell, not doing sex scenes with the best-looking bloke in Britain.'

'So this is about your insecurities and not her success?'

'I suppose.'

'The thing is, Jack, at the moment she loves you. You're engaged to be married regardless of her success, but if you keep pushing her away because you're afraid of what might happen, then you'll lose her. It's ironic, but the fear of failure is often its catalyst.'

'How did you become so wise?'

Mum looked at me with a smile, a smile that for an instant made her look young again. Her face lit up, her eyes sparkled and the wrinkles seemed to vanish just for a second and there on the sofa was my mum. The mum I'd known growing up. She looked beautiful, like an old film star from the fifties.

'It isn't wisdom, Jack, it's age. When we're young we often can't see what's right in front of us, but with age comes perspective. You know your dad once said something that's always stayed with me.'

I sat forward on the sofa at the mere mention of my father. I looked up briefly at the old black-and-white photo of him and Mum on their wedding day that had pride of place above the fireplace.

'What's that?'

'I was having a bad day and having a go at him about something trivial and he said, "We should love blindly without question, without regret and selflessly."'

'And what did you say?'

'I said I was sorry, but then he said, and typical of your father, "But right now, love, you're being a right pain in my arse, so I'm off to the pub."'

Mum and I laughed, but we were both lost in our own worlds. Mum was, I'm sure, thinking about Dad, while I was thinking about Emma. Mum was right: I would lose her if I didn't support her and I couldn't let my fears get in the way of our happiness. I was going to go home, apologise and let her know how proud I was of her and how much I loved her. Before it was too late.

## EMMA

As soon as I walked into the small and upmarket café in Swiss Cottage, I saw Rhys and my heart dropped. He was reading a book at a table in the corner and looking every inch the archetypal film star. I forgot I was soon to be acting opposite him and I became a silly teenager again. He was wearing a blue cable-knit jumper and a pair of faded jeans, his hair was its usual beautiful mess and he had a few days' stubble hanging around his chin. There was no getting away from the fact that he was drop-dead gorgeous and every young girl's dream. I, of course, was almost thirty and should know much better.

I was still pissed off after the argument with Jack. I couldn't believe how callous he was being about the film. I'd been waiting for this moment my whole life and the one person who should have been supporting me was the one person who was acting like a complete and utter dickhead. I didn't want Rhys to know anything about it and so I put on a smile, threw my shoulders back, took a deep breath and made my way over to his table.

'Em,' said Rhys as soon as he saw me. He got up and gave me a theatrical kiss on each cheek and a warm hug, as if we'd been friends for years. He smelt fantastic and I could feel the taut muscles beneath his jumper. I noticed people at nearby tables were furtively watching us. They'd obviously spotted Rhys and were probably trying to work out if I was famous too. To be honest, I felt a little bit out of my depth. For Rhys this was just another lunch and just another co-star, but for me it was the beginning of everything. 'How are you?'

'Good thanks,' I said, putting my handbag down on the table next to me. 'You?'

'Fantastic. Bit tired. Up all night going through a script for an American thing my agent wants me to do. It's shit, really, but big-budget and has some huge names attached to it. I just don't know if I want to go down that route, the big-budget action films, or do things a bit more, you know, eclectic.'

'Then don't do it,' I said, giving advice as though I knew what I was talking about. This from the actress who had recently been turned down for such esteemed roles as 'girl on phone', 'girl on train', 'second friend from the left' and, most recently, 'girl in lift'. I was a classically trained actress who'd been turned down for roles that basically required me to stand still.

'I know, but it's five million for six months' work and it's set in Hawaii, which wouldn't be a bad place to spend a few months . . .'

'Five million?' I said incredulously.

'Yeah.'

'As in pounds?'

'Yeah.'

'And you're asking me for advice?' Rhys looked at me and laughed. He had a horribly gorgeous laugh that made me fancy him even more than I already did. I tried to put all naughty, inappropriate thoughts out of my head. I was engaged. I loved Jack with all my heart even though he'd been an utter pig all morning, but Rhys had a way about him. Sort of like a young Sean Connery. He had a raw sexiness that wasn't forced, but a natural quality which ran through every-thing he did. He could probably make brushing his teeth sexy.

'Why are you laughing?'

'Oh, Em, you're priceless. Let me buy you lunch. What do you want?'

It was only ordering lunch, but it somehow felt like a trick question. What did I want? I looked down at the menu and I quite fancied a hamburger or perhaps the pie and mash. I'd been so nervous about meeting him I hadn't eaten a thing all day. I felt like I should stick to a salad or maybe at most a light sandwich on wholegrain bread, but then again, did I want to be that girl? The girl who ate nothing, lost too much weight and ended up in one of those God-awful magazine spreads about actresses who get too thin. They'd somehow find a photo of me before I was famous where I was a stone heavier and say how healthy I looked, and then a new photo of me from a terrible angle where I looked like I hadn't eaten in six months. The next thing I knew I'd be labelled as bulimic and a bad example to all young girls. There was also the chance I was completely overthinking things and Rhys didn't give a shit what I ate.

'Burger and chips please,' I said and I noticed the look on his face. 'Sorry, what should I have ordered? The side salad? Soup? A glass of water?'

'No, not at all. I was just thinking how refreshing it is to be with someone like you.'

'A complete pig?'

'No, an actress who eats real food, doesn't get all mental and stick thin at the first sight of success and looks absolutely stunning just as she is.'

His Welsh accent turned me to jelly and I went a deep shade of burgundy, which was bad enough, but became worse because Rhys noticed straight away. He smiled at me and I didn't know where in the world to look. I excused myself and went to the toilet while he ordered.

'What kind of actress do you want to be?' said Rhys when we were tucking into our food.

'When I was young and fresh out of university I wanted to be just like Kate Winslet. Picking and choosing great roles, powerful roles in cool indie films, but my last audition was for a dead person in *Casualty*. So, to answer your question, anything.'

'After this film, let's hope you won't have to play any more dead people.'

'Oh, I didn't get it. Apparently, I didn't look quite dead enough,' I said and Rhys burst out laughing.

Sitting with Rhys and going through the script over countless cups of coffee was like a dream come true. It was the life I'd always craved and I had to pinch myself; I was actually living it. During the three hours we sat talking, drinking and getting to know one another, a few young girls came by and asked for his autograph. He was polite and affable and had his photograph taken with a smile. I sat in my seat feeling like the luckiest girl in London. Somehow I was sharing lunch with Britain's most eligible bachelor and *Heat* magazine's hunkiest bloke of the year. It was almost five o'clock when we finally stood up to leave.

'Fancy a drink? I'm meeting a couple of mates in Soho,' said Rhys, putting on his jacket.

'I shouldn't.'

'Which means you will, right?'

It meant I shouldn't. Jack would be home from his mum's already and what would I say to him? Just popping out for a drink with Rhys Connelly and some of his mates in Soho, you don't mind, do you? I'm sure given his already frosty reaction to my sex scenes with Rhys and his general ill-feeling towards the film he wouldn't appreciate me having a drink with him too. Just as I was on the verge of saying no and slouching off home to Jack, something stopped me. He had no right to be jealous. I'd done nothing wrong and if he couldn't be happy for me then that was his fault.

'I'd love to,' I said and we walked out of the café and straight into a paparazzi ambush. No sooner had we left the café than four cameras were taking our photo and questions were shouted at us two at a time. Who's your friend, Rhys? Is she your girlfriend? What's your name, love? Where you going, Rhys? What did you have to eat, Rhys? What did you eat, love? Is that a Mulberry handbag? What film you doing next, Rhys? I heard something big in the States? They went on and on as the cameras flashed and flashed, until Rhys grabbed my hand and whisked me away to a waiting cab. My mind was a whirlwind. What had just happened? Did this happen everywhere he went? Did my Zara handbag really look like a Mulberry?

'You'll get used to that,' said Rhys, as we climbed in the back of the black cab.

'I think I'm going to enjoy this,' I said with a breathless smile as we started off towards Soho and a night out on the town with Rhys Connelly and his fabulous friends.

**To: Kate Jones**
**From: Emma Fogle**
**Subject: Re: I made it!**

K,

I got the part! I couldn't believe it at first. I still don't. It was so surreal. There we were at the restaurant with Matt Wallace, the famous director, and he offered me the lead role opposite Rhys Connelly! It's still sinking in to be honest. Rhys turned up at the restaurant too and yes, he's just as sexy in real life. Probably sexier, actually. I think Jack felt a little bit overwhelmed by it all.

He's been a bit weird since. I'm not sure what his problem is and, typical Jack, he's not talking about it. Agh . . . men! Still, I'm finally living my dream and you're living yours too! It's so strange how life works itself out.

I wish I could pop over and pay you a visit. I miss you too. After I found out about the film you were the first person I wanted to tell. I wanted to give you a big hug and then break open the champagne and get plastered. Instead I had to make do with just a grumpy Jack. Mother's over the moon, obviously. I think she phoned everyone she knew after I told her. She's even been ringing me up, so I know it's a big deal. Still, as soon as you get back we're going to celebrate! I'm looking forward to seeing some photos too young lady, so make sure you send me some ASAP!

Ed was pretty quiet on the drive back to London. He's definitely missing you. I haven't seen him since you left, but Jack met him for lunch a couple of times and said he was looking a bit depressed. Still, he had the chance to come with you and he didn't so it's his fault. Don't feel bad for him or regret going. Like you said, you're doing this for YOU!

So Jez, eh? A bit of a dish? It's probably better travelling with a bloke anyway. It's safer. I'm so jealous. I haven't had a decent holiday in ages. We're always so broke. After the film things will be different! We're definitely going somewhere lovely and warm for our honeymoon and I'm going to make Mother pay for it. Maybe the Seychelles.

I'm going away with the cast to a mansion in Berkshire for a week in February, which is quite exciting! I haven't had the guts to tell Jack yet. He's being all weird and I don't want to make things worse. I'll tell him soon, when he's stopped being such a baby. What is it with men? It's like they've never properly grown up or something and as soon as something doesn't go their way they sulk.

Well, that's it from over here. I have a script to read. I'm a very important actress now don't you know!

Make sure you email again soon. I want to hear all about the islands with Jez! Miss you.

Love Em X

# KATE

When I was back in England, dreaming about my trip, I always envisaged a moment when it would all make sense. An epiphany, I suppose, when I knew I'd accomplished something special. That moment came during the second week of my trip. After Jez and I left Bangkok, we boarded a bus at the Southern Bus Terminal and headed south. It was a tumultuous journey: a challenging bus trip of nearly fourteen hours and then a two-and-a-half-hour boat ride, which I was a little apprehensive about as the last time I was on a ferry I spent most of the time throwing up.

We left Bangkok at six o'clock in the evening and we wouldn't be in Koh Phangan until early afternoon the following day. It was a long journey, but we soon settled in. The bus was far more comfortable than I'd imagined and it went by fairly quickly with card games, sleep and talking about what we were going to do for the next ten days in paradise. I'd had fun in Bangkok and it was the perfect introduction to my trip, but I was ready for a change of scenery. Once we left behind the craziness of the city and headed into the country, it was a bit of a watershed for me and I almost cried. I had made it. I was doing it, not quite on my own, but as good as. I felt like a proper backpacker.

The moment that really brought it all together and made me pinch myself came the next day. Jez and I were on the ferry heading out towards the island of Koh Phangan. It was a bright sunny day and mainland Thailand stretched out, disappearing ever further into the distance, its rainforests, beaches and cities left behind as we headed out to an island in the Gulf of Thailand. I was sitting on the back of the boat next to Jez, the wind in my hair and the smell of the ocean filtering through my nose. A ray of sunshine created a dappling effect on the ocean and then I smiled. I smiled because I knew that was it.

On my old office computer back in London, I had an image of Thailand as my screensaver. I looked at it every day, and it was almost the same image as I saw in front of me. It wasn't exactly the same place, but it looked so similar and suddenly it hit me. I'd done it. I'd made my dream come true and no matter what happened on the rest of the trip and for the rest of my life, I'd done that. It was truly an incredible feeling and one that was worth every penny, argument and mile travelled. I felt for the first time, perhaps in my whole life, like I was actually living instead of just existing. Jez had been telling me all the way down that Koh Phangan was absolute paradise and he wasn't wrong. As soon as we stepped off the boat and onto the perfect sandy beach, I was awestruck. The turquoise water was so clear and the sand was a golden yellow and warm between my toes. Small Thai fishing boats sat in the water looking like props on a film set and palm trees hung over the beach, creating shadows that disappeared into the sea. We took a bumpy old minivan to the resort Jez had stayed at on his last visit. It was right on the beach and we had our own little bungalow, surrounded by lush rainforest and a thirty-second walk to an incredible secluded bay. There was, however, one slight problem.

'Just one bed?' I said to the lady at reception. She was a small Thai lady with a face of adamantine stillness. 'And you have nothing else?' She continued looking at me as if I'd asked her to unravel the mysteries of the universe in a language she barely seemed to grasp. She only spoke in short, sharp snaps, which sounded like she was trying to clear her throat, not communicate.

'We'll take it,' said Jez, handing over the money before I had the chance to say anything else. 'Trust me. It will be worth it.'

This was how Jez and I ended up sharing a bungalow on the beach with only one bed, which would have been fine if the bed hadn't been a small twin and we had to sleep with almost nothing on due to the heat. It was a situation designed to cause the greatest amount of sexual tension between two young people of the opposite sex in paradise for ten whole days. Throw in copious amounts of alcohol, applying sun screen, trips to and from the shower and the fact we definitely quite fancied each other and things didn't look good. Maybe I should have got out while the going was good, but I couldn't. I told myself again and again that we could do it. We could be platonic. Jez was just my friend. My travelling buddy. Mates.

'So this was your evil plan,' I said.

'I should probably have booked ahead or something.'

'Really?'

'You take the bed. I'll be fine on the floor.'

Jez looked at me with a solemn schoolboy face. I could tell he felt bad, but he also knew I wouldn't make him sleep on the floor. I looked down at the hard uneven boards, scattered with dust, bugs and the occasional stray nail. Ten days on that floor and his back would be ruined for life. Not to mention the possibilities of spiders and mosquitos.

'No funny business,' I said with a stern face.

Jez smiled and threw his backpack on the bed next to mine; a strange prequel to our actual bodies lying there that night.

Despite the bed situation, life on Koh Phangan quickly fell into an easy routine. We'd get up around nine or ten, usually a bit hung-over, and have breakfast at the hostel. Most days it was just fruit and cereal, a cup of coffee and toast. Then we'd go to the beach and read our books, swim in the crystal-clear water, snorkel, go kayaking or take a walk through the rainforest. On the first morning we were still quite tired from the journey and so after breakfast we camped out on the gorgeous beach. Jez had brought along his guitar, and I was leafing aimlessly through my Lonely Planet travel guide. Jez was strumming along and started singing the first few lines of a song. I didn't recognise it and so assumed it must have been one of his.

'I like it.'

'It's just something I'm working on.'

'Play me the rest.'

'It isn't ready,' said Jez, looking at me coyly from under the brim of his straw hat.

'Oh go on. For me. Please,' I said, giving him the face that always worked on Ed.

'Fine, just for you,' said Jez. 'It doesn't have a title yet and I still have work to do on the chorus, but here goes.'

Jez launched into his song and it was incredible. He had a really amazing voice, a bit raspy, but soulful and full of passion. It was the first time I'd heard him sing one of his own songs all the way through and it blew me away. I sat there in awe until eventually he finished.

'Fucking hell, Jez.'

'Terrible?'

'No, it was amazing. You're really good.'

'Thanks,' said Jez and even with the heat of the day, I could see his face go red and I felt myself fall slightly more in like with him than I already was. The memories of sitting next to my dad when I was very small, listening to him play the guitar and sing me songs popped into my head, but I managed to squash them quickly. I was trying to keep any thoughts of my father as far away as possible.

'What do your parents think about Jez the musician?'

'As opposed to Jez the doctor?'

'Yeah.'

'Dad would like me to go into medicine like him. Mum thinks I'm wasting my time. "You're too clever to throw it all away on a silly pipe dream, Jeremy," she says every time I see her. I don't expect them to understand me in the same way I don't understand them. And it's worse since . . .' he said, and then stopped.

'What?'

'Nothing. Fancy a drink? I'm gasping.'

'Sure,' I said and we headed to the hostel pool bar, but I was left wondering what it was he didn't tell me. Trying to imagine what small piece of his jigsaw he wasn't prepared to give away just yet.

We hired scooters on the fifth day and drove up to a bar Jez knew called Amsterdam. Riding the scooter was quite an experience. The little Thai man who rented it asked me if I'd done it before and, of course, I nodded confidently and said yes, sure, no problem. This was apparently the only comfort he needed to make sure I would return in one piece.

It was incredibly exciting as we rode around the island on our little scooters, albeit almost crashing a few times. Bar Amsterdam was at the top of a huge hill and from there you could see over the rainforest to the ocean. It was an incredible place for a drink. It wasn't too busy when we got there so we settled in and had a few beers. It gradually filled up as the afternoon wore on, but it gave me the chance to ask Jez something that had been on my mind since we'd met in Bangkok.

'So, Jez, is there anyone waiting for you back home?'

Somehow, and despite spending the last few weeks practically living together, I hadn't broached the topic of his love life. I think because in my head I didn't want to sound like I had ulterior motives. I didn't want him to think I was interested in his availability. I was being typical me. Overanalysing, overthinking and making a nothing into a something. In a way, it was worse than not asking him before because in Bangkok we weren't sharing a tiny bed in just our underwear. Two weeks before, we barely knew each other and still had a distance between us. Two weeks before, he was just Jez, the bloke who rescued me from Bangkok airport in my hour of need, but now he was Jez, the sexy young bloke I was travelling with and basically dating, but without the complication of sex.

'You mean apart from my parents and a Labrador named Rusty?'

'Yeah.'

'Not really. I was sort of seeing someone before I left but I doubt she's waiting for me.'

'Why do you doubt it?'

'Because I said, "Claire, please don't wait for me,"' said Jez, causing us both to giggle.

'And why didn't you want her to wait for you? So you could sow your wild oats? Travel the world and shag lots of foreign girls in exotic locations?'

'Hardly,' said Jez quietly. I suddenly felt a tension between us I hadn't felt before. He was looking directly at me, holding eye contact and looking as if he was about to tell me something really important. 'The reason I came travelling, Kate, wasn't to sow my wild oats or to avoid work, extend university or drink myself into oblivion. I came away because my brother died.'

My heart sank and I wanted to hug him with everything I had.

'Richard was at university in Durham,' Jez started and his face changed. A deep sadness seemed to lay itself over him, shrouding his smooth skin and bright blue eyes with a vulnerability. 'Even though he was younger than me, I always looked up to him, you know. He was funny, clever, brilliant really. I probably should have hated him. He was always everyone's favourite, including my parents, but I never could.' Jez took a long gulp of his beer and lit a cigarette. 'He was driving down to see me for the weekend. It was late and wet and he probably should have taken a break, but he didn't. A lorry jack-knifed in front of him and he was killed instantly, or so the police said.' Jez stopped and I could see pools of tears beginning to form in his eyes. He wiped them away quickly and gave me a smile. 'We'd always planned on travelling together when he graduated, so when he died I took off. I didn't even wait around for the funeral. I couldn't sit in a church or watch him being buried and so this is my tribute to him. One year to remember him, do everything we should have done together, before I go home and start over.'

'Oh God, Jez, I don't know what to say. Is this what you were going to tell me the other day at the beach?' I reached over and held his hand.

'I just didn't know how to come out with it. It's still pretty raw.'

'Of course and if you don't want to talk about it that's fine, but I'm here for you,' I gabbled. I didn't know what to say. I'd had emotional upheaval in my own life, but nothing like this. I looked at Jez and he suddenly looked so young, so fragile.

'It's actually good to have someone to talk to about it who didn't know him. Everyone back home is too close. That probably sounds crazy.'

'No, not at all, it's understandable.'

'Is it though? Is it OK to just leave? Not say goodbye to him? Not go to the funeral?'

'It's death, Jez, there are no rules.'

'I wish my parents felt that way.'

'They will.'

'They're pretty pissed off. I left Mum in tears and Dad wouldn't speak to me at all on the drive to the airport. They don't understand.'

'Give them time.'

Jez looked across at me and smiled, a tear suddenly falling down his cheek.

'Thanks, Kate,' he said, wiping away the tear, but it was quickly replaced by another and then another.

'Let's have a drink,' I said with a thin smile, raising my glass. 'To Richard.'

'To Richard,' said Jez and we both downed what we had left of our drinks.

## ED

The drinks with Georgie started on her first day. We went to a pub near work and it snowballed from there. We had a good time together. Despite being absolutely gorgeous she was fun and didn't act like a twenty-two-year-old. We got on so naturally, as if we'd been friends our whole lives instead of for only a few hours. I think because she was completely out of my league and I had Kate it made it easier because it stifled any remote suggestion of something sexual happening.

Of course, our post-work drinks led to the normal office rumours, which began to circulate like wildfire. Ed Hornsby, the dirty old dog, was conducting an illicit affair with the beautiful and much-younger Georgie Hays, while his girlfriend was away travelling. Georgie and I tried to laugh it off, but I was soon standing in front of Hugh, hands nervously in my pockets, explaining myself like a naughty schoolboy.

'What did I say, Hornsby, eh? Hands off. No funny business. I thought you of all people would know better. Tremendously disappointing to say the least.'

Hugh was sitting behind his enormous wooden desk, looking annoyed and agitated, his bulbous face getting redder and redder. Hugh didn't like anything that detracted from his sole purpose: work. I'd seen other people in his office brought to tears for far less. I'd committed the worst possible sin in his eyes. I'd taken his mind off work and onto something far less honourable.

'Hugh, honestly, it's nothing. Just mindless office gossip. You know I'd never do anything to betray you or the company.'

'So you haven't been having cosy drinks with her after hours then, eh?'

'We've had drinks, yes, but purely social and completely friendly. Nothing funny going on at all. She needed a friend . . .'

'Listen, Hornsby, because I'm only going to tell you this once. Men and women don't just go for friendly social drinks. You can call it that until the cows come home, but it doesn't happen. No such thing. Either you want to bang her or she wants to bang you. Stop it now.'

Somehow his use of the word bang seemed to make the whole thing so unsavoury. I imagined Hugh at home demanding that Mrs Whitman stop watching the bloody *Antiques Roadshow* and bang him right away.

'Yes, sir,' I said and walked out of his office, hoping the entire floor wasn't looking at me. Luckily they weren't, but one pair of eyes was.

We'd already agreed on lunch, but I decided it was best to stop things right away. My plan in Kate's absence had been to get ahead and definitely not find myself in Hugh's bad books. Hugh didn't give people the benefit of the doubt and he wouldn't give me a second chance. I emailed Georgie as soon as I got back to my desk.

**To: Georgina Hays**
**From: Edward Hornsby**
**Subject: Extra-curricular drinks**

Had words with Hugh. We need to stop the after-work drinks. It was fun.

Ed

**To: Edward Hornsby**
**From: Georgina Hays**
**Subject: Re: Extra-curricular drinks**

Why???
  G x

**To: Georgina Hays**
**From: Edward Hornsby**
**Subject: Re: Extra-curricular drinks**

Apparently it looks bad and can only lead to a life of debauchery
and vice.
  E x

**To: Edward Hornsby**
**From: Georgina Hays**
**Subject: Re: Extra-curricular drinks**

But it's been fun and nothing's going on. Just friends, right?
  G xx

**To: Georgina Hays**
**From: Edward Hornsby**
**Subject: Re: Extra-curricular drinks**

Best to knock it on the head. Don't want to upset Hugh and get
you in trouble.
  E xx

**To: Edward Hornsby**
**From: Georgina Hays**
**Subject: Re: Extra-curricular drinks**

I'm sad. One last drink? Friday night, somewhere different where
no one will see us?
  G xxx

I should probably have said no. It would have been the sensible thing to do, but it was just one last drink. Two friends having a couple of pints. It was nothing.

**To: Georgina Hays**
**From: Edward Hornsby**
**Subject: Re: Extra-curricular drinks**

Sure. One last drink sounds good.
E xxx

So it was I found myself sitting in a Clapham Common pub on a Friday night with my boss's niece. Before, our drinks had been a couple of pints at one of the pubs near work, but this felt different. We were out of our comfort zone – and underground zone too for that matter. We'd specifically gone somewhere to have a drink and I knew it was wrong. We were sneaking around like lovers.

Once we were at the pub it became clear something had definitely shifted in our relationship. It was easy to discard a casual drink after work because we didn't have to alter the course of our lives to do it, but this was something else. This was deceitful. This wouldn't end well.

'Can you believe what Hugh said?'

'It's ridiculous. We're adults and yet he's treating us like his children,' said Georgie.

'I think to him we sort of are.'

'That's so yucky,' she said and we laughed. We were sitting across from each other at a table. We'd already had a couple of drinks and had kept clear of anything too personal so far. I hadn't asked about boyfriends and she hadn't mentioned Kate. Everything was going to be fine.

'So what happened to your girlfriend?'

I spluttered. 'Kate?'

'I remember you briefly mentioned she was away but didn't elaborate. If it's too weird . . .'

'No, it's fine. She's off travelling for six months.'

'And you didn't go because—?'

'I couldn't leave work. This was something she wanted to do. It was her dream, not mine.'

'And she left without you for six whole months?'

'Yeah.'

'Were you angry?'

'I suppose I was, but when she left I think I was more disappointed than angry. I couldn't believe she'd gone through with it.'

'I don't think I could do that to someone.'

'Leave them?'

'It's just not right,' said Georgie, looking more beautiful the longer we sat there. I'd already seen other men looking over and checking her out. All probably wondering what she was doing with me and I understood. I didn't know why she was with me either. I was older than her, not anywhere near as attractive and I had a girlfriend. What could she possibly gain from hanging around with me? But despite all notions to the contrary, here she was. Georgie Hays and I were friends.

'She had her reasons,' I said, trying my best to defend Kate.

'I'm sure, but she still left you.'

'I suppose.'

'I'd be livid if a man left me like that.'

'And what would you do about it?'

'Probably sleep with someone else to get my revenge,' she said, and suddenly the air around me became a million times heavier. Had she really just said that? Was I taking it the wrong way or the right way? I didn't know, but suddenly I was getting redder and goosebumps spread up my arms and down the back of my neck.

Was she flirting with me?

Did she want to have sex with me?

Did I want to have sex with her?

The alcohol was starting to pickle my brain from its usual state of logicality into a place where anything was possible. I looked at her and instead of looking sheepish or embarrassed by such a brazen statement, she looked deadly serious.

'You, umm, think that's what I should do?'

'What do you think Kate is doing right now?'

Up until that moment, I hadn't really been thinking too much about what Kate had been doing for the past few weeks. We spoke on the phone and she'd mentioned she'd met a guy called Jed or something, but I hadn't or didn't want to think about her living without me. Just the thought of Kate in Thailand and what she was doing made me nauseous. Not that I didn't trust her, because I did, or I thought I did. But the fact was she'd chosen to leave me and if she could do that, what else was she capable of?

'I should probably get another round in,' I mumbled, before getting up and walking off towards the bar.

As it turned out, Georgie only lived a five-minute walk away from the pub. It was gone eleven and we were stumbling through the streets together. I was going to walk her home before getting a taxi back to Wandsworth, like a proper gentleman.

'I'm sad,' she said as we reached her front door step.

'Why?'

'Because we can't do this anymore. I like you, Ed.'

'I like you too.'

'How much?'

'A lot. Very much. This much,' I said, stretching out my arms as wide as they would go.

'Too much?'

I was going to say something, but before I had the chance she leaned in and we were kissing. I should have pulled away. I should have said no and left, but I didn't. Georgie was young, beautiful and for some reason only known to her, she found me attractive. She wanted me and I couldn't say no. The alcohol didn't help, but it wasn't an excuse. I knew what I was doing and I wanted it. Her lips were so soft and she kissed me like she wanted me more than anything in the world. But the elation didn't last. It couldn't. The longer we kissed the more I thought about Kate – the love of my life. The girl I planned to marry and spend the rest of my days with. What if she didn't cheat? Then would I always be the one who had wrecked our relationship. I wasn't that man. I quickly pulled away.

'I'm sorry. I can't do this.'

'What's the matter, Ed. Don't you want me?'

'Of course I do. You know I do. This isn't about you, it's Kate, I can't cheat on Kate.'

'Even though she's probably cheating on you right now?'

'Even so.'

She gave me a look I couldn't decipher. I felt terrible. I wanted to say, 'Fuck it, let's go upstairs and get naked,' but I didn't. I couldn't. The guilt would have torn me apart. I wasn't equipped for the life of a philanderer. I was too weak or maybe too strong, I wasn't quite sure which.

'Your loss,' said Georgie, who turned around without another word and slammed the door in my face.

I found a taxi and spent thirty minutes in the back racked with guilt. Should I tell Kate what I'd done? Was it worth it?

Eventually, as we pulled up outside my house, I decided it was best not to. I hadn't done much and it wasn't worth the arguments it would no doubt create. I wouldn't go out with Georgie again and so that was it. I would focus on work and I definitely wouldn't kiss her again. I took a deep breath and realised I'd just dodged a big bloody bullet. I'd been a fool, but somehow I had escaped by the skin of my teeth.

## JACK

Writing has always been my coping mechanism. I can lose myself in words and ideas so easily and when I do, everything else in the world seems irrelevant. It helped a lot when Dad died. I spent ages writing after the funeral. Most of it was nonsense, lots of wistful poetry and mawkish stories about death and loss, but some of it was useful.

I was at my desk trying to work through a few minor kinks in the synopsis before I sent my novel off to agents: my last chance to have the life I'd dreamed about since I was a teenager. It was terrifying to think it was my last throw of the dice, but I didn't have a choice. Having a dream was one thing, but at the expense of everything else was too much of a sacrifice.

I was happy to have writing to do because I was keeping out of Emma's way. It had been a tumultuous week; it started badly, with an argument about her late-night drinking session with Rhys. It wasn't that I minded her going out with him, not that I was thrilled about it, but she didn't think to even call me. I was at home with dinner ready, waiting to apologise about our earlier argument, while she was boozing it up with Rhys and his media mates in Soho. I waited until ten before I threw her dinner in the bin and went to bed in a strop. She came home past midnight and sneaked into bed reeking of alcohol.

I had to be at work early the following day and so I didn't see her until the next night. We spoke, but it was tense and we

83

both said things we probably shouldn't have. Then on Tuesday on page thirteen of the *Sun* there was a picture of Rhys and Emma leaving a café together hand-in-hand. She was referred to as a 'mystery blonde' and perhaps Rhys's new flame. She explained it was nothing, just typical paparazzi looking for a story where there wasn't one. Since then it's been a week of avoiding each other, monosyllabic conversation and mainly not speaking at all. Neither of us, it seemed, knew where to begin.

'I need to tell you something,' said Emma suddenly.

I stopped what I was doing and spun around in my chair. She looked serious. Had she cheated on me with Rhys after all? It was the first thought that popped into my head. I tried to remain calm and not jump to any conclusions because I had no reason for not trusting her. Mum's words echoed in my ears, 'It's ironic, but the fear of failure is often its catalyst'. I didn't want to be the man who ruined a perfectly great relationship out of fear of losing it.

'OK,' I said calmly.

'I have to go away for a week with the cast. It's not until the middle of February, but I really need to go. Do you mind?'

Did I mind? I spent a moment thinking about it and the truth was I didn't. I don't know what she thought of me or what had happened to us over the past week, but I didn't want her to think I was annoyed or jealous of her success. I didn't know how to tell her it wasn't her success I feared, but losing her because of it. Just looking at her sitting opposite me, so meek, it made me feel awful. I'd done that. I'd made her that way. Change was hard and the realisation I hadn't handled it well made me feel like a prize idiot. My father's words quickly followed Mum's in my head, 'We should love blindly without question, without regret and selflessly'. I'd been a selfish prick and I knew it. I looked at her and smiled.

'Of course I don't bloody mind,' I said and we fell into a mad embrace. We kissed deeply before she pulled away and looked at me, tears washing around her eyes.

'I'm sorry if I hurt you, I . . .'

'It's me who should be apologising. I'm sorry. I should have been more supportive and I wasn't. I was stupid and a real prick about things.'

'You were a bit,' said Emma, with a ridiculously cute smile.

'But not anymore. I'm going to support you and give you whatever you need. I'm so proud of you, Em and I love you so much.'

'I love you too,' she said and before I knew it, my writing was all but forgotten as we stumbled, kissing and pulling each other's clothes off, towards the bedroom.

'So that's what it's like to shag a film star?' I said as we lay in bed afterwards.

'Oh, stop it.'

The sex had been incredible because when we finally orgasmed together, it wasn't just a regular orgasm, but one filled with relief and awash with love. There had been moments, albeit fleeting, but moments nonetheless when I thought we might never have sex like that again. However, lying there wrapped up together under the duvet, our naked bodies curled around each other, I felt nothing but calmness. Her head was on my chest, bobbing up and down slowly to my breathing, her body fitting perfectly against mine, and everything felt right again.

Our cocoon of happiness didn't last quite as long as I'd hoped though as my phone suddenly stirred into life. I reached across to the nightstand and had a look at the caller. It was Ed.

'You'd better get it,' said Emma. 'I'll jump in the shower.'

I watched as Emma hopped out of bed and walked off towards the shower; her perfect little bum wiggling away brought a smile to my face. I was a lucky man.

'Ed, mate, how are you?'

'Good thanks, you?'

'No complaints. How's life without the missus?'

There was a brief pause and even on the phone I could sense a tension in his voice.

'Oh, you know, dull. I was calling to see if you wanted to get a drink.'

'Yes, of course, when and where and I'll be there with bells on?'

'Tomorrow night?'

'Sounds perfect, mate,' I said. 'About seven-thirty?'

Ed and I agreed to meet at a pub on the Southbank and go from there. I was looking forward to it and maybe a night out with Ed was just what I needed.

I liked and admired Ed so much because in many ways he was my mirror opposite. At twenty-nine, I was still chasing a dream and working in a crap service job while I waited for my big break, whereas he was doggedly settled into a life of hard work – not necessarily doing a job he loved, but one he knew would pay the bills. He definitely wasn't a dreamer, but a realist who didn't want to rock the boat and make any mistakes. That's why I wasn't surprised he didn't go with Kate. I would have been more surprised if he had. I used to think he was a bit boring, but now I saw that above everything else, he was just afraid of failure. Afraid that with one wrong move the whole bloody house of cards would come falling down.

## EMMA

There was something I didn't want to tell Jack. It was nothing really, just a silly misunderstanding. It was one of those things that happened with people like Rhys. I'd had enough experience with other actors to know what it's like and Rhys apologised profusely and promised it wouldn't ever happen again. We even laughed about it afterwards because it was so ridiculous. I felt awful though because I shouldn't have let it happen at all and now I was keeping it from Jack.

After we left the café in Swiss Cottage and headed to Soho, I was so excited and wrapped up in a glow of exhilaration. Having my photo taken with Rhys and then being whisked away in a cab to an exclusive club, I felt like a proper celebrity. I know it's all a bit superficial and silly, but as the flashes of the cameras were on me, blinding me with their hunt for a story, I felt like the little girl who had put on a play for her mummy.

Once at the club, I soon realised it wasn't like anywhere I'd been before. For a start, it was impossible to get in unless you came on the arm of Rhys Connelly and inside it was wall to wall celebrities, and I was one of them; part of the inner circle.

After we were settled in and got drinks, Rhys introduced his friends. There was Paul, an old friend from Wales, who lived with him to help 'keep his feet on the ground' and there was Eloise, Rhys's fabulous agent. I asked her where she was from and she just smiled and said, 'Everywhere, Emma, and nowhere.' It was probably why she seemed to have an accent that sounded like South African crossed with French, topped with a dollop of American and finished off with shavings of high-society English. She was lovely though and kept telling me how beautiful I was.

The night changed at just gone ten. Paul and Eloise had to leave. Paul was heading back to Wales early in the morning and Eloise had to catch a flight to LA. Eloise gave me a long hug goodbye, followed by a kiss on the lips and told me to stay in touch. They both disappeared, leaving Rhys and me alone. By that point we'd both had quite a few. I was still on cloud nine and alcohol was running through my body like liquid excitement and so when Rhys asked me to dance, I didn't think anything of it.

I'm sure in most clubs the sight of Rhys dancing would have drawn looks and hushed comments, but in there, in a room packed with celebrities, he was just another body and I was just another body dancing closely next to him. We danced for what felt like an hour, but was probably more like fifteen minutes, gradually getting closer, moving together, until suddenly we kissed.

Maybe it was the alcohol, the adrenalin, or that it was Rhys Connelly, I don't know, but when he leaned in and kissed me, I didn't stop him. Not right away. It didn't last longer than a few seconds and then he pulled away once he realised I wasn't really kissing him back.

'Shit, sorry,' he said. 'Got a bit carried away.'

'It's fine.' I smiled. 'I understand. You're Rhys Connelly, big movie star. You're probably used to getting whatever girls you want.'

'But not you, eh.'

'That's right,' I said and we carried on dancing.

Rhys apologised again at the end of the night as he put me in a cab and paid the driver. I said it was fine because it was. It was nothing. Just a silly, drunken kiss.

I felt awful when Jack was apologising to me, but I couldn't tell him and, honestly, it was never going to happen again, so what was the point? It meant nothing.

'Sure you don't mind?' said Jack, standing in the doorway, looking gorgeous in his going-out clothes. He had on a pair of faded blue jeans, a pale green gingham shirt and he smelt wonderful.

'It's fine, you have fun with Ed.'

'But what about the wedding stuff?'

'Right, the wedding stuff, and you're going to do what exactly? The flower arrangements? The invitations?'

Jack looked at me with those gorgeous eyes of his and then smiled. The wedding was six months away and so far we hadn't done anything except save the date and book the church. We still had everything else to do and on top of the film, it was starting to feel like it would never get done. So, in our hour of need, and desperate, I had called my mother.

'I really am sorry about being such an idiot about the film,' he said, sitting down on the bed next to me, grabbing my heart and yanking it around the room. I kept thinking about the kiss and whether I should tell him. It didn't mean anything and it wasn't going to happen again, but I hated lying to him.

'It's all right, honestly.'

'No, no it's not. I was stupid and your basic twat of a bloke. I want us to be happy, honest and proud of each other regardless of what we're doing. I want us to tell each other everything, the good, the bad and the ugly. I want to be the one to support you and help you and the fact I wasn't makes me feel like an idiot. I love you and I'm so proud of you . . .'

'Rhys kissed me,' I said suddenly. Jack let go of my hand

and stood up. 'He kissed me at the club and it didn't mean anything. It was a silly, stupid kiss, we were drunk and . . .'

'Did you kiss him back?'

'For a second, maybe, but then I stopped it and I'm so sorry, Jack. I wanted to tell you right away, I did, but . . .'

'But you didn't, did you?'

He was looking at me, his face bristling with contempt and anger. It was a face I'd never seen before and it scared me. I'd betrayed him, betrayed us. I was terrified I was going to lose him over nothing. I suddenly wished I hadn't told him because then he wouldn't have that face. That look of hatred.

'Because it meant nothing. Was nothing. Just a stupid mistake that won't ever happen again. I love you, Jack, and no one else. I just want to be with you.'

'Then don't do the film.'

'What?'

'If you love me so much, don't do the film with him.'

'But it's my dream, Jack. The moment I've been waiting for my whole life.'

'And if you love me, you won't do it,' he said again, grabbing his coat and heading towards the door. 'I'd do anything for you, Em, anything.'

And then he was gone.

As soon as the front door closed, I burst into tears. I had been such a fool. Why did I have to tell him? The answer was simple: because I loved him and not telling him would have eaten away at me until eventually I would have broken down and told him anyway. It was better done now than in two months or, worse, after the wedding. It hurt though. How could he ask me to give up the film? He knew what it meant to me and how hard I had worked to get it. He was probably just overreacting. He didn't mean it.

I got up, dried my eyes, splashed some water over my face and walked into the kitchen. I sat down with a glass of wine and waited for Mum to show up.

'Why isn't Jack here?' said Mum. 'He should be here. He is the groom, after all.'

'He had to go and meet Ed.'

'Now, there's a funny business. What sort of man lets his girlfriend waltz off across the globe by herself? Still, Jack should be here, darling.'

I loved Mum dearly, but she could be shallow, petty and more judgemental than anyone I knew. She'd never really warmed to Jack. I think because he worked in a coffee shop instead of doing something proper, she thought him a failure. I think she only let me pursue my acting dream because she'd hoped I would meet a tall, dark and very rich man who'd take care of me. She wanted Mr Darcy and instead she got Jack and he wasn't good enough for her little girl.

'Well he isn't. Shall we get on?'

'I suppose,' said Mum and she started going on about the reception and a friend of hers with a huge mansion in Oxfordshire, but all I was thinking about was Jack.

From the moment I met Jack, I had no doubt he was my soulmate, my one true love. I don't think I even believed in soulmates before him, but as soon as we met that was it – the search was over. We never just dated; it was always so much more than that. We were always so sure about each other, so intent nothing would ever come between us. Now that it had, I didn't know what to do. I was lost.

'What do you think, darling?' said Mum suddenly.

'About what?'

'You weren't even listening were you? About the Oxford house for the reception and Uncle Peter's Rolls for the car.'

'Yeah, sounds fantastic,' I said, but my head or heart wasn't really in it.

'Don't say yeah, darling, say yes. It sounds so common and your father and I raised you better than that,' said Mum, her usual snobbish self, but I didn't have the heart or the patience for a fight.

'Sorry,' I said and we moved swiftly on to the flowers.

**To: Kate Jones**
**From: Emma Fogle**
**Subject: Re: I made it!**

K,

Oh my God! Rhys Connelly kissed me!

Let me start at the beginning. We met up at a café to go over our lines. This in itself was crazy enough. I was sitting with Rhys Connelly having lunch for Christ's sake! He's actually a really sweet and funny man. Yes he's gorgeous and sexy, but after a while I almost forgot who he was and we were just having a good time. I was actually more excited about going over the script together. I felt like a proper actress. It felt so good, Kate.

Anyway, after we finished, he invited me out for drinks in Soho with some friends of his. I felt bad for Jack, stuck at home waiting for me, but this was the chance of a lifetime. The club was A-mazing. Seriously. You'd have loved it. I wish you could have been there too. I met his friends but they had to leave early and so it was just me and Rhys. We were dancing when he just leaned in and kissed me. I couldn't believe it. I mean, since I started dating Jack, no one else had tried to kiss me. Especially not an A-list movie star! This was probably why I didn't stop him right away. I was in shock. It didn't last long and we had a giggle about it afterwards. He even apologised and I could see he felt bad. I did feel guilty about it, of course, but it was nothing. We'd had a few drinks and it lasted seconds.

But then I told Ed and he flipped out. I suppose because in my head it really was just a bit silly, I thought he would see it in the same way. He didn't. He went ballistic and told me not to do the film! What am I going to do, Kate? I love Jack so much, but this is the role I've been waiting for my whole life. I wish you were here. I know that's supposed to be the other way around, you're supposed to be the one saying, I wish you were here, but I need you.

I've also been trying to organise the wedding with Mother, which is, as you can imagine, a total nightmare. She's taking over and trying to do everything her way. The trouble is I have so little energy and fight that she's probably going to get her way and we'll end up having the wedding of her dreams!

I hope all is well in paradise! I can't wait to hear from you again soon. Don't forget the photos! I want to see what Jez looks like and how tanned you are!

Love Em X

## KATE

'Ready?' said Jez with a huge smile on his face.

We were heading off to the full moon party. We'd been drinking steadily all evening and were both a bit tipsy. It was only nine o'clock and I couldn't imagine staying up all night but I was going to try.

'Ready as I'll ever be.'

We arrived at a huge party, dance music blaring out from all corners, drowning us in its earth-rumbling bass.

'This is mental!' I shouted. We were surrounded by tens of thousands of other revellers, all here looking for that elusive traveller experience. We'd done the full moon party. It would be something to look back on. Something to tell the grand-kids when they were convinced we didn't understand them. A proper backpacker experience that for some reason made me think back to the day I almost died.

I was fifteen and it was typical teenage folly. I was loitering around after school with a couple of friends, delaying going home where I'd be forced to do my homework before dinner. We'd recently discovered the joys of smoking, although it wasn't really that joyous, just three girls coughing and splut-tering and trying to look cool behind the Co-op. I was about to leave and head off home. I said goodbye to my friends and then stepped out into the road without looking and was hit by a car. Luckily the car wasn't going very fast, but I still ended up in hospital, surrounded by my family with doctors telling them I was a very lucky girl indeed. I had broken ribs, a broken arm, a whole smorgasbord of brown and sickly looking bruises and internal bleeding. It could, they stressed so many times before I eventually left, have been much worse.

After my near-death experience, Mum fussed over me so much. She seemed terrified I was going to drop down dead at any moment, which obviously caused me a great deal of annoyance, being a teenager in the throes of puberty. Maybe I didn't fully realise it then, but I changed after my brush with death. I started making plans and thinking about my future. I stopped messing around at school and I knuckled down, because I realised life was short and I wanted to do so much.

I can still remember the exact moment the car hit me with incredible clarity. And the shock of suddenly finding myself on the ground, trapped under a car, while panic surrounded me. I wasn't that conscious because I'd hit my head on the ground, but there was a split second when I was totally lucid and in that moment, the life I wanted to have seemed to flash through my mind.

Since then I'd always been on the run. Running from one thing to another, terrified that if I stopped, my near-death experience would have been for nothing. I guess in some ways Ed and I were both running, but his version of running meant staying still, not changing, out of fear of the unknown, while my version meant running off around the world, chasing a dream I'd had since I was fifteen.

By two in the morning Jez and I were both far too tired to keep going. We'd stopped drinking already and the prospect of staying up for another four or five hours seemed beyond us.

'Flagging?' said Jez.

'Just a bit. Shall we make a move?'

Make a move? I sounded like my mother.

'I'm never going to last until sunrise and we have a travel day tomorrow.'

'Let's go,' I said and offered him my hand, which he took, and we headed off along the beach. 'I can't believe this is it.'

'What?'

'This. Us. Our last night here and then we go our separate ways.'

'We don't have to,' said Jez, looking across at me.

'What do you mean? You have to leave Thailand and I'm heading up to Chiang Mai.'

'I could cross the border and come back for another thirty days . . .'

'And why would you want to do that?' I said with a naïve little giggle, stopping and turning to look at Jez. I felt fifteen again.

'Because I like you, Kate.'

'I like you too.'

'No, I *like* you,' he said before he left a pause and then said it again. 'Like you.'

'Oh.' That was the last thing either of us said.

Thousands of miles from home, under the moonlight, Jez and I kissed passionately for what seemed like forever. It had been so long since I'd kissed anyone except Ed, and it felt strange at first, but then suddenly it didn't. Suddenly it felt like the most natural thing in the world. We stumbled back to our bungalow and to the bed that had seemed like a bad idea at the time.

We lay there and it seemed only a matter of time before our kissing led to something else, but I didn't know if I could. A part of me wanted to. I sort of ached for it and I knew with Jez it wouldn't be awkward or strange and it would mean something. But I couldn't do it. I'd hurt Ed enough already just leaving. I couldn't do this to him as well. I liked Jez a lot. More than a lot, actually, but whether I had sex with him or not wasn't going to change that. I was afraid, though, that it might change things with Ed forever and I wasn't ready to do that. I wasn't ready to just give up because I was so far from home. 'I'm sorry, Jez, but could we just cuddle?' I said.

'It's him, isn't it? The boyfriend who hates to travel.'

I nodded.

'I'm sorry, Jez, but I love him and I don't want to do anything to risk what we have.'

'Even though he wouldn't come travelling, obviously loves work more than you and even though we kissed?'

'Even so.'

'He must be special.'

'He is, Jez, and so are you.'

'Really?' he said, looking across at me, the moonlight catching the side of his face.

'Yes really. You're wonderful, funny and sexy and if it wasn't for Ed . . .'

'You'd spend the rest of the year travelling with me, we'd fall in love and live happily ever after?'

'Maybe.'

A part of me wanted that. I could see it all in an instant. I could see the next six months and probably longer travelling the world, experiencing life and living the dream. I'd always thought about backpacking and in my head there was always a man. Tall, dark and handsome, just like Jez, and we'd fall in love on a tropical island like Koh Phangan. When I was fifteen it was all an incredible dream, but now I was actually living it and in that moment with Jez, lying in that bed, I think I could have gone with it. It was a close call. Instead we lay listening to two cats screaming outside and to the sound of the over-head fan slowly cooling our bodies.

I used to go to the park with Mum when I was little. We'd go there nearly every day in the summer before autumn came with the rain and winter with the cold. I used to love going on the swings and swinging as high as I could. Mum would get scared and yell out my name from the bench, 'Kate Marie Jones, stop it now; don't go any higher!' I would go right up until the point when it felt like I was about to go all the way around. I loved that feeling of flying so close to the edge and wondering if one day I'd go too far. I had the same feeling again with Jez. I felt like if we kept going, we'd go all the way around and we'd never be able to come back again.

'Richard would have been proud,' Jez said through the darkness.

I turned and looked at him and I could see he was smiling.

'Why's that?' I said, reaching across for the packet of ciga-rettes on the nightstand.

'He said one day he'd like to have an affair with an older woman. Something else I've crossed off the list for him.'

'Cheeky bastard,' I said, hitting him gently on the shoul-der. 'You know, just for the record, I really admire what you're doing.'

'What do you mean?'

'This. Travelling the world for Richard. I can't think of a better way to remember someone.'

'Thanks,' said Jez quietly. There was a small pause as he lit a cigarette. 'It . . .' he started and then I could sense he was on the verge of tears again. 'It's guilt, mainly.'

'Guilt? Why?'

'Because he was coming to see me when he died. It was a weekend I organised and made him drive down for. You know he called me on the Friday because he wasn't going to come. It was our last conversation. He had too much to do, but I convinced him to come anyway. I made him come, Kate, and he died.'

'But it isn't your fault. Surely you can see that.'

'I still feel guilty though and maybe that's why I had to get away so quickly, because I couldn't face it. Running away seemed like the only choice.'

'Maybe it was. You did what you had to do, and what good would have come from being there? Going to the funeral. Dealing with all the tears and grief, talking about it over and over again. At least this way you're grieving on your own terms and paying your last respects to Richard the way he would have wanted.'

'I just . . .'

'Just what?'

'I just wish I could see it like that.'

'And you will, in time.'

Jez and I lay smoking and talking until we both fell asleep near dawn to the steady moan of dance music in the distance. We'd planned on staying up to see the sunrise, but neither of us made it. We awoke around ten, still wrapped up in each other. Jez smiled at me.

'I suppose this is it.'

'I suppose,' I said and a part of me wanted to cry.

We packed our bags and said goodbye to our little bungalow. In some ways it felt like an absolute age since we'd arrived, cautiously navigating the single-bed situation, but in others it felt like only yesterday. We took the boat back to the mainland and I thought about the moment I'd had on the way out to Koh Phangan – my epiphany. It had been a wonderful moment, but going back felt even more monumental because I had changed. I had cheated on Ed, but it had made me closer to him, if that made sense. I thought about my kiss with Jez and if I regretted it. I didn't. I didn't because he made me realise, despite everything, just how much I loved Ed. If going travelling was something I had to do, then so was being with Ed. If I was still running, then Ed was the constant that would always keep me coming back.

Jez and I stood facing each other at the bus terminal. I was heading one way and he the other. I didn't know what to do or what to say. I wanted to keep in touch, but I knew it wasn't possible. I'd shared moments with Jez I'd never forget. He would always be the one who saved me. My Bangkok hero. We stood in an awkward silence, neither friends nor lovers, but caught somewhere in between.

'I have one question,' I eventually said.

'And what's that?'

'Why did you spend the last three weeks with me?'

Jez smiled and looked at me with those gorgeous blue eyes. Jez had a certain smile, my mum would call it cheeky; the smile of a boy who knew he was handsome and could get away with blue bloody murder because of it.

'Isn't it obvious?'

'Because you thought I'd have sex with you?' I said and then laughed a horribly girlie laugh.

'Kate,' he said, holding my hands in his. 'It was never about the sex.'

'You just liked being with me?'

'Is that so hard to believe?'

'Maybe,' I said and we kissed again, only this time it was different. The passion was still there, but, knowing I wouldn't ever kiss him again, I felt a sadness that would linger on my lips long after we said goodbye.

# Happy Endings

To: Emma Fogle
From: Kate Jones
Subject: Re: I made it!

Em,

I can't believe you kissed Rhys Connelly! That's incredible. Was it amazing? I bet it was. I know you probably felt guilty, but shit, Rhys Connelly! And if it really was nothing then Jack shouldn't be that bothered. I mean, yes, you kissed him, but you're going to be kissing him in the film, so what's the difference? I think with men it's mainly ego. I'm sure Jack will come around once he's calmed down. And, talking of kissing, I ended up snogging Jez! What's wrong with us? Let me explain how it happened and what I've been up to since the last email.

Jez and I travelled down from Bangkok to Koh Phangan. It was a long journey but so worth it. It was so beautiful, Em. When we arrived we checked into this hostel that Jez had stayed at before. It was gorgeous, right on the beach, but the only problem was that we had to share a bed! OK, fine, I should have guessed something was going to happen, I suppose, but it felt sort of innocent at the time.

The island was just perfect and we spent our time snorkelling, taking little trips on the death scooters (so dangerous but such fun!) and sunbathing. I have an A-mazing tan already. Just have a look at the photos I've attached – you're going to be so jealous! It took us ten days to finally kiss, but it was really magical. I don't know how it felt to kiss Rhys, but kissing Jez felt so good and so right it scared me. I felt guilty straight away because I hadn't meant to cheat on Ed. We just kissed though, nothing else. I mean we cuddled in bed, which is bad, I know, but, and it isn't an excuse, but when you're so far away it feels different. I'm not going to do any more though. I didn't come away to cheat on Ed. I love Ed. This was just a blip.

I just arrived in Chiang Mai, which is in the north of Thailand, after another very long trip. I'm loving it though, Em. It's hard to put into words, but I feel a connection to my old self again. That probably sounds a bit weird, but I think working the last eight years and living in London, I sort of lost a bit of who I used to be. The old, pre-university, back-in-Oxford, teenage me. But coming away and doing the trip I planned when I was fifteen, I feel closer to that me again. It feels silly writing it, but it's you, probably the only person who understands what I'm waffling on about so I don't care.

I have lots of cool stuff planned for Chiang Mai. I'll write again soon with more details. I've attached a few photos – a couple of Jez, so make sure Ed doesn't get a whiff. Let me know how things go with Jack and with the wedding. Make sure you stand up to your mum. This is your wedding, not hers!

Love K X

# february

## ED

Jack looked like he had the weight of the world on his shoulders. Something had obviously happened with Emma because as soon as he arrived, he ordered a pint and a whisky and they were both gone in a matter of minutes. I got us another couple of pints and we sat at a table by the window. Outside, the Thames was a slow-moving grey mass and the sky was the colour of charcoal with not a star in sight. It was good to see Jack, although by the expression on his face, maybe it wouldn't be the light-hearted lad's night out I'd hoped for.

'Do you want to talk about it?'

Jack was twirling a beer mat between his fingers and he looked like he wanted to punch something.

'It's Emma. She kissed Rhys Connelly.'

It was then I guessed that what he actually wanted to punch was some*one*.

'The actor?'

'They went out for lunch, then to a club in Soho. One thing led to another. Long story short, they kissed.'

'Blimey. I never thought she'd do something like that.'

'Me either.'

'And she told you?'

'She said it was a mistake and it wouldn't happen again, but they're doing a film together and there's sex scenes and nudity and so of course it's going to happen again.'

'Mate, I'm sorry.'

I immediately started thinking about Georgie. Was it just a kiss? Did it mean nothing? I wasn't so sure. I think it always means something when you cheat on your partner. People throw around hollow phrases like, it meant nothing, it won't happen again, I felt trapped, but what does all of that really equate to? Aren't they just pitiful excuses because we were too weak to turn down the offer of someone who made us feel attractive? I knew what I was doing with Georgie was wrong, but I did it anyway. I stopped before we went too far, but I still cheated on Kate and I was sure it definitely meant something.

'I told her she couldn't do the film,' Jack said suddenly.

'Oh.'

'Too much?'

'It's your life, mate, and your girlfriend.'

'But you think I went too far?'

'It's just . . . that's always been her dream and she's finally made it. I'm not sure you can take that away from her.'

'Bit like you and Kate.'

'Exactly like me and Kate. I couldn't stop her leaving and I have to trust she will come back to me.'

'But what if she doesn't? What if she meets someone else?'

'Then I suppose that's it.'

'You can be that clinical about it?'

'Not clinical, just a realist. We can't make people stay with us, love us. It doesn't work like that.'

I wasn't sure I believed a word I was saying. It sounded right, like it might be true and that I should believe it, but I wasn't convinced. I loved Kate so much. She gave me meaning. Without her I'd be a shell of myself and it would kill me if she didn't come back. I'd be crushed. I knew I couldn't make Kate love me and be with me any more than Jack could stop Emma from doing the film, but if she didn't, I didn't know what else I'd do.

'What do you think I should do?' said Jack, downing the dregs of his pint.

'I think you already know the answer to that one, mate. Another?'

'Please.'

Ever since our kiss, Georgie and I had kept our distance. There had been a few furtive glances and awkward moments at the photocopier, but we'd seen the error of our ways and I assumed it would disappear into my forgettable past like my brief foray into the office five-a-side football team. However, while I was standing at the bar waiting for our pints, Georgie had other ideas. My phone buzzed in my pocket to let me know I had a text.

Home alone, bored and thinking of you.
G x

I felt a prickly heat rising up inside of me. It was silly, but it felt like every person in the room knew what was going on. I quickly looked around and, of course, no one was looking at me. They were all drinking their pints or talking and not paying me the slightest bit of attention. I quickly stuffed the phone into my pocket and headed back to the table with our drinks, desperately trying to work out what Georgie wanted from me.

'How're you doing without Kate?' said Jack once I'd sat down again.

'I'm not going to lie, it's been tough.' I said. 'Tougher than I thought.'

'Do you regret not going then?'

It was a good question. Did I regret not going? Did I regret what had happened with Georgie? Did I wish I was sunning myself on a beach in Thailand with Kate rather than sitting in a pub trying to decide whether I should send a reply that would cause more harm than good?

'No,' I said, taking a sip of my pint. 'It was Kate's thing. She needed to do it for her. If I'd gone, I'd probably have ruined it for her.'

'You're right. You'd have dragged her down with your constant whining.'

'Cheers, mate.'

'At least if it all does go awry and it isn't what she'd hoped for, she can't blame you.'

'It's a win–win. Either she has the time of her life and she thanks me for letting her go, or she has an awful time and can't wait to get back to me.' If only I was that confident everything was going to turn out so well.

'I wish my situation was that simple,' said Jack and his face dropped again. 'And on that note, I'm off to the loo.'

Once Jack had gone, I took out my phone and stared at the text. Why would she have written it? Maybe she was drunk? or maybe she meant to send it to someone else. Just as I was pondering whether to ignore it, delete it or reply to it, another message suddenly appeared in my inbox with a ping.

Are you ignoring me Ed? G x

Obviously the message was for me. What could I say? Was I ignoring her? Yes and for good reason. She was beautiful, home alone and thinking of me and I was out, drinking, my girlfriend was ten thousand miles away and I hadn't had sex in forever. I decided it wouldn't hurt to have a bit of friendly banter.

Of course not. Just out with a mate having
a few beers. Why aren't you out? E x

Before I had the chance to put the phone back in my pocket, it buzzed again.

No one to play with. At home in my pyjamas, bored and wishing you were here.
G xx

I quickly typed a reply before Jack came back.

And what would we do? Film? Takeaway?
Other? E xx

It was wrong and stupid, but at that moment, I didn't care. I felt out of control and maybe it was what I needed. Maybe what I needed was Georgie. Obviously I wasn't thinking clearly, but before I managed to text myself further into a hole, Jack came back to the table.

'How's the writing going?' I said nervously, hoping he wouldn't spot the look of embarrassment and guilt that seemed, to me at least, plastered like a billboard across my face.

'All done. Sending off the agent letters on Monday.'

'And this is definitely the last one?'

'For a while. I'm so bored of being broke, of feeling like a complete and utter failure. If this doesn't work, it's back to the drawing board.'

'Like I've said before, you can always come and work with me.'

'Another pint here or do you want to go somewhere else?' he said, ignoring me.

'We can stay here if you want; get pissed like a couple of old codgers.'

'You don't fancy going somewhere a bit, I don't know, live-lier?' said Jack with a disappointed shrug.

I looked around at the pub and it was lively enough. Admittedly, the people were mainly City workers who came here because they could sit down and talk, eat some half-decent food without being elbowed out of the way by pissed tourists, students and people under the age of twenty-five. The pub was full of people like me. People who sat in comfortable chairs all day and didn't want that to change by night.

'Fine, let's go somewhere a bit livelier,' I said, downing the last inch of my pint.

'While the Kate's away, eh.'

I smiled and grabbed my coat. Maybe it was time I took a chance and had a bit of fun. Maybe it was time I stopped living the easy life in easy pubs full of middle-aged people living middle-aged lives. After all, I wasn't yet thirty. I was sick and tired of always doing the right thing, the sensible thing, and acting as though I was past it. Kate wasn't the only one who could be impulsive and have fun.

Four hours later I ended up drunk and standing outside Georgie's flat in Clapham, throwing small stones at her window. Maybe if I'd have stayed with the commuter-belt bunch, I'd have gone home like a good boy, bought a kebab and fallen asleep on the sofa thinking about my girlfriend. As it was, I spent the night with Jack, getting steadily drunker, texting backwards and forwards with Georgie until I couldn't take it anymore. Jack and I left the club and after I said good-bye and wished him well with Emma, I hopped in a taxi and headed to Clapham.

From the age of eight to sixteen Alex Holloway was my best friend. Alex's family moved to Wales just before sixth form and we lost touch, but before that we were inseparable. For Alex's fourteenth birthday his dad bought a video camera and spent the whole party videoing us. This was in the days before cameras on mobile phones and no one I knew had a video camera.

What I remember most about the party wasn't the cake, the snooker competition or even that he'd invited Hannah Callaghan, the best-looking girl at our school, but watching the video footage back afterwards. It was the first time I'd ever seen myself on video and I couldn't believe it. Was that what I really looked like? Was that how I smiled? Moved? Spoke? Was that how everyone else in the world saw me? In our heads we have a certain image of ourselves, but when we see how we actually are, it's so different. It made me wonder who I really was.

Fifteen years later, I was thinking the same thing as I stood on Georgie's front door step. Who was I and what the fuck was I doing?

'You came,' said Georgie as she appeared at the door.

She was wearing a simple floral dress that stopped just above her knees. She looked at me for a moment, her lovely face and incredible body just waiting for me to step over the threshold. 'I did,' I said, and then she grabbed my hand and pulled me inside.

The minute I stepped into her flat it was like everything accelerated. The pretence I was there for anything other than sex quickly washed away. The pretty floral dress fell to the floor, revealing Georgie's wonderful body beneath. She was wearing a matching blue and white polka-dot bra and panties.

'What do you think?'

'Incredible', was the only word I could think of.

'Just give me a moment,' she said, planting a delicate kiss on my lips before she bounced away and disappeared into what I assumed was her bedroom.

While she was gone I had a quick look around her flat. It was your typical just-graduated-from-university flat. The walls were adorned with posters of bands, films and the mandatory Gustav Klimt poster. The various eclectic knick-knacks and ornaments that didn't quite fit together; the combination of two different people bringing with them their histories and childhood memories; photos of young girls with their ponies, on holiday with their parents, boyfriends, brothers, I didn't know. The scattering of old books on shelves and on the coffee table. The wine bottles stacked up on a sideboard and the IKEA rugs plastered across most of the old wooden floor. It screamed of lives just beginning, of unanswered questions, of youth and promise. Then, over the fireplace, I saw a picture of Georgie, with what I assumed were her parents, on graduation day; she was beaming from ear-to-ear, a beautiful young lady and her proud mum and dad.

'Ready?' said Georgie, suddenly reappearing around the doorway.

To be honest, I wasn't. The alcohol had done a fairly decent job up until that point, but, now we were about to disappear into her bedroom, the realisation of what I was going to do seemed to hit me like a bus. I walked towards her until we were face to face.

'What now?'

'Now, Ed Hornsby, you fuck my brains out.'

It was a strange experience if I'm honest. The sex was great. It was natural, raw and spontaneous, and I did things with her I hadn't done with Kate in years. Whereas with Kate I didn't go that extra-mile, try that different position, because we had our system and it worked, with Georgie it was different. Afterwards we lay in the dark looking up at the ceiling and the orbs of light that crept in from the streetlights outside.

'Can I ask you something?' I said through the darkness.

'Sure.'

'Why me? Why did you pick me when you could've had anyone at work?'

'Because there was something about you. A vulnerability. A sadness. It was as if from the moment I met you, I could feel it. You were desperate for something and I thought maybe it could be me.'

She rubbed her leg along mine and then reached across with her hand and ran a finger down my stomach. I suddenly thought of Kate and a huge wave of guilt swept through my body, making me feel nauseous. The alcohol had worn off and I was looking up at the mountain face of reality and it went on forever. It suddenly dawned on me that I would have to tell her. She would come back ready to settle down, get engaged, start our life over and I'd have to tell her. I had cheated and suddenly I regretted it more than anything in the world.

'I should go,' I said, looking down at Georgie's body outlined against the white sheet.

'No, stay, Ed. I want to go again.' Her hand quickly reached towards me, but I shifted myself in the bed.

'I should . . .'

'Feeling guilty? Don't. You've already done it so another once or twice isn't going to hurt.' Her hand tried to find me again but I stood up and searched the floor for my clothes.

'I'm sorry.'

'Ed, stop being ridiculous and get back in bed,' said Georgie, kneeling up so I could see her body in full. But it didn't matter. Nothing mattered except leaving. I managed to find my jeans and then my shirt. I got dressed while Georgie slumped back into bed.

'Seriously, you're leaving?'

'It's not you, Georgie, it's me. It's Kate. I can't do this. I love her.'

'It was fine ten minutes ago when you had your head between my legs; why isn't it fine now? What's changed?'

'Nothing. I just feel like I should leave.'

'But I don't want you to leave, Ed. Stay. Please. For me?'

Georgie got off the bed and wrapped herself around me, kissing my neck and making my escape that much harder. But something had triggered inside of me. I didn't want this anymore. I didn't want Georgie. I wanted to go home and wrap myself in the duvet that still faintly smelt of Kate.

'I'm sorry,' I said and walked out.

## JACK

I reached across and felt nothing but a slightly creased sheet. The bed was empty. My head felt like someone had attacked it with a hard, blunt object from the inside. My eyes were stuck together with sleep and my stomach felt like a washing machine of salt and vinegar. It had been a good night with Ed, but now I was paying the price. I wondered what time it was. I stretched myself across the bed so I could see the alarm clock. Ten thirty. No wonder Emma was up.

I got out of bed, put on some clothes and headed into the lounge in search of Emma but she was nowhere to be seen. Instead, all I found was a note on the fridge. She'd gone out and wouldn't be back until later. There was no mention of where she'd gone, with whom or what time I should expect her back. I had, it seemed, been abandoned. So, in my hour of need and desperate to stop the pain that was beginning to encircle my body, I headed off to the café around the corner for a full English breakfast and at least two mugs of very strong coffee.

Frank's Café was the top dog when it came to upmarket greasy spoon breakfasts. I liked Frank's because Frank was Italian and so even though it was traditional café grub, it was served as if you were in a café in Naples. He also made incredible Italian coffee. I ordered the Frank special breakfast and a cappuccino. I picked up a copy of the newspaper and scanned the headlines, but I couldn't concentrate. Partly because my head was pounding, but also because I felt so guilty about Emma.

I'd been a monumental idiot. There was no doubt in my mind I'd made a complete and utter mess of everything. Emma shouldn't have kissed Rhys, but it was nothing, just a silly, stupid moment of weakness. If I hadn't been so against the film in the first place, then perhaps she wouldn't have felt the need to seek comfort and solace in the arms of Rhys Connelly.

Frank brought over my food with a smile, the plate overflowing with bacon, eggs, sausage, black pudding, toast, beans and hash browns. I began eating almost as soon as the plate touched the table.

'Feeling a bit worse for wear?' said Frank, holding an oversized pepper grinder.

'Just a little. Bit of a big one last night.'

'Still, good to get out though, eh. Pepper?'

Frank always waved his big phallic wooden pepper grinder at me and I always said no. I didn't like pepper, but Frank liked to wave it about as though he were offering me an expensive bottle of wine. It was a grand gesture for something so simple. If there had been a little pot of pepper on the table I could have ignored it, but when Frank came over so happy to see me and offered me the chance of extra pepper with a sort of theatrical, Shakespearean pomp, I felt terrible for saying no. But on that morning and with the guilt of Emma already weighing heavily on my shoulders, I couldn't let Frank down too.

'Please,' I said and a huge smile spread across Frank's face.

'Just say when,' said Frank, going to work; little pellets of black pepper cascaded onto my plate and covered my food.

Stepping out into the chilly but bright day, I felt a sense of happiness, and the darkness that had encircled my morning began to filter with light. I'd been a fool, but I could fix it. I had made Frank happy and I was going to make Emma happy too. I was going to let her do the film, fulfil her dream and I was going to be happy about it. It would make everything all right. I guess the whole point was that I trusted her, always had, and whatever happened, I had to keep on trusting her.

I was on the dreaded one-to-close shift, which meant I wouldn't be home until gone midnight. This also meant I wouldn't see Emma. I was feeling a bit better after breakfast and I even had a surge of optimism about my book. Sitting on the tube, I started imaging our life if I actually achieved the impossible and got published.

The tube was a great place to think, dream and imagine a better life. Maybe because it's underground and easy to get lost in your own little world or because it's like a return to the foetal state, as the gentle rhythmic swaying and rattling puts you into a sleepy trance. It worked. I was daydreaming about not having to work at To Bean or Not to Bean again. About the day I could go in, hand over my apron and walk out, head held high and with the knowledge I would never have to work there another day in my life. As I took the escalator to the surface and walked out into the sunshine, my dreams began to fade away and the reality I was going to spend the next ten hours behind the counter serving terribly named coffee to tourists slapped me around the face. I was suddenly wide awake.

The only good thing about working at To Bean or Not to Bean was the occasional team member who made it a bit less like hell. Therese O'Donnell was twenty and fresh off the plane from Ireland. She had dark Irish hair, fair skin, huge green eyes and high cheekbones. She also had a laugh I could hear every day for the rest of my life.

'You look terrible, what happened, get hit by a bus?' said Therese when I walked into the office behind the counter. Therese was having a cup of coffee and reading a Rough Guide to Thailand. Therese wanted to travel the world and I had no doubt she would. Probably not on the wages she earned at To Bean or Not to Bean, but she'd find a way.

'Not exactly. Late night, too many drinks and old age.'

'Jesus, Jack, you're not old. You're what twenty-seven, twenty-eight?'

'Twenty-nine, actually.'

'Shit, better call the old people's home. There's a man in his late twenties, could die any minute,' Therese said and then laughed that laugh. 'Where'd you go, anyway?'

'Just out with a mate. A couple of pubs and then a club near Covent Garden. I didn't get home until nearly two in the morning.'

'Not a great example for your staff now is it?'

'And you'll be fired if you're not back from Thailand and out there serving coffee in five minutes,' I said. She smiled at me and her eyes sparkled and lit up the room.

'Better not piss off the boss – hung-over to hell,' she said, putting her book away before she walked past me with a smile.

The ten hours at work went by slowly, but at least with Therese working next to me it was fun. I was technically her manager, but because I didn't care much for my job and would be leaving soon one way or another, it didn't feel like that. By eleven o'clock I was dead on my feet and itching to get home and into bed. Therese had other ideas.

'I'm going out for a few drinks with friends, fancy coming along?' she said with a glint in her eye.

I looked at her for a moment and a thought floated around my subconscious. She was exactly my type of girl. If I was twenty-one again and she had asked me out for a drink, I'd have bitten her hand off. She was still just my type in many ways: a raw bundle of dreamy flotsam hoping the wind would blow her some place nice.

'I probably shouldn't. Don't want to cramp your style.'

'I don't have style,' she said, smiling, and then she looked right at me. I've never been one to think girls fancy me. In fact, I've always been the opposite. Therese, however, was giving me a look that definitely made me feel like she might. 'I have something much better than style.'

'And what's that?'

'Come out and I'll show you, old man.'

It was late and we were alone in the shop and suddenly I found myself feeling vulnerable because I thought how easy it would be to do something silly. How easy it would be to make a mistake. I felt vulnerable because for the first time since I started dating Emma, I had that pang of lust and desire for someone else.

'Maybe next time.'

'You're on,' she said with a smile. 'Now you'd better get home before the clock strikes midnight.'

'Night. Have a good time.'

'Would be better with you there.'

'I doubt it.'

'Next time, then,' she said with the same flirtatious glint and I found myself reddening. Luckily, before she could see how embarrassed I was, she blew me a kiss, turned around and walked off into the night. For a brief moment I considered going for a quick drink, the lights of London were still burning brightly and in the distance I could hear the melodious bass of club music, but I could also imagine Emma lying in bed waiting for me. I closed up and walked towards the tube station alone.

On the ride home, I thought about Therese, just starting out, just beginning her journey, and although I was only eight years older than her I felt so much farther along. So much more complicated than just a drink and a shag on a Saturday night. I would have neither. I'd go home, where Emma would already be asleep. I'd probably have something to eat before I slipped into bed next to her and dozed off, the bright lights of the big city fading quickly to dreams.

## EMMA

Something wasn't right.

It had been two days since I waved goodbye to Jack outside the flat. They'd sent the car as promised, a sleek, silver Mercedes that appeared at eight o'clock on a Monday morning, slipping through the mist while we peeked through the curtains. Jack was doing his best to be supportive, but he was tense and awkward. He'd told me I could go and that he was happy for me, but I knew deep down he didn't want me to leave. The thing was, I didn't just want him to tell me it was all right to go: I wanted him to *want* me to go.

We drove for just over an hour until we arrived at the huge mansion in Berkshire where the film would really begin. The house was gorgeous. It looked like something straight out of a Jane Austen novel. There was even a huge lake in front of the main house and acres of garden to explore. I was so excited and energised by the thought of it; the magic of the silver screen had finally touched me.

But that was two days ago, before I realised my period was late. I'd been as regular as clockwork since I was a thirteen-year-old girl. I was never late. My period hadn't come and I knew what that meant.

At first I put it down to the stress of everything with Jack, the wedding planning with my mother and the film. Then I sort of forgot about it and pushed it to the back of my mind, hoping it would go away by itself, or rather come. But on the second morning I woke up in a mad panic. My room was beautiful, I was living the dream, but it could all be about to come crashing down around me. I burst into tears. How could it have happened? I'd been on the pill since I met Jack. Why when my life was about to take off, when I was about to realise my dream, would I get pregnant? In what sick, twisted world was that fair?

There was a knock at my door. I quickly sniffed up my tears, grabbed a tissue and blew my nose.

'Em.' Rhys's whispered voice came through the door. 'You all right?'

I was only in my pyjamas and I looked awful, but I got out of bed and let him in. I needed someone.

'Morning,' I said and attempted a brave smile.

'I heard tears – you all right?'

I attempted another smile, but I couldn't do it and fell into tears again. Rhys pulled me into his shoulder and I wept thinking about the possibility of being pregnant until he walked me into my room and closed the door. We sat on the bed for a minute. I was trying to wipe my face and stop the waterfall of tears that were desperate to escape and rush down my face. Rhys sat with his arm around me.

'Do you want to talk about it?'

I didn't know what to say. Did I want to talk about and, if so, did I want to talk about it with Rhys? It was strange, but if there was one person I could talk to, it was probably him. He understood what this would mean for my place in the film. As much as I loved Jack, I wasn't sure he could be so pragmatic about it. Jack knew what acting meant to me. He understood the sacrifices it took to be creative, he'd gone through enough of his own, but this was his child and I wasn't ready to talk it over with him yet. Rhys shared some of the same qualities as Jack, but it wasn't his baby and so he could be completely impartial.

'I think I'm pregnant,' I said, and the tears came again, gushing out, uncontrollable and raging.

'Shit,' said Rhys. He gripped me tighter because he knew what it meant too. He knew if I was pregnant I wouldn't be doing the film. Shooting didn't start until June and by then I'd be at five or six months, I wasn't sure, but I'd be showing. I'd be far too big to play the beautiful, petite role in a romantic comedy. I was at that point in my life, at the moment when I had to decide what was important to me, what mattered and what sort of life I wanted. I was at the precipice and it was terrifying. 'Are you sure?'

'No, I mean, I haven't taken a test, but I'm late.'

'That's all? It's probably nothing, Em, and it doesn't mean you're pregnant. We'll do a test, together, today, and we'll get this sorted out.'

He said it with such conviction, such certainty, that for a moment I thought maybe he was right. Maybe I wasn't pregnant after all. Maybe I was panicking about nothing.

Maybe.

I wanted more than anything to believe him. But the truth was, I knew. Something inside of me had changed and I could feel it.

'I'll pop out and get a pregnancy test,' said Rhys. 'No one will have to know.'

'No one will know? You're Rhys Connelly. I think if you just pop to Superdrug and buy a pregnancy test, someone will know. Probably the whole world in about the time it takes some crazed stalker to tweet it. How about I go and you stay here?'

'Good idea,' he said with a smile. He hugged me tighter still. 'But you aren't doing this alone. I'm going to be here with you, all right?'

'OK,' I said and that was how I ended up, three hours later, sitting on the bathroom floor with Rhys looking at a white plastic stick, holding Rhys's hand hard, because I desperately wanted it to be negative. I so desperately wanted not to be carrying Jack's baby.

If there's one thing I've learnt in my life it's that we can't always get what we want. Maybe that's a good thing, because if we always got what we wanted, where would the fun be? The hope of a better life? The desire to travel to distant shores and experience new things? When Kate told me she was going travelling for six months, I was so happy for her because I knew how much she had wanted it. People questioned why she would leave a seemingly idyllic life to trot off across the globe, and in search of what exactly? But I didn't. I didn't because I remember her telling me after she was hit by that car how she wanted to travel. I knew what it meant to her.

'Pregnant,' said Rhys. We'd been looking at the white plastic stick for about a minute in complete silence. The word Pregnant had appeared and neither of us seemed to know what to say. In the end Rhys said the obvious. 'Do you think it could be wrong?' he asked gently.

'I don't think so.'

I was pregnant. It was official and no amount of praying, wishful thinking or pretending otherwise was going to change it. There was just one question that needed to be asked. This was why I needed Rhys, because only he would have the balls to ask it.

'Are you going to keep it?'

I looked at him and burst into tears again, smothering myself in his shoulder and feeling the dampness of his T-shirt shroud my face.

'I'm sorry. I didn't mean to . . .'

'No, it's OK. I was crying because I was thinking the same

thing,' I said, a blubbering snotty mess. 'Aren't I an awful human being?'

'No. God, no. It's perfectly reasonable to think about it, Em.' Rhys had his arm around me again. 'This is your whole life we're talking about. Your whole career. This film could be the making of you. It will be. I know it. You're beautiful and talented and you need this film. We need you to make this film.'

'But if I have the baby then . . .'

I looked at him and he looked at me and we didn't need to say anything because we both knew. If I had the baby, I couldn't do the film. That would be it.

'It's a tough choice, Em, I get it, but think about it this way, and it might sound harsh, but you can have another baby. There will be other chances to start a family, when you and Jack are ready, but this film could be it. It might be your only chance. Don't let one mistake ruin it for you because I know you'll regret it for the rest of your life.'

The words seemed to make some sort of sense, but I couldn't process them properly. Could I really have an abortion just to further my career? Was that all right? Women had abortions all the time and for many reasons. It wasn't like I had anything against abortions. Not that I thought of them flippantly, but this was my whole career. Was it all right to give up a baby, a whole life, for another life? Then came the memory of the other one. My first baby. The one I'd had to get rid of because I was too young. That was different though. This was with Jack and I was almost thirty. Could I do it again? Could I lose another baby just because the timing wasn't right?

Then, of course, there was Jack. Wonderful Jack. We had discussed having children one day, but it felt like that dream holiday you always talked about, to the tropical paradise in the Indian Ocean. One day. But that day was now and what would he want? I couldn't do it without telling him, but it was my body, my life and my decision. Jack was a factor, but not the deciding one.

**To: Kate Jones**
**From: Emma Fogle**
**Subject: Re: I made it!**

K,

I have something to tell you. I don't even know where to begin or how to say it. I'm pregnant. Even writing the words, it doesn't seem real. I'm at the mansion in Berkshire with the cast of *The Hen Weekend*. The week that should have been the best week of my life. The week I was supposed to become a proper actress. A defining week, but as it turns out, it's defining me in a different way. It feels like I'm destined never to achieve my ambition because I'm pregnant and I can't get another abortion and I can't do the film if I'm pregnant. I can't get rid of another baby. I still think about the first one and it hurts enough. I'm not sure I could handle going through that again.

But, if I keep it then my film career will be over before it's even started. I'm so torn, Kate. I really wish you were here. I can't talk to Jack about it yet, but I need someone. I've been talking to Rhys, he's the only person who knows, but I can't help but feel like his advice is a little one-sided. He told me I shouldn't keep it because there would be other chances to have children, but maybe only one chance to be a film star. I understand where he's coming from, I do, but having an abortion isn't as simple as just going in, having it done and then getting on with your life like it never happened. It's the pain of knowing you stopped a life before it had the chance to even begin. The potential that little embryo had that was crushed because of a decision made by me, their mother, the one person who should have been protecting them. I'm sorry I'm going on. I'm just such a mess and writing to you felt like the only way of getting it all out.

It feels like the rug has been pulled out from underneath me, which is terribly sad because that's not how you should feel when you find out you're pregnant, is it? It should be one of the greatest moments of your life, not the worst. I love and miss you so much. I'm sorry this is how you had to find out. I wanted to call you, but when I looked up the time difference it was like two o'clock in the morning and I had to get this off my chest now.

I hope all is well and you're having a ball in Chiang Mai. I can't believe you kissed Jez. Although I had a look at the photos and I can see why. Still, at least you didn't have sex with him. A kiss is one thing, but sex is something else. I hope we can talk soon. Your BFF.

Love Em X

## KATE

'Down in one,' said Orla with a devilish grin.

I picked up the shot glass, full to the brim with something called a multiple orgasm, and felt my head, already swimming with other saucily named cocktails, give me a little warning. I was going to feel like absolute shit in the morning. I didn't care though. I was in Sydney with my newest backpacker buddy and I was enjoying myself. Tomorrow could wait.

'Ready,' I said and the next moment the multiple orgasm was working its way down my throat, burning me with its high alcohol content and then making me almost vomit, but I managed to keep it down.

'Another multiple orgasm!' yelled Orla to the barman and my head groaned. Two young boys looked across at us.

'I'll give you a multiple orgasm, love,' one of them said with a pithy grin in a Yorkshire accent.

'I doubt you could give me one,' Orla replied in an instant, cutting the boy down with a single line. His blokey smirk turned quickly to a boyish frown and he turned back to his mate and they walked away. Orla looked at me and we burst out laughing.

After Jez and I said goodbye, I embarked for the first time on travelling solo. I took the sleeper train up to Chiang Mai in the north of Thailand. Chiang Mai was beautiful and because I signed up for an organised tour I wasn't alone for very long.

I did an elephant hillside trek with a small group of ten people for three days, which was spectacular. I met a couple from Brighton and we bonded straight away. Marc and Jo were lovely and made being without Jez bearable. After our trek, I spent the rest of the time in Chiang Mai with them, before we travelled back to Bangkok together. The only downside of being with them was they made me think about Ed. Marc and Jo were having a wonderful time. They were so happy, and loved travelling together. It made me wish even more that Ed had decided to come with me. They gave me a glimpse of the life I had dreamed about. After I said goodbye to them in Bangkok, I hopped on a plane to Sydney and left Asia and all my memories of Jez behind.

After the relaxing, chilled-out vibe of Thailand, being back in a large cosmopolitan city like Sydney was a bit of a shock. Every day became a routine of introductions, trips to tourist attractions and trying to find that elusive travelling friend. I soon realised how lonely travelling could be. I spent two whole days without talking to anyone. I spent a lot of time at the Travellers' Contact Point on George Street so I wouldn't feel utterly alone. I was ten thousand miles from home and knew no one. It was at that point I realised I had to make a bigger effort to meet people. I spent the best part of a week going through the same generic conversations trying to find a travelling mate before I met Orla.

I was on the ferry coming back from Manly, one of Sydney's beautiful northern beaches. We had the usual backpacker conversation about where we'd been and what our plans were before we swam into the deeper waters of personal history, and it was there I always started treading water.

It would have been easier if my father was dead because then at least I'd have some level of closure, of sentimentality. I'd be able to tell people about him without that all-too-familiar pang of embarrassment and anger. My dad? Oh, he fucked off when I was ten years old because he was too much of a coward to hang around and be a proper father. Because he thought his band was going to be the next big thing, the new Beatles, and he couldn't do that and raise a family. I knew Orla and I were going to get along when we bonded over absent fathers.

'Dad left when I was five,' said Orla. 'Haven't seen the good-for-nothing bastard since.'

'Mine left when I was ten. He tried for a few years, if you call trying turning up on birthdays and the occasional weekend with useless presents.'

'Men. Complete shits or what? You won't catch me in a relationship anytime soon,' said Orla as the Sydney harbour bridge and the opera house suddenly came into view. It was the first conversation we had and I felt like I'd known her my whole life.

Orla was exactly what I needed in Sydney. She wanted to have fun and so we did. We moved into a house together in a suburb called Glebe. It was trendy and cool, a bit bohemian and perfect for my six-week stay. It felt more like a little town with wonderful cafés, pubs and a market at the weekend. It was a bit like living back in London, but so much better.

Orla and I hit the town nearly every night. I hadn't done that much drinking since university, but I needed it. If being with Jez had been an experience in relationships and love, Sydney was cathartic in that it gave me the chance to let my hair down and feel young again. There were plenty of days when I would have put my feet up, made a cup of tea and read a book, but Orla would drag me off to do the Coogee to Bondi walk or to a gig in the city. She made me realise that what I had in London wasn't living, it was accepting without asking if I could do better. If Jez made me see how much I loved Ed, Orla made me realise how much I didn't want life to just stay the same when I returned.

I spent a few days thinking about changing everything when I got back, but the one person I really wanted to talk to was Ed. Trouble was, I knew Ed. He wasn't the type to crave change, to stop what he was doing and choose a different path. Ed was stuck in his rut, but, more importantly, I think Ed quite enjoyed it.

'I can't take it anymore,' I said to Orla.

After our third multiple orgasm, we'd gone on to a club to dance till we dropped and it was nearly three in the morning when we finally staggered home.

'You don't have to take it,' said Orla. 'Stand up for yourself. Girl power!'

'But you don't know Ed. He hates change. He won't do what I say and jack it all in and start over. I'll forget what this feels like and I'll slip back into my old life again. I know it.'

'Stop it, will you. Stop talking bollocks and look at yourself. There's nothing you can't do and if Ed doesn't want to join you, then fuck him.'

'But I love him, Orla. I do love him.'

'And if he loves you, he'll stop sitting around on his arse and do whatever you want.'

'But that's the problem though, isn't it.'

'What's that?'

'I don't know what I want. I used to think I wanted our old life in London, but then I didn't. I used to think I wanted to settle down, be a housewife, have kids and all that, but now I don't know. Maybe I'll never know what I want. Maybe I'm destined to always be running. Destined to be like my fucking dad.'

'Don't say that. Just because you don't know what it is you want, doesn't mean you're anything like him. He left a little girl, a whole family.'

'But what if it's just in me? Maybe we can't help who we are. Perhaps we're destined to be like our parents whether we want to or not.'

'You don't believe that.'

'Then why did I kiss Jez in Thailand? Why am I running away from everything back home?'

'You're not running, Kate, you're living. There's a difference. Just because you want something different, something more, it doesn't mean you're running. It means you're searching. Most people piss about through life, do fuck all, have a couple of kids, work in shit jobs they don't like to sustain a life they don't care much for. Just the fact you've realised that and want more means you're miles ahead of all the eejits back home, digging holes and burying themselves deeper and deeper without even realising it.'

We staggered along further, the slight chill of the night air keeping us going and sobering us up slightly. I didn't know what to think anymore. I didn't know if I was running, living or doing something else, something worse or something better.

'I suppose I've always blamed myself in some ways for Dad leaving.'

'But that's crazy. You were ten. I stopped blaming myself years ago, when I realised it was all his fault. He was a drunk, lazy bastard who couldn't handle having kids. Not my fault.'

'Do you think it's part of why you've been travelling so long?'

'God no,' said Orla with a smile. 'I'm having the time of my life. After Dad left, Mum spent her days raising kids, working two, sometimes three, jobs to pay the rent, blaming men for everything and being miserable. I knew I didn't want that for me. I wanted freedom. You only get one shot at life, best not to spend it miserable.'

I'd spent the best part of my childhood sitting at the top of the stairs or locked in my bedroom listening to my parents fight, fingers in my ears, praying it would be over soon. Then I spent my teens wishing Dad would come back because the arguments were better than feeling abandoned. It seemed better for Mum to be crying because he was there than not. I felt trapped in the middle of their relationship. It was no wonder I wanted to run away as fast as I could, but maybe Orla was right. Maybe this wasn't running and perhaps for the first time in my life, I was actually just living. The problem was, I didn't know.

I was at a café on Glebe Point Road the following morning. Orla had to go into work. She worked illegally at an Irish pub in Bondi and would go in randomly whenever the owner called her. All cash-in-hand. I was feeling a little worse for wear, but it was February and back home it was probably cold or wet, while I was bathed in a beautiful warmth. I had a cappuccino and a bacon roll and I started thinking about my father.

I knew Orla was right about it not being my fault he left. How could it have been? I was only ten. It didn't stop me spending most of my teens blaming myself though. I've always hated him for that. For making me feel like it was my fault when it was all about him and his dreams. When you're a kid, you idolise your parents. You put them on a pedestal and think of them as these all-knowing super beings that can do no wrong. We think our parents are infallible, but in reality they're people just like us, doing their best, making mistakes and making it all up as they go along.

Dad was only thirty-two when he left. Just another useless bloke having another mid-life crisis and chasing a teenage dream. That didn't stop his little girl from lying awake night after night, listening and hoping to hear the front door open and her daddy's voice. When I look back, I realise now just how much his leaving shaped my life and my relationships. Maybe to him he needed to escape and that meant more than two broken hearts. I had to get away, but I wasn't breaking hearts or leaving behind a child. If I'd stayed with Ed, who's to say that five or ten years down the line I wouldn't have run away too and left behind far more than just a pissed-off and disappointed boyfriend. I was doing this now to stop that from ever happening.

**To: Emma Fogle**
**From: Kate Jones**
**Subject: Oz**

Em,
   Oh Em. It does seem like a cruel twist of fate, but you shouldn't think for a moment like this is the deciding moment in your life. I understand it's a big decision, but remember: you're young, beautiful and talented. I don't think this is your one chance at being an actress. If you decide to have the baby then you will figure out your career later. If you decide to have the abortion, you know I'll support you and be there for you every step of the way. Whatever you decide, you have me. And Jack and Ed too, of course. And maybe instead of thinking of it as this awful thing, think of it the other way. You're the lead role in a huge film production opposite Rhys Connelly or you're going to be a mum to a wonderful little baby. Either one is something I know you'll be brilliant at and love to pieces. Try and think of this as a positive thing instead of something negative.

## *Happy Endings*

I remember how you felt after the first abortion. I remember the look on your face when you told me. I just, and I'm not trying to tell you what to do or persuade you either way because this is your decision, but if I was there and you asked me straight out what you should do, I think you know the answer. I know you, Em. And if you do decide to keep it, Jack will be a wonderful dad and you'll be the best mum in the world.

Sorry I missed your call again. My reception is a bit patchy. I hope we can talk soon.

I'm in Sydney at the moment and having a blast. It's incredible, such a cool city and I feel at home here already. I met an Irish girl called Orla and we have so much in common. She's a little crazy but I think that's what I need at the moment. She certainly keeps me on my toes! We moved into a house in a suburb called Glebe, which is so hip and bohemian, you'd love it. I'll email again soon. Just remember that whatever decision you make, do it for you. If you need to talk, call me. Love you.

K x

## JACK

When Emma left there was so much I didn't say. I felt like it was becoming a reoccurring theme in our relationship. We looked at each other but didn't say anything important. I knew she was still angry with me. I told her it was fine she was going, but I don't know if she really believed me.

I had a cup of coffee and some toast and sat down on the sofa. I scrolled through the TV channels, but nothing was on. It was midweek and my day off work. I'd usually spend the day with Emma. We'd walk to a local café for breakfast or take the tube into central London and visit a gallery or museum. Sometimes we'd just potter about at home doing nothing, but nothing with Emma was still something. Without her it was dull and I didn't know what to do with myself. Normally I'd write, but my book was finished and I'd sent letters begging agents to give me a shot. All I could do was wait. Wait for the rejections before I decided what to do with the rest of my life.

After an hour of thinking and another cup of coffee, I decided to give Emma a call. It was almost nine o'clock and I hoped hearing her voice would lift the gloom that had descended upon the living room. I grabbed my mobile and dialled.

'Hello?' said a voice.

'Is Emma there?'

'She's in the shower. Who's calling?'

'Who's this?'

'Rhys. Who's this?'

The moment I heard his name, a hundred irrational thoughts went flying through my mind, forming a whirlpool of ridiculous paranoia that threatened to pull me under.

'It's Jack. Her fiancé,' I said, not attempting to hide my anger and mistrust. 'Why are you answering her phone?'

'I was in her room . . .'

'While she's in the shower?' My voice wobbled with a raging jealousy.

'Listen, mate, it's not what you think . . .'

People only said 'it's not what you think' when it was. If he didn't have a reason to feel guilty, he wouldn't have said anything. I didn't know what to think, but I knew that whatever was going on, it wasn't innocent. I was a bloody fool. Of course something was going on. It was Rhys Connelly. Every woman's perfect man and he was in Emma's bedroom while she was having a shower. I threw the phone across the room. I had to get out of the flat and away from everything that reminded me of her. I got dressed, grabbed my jacket and left the flat before standing outside on the street with no idea what to do next.

'Do you want to talk about it?'

'Not really. I just want to drink.'

'We can definitely do that,' said Therese with a smile. That smile.

I was tired of talking. I was tired of going over things in my mind, trying to figure everything out and be everything to everyone, but mostly I was tired of feeling like a failure. I wanted to get drunk. I wanted to act without thinking, without thought, without fear, without the future hanging over me, without the past judging me, without a plan, without a way home and without thinking about Emma. I wanted to be twenty again, before life became complicated and mixed-up. I guess I wanted to be just like Therese.

'Then it's my round,' I said, downing half of my pint in one go. 'Back in a sec.'

I looked back at Therese from the bar and she smiled a gorgeous, seductive smile. I felt that pang of lust again. It wasn't so much a deep need for Therese, but for youth. Why did that always happen? Why did life seem so much better then? Why did I yearn to be twenty again and why did Therese make me feel that way? Maybe it was inevitable. I was fast approaching thirty, my fiancée was off making her life, while mine was stalled, and the only thing that made sense was to go back to a time when things weren't like that.

'It's just . . .' I started as I returned to the table with our drinks.

'Just what?' said Therese.

'Things were fine, they were. We were fine, but now she has the film . . .'

'You feel a bit like a spare part?'

'Exactly,' I said, drunkenly pointing at Therese across the table. 'Like a spare part. You got it in one. And there's Rhys. He's gorgeous.'

'I'd do him,' said Therese and then she laughed. 'Sorry but I would.'

'I know. So would I, if I were a girl. And I trust her, I do, but it's him. How can she resist him?'

'But she loves you, Jack. Just because he's gorgeous, it doesn't mean she doesn't have any willpower.'

'I know and I've gone over it in my mind a hundred times.'

'And what did you come up with?'

'It's obvious, isn't it?'

'Is it?'

'Yes, of course. She's going to be a famous actress and I work at a shitty coffee shop. Eventually, whether it's today, tomorrow or next month, she will leave me for someone better. She has to . . .'

'Why does she have to?' said Therese, looking more and more tempting with every passing moment.

'Because that's what happens. It just happens. You'll understand one day.'

'What, when I'm as ridiculously old as you?'

'Exactly,' I said and we both laughed.

'A campervan,' said Therese, twisting the straw around in her mouth. 'All across Australia for like six months.'

'My dad had one of those.'

'They're so cool,' she half-shouted through the semi-darkness. We were in a club near Leicester Square. I didn't know which one. She'd led me there by the hand, stumbling through the dark, noisy streets of London. We were standing at the back of the room together, our bodies touching, still somehow holding hands and talking. A song I didn't recognise came on, but she suddenly jumped up in the air and made a sort of squeal. 'We have to dance,' she said, pulling me towards the dance floor.

I didn't have the chance to tell her I didn't dance. It was too late.

Except for the occasional wedding, I hadn't danced in years. But before I knew it, I was giving it everything. I'm sure the alcohol had loosened me up, but I was spinning around, flailing my arms around like a lunatic and jumping up and down with everyone else. I was actually enjoying myself. Therese was a far better dancer than me and soon attracted the attention of a couple of men and so she danced against me and they soon understood and tried their luck with another girl. Therese and I danced together, getting closer, touching more and before I knew it, she had her bum rammed into my groin and was gyrating backwards and forwards and I seemed to lose all control. I was running my hands up and down her body, feeling her breasts and her legs, until eventually she turned around and we were face to face.

'You're getting married, you know.'

'I know.' She was barely an inch from my face. 'What are you trying to say?'

'Just . . .' she said, and then stopped.

She had her arms around my neck and then the next moment she leant in and kissed me. The music was blaring in the background while Therese and I were locked in our little world, our mouths together and our hands moving over each other's bodies. It felt frantic and passionate and intense. I hadn't felt anything like that for a long time and I didn't want it to end. The alcohol made my head swim and we seemed to kiss forever. Through one song and then another, until eventually we pulled away, both gasping for air.

'Back to mine?'

'You sure?'

'Definitely,' I said and grabbed her by the hand, leading us through the maze of people and then out into the dark, cold night.

We kissed in the back of the taxi. It wasn't a black cab, but just an Indian man in a beat-up old Toyota that smelt like kebabs and vomit. It wasn't the most romantic place in the world but then again young love isn't romantic, is it? Not that it was love or anything close, but late-night sex with strange girls was never about romance. Sex in your late teens and twenties was about needs and alcohol and when the two collided, it didn't matter when or where you were. It was the polar opposite to sex with Emma. In a relationship sex becomes like food: it's a necessity and sometimes you get all dressed up and go out somewhere nice, but usually it's just something convenient and quick between TV shows.

We slammed in through the front door of the flat, ripping and tearing at each other's clothes, kissing and frantically trying to devour each other. We were half-naked before we fell onto the sofa. I couldn't believe what I was doing, but I couldn't stop myself either. I was too far gone to put an end to it.

'You want to do it here?'

'I don't care,' said Therese before she grabbed at my head and pulled me down on top of her. The rest of our clothes quickly gave way, falling on the floor in a pile. We were naked and I was about to do something I never thought I'd do. I was going to have sex with someone other than Emma.

I closed my eyes and felt Therese's body beneath me and it felt good. Suddenly, through the darkness of the room, I heard my mobile buzzing in the corner. It was still lying on the ground where I'd thrown it that morning. That morning that felt so long ago. Therese and I stopped for a moment and I looked up quickly. It was probably Emma.

'Do you have to get that?' said Therese, her voice breathless and suddenly so young.

'No,' I said before I closed my eyes and sank into her.

## EMMA

'Who was on the phone?' I said, walking back into the room and leaving the steam of the bathroom behind me.

'Jack, and he sounded a bit weird.'

'In what way?'

'Mad, angry, jealous maybe?'

'Oh shit, he probably thought . . .'

'Thought what?' said Rhys, who was lying across my bed looking his usual gorgeous self. His hair was a tangled mess and his firm, muscular body was stretched out like David relaxing between poses for Michelangelo.

'That we were . . . you know. I told him about our kiss and then you answer my phone while I'm in the shower.'

'I can see why he'd be jealous . . .'

'Oh and why's that?' I said, drying my hair with the towel and suddenly realising the top of my legs were poking out through the dressing gown and Rhys was looking. I quickly flicked the dressing gown to cover myself.

'A girl as beautiful as you, stuck in a grand old mansion with me for a week. I could see how he'd think something might happen. It isn't so hard to believe.'

I felt myself getting warm and blushing wildly.

'You're trying to seduce a pregnant woman?' I said with a silly little giggle. It was the first time I'd laughed or even smiled since I'd found out. 'That's a low, even for you.'

'Barely pregnant,' said Rhys, sitting up and looking at me. 'You still look incredibly shaggable.'

'Rhys, stop it,' I said with a stern smile. 'You know we're not going to happen. Why don't you go and shag one of the sound girls or that pretty young thing playing your sister?'

'That's a bit incestuous don't you think?'

'She isn't really your sister and she does have a great pair of tits.' I couldn't believe what I was saying, but I didn't want him flirting with me. It made me feel guilty about Jack and I didn't want to encourage him. I didn't come here to sleep with Rhys. I came here for the film. I felt the tears again and suddenly wanted Rhys to leave. I had to call Jack and talk to him. I had to tell him about the baby.

'They are a pretty fantastic pair,' said Rhys, staring off into space. 'Are you going to be all right?'

'I'm a big girl. I'll be fine,' I said with a reassuring smile. 'Now go and seduce that poor young girl and break her heart.'

'Right, will do,' said Rhys with his gorgeous smile and then he left.

After he was gone I fell onto the bed and cried again. I wasn't crying because of the baby anymore, but because I'd finally come to a decision. I was crying for that.

Sara Gifford was in the same year as me at school. She was one of the popular girls, always dressed fabulously and she seemed to have everything: poise, confidence, intelligence. Meanwhile, I was the ugly duckling still waiting to grow into my body. I didn't quite fit. I would blossom at eighteen, but at fifteen Sara Gifford was the girl all the others wanted to be and all the boys wanted to do. Then she got pregnant and vanished without a trace.

Rumours flew around the school. She'd been sent to Coventry. We didn't know what that meant, but apparently it was awful. She'd been sent to a home for pregnant girls. She'd been taken to far-flung north Scotland. She was suddenly an outcast because she'd made the mistake of making a mistake. She left school on a Friday, got in the back of her dad's Range Rover and never came back.

A few months later I was walking past her house and saw a Sold sign up in the garden. I realised then that babies didn't just change lives, they made lives. I was twenty-nine, not fifteen, but I felt the same. This baby wasn't planned, it wasn't expected, but it was going to define and shape of the rest of my life.

That morning, I called Jack numerous times but it kept going to his voicemail. He was obviously angry and ignoring me, having assumed I was cheating on him just because Rhys answered my phone. That hurt. Why didn't he have more faith in us? In me? As the day went on, I began to worry and thought about going home, but I needed to see the day through first. We were scheduled to have a read through after lunch and so I spent the late morning wandering the gardens. I felt like Elizabeth Bennett as I strolled among the manicured gardens and around the grounds. I imagined Mr Darcy walking up from the lake, just as Colin Firth had done, but it wasn't him, or even Rhys Connelly, it was Jack. My Jack. It had always been Jack.

I knocked on Matt's door.

'Come in,' he said. I walked in and as usual he was tapping away on his laptop. While the rest of the cast and crew had been meeting, relaxing and going through the script, Matt had generally been locked away in his room, head down and fingers frantically typing. 'Em, darling, what's up?' said Matt, spinning around and looking at me. 'Fuck, what's up?'

'I have something to tell you.'

'Right. And whatever it is, we can work through it.'

'I'm pregnant,' I said, before letting go of the tears.

'Oh shit.'

'I'm so sorry. I don't know how it happened. I'm on the pill and it wasn't planned and Jack doesn't even know yet and I'm freaking out because I want to do this film so badly, I do, but I know I can't if I'm pregnant. I'm just . . .'

'It's all right,' said Matt, getting up and walking over to me. He put his arms around me and gave me a hug. He knew right away that I couldn't do the film. 'The film will go on. You'll have other chances if that's what you want. You're a brilliant actress, Emma, and it's been a pleasure.'

'Thank you,' I managed to sniff out.

'You're definitely going to keep it?' said Matt suddenly. 'Sorry, just checking.'

'I have to. I want to.'

'Stay tonight. We're having a huge meal and you should stay.'

'I'd like that.'

The film and everything that came with it was what I'd always wanted. It was in many ways my happy ending. At least that's what I always thought. Then, as soon as I knew I was pregnant, something inside of me changed. Acting had been my dream, but it wasn't all about me anymore; it was about the baby growing inside of me. They were a part of Jack and me. A small, tiny, little version of us and I couldn't let that go.

It was just before midnight when I sat down on my bed. I checked my phone but Jack hadn't called. It would be fine when I got home and told him the news. Our news. I wanted to try him one more time before bed. I rang his number and waited. It rang and rang before eventually going to voicemail.

'Jack, darling, it's me. I hope everything's OK. I really miss you. I don't know if you're angry with me or jealous about Rhys, but there's nothing to worry about. I love you so much and I'm coming home tomorrow. Let out for good behaviour. Sorry, bad joke. I have some news though and I can't wait to tell you. I love you, Jack. Always have, always will. Good night.'

I lay in bed and thought about Jack and the baby. Our little baby. It wasn't the life I'd ever imagined, but I knew it was the life I wanted. It seemed so obvious. Jack was always going on about defining moments. He thought we all had a pivotal moment in our lives – a piece of random luck, good or bad timing, a pivotal decision that made us who we are – but I hadn't always agreed with him. I thought life was like a film: just a series of shots worked together to create a whole. It had a beginning, middle and an end and within that framework were important milestones: first steps, first words, first kisses, first loves, first jobs, marriage, kids. It all rolled into a life.

It dawned on me that when I was sixteen and had the abortion, had lost the baby that Mum said was impossible to keep, that was my defining moment. That baby would have been thirteen now. My life would have been unrecognisable from my current one. I always thought back to that and a part of me regretted it, felt awful for doing what we did, but another part of me knew Mum had been right. That baby was impossible, but this one was different. Once I knew I was pregnant, I knew I had to keep it. It wasn't really a choice and maybe, just maybe, it would help heal the wounds of the first one.

I fell asleep thinking about Jack, holding my phone in my hand, hoping that tomorrow, when the sun came up, everything would be all right. The last noise I heard before I closed my eyes was giggles on the landing and then Rhys's whispered voice telling someone to be quiet, before I heard the door to his room open and another young heart about to be broken creep inside.

**To: Kate Jones**
**From: Emma Fogle**
**Subject: Re: Oz**

K,

    I'm going to keep the baby. In the end it wasn't even a choice. It's Jack and me and we made this life and whether we meant to or not, it doesn't matter because we did. And I'm really excited about it.

    It's strange, and I don't want to go all weird and girlie about it, but something biological shifted in me and I can feel it. It's like once I was pregnant my motherly hormones just kicked in and I know more than anything in the world I have to take care of and protect this little life. It isn't something I thought I'd ever feel, but I don't miss the film because this is so much more important. And you were right about that too. I'm young and I got this role, I can get other parts. This isn't the end of my acting career, but the start of something else.

    It's my last morning at the mansion and it's early because I couldn't sleep. I've been up most of the night thinking about Jack. I have to go home and tell him now and as happy as I think he's going to be, I'm still worried. This baby wasn't planned and a part of me is terrified because we can't afford it and I know it's going to put even more strain on Jack to do something. I know he's going to be a brilliant dad, but I'm just concerned because he's already been acting weird about the film and now this. I'm probably worrying about nothing, as usual. Wish me luck.

I hope you're having fun and still enjoying yourself in Australia. I'm so glad you found a suitable travelling buddy – and a girl this time! I'll write again soon. Your pregnant and happy BFF. Love you.

Love Em X

## JACK

I didn't know what it was. I couldn't place the sound. I turned and felt my spine concertina as if I'd been sleeping inside a small wooden box, but then I realised it was almost as bad – I'd slept on the sofa. The small two-person sofa we'd been meaning to replace for ages, with the lumpy bits that dug into my back. I could still hear the noise like a gentle tapping on wood. I tried to open my eyes and get my bearings, but my head was banging and a sharp pain sat just behind my eyes waiting for its cue to go on. I opened my eyes and the sharp pain suddenly released itself upon the rest of my head. A blurry but familiar image was standing in front of me.

'Oh my God, what happened to you?' said Emma. I sat up slowly and it was then, as Emma leant down to kiss me that I remembered. Everything came flooding back in a millisecond, crushing me beneath its sheer weight of awfulness. Memories like snapshots of another life flashed through my mind. Emma. Rhys Connelly. Depressed. Therese. Drunk. Dancing. A club. Back to mine. Naked on the sofa. Sex? I stopped and looked at Emma in horror. 'What's the matter?'

'It's not what it seems,' I managed to garble out as Therese came walking out of the bedroom in a pair of Emma's pyjamas. Emma's face dropped. It looked terrible. It was terrible. 'Emma,' I said, but it was too late because she was already turning around and walking out, slamming the door behind her.

'Sorry,' said Therese from behind me. 'I thought she was gone for the week.'

'Me too,' I said, grabbing my crime scene pile of clothes from the floor and getting dressed.

The night before on the sofa, Therese and I had started out with an almighty passion. We'd grabbed and pulled at each other until we were naked. It seemed for all the world like it was just a matter of time before we would go that extra mile. But I couldn't. I pulled back at the last moment because something deep inside of me knew that if I had sex with Therese, I wouldn't be able to forgive myself.

'What's the matter?' Therese said breathlessly.

'I can't do this. I'm sorry. It isn't you, it's me. It's Emma,' I said and then we were getting up and covering ourselves with a sort of awkward embarrassment; our nakedness, which only moments before had seemed so natural, suddenly felt like the strangest thing in the world. The darkness of the room was replaced with light as the world in all its complicated glory stopped us in its tracks.

We sat and talked for a while and she wanted to get a taxi home, but it was late and so I told her to stay the night in the bed and I would take the sofa. I didn't think Emma would be back for days and so I didn't think it would matter. I didn't think and that was the problem.

I caught up with Emma just as she was getting into her car, tears streaming down her face.

'Emma, please don't do this.'

'Do what, Jack?'

'Let me explain.'

'Five minutes,' she said, the tears replaced with a face of sheer calm. She looked shocked, not angry but disappointed, and that was far worse. When I was little and I did something so terrible that Dad didn't even shout, but just stood and looked at me, disappointed, it was the worst feeling in the world. When you did something so awful it was beyond punishment, you felt it and I had the same feeling again. I wanted Emma to shout at me, punish me and then forgive me. What I didn't want and couldn't stand was the quiet, sullen disappointment.

We walked around the corner to Frank's Café and took a seat outside. I ordered us a couple of coffees and we sat and looked at one another. Emma and Jack. Jack and Emma. We were getting married in a matter of months. We were going to spend the rest of our lives together, but at that moment, nothing was further from my mind.

'I called and Rhys was in your room,' I eventually said. 'And I thought, after your kiss . . .'

'You thought I was shagging him.'

'I'm sorry, Em. I freaked out. I made a mistake. I should've trusted you.'

'So you thought, Emma's screwing Rhys, I'll go out, pick up a random girl, bring her home and fuck her in our bed. That will teach her.'

'We didn't have sex.'

'You didn't?'

'No.'

'But something happened. A girl in a pair of my pyjamas did walk out of our bedroom if I'm not mistaken.'

'Her name's Therese. We work together. It was just a stupid drunken thing, Em. It didn't . . .'

'I know, "It didn't mean anything". But you know what, Jack, it usually means something,' she said, her face cracking again. A tear leaked out and slid down her beautiful pale cheek.

'I don't know what to say to make it OK. I just want to go back and change what I did, make a better choice. I love you,

Em, so much and I hate that I hurt you, hate that I did what I did.'

'And what did you do?'

'Nothing, we just kissed.'

'Just kissed?'

Perfectly balanced moments like that didn't come along very often. I had an opportunity. The truth was that we didn't have sex and surely that was all that mattered. We were drunk, it was foolish, but why should I ruin everything because of a stupid, silly mistake? People talk a lot about the importance of truth and honesty in relationships, but what good was the truth if it was going to hurt Emma and possibly ruin the rest of our lives?

'We just kissed. We were drunk and that's why she stayed over because I didn't want her going home late at night. She slept in our bed and I slept on the sofa. It was nothing, Em. A stupid, stupid kiss that meant nothing. I would never cheat on you. You're going to be my wife.'

She looked at me and I could see she was breaking. I felt rotten, but I couldn't risk losing her because of one night.

'And it's never going to happen again?' she eventually said, wiping the tears from her cheeks.

I smiled and a great weight suddenly fell from my heart, breaking off like an iceberg and floating away before being dissolved in the ocean. Emma would never know the complete truth about Therese, but it was all right because it didn't matter. It was nothing. The shameful truth is that sometimes one-night stands do mean nothing. Sometimes it's just a senseless, thoughtless, rash concoction of alcohol and irresponsibility.

'Never. I love you too much.'

'Love you too and I'm sorry, I . . .'

It suddenly dawned on me I still didn't know why she was back so early. What had happened with the film, the week away and why was she looking at me like that? Her face had changed again. Only this wasn't an expression I'd seen before. I couldn't read it and I didn't know what she was going to say next. How could I have known?

'What's the matter?' It was then that she broke down again, the tears flooding out of her. People at nearby tables looked across at us as I got up and knelt in front of Emma and held her. She sobbed into my shoulder for what seemed like an age. I felt her body shudder and shake uncontrollably. It scared me. She eventually pulled herself from me; I wiped her eyes and nose with the back of my hand, before she looked at me with a smile.

'I'm pregnant, Jack,' she said, searching my face for a reaction. 'We're having a baby.'

Suddenly everything seemed to tumble and fall away beneath me. Everything I thought I was and had seemed different and changed forever. How could she be pregnant? She was on the pill and we'd been together for so long and I didn't understand. I was going to be a father. I wasn't ready. I didn't have a proper job. I hadn't made it as a writer. I couldn't support them like my own father had with us. But then suddenly it didn't matter. Emma and I were having a baby. All the negative thoughts and worries evaporated and a huge rush of love and protection shone like a lighthouse through my body, illuminating everything around me.

I'd thought about having kids one day, when our careers were sorted, when we could afford it, when it seemed right, but sitting there at Frank's, it felt right. It wasn't planned, we couldn't afford it, our careers were far from sorted and maybe we weren't ready, but it felt right.

'Seriously?' I managed to mumble out between the tears that had suddenly appeared on my face. 'I'm going to be a dad?'

'Seriously,' said Emma and I buried myself in her knowing that nothing in the world really mattered anymore except Emma, me and the little person growing inside of her.

## ED

I love Kate. I love Kate. I love Kate.

I was sitting at my desk repeating the same three words over and over in my mind, trying desperately to erase in some way the waterfall of guilt that kept tumbling and cascading unrelentingly down my body. Since my night with Georgie, I'd felt sick nearly every moment of every day. I'd wake up in the middle of the night in a cold sweat, hoping and praying it had all been just a horrible nightmare, then realising it wasn't a bad dream at all but my actual life. I'd see Georgie at work, smiling, laughing and without a care in the world and my heart would sink. It meant nothing to her. I had been just a casual shag, another notch on her bedpost.

'Do you have those numbers?' barked Hugh, suddenly standing in front of me. His bear-like silhouette blocked out the sun that was coming through the window.

'Sorry, sir, what's that?'

'The numbers, Hornsby. The numbers we spoke about this morning,' said Hugh again. The hostility in his voice because he'd been forced to repeat something spat at me and I was surprised not to find my face suddenly damp. I could see his brain ticking over as he waited, calculating the seconds he'd wasted having to repeat himself. Oh, the humanity.

'Right, yes, the numbers. I'll email them to you. Five minutes?'

'To the second, Hornsby. To the second!' he said in the same venomous tone and then he turned around and marched towards his office. I quickly started working on the numbers he'd requested and managed to email him in a little under five minutes. My heart was racing, my hands were sweaty and I needed a quick break. I didn't smoke, but grabbed my coat and headed outside anyway.

Kate and I were walking along the Thames path in Putney. It wasn't long after we officially became girlfriend and boyfriend. We talked about everything and nothing and stopped for lunch at a little pub. I was twenty-one and I didn't think life got any better. Growing up in Slough, this was what I had always dreamt about. I had a beautiful girlfriend, I'd just graduated university and I had my whole life ahead of me. I remember it so clearly and the conversation we had that day.

'Love you,' I said for the first time.

It had been on my mind for days and the moment felt right. I'd known I loved Kate so quickly it had taken even me by surprise. I hadn't intended to fall in love so soon. I always thought I'd get my career on track first, make some serious money before I delved into a proper relationship. However, from the moment I met Kate in the student union, I just knew.

'Love you too,' she said, her eyes glistening with pure, unadulterated happiness, but then her face dropped and she held my hands and looked at me. 'Just promise me one thing.'

'Anything.'

'Promise me you'll never hurt me.'

One of the happiest moments of my life and Kate still had those doubts. The doubts put upon her by her useless father. This was what happened when parents got divorced. There I was, from a fully functioning two-parent family, wrapped up in layers of love and the future all mapped out: a wedding, a house, kids and a whole lifetime of happiness, because in my world that was what happened. But Kate was worried it was going to nosedive into disaster and we were going to end up like her parents, because that was all she knew.

I promised I wouldn't let that happen. I told her I'd protect her, give her the life she craved and that I'd never hurt her. Maybe it was youthful folly or just wishful thinking, promising something I could never guarantee, but I had let her down. Let us down.

'Could I?' I said to a bloke I barely recognised. He offered me the packet and I took out a cigarette. He sparked up his lighter and I inhaled, taking in the smoke and then almost coughing my guts up, but I managed to keep it in.

I smoked for a few years when I was younger, but quit during university. My father was a lifelong smoker and I didn't want to end up like that: the gravelly voice, coughing every morning, the yellow-stained fingers and not being able to walk up a flight of stairs without wheezing.

'Cheers,' I said and then stood there with the rest of the smokers in the cold.

We were like a police line-up. All clutching our cigarettes, trying to finish them quickly so we didn't get in trouble for being a minute too long, but trying to draw some happiness from being out of the office for a moment. I usually walked past the smokers line-up on my way out to grab lunch and always felt a sense of pity for them. But here I was, one of them, clutching my cancer stick, tapping my feet to an imaginary beat to keep warm and trying to enjoy it.

'I didn't know you smoked.' The voice came from nowhere. An instantly recognisable voice. Georgie was standing next to me looking her usual gorgeous self in a warm coat and scarf. She sparked up a cigarette.

'Oh, you know, occasionally.'

'Stress?'

'Something like that.'

We hadn't spoken much since our night together. She'd rung me a couple of times, but I'd ignored it and let it go to voicemail. She hadn't left any messages. The truth was I didn't want to speak to her again. Strictly professional was the only way I could cope.

'You shouldn't be stressed, Ed,' she said with a salacious grin. 'Not about us anyway.'

'I'd better get back.' I had a last toke on my cigarette before I stubbed it out in the smokers' bin.

'Wait,' said Georgie, grabbing my arm. 'Don't leave because of me.'

I noticed a couple of heads look across from the line-up. The last thing I needed was a smoking-break scene. It would be all over the office by lunchtime and I'd be standing in front of Hugh before the end of the day.

'No, it's not you. I just have a lot to do,' I said with a smile. 'You know Hugh.'

'More than I'd like,' said Georgie, giggling. 'Listen, Ed. I'd hate what happened to get in the way of our friendship.'

'Right, yes, of course,' I said, but knowing there was no way we could be friends. Just seeing her face at work was a constant reminder of what I'd done. Talking to her was worse. 'Friends.'

'Good. Friends,' said Georgie and then she leaned across and gave me a hug, pushing her body against mine. The smell of her perfume tickled my nose and the feeling of her hands around me made me want to pull back and run as far away as I could. I didn't though. I couldn't. Keep it together, Ed, I told myself. Just smile and walk away, and that's exactly what I did.

march

## KATE

I was standing at the open door of an aeroplane, fifteen thousand feet in the air, and looking down at the ground far below when I realised two very important things. One: death was only a failed parachute opening away. Two: I wasn't ready to die.

Until twenty-fours before, I wasn't even thinking about skydiving. It wasn't on my bucket list because I was a scaredy-cat and my bucket list didn't contain things that could lead to my death. I saw it as slightly counterproductive to have things that might actually kill me on a list of things I wanted to do before I died. I didn't mind the occasional bit of risk, but jumping out of a perfectly good aeroplane didn't seem like the best way to spend a Wednesday afternoon. If it hadn't been for Orla and what happened with Ed, I wouldn't have even thought about it, but there I was about to take literally the biggest leap of faith and I was shitting myself. Orla, on the other hand, who was standing just behind me with her burly Aussie attached to her like an oversized snail shell, couldn't wait.

'Ready?' said Andy, the Australian crackpot whom I entrusted with my life.

'Not really.'

'Too late to back out now,' said Andy salaciously, and that's when it happened. We jumped.

## Twenty-four hours earlier

I hadn't spoken to Ed in over two weeks and I was starting to feel uneasy about it. Maybe it was because of Jez, but I felt like I was losing touch with him in more ways than one. Ed seemed to belong to an old life that had no relevance to my current one, but I still missed him terribly, or at least the idea of him.

I was sitting on the beach in Byron Bay when I decided to give him a call. It was just past nine o'clock in the evening back home and so I figured he'd be back from work and probably parked in front of the telly. I imagined him in my head: feet up on the coffee table, glass of wine in his hand, a tired frown on his face and falling asleep to the news.

It was strange to imagine our house. It was even stranger to imagine myself back there again. Cutting and pasting myself back into my old life was going to be much harder than pushing a couple of buttons on a keyboard. Maybe that's the problem with our generation. We're so used to controlling everything with the click of a button and yet the one thing we can't control is our lives. We think we can break hearts and then magically erase the problem, but love doesn't work like that. I'm part of the Ctrl+Alt+Del generation and it feels like I'm the pair of tits they hired to be the spokesperson.

'Ed,' I half-shouted along a crackly line.

'Hi.'

'What you doing?'

'Just watching TV, drinking a bottle of red and wondering where in the world my girlfriend is.'

'Byron Bay, between Sydney and Brisbane.'

I went on to explain how Orla and I had left the comforts of Sydney and taken an overnight coach to Byron Bay. It was the first stop on our girl's tour up the east coast of Australia:

four weeks of hedonistic partying and seeing as much as we could until it was time for me to head to Melbourne.

Byron Bay was a gorgeous little surf town and we were staying at a hostel a hop, skip and a jump over railway tracks to the beach. It wasn't quite as idyllic as Koh Phangan, but it had a nice relaxed vibe and we quickly got into the habit of waking up and going to the beach before walking into town for night-time fun and giggles. Being in Byron Bay reminded me of the holiday I took to Newquay when I was seventeen. I went with Emma and another couple of friends from sixth form. It was our first holiday without our parents and so we all went a bit crazy, the liberation making us feel like proper adults. It had been a real rite of passage and being in Byron Bay gave me the same feeling.

'Sounds great,' said Ed and I could detect a shard of something in his voice.

'You all right?'

'Tired. Not sleeping well without you.'

'You should try sleeping on some of the hostel beds I've been in, more like planks of wood. It's doing my back no favours.'

'It's one of the reasons I didn't come.'

'Yeah, right. We could've stayed at five-star hotels and you still wouldn't have budged from the sofa.'

'What's that supposed to mean?'

'Nothing, I was joking. Are you sure nothing's bothering you?'

'Just tired,' he said again and then there was a silence.

Neither of us knew what to say to each other. It was pitiful. We'd gone from living together and longing for each other to almost complete strangers in less than three months. I didn't want to go on and on about what I was doing and it seemed like he didn't want to talk about anything. I felt like I was losing him when we didn't talk and completely lost when we did. Maybe it wasn't meant to work. Could being apart for such a long time ever really work?

'Glad I called then.'

'And what do you want me to say, Kate? How's the trip? Tell me about all the drinking, partying and blokes you've been messing about with?'

His tone took me completely by surprise. It was angry and short, but what threw me the most was the unwitting reference to my fling with Jez. He shouldn't have had any right to be angry or jealous, but he did. I felt awful and a part of me wanted to tell him. He deserved to know the truth, but I was too afraid. I didn't want to lose him. Technically, it was only a kiss and a shared bed, but I suppose deep down it was more than that. I had felt something for someone else and thought about being with them and surely that was a lot worse than just a kiss.

'It's not like that . . .'

'And what's it like, Kate?'

'Do we have to do this? I just wanted to hear your voice. I don't want to argue.' There was another long pause. All I could hear down the line was the noise from the TV in the background. 'What are you watching?' I wanted to talk about something mundane. I was bored of having the same conversations with Ed. Ten thousand miles between us and all we could do was argue.

'I don't think I can do this,' he said suddenly.

'Do what?'

'This. Us. Being apart. Just talking on the phone. Always wondering where you are and what you're doing. It's killing me.'

'What are you saying?'

'We can't keep doing this to each other. You need to be free of me and I . . .'

'You what, Ed?' I said, suddenly holding back tears.

'I need to be free of you.'

'Are you breaking up with me?'

I could feel the tears about to break and wash over my face.

'Not breaking up, exactly. Taking a break. Let's be honest, this isn't working. It can't. If we don't talk to each other while you're away, then when you get back we can just see what happens.'

'What the fuck does that mean?'

The tears quickly turned to incredulous anger.

'It means exactly that. I feel like I'm holding you back, like you're calling me just to check in and all I can think about is you and wondering, is she going to call? What's she doing? I just think we need a break and then when you get back . . .'

'I know, see what happens.'

I couldn't believe what he was suggesting. Ed was the least 'let's just see what happens' man in the world. It wasn't Ed talking. At least the Ed I knew. Ed hated anything that wasn't rubber-stamped and official. Ed didn't make decisions at the drop of a hat. Something had changed. Ed had changed.

'You know it makes sense, Kate. I'm just trying to do something now so when you get back we can work.'

'But why? I don't understand.' There was a pause and all I could hear was him breathing down the line. 'Ed?'

'Just leave it, Kate, please. Can't we just see what happens . . .?'

'Oh, God, stop, just stop it! Do you hear yourself? This isn't you talking. You begged me not to leave. You proposed marriage. You told me you didn't want me to change because you wanted to marry me just as I was and now you want to see what happens? No, Ed, no. What's happened? I know you and this isn't you.'

'Maybe I've changed.'

'Oh, so I leave and you're the one that's changed?' I was suddenly crying and people nearby were looking across at me. I was the crazy person on the beautiful, sunny day at the beach, crying and shouting at her mobile phone.

'I think it's for the best.'

'For who? For me? For you? Who, Ed?'

'For the both of us.'

'What happened?'

'What do you mean, what happened?' he said and I noticed a crack in his voice. A stain on his otherwise brilliantly professional performance.

'Something happened you're not telling me. What is it?'

Again the pause, only this one was different. There was a tension that lingered between us until finally Ed said 'I'm sorry, Kate. I didn't mean to do it, things just got out of control . . .'

'What happened?'

'I slept with someone. I'm so sorry.'

I couldn't believe it. Ed, my Ed, had slept with someone else. I should have been angrier. I should have wanted to slam the phone down and never see him again. Except, of course, I couldn't, because I'd been unfaithful with Jez. Not quite three months apart and we'd both been unfaithful. What did that say about us? What did that say about our future together? 'Do you like this girl?' I said, suddenly feeling tears sting my eyes.

'No, Kate, it was nothing like that. It was just . . .' Ed stopped for a moment. 'I think I was missing you and I was angry at you for leaving. It's not an excuse for what I did, I'm not trying to say it is, but I don't like her, Kate, not like that. It was just sex.'

In some ways that made it harder because I knew I could forgive just sex. That might sound crazy, but just sex was a mistake, an error in judgement, but feelings like I had for Jez, that was worse. Feelings aren't a mistake or a simple error; they're deep within us and they mean something.

I looked around me. It was so warm and beautiful. People were stretched out, enjoying themselves, so care-free and unaffected by the troubles of the world. Laughing, swimming, playing football and chatting each other up; these were my fellow backpackers and I wanted to join them. I wanted to dive in and swim in their cool uncomplicated waters. I wanted to be twenty instead of almost thirty and wanted my old life back. I wanted to push Ctrl+Alt+Del, stop this program and restart. Why couldn't I? After the tears had slowly faded away, I laughed a little.

'What?' said Ed. 'Why are you laughing?'

'Because I kissed someone, Ed. In Thailand. I wanted to tell you, I did, but didn't have the courage.'

'I am so sorry.'

'I know. Me too.'

'So where does this leave us?' said Ed. He sounded shell-shocked. His voice was hollow.

'I think you were right. Maybe we should take a break and see what happens.'

'Love you,' said Ed desperately.

'Love you too,' I said, but neither of us sounded that sure.

There was a long pause, neither of us sure what to say next. It felt like one of those moments back home where we'd sit down by the Thames, holding hands, enjoying the moment without having to say anything. The difference was that we were so far apart. We were holding hands across the ocean, not sure what was going to happen next.

'You know, I never meant to hurt you,' I eventually said. 'Coming away. It was just something I needed to do.'

'I know.'

'Then why were you so grumpy before I left? Why did you try and stop me?'

'Why do you think?'

'Because you're a miserable sod?'

Ed laughed a little.

'No, Kate, because I was afraid of this. I was afraid I'd lose you.'

'You haven't lost me, Ed.'

'Haven't I?'

'Not unless you want to.'

'Why do you think I suggested taking a break? I was doing it to try and save us.'

'It's going to be weird not talking,' I said.

'It will, but it's been pretty weird talking too so maybe it's for—'

'The best. I know.'

Another pause.

'So I guess this is it.'

'Can I text you though, from time to time?'

'Sure,' said Ed. 'Let me know where you are.'

'Make sure I'm still alive,' I said with a giggle.

'Exactly,' said Ed and he chuckled, but it just sounded sad.

After we said goodbye, I sat on the beach, looked out at the ocean and felt the gentle breeze on my face. If there was ever a moment I needed to press Ctrl+Alt+Del, now was the time. Not only was I miles from home, but I was, to all intents and purposes, single for the first time in a very long time.

**To: Emma Fogle**
**From: Kate Jones**
**Subject: Re: Oz**

Em,

I'm so happy you decided to keep the baby. I thought you would. Back when you were sixteen you made the right decision too. I know it's been hard for you so hopefully now you can feel some sense of closure. I'm SO happy for you and Jack. I'm also very annoyed that I'm not going to be there during the first half of the pregnancy, but I'll definitely be there for the birth! Just you try and stop me.

Unfortunately, things aren't great with Ed at the moment. We spoke the other day and agreed to take a break. I don't really know how or why it happened. We talked and we both told each other a few things and the next minute we were on a break until I get back. I'm starting to wonder whether coming away was worth it. What if Ed and I don't make it because of this? I still love him so much, but there's a distance between us now and not just the physical one. It's so strange because I don't feel any different with you, but with Ed it's like being so far apart is destroying everything we've spent so many years building up. It's funny that our friendship is stronger than my relationship with Ed. Not Ha Ha though.

Orla and I are in Byron Bay at the moment. It's a gorgeous little seaside town and we're having the best time. Byron sort of reminds me of Newquay. Orla and I found a pub/club here called Cheeky Monkeys, it's a bit of a meat market, dancing on the tables and all that, but it's fun and cheap. Remember that club we went to in Newquay where we met those boys from Southampton? I think it was called Berties or something. I remember it was cheese-tastic! You got off with that guy, Steve, and I ended up with Stuart, the boy with the wandering hands!

That was so much fun. I guess I was thinking about it because I'm here and also because life was so uncomplicated then. Why does it have to be so difficult now?

I intend to enjoy the rest of my trip and not think about Ed too much. I can't let him ruin this for me and hopefully we can sort things out when I get back.

Missing you, Em. Say hi and congrats to Jack. Have you told your mum yet? I wonder what she's going to say. Still, whatever she says, remember it's your life and not hers. We're heading off up the coast tomorrow to Brisbane and then to a place called Fraser Island to camp for three days. It's the world's biggest sand island! How cool is that?

Love K x

## ED

It was Friday and the office was winding down for the week; the giant juggernaut was slamming its brakes on for the two-day hiatus. It was just gone seven and the only people left in the office were the new recruits trying to gain favour and, of course, Hugh Whitman. Then there was me, who didn't want to leave because I had nowhere else to go. Home reminded me of Kate and I wasn't in the mood for the pub. Work was my only shelter amid the chaos of my life. Kate had never understood my relationship with work in the same way I'd never understood her need to go travelling. Kate was desperate to escape the day-to-day confines of work, while I lost myself in it to escape the unknown beyond. I needed the drudgery while she needed freedom, but somehow we had always needed each other to make it work.

'Drink?' said Georgie, suddenly appearing at my desk.

I noticed Hugh look up from his computer and give me the evil eyebrows, furrowed, deep and questioning.

'Probably not a good idea.'

'Just a quick one. I need to ask you something.'

'You can't ask me here?'

'Just one tiny little drink,' she said with an eager, school-photograph smile.

Hugh walked past, briefcase in hand and a Himalayan expression of irritation and displeasure plastered all over his face. He had warned me about any extra-curricular activity with Georgie and he certainly wouldn't warn me again. He didn't have to use actual words; his face said it all, crushing me with the sheer weight of its disapproval.

'Night, Hornsby,' he boomed like an old headmaster.

'Sir.'

'Good night,' said Georgie, smiling sweetly.

For a moment Hugh's face cracked; a tender smile gave the slightest hint of humanity beneath.

'Georgina,' he said before he looked back at me, his whole face contorting into a look of absolute annoyance. His eyebrows were like heavy leaden storm clouds bearing down on the thin slits of his eyes and the jagged rolls of floppy flesh that made up the rest of his face. The red veins of deep burgundy wine on his nose and cheeks seemed to deepen and threatened to rip and stream down his already bloodshot face.

When he was firmly out of earshot I turned back to Georgie, who was now perched upright on my desk. She was wearing a white cardigan over a flowery blouse that hung loosely down towards her perky young breasts. I got a sudden flashback of our night together. It would've been so easy to give in, to go out for one tiny little drink, but I didn't want to. I didn't want her. It was something I realised during our first time together. It didn't matter that she was gorgeous and wanted me, none of that mattered because she wasn't Kate.

'I don't think we should.'

'But, Ed, I want to. Just one. Please. For me.'

'No, Georgie, I don't want to.'

'You don't want me?'

'I love Kate and what we did was a mistake.'

'Dearest Ed, you're talking absolute drivel. It wasn't a mistake. Turning me down will be a mistake.'

'Oh for God's sake, Georgie, just fucking grow up!' I found myself half-yelling.

'You're telling me to grow up? Mr "my girlfriend has abandoned me for a trip around the world". How pathetic.' I suddenly hated her. She wasn't a sweet, innocent little girl after all, but an annoying, spoilt little brat. I hated myself even more for sleeping with her in the first place. 'You're going to regret this.'

'I doubt it,' I said, standing up. She was poison. A beautiful, angelic-looking devil. 'Have a good weekend,' I said, brushing past her on my way out.

I walked outside into a dreary, wet London night. I pulled up the collar of my coat and walked towards the tube, little pellets of rain spitting against my face making me wince, but I didn't care. I was smiling because I realised something. I wasn't like those other men who cheated on their wives and girlfriends and bragged about it to their mates. I was different, better perhaps, and just because I'd had one weak moment, one lapse in concentration, it didn't mean I loved Kate any less or that we couldn't work. Kate wasn't perfect and neither was I, but maybe we were perfect for each other and that's all that mattered.

The early morning sun crept through a narrow crack in the curtains and tapped me gently on the forehead. I opened my eyes and felt the warmth envelop my face. It was just past seven o'clock on Monday morning and I was awake before the alarm clock. I had to be at work by nine and so I had time for a leisurely shower and a decent breakfast in front of the television. I felt refreshed.

It had been a good weekend. I went to the pub on my own, had lunch, read the papers and watched football, drank a few pints and it was cathartic. I chatted with a few of the locals and when I left, I felt different. I knew I couldn't just sit around waiting for Kate to come back. I'd been wallowing, but no longer. I was going to seize the bloody day. Ed Hornsby didn't wallow. As Hugh Whitman drilled into us from day one, there are no problems, only solutions, and if you aren't part of the solution, you're part of the problem.

I strode into the office and sat down at my desk and Georgie looked across at me sheepishly. I turned on my computer and stood up to walk across and get a cup of coffee; Hugh was in his office, face like thunder, and he beckoned me over. My early-morning optimism was wiped away in an instant. It wasn't going to be good. I walked over, trying to work out what it could be and what I'd done. All of my accounts were doing great, a couple of clients had issues with under-performing stock, but we were in a recession, it happened.

'Come in. Close the door. Sit down,' barked Hugh.

'Problem, sir?'

'Yes. A big fucking problem, Hornsby. Young Georgina Hays has submitted to me personally a complaint of a sexual nature against you.'

I felt my face flush with a potent mixture of embarrassment, fear and incredulity.

'What? I . . . err . . . don't understand, sir. What sort of complaint?'

'Details, Hornsby, details. Problem is I can't let it go. I warned you about any funny business, but you couldn't do it, could you, eh. You had to eat the bloody apple.'

'But sir, what we did was . . .'

'So you don't deny it?'

'I . . . I . . . I . . .'

'You had intercourse with her?' It sounded so horrible coming from his mouth. 'And you forced yourself upon her?'

'No, no I didn't. I wouldn't. We were drunk, it happened. It was her idea. I . . .'

'Listen, Hornsby,' said Hugh, leaning forward slightly but without whispering. 'You've been a good worker, punctual, hard-working, a team player, but you fucked up big time and I can't let it go. Now, we could have a hearing, work out the facts and all that, but this is my department, my team and I'm not going to drag Georgina through all that. I'm going to offer you a decent settlement and you're going to take it. You don't talk to anyone. You get up, leave, go home and I don't want to see you ever again. Understood?'

I was literally speechless. That evil, vindictive little bitch had got me fired and there was nothing I could do about it. I was unemployed. I wanted to cry, but I couldn't let Hugh see me like that. 'I just want you to know, I didn't do anything wrong. We went out, had a few drinks and a one-night stand and now she's lying about it. I would never do anything to cause you or the company any distress. I love my job. Please, Hugh, don't fire me. I'll do anything.'

I needed this. It was all I had to keep me sane. Unfortunately, Hugh's face didn't waver and he just stared at me with those glassy, bloodshot eyes.

'It's already done. HR already have your final cheque. Six months' pay. Take it and do something useful with it. Now get out.'

For a moment I thought about fighting it. I could battle Hugh and the rest of his cronies, but it wouldn't save my job. I could threaten to sue, take this all the way to the top, but something inside of me knew I didn't have it in me. Instead, I stood up and walked out, my mind completely and utterly frazzled. It felt like I was living in a nightmare, my hearing seemed distorted and I moved seemingly without using my legs. I floated back to my desk, grabbed my bag and my jacket, and turned to look at Georgie one more time, but she was too busy laughing and talking to one of the new young male recruits. I'd been a bloody fool.

I took the lift down to the ground floor and then stepped into the foyer for the last time. I took one final look up at the impressive structure they'd paid millions for. The open-plan office resembled a beautiful cruise liner crashing into a gothic cathedral and a sudden fear created a numb pain in my chest. I'd always feared failure and loneliness. I feared ending up with nothing and no one and as I walked out into the chilly streets, it became quite clear I was singularly, completely, horribly alone and, worse, a failure.

## JACK

'Ready?' I said.

Mum was sitting at the bottom of the stairs putting her shoes on. It was the anniversary of Dad's death and we were about to head off and lay flowers on his grave.

'Ready,' said Mum, standing up with coat, scarf and gloves on. She also wore a small, thin smile.

'Let's go and see Dad then, shall we.'

Outside I offered her my arm and we set off on the half-mile walk. I was itching to tell her about the baby, but I'd promised Emma I wouldn't. She wanted to wait a bit longer and do it together. I understood, but it was such a solemn day and I knew it would cheer Mum up. The promise of a new life; her first grandchild. She'd be over the moon.

'How's everything with you and Emma? All right?'

'Good thanks.'

'You over all that nonsense about the film?'

'Yes. I was just being a bit of a prat, but we're fine now. Couldn't be any happier.'

'That's good to hear,' said Mum as we turned the corner and set off up the hill towards the church.

'And how are things with you?'

'Oh, you know, can't complain.'

'And what about that bingo business?'

'It's a disgrace, Jack, an absolute disgrace. I've spoken to Greg Bishop about it, you know, he runs the bingo nights. It's all Doris. You know Doris.'

179

'Blue hair, small . . .'

'Face like a weasel and acts like one too. Cheating she is, Jack. There's no other word for it. I'm getting a petition together to get rid of her. Get her banned for life from the bingo hall. We've only got five signatures so far, but we'll get there. Bruce has been a big help. Since his wife passed, I think he's just throwing himself into the bingo to keep his mind occupied.'

'Right,' I said. 'Sounds like it's chaos down there.'

'It is, Jack, it is.'

It was nice to talk about something mundane.

'Here we are,' I said as we arrived outside the church.

It was a beautiful day. There was a brilliant blue sky overhead, which was only broken up by a few stringy white clouds, and somewhere nearby birds sang, almost like a choir, as we began the slow march through the graveyard. Dad's small plot was near the back, just under an oak tree. We walked past the graves of strangers, people whose names I knew only because I'd walked past so many times on my way to see Dad. Long-gone fathers, wives and children, all remembered by someone. Eventually, we came to the small plot where my father's ashes were buried. Mum and I stood in silence and then Mum lay the flowers down next to him.

'There you go, love,' said Mum, breaking my heart the way she always did when she spoke to Dad. Like he wasn't really gone. 'He would have been sixty this year,' she said, turning to me.

'I know,' I said.

'I just can't believe it's been fifteen years.'

'Me either.'

I kept thinking about my baby. His grandchild that was on the way. I was also thinking about my writing. I wanted it to happen so badly. I needed it to happen for many reasons: for me, for Emma, for our baby, but I think, most of all, I needed it for Dad.

'He's says he's going to be a writer,' said Dad in his clear, confident voice.

Dad was in the lounge talking to our neighbours, Joyce and Karl. Karl was a doctor at the nearby hospital and Joyce taught at my school. They didn't know I was sat at the top of the stairs listening to their conversation.

'Not going to take over the family business then?' said Karl.

'Not really Jack's strength,' said Dad.

'Must be a bit of a disappointment for you,' said Joyce. I never did like Joyce. I didn't have to worry though; Dad and I had already talked about my writing ambitions and he said he was proud of me. I'd been nervous to tell him because I know he'd always assumed I would go into the family business, keep the legacy going. A part of me felt guilty because I knew deep down he would have loved me to follow him into real estate, but despite his disappointment, he was happy for me. Proud I was following my dreams, just like him.

'No, no,' said Dad. 'It took me a bit by surprise if I'm honest, and of course I worry about him.'

'Understandable,' said Karl. 'Not a proper career, is it.'

'Probably just a phase,' said Joyce.

'Hmmm, maybe,' said Dad.

I was seething. Why wasn't Dad standing up for me? I couldn't believe what I was hearing. It had taken every ounce of courage I had to tell him and I thought he supported me. I thought he understood, but most importantly I thought I knew him better than anyone.

'Give him time, he's only young,' said Karl. 'We all have crazy dreams at that age. I wouldn't worry, once he grows up and realises the money is in real estate, he'll be begging you to show him the ropes.'

'I wanted to be an actress for a while,' said Joyce with a high-pitched giggle. 'I even went to a couple of auditions back in the day.'

'And what happened?' said Dad.

'What do you think? Luckily, I decided to become a teacher instead, otherwise I wouldn't have met this one,' she said, leaning across and giving Karl a kiss.

'I'm sure he'll be fine,' said my father. 'You never know, he might still take over the business when I'm old and grey.'

They all laughed and drank their gin and tonics.

Tears suddenly stung my eyes. I couldn't believe what I was hearing. I got up, walked back to my bedroom and closed the door. I put on some music and lay down on the bed. Dad just thought I was some immature kid who had a stupid pipe dream? I'd always looked up to him. I thought I wanted to be just like him, but hearing him say those words I realised he was just like all the other adults. He didn't understand me in the way I thought he did, and I didn't understand him either.

Mum got home shortly after and then Karl and Joyce's daughter Ashleigh came over. We had the barbecue and I didn't say anything to Dad. I didn't know what to say. I felt determined to become a writer and then he'd be proud of me, and not because I was like him and was following in his footsteps but because I was making my own.

Two weeks later Dad died and I never got the chance to talk to him or get over hearing that conversation. In my mind, he was still the same man to me he was when I was a teenager. I still needed to show him I could be a success on my own terms. I still needed his approval.

# EMMA

I knew Jack wasn't telling me the complete truth about the pretty young girl in our flat. I could see it on his face. I didn't know how far they'd gone, whether they'd had sex or not, but it didn't matter. I knew he loved me and that was all I needed. None of us are perfect, but at the end of the day, when you close your eyes and feel the person next to you in bed, if you know they love you more than anything in the world, what does one mistake really mean? I'd kissed Rhys and Jack had made a similar mistake. The most important thing was that Jack and I were having a baby together.

'Ready?' said Jack, walking into our bedroom.

I took a deep breath and looked at myself in the mirror, trying to see any signs of change. I knew it was silly, I didn't look any different really, except being a bit puffier in the face, but I hadn't gained any weight. In fact, due to the morning sickness, I'd actually lost some. I felt different though. Just knowing seemed to change everything about me. I felt like a grown up for the first time in my life.

'Ready as I'll ever be.'

We had our first appointment at the doctors and I was terrified something was wrong. Scared to death I wasn't pregnant at all and the brave new world we'd created would mean nothing. After I told Jack, our plans had changed so quickly. We'd discussed the film briefly, but it was over. Jack was already planning beyond working at To Bean or Not to

Bean. He was going to get something better and I was going to try and get some acting parts to help. It was so much more than that though. Our relationship had evolved. Suddenly it wasn't just about us; it was about nine months later when our world was going to be turned upside down. Jack became different too. No longer the boy I'd known; now a father-to-be and more protective over me than ever before.

We created a bubble, our own little world, and I didn't want it to end. For my whole life, I thought I'd needed my career so badly and needed it to be a success, but then I didn't. All I needed was in that bubble and everything in it mattered more than anything had before. The trouble was, when you finally had something you were so afraid to lose, it laced the happiness with a terrified, over-protective sadness. I could lose the film, it didn't matter, but if I lost Jack or the baby, I didn't know what I'd do. Going to the doctors was the first step on a staircase that went on forever.

The surgery was on a quiet tree-lined street near Regent's Park. We got out of the car and stood outside the building, holding hands before we took deep breaths and walked inside. I checked in and we sat down in the waiting room. Jack held my hand and I looked around at the other women. One of them was heavily pregnant and looked like she was going to drop at any minute. Her huge belly sat in front of her making her grimace in discomfort. The other two women were in different stages of pregnancy and then there were two very young-looking girls. I didn't dare ask if they were having check-ups or were actually pregnant. One couldn't have been more than fourteen and both were alone, trying not to look too nervous, but they weren't fooling anyone.

I idly rifled through the stack of magazines on the table in front of us but I wasn't really looking, just trying to stop my brain from cycling through the hundred or so petrifying thoughts that were clouding my mind.

'Emma Fogle?'

I looked up and a nurse was standing smiling at me. I smiled back and Jack helped me up. I wasn't sick, but I think he just wanted to support me and it was the only way he knew how. It was only then I realised that Jack was the only man in the waiting room and I suddenly felt a deep pang of love for him.

'Miss Fogle, let's have a look at you shall we,' said Doctor Simpson as I lay down on the table; Jack was by my side holding my hand. Doctor Simpson squeezed a pea-sized ball of cold jelly onto my stomach and started the ultrasound. It was easily the tensest thirty seconds of my life. I squeezed Jack's hand so hard I could see him grimacing with pain.

Before all of this happened I'd thought about having children. 'One day' seemed to be the common theme that ran through most of my thoughts. But lying on the table, waiting to hear the indescribable heartbeat of my baby, one day became now and I'd never wanted anything so badly in my entire life. Doctor Simpson moved the ultrasound probe around but the only noise we could hear was static, until eventually we heard it.

'There's the heartbeat,' she said. 'Sounds perfectly healthy.'

Suddenly both Jack and I were in floods of tears. It was really happening. We still had a long way to go, but I definitely had a baby, our baby, and it had a healthy heartbeat. The relief washed over me faster than any wave, catching me quickly and dragging me along with it. I was finally able to relax. The rest of the examination went smoothly and we made an appointment for our next check-up. Afterwards we went out for an early dinner.

We were at Pizza Express in Notting Hill, just a short walk from our flat so Jack could have a few drinks. My drinking days were over, for nine months at least, which made me realise I had so much to learn before the baby came. I would need books and to find classes, but above all, we needed a bigger place to live.

'You know we can't raise a baby in our flat,' said Jack.

'I was just thinking the same thing.'

'And I know your parents will probably want to help, but I want us to do this on our own, Em. This is our baby, our life, and it's time I supported us.'

I'd always known Jack hated living in a flat paid for by my parents. He needed to be the man and he wanted us to be self-sufficient, but it was easier said than done. I didn't earn much from acting and Jack's wages from To Bean or Not to Bean would barely be enough for a studio flat in a far worse part of London. As much as I knew it killed him, we needed my parents. I felt awful for him because I knew how much it hurt him, ripped him apart, but what good were words and good intentions without anything to back them up.

'I know, love, and we do have to move, but with me not working at the moment and you at the coffee shop, I don't know what we're going to do. I'll try and get something quick like a commercial and maybe my parents could help us initially,' I started but Jack leapt in, his face more determined than I'd ever seen him before.

'I'm going to sort this out,' he said. 'One way or another, I'm going to support us and give us the life we need. We don't need your parents. I'm going to be your husband soon and a father and I'm going to do this,' he said and all I could do was smile and play uneasily with my cutlery.

'Emma?' said a voice suddenly. I looked up and there was

a waiter dressed in the restaurant's black and white stripes. He was handsome, probably in his early twenties, and had striking cheekbones and piercing deep blue eyes. He looked vaguely familiar. 'Sorry, Stephen Croft. I'm in *The Hen Weekend*, just a lowly old friend of a friend, but we had a line together. Shit, you don't remember me, so embarrassing, I'm sorry . . .'

I did remember him. Suddenly his face came back to me. We'd gone over our line at the mansion the day before I left. Young Stephen Croft, fresh out of university, desperate to be an actor and exactly like me ten years before. He had the world at his feet and nothing was going to stand in his way.

'Of course I remember you, how's things? How's the film?'

Suddenly Stephen was going on about the film and who was in line to replace me and script changes and rehearsals. As he was talking and I could see how completely wrapped up in it he was something fell over me: a blanket of calm, because I realised I didn't care anymore. The film was my past and even though I'd moved on, a part of me had still been worried that somewhere along the line, I'd regret giving up my big chance and having a baby. Stephen went on for ten minutes before his manager gave him the evil eye.

'Must go, great seeing you again, Em. See you around,' he said, but as soon as he said it, I thought to myself that he probably wouldn't.

'You OK?' said Jack, reaching across and placing a hand over mine.

'Yeah, I am,' I said with a smile, but it wasn't forced and I meant it. I really was going to be OK. 'You do realise what this pregnancy means?'

'What's that?'
'I'm going to be an absolute whale at our wedding.'

**To: Kate Jones**
**From: Emma Fogle**
**Subject: Re: Oz**

K,

I was just reading back the first email you sent me – shit that feels like a lifetime ago now – and you were right, this is strange. I also read the last one and then I started thinking about how everything is changing and it's scary, Kate. Don't get me wrong, things are changing for the better. I'm super excited to be a mummy (I know Jack will call me a yummy mummy!) and you're off travelling the world. I guess I was just thinking how as you get older changes become scarier because they mean so much more. It's like you said, when we were kids, having fun, kissing boys, none of it felt like a big deal. But now everything seems so important and that's terrifying.

I'm sorry to hear about you and Ed. I can send Jack on a scouting mission if you want. Check out the lie of the land? I'm sure you'll work it out though. I mean the man proposed to you not that long ago. Surely that means something, right? It must be hard being so far apart. I can't imagine being that far away from Jack. The important thing though is that you enjoy yourself and worry about Ed when you get back. Remember what you used to always tell me whenever I didn't get an acting part? Only worry about the things you can control and let everything else go. You were right then, Kate, so take your own advice!

I feel so boring now. Just a pregnant woman. I sit at home watching daytime television and reading pregnancy books – such a cliché! I haven't managed to get any acting jobs yet. My agent is trying, apparently – I think he's still quite pissed off about me getting pregnant. Oh well. I hope the world's largest sand island was fun. I look forward to seeing some more photos and hearing about the rest of your A-mazing adventure soon!

Love Em X

april

## KATE

'I feel like death,' said Orla.

She had on her big sunglasses, a hoodie top and definitely looked a lot like death. I didn't feel much better myself. Not quite death, but maybe a severe cardiac arrest, still in critical condition. We were sitting at a café across the street from our hostel in Cairns. Our east coast trip was almost up. After Byron Bay we'd visited Brisbane, camped on Fraser Island, spent a few relaxing days on lovely Magnetic Island, sailed around the Whitsunday Islands on a catamaran and rented a car and driven to Cape Tribulation. Cairns was our final stop. Our last hurrah. We checked into Gilligan's backpacker resort and last night, even for us, had been a big one.

'I know what you mean. I don't know if I can eat this,' I said, looking down at a plate of bacon, eggs, mushrooms, tomatoes, hash browns and toast. I was already on my second coffee and itching for a third.

'Get it down you; you'll feel much better.'

I grunted back. I wasn't so sure.

We only had one more night together and that was it. One more night and then Orla was staying in Cairns to find a job and I was flying to Melbourne. I'd been with Orla for just over two months in total. In backpacker terms we'd been friends forever. We'd been drunk so many times, shared every facet and side street of our lives and now we were about to go our separate ways. Maybe we'd never see each other ever again. The strange transitory nature of backpacker relationships never failed to surprise, delight and depress me.

'Before we go, I have to ask you something,' said Orla as we neared the end of our breakfasts. I was faring better than expected, but still couldn't stomach the mushrooms, which had a sickly brown look about them and a snail-like juice that ran and mixed with the tomatoes.

'Anything as long as it doesn't involve alcohol. I don't think I'm ever going to drink again.'

'How many times have you said that during the last few months?'

'Not enough, apparently.'

We giggled and then Orla looked at me with a solemn, thoughtful face.

'Why is it you love Ed so much?'

'What do you mean?'

'Why do you still love him? Maybe it's just me, but it seems like you're travelling on your own, falling for hunky, young traveller guys in Thailand . . .'

'Guy,' I corrected her.

'All right, guy. It sounds to me like he's holding you back, making you feel guilty and miserable and yet you still claim you love him. Why?'

I felt a dull pain in my stomach every time I thought of Ed. I didn't know what it was. Guilt, perhaps, or sadness? It felt like I had a football sitting in my stomach. Did I still love Ed? It was a question I'd asked myself a hundred times since Byron Bay. Of course, after I got off the phone with Ed, I spent the rest of the day crying with Orla, telling her every last detail of my relationship with Ed and my feelings for Jez. Orla listened and then we went out and got hammered – her idea, not mine. I'd spent every day since going over and over in my mind the conversation with Ed, trying to fathom how we'd arrived at that point and what it meant to my future. To our future.

So when Orla asked why I still loved him, the truth was, I wasn't entirely sure. I did though. I loved him. We'd been through too much together and shared too much to just stop. Relationships and love didn't come with brakes, brakes that worked anyway.

'It's complicated,' is all I could say.

'No offence, Kate, but people only say it's complicated when what they really mean is, I don't know how to finish it.'

Was she right? Was Ed just a habit I didn't know how to quit? Was Ed just like smoking and all I needed were some Ed patches and then everything would be all right?

'Well, that isn't the case with us, I can assure you. If I wanted to finish it, I would,' I said, not sure whether my performance was that convincing or if I even believed it myself. 'Like I said, it's complicated.'

'As long as you're sure,' said Orla with a supportive smile. 'I just want you to be happy.'

'I'm sure,' I said. 'Now how about a hair of the dog?'

'I thought you weren't drinking ever again?'

'And how many times have I said that during the last few months?'

'Not enough, apparently,' said Orla with a huge grin.

As we got up, the stomach-football sank down and disappeared for a moment, but I knew it would be back. I really didn't want to drink again, but it was the only distraction I could think of. Maybe alcohol would help uncomplicate things or at the very least take my mind of it for a few hours.

'He isn't your usual type,' said Emma.

'What do you mean? I don't have a type,' I replied.

'Oh, come on, Kate. You definitely have a type. Slackers, bohemians, arty types. Tall, good-looking and usually danger-ous. They're always a bit alternative, but he is just very . . .'

'Very what?'

'Straight. If your history of boyfriends was Take That, you've finally landed Gary Barlow.'

I looked at Emma and we giggled, but inside the mecha-nisms started to turn and my usual doubts and worries started to grind away. I really liked him, but I also knew Em was right: he definitely wasn't my usual type.

'Well, maybe I'm ready for Gary Barlow.'

'After Dan, you mean?'

'Yeah,' I said, looking down briefly at the table, feeling that same mixture of regret, embarrassment and anger I'd felt every day since we'd broken up.

'He was definitely a Robbie.'

'But the worst version of Robbie. Post-Take-That-break-up Glastonbury Robbie.'

'You're well shot of him, and maybe this Gary Barlow wannabe is just what you need.'

'I don't think he's a Gary Barlow wannabe, Em.'

'Then what is he?'

'He's an Ed.'

It was a few weeks after Ed and I met in the student union and things had been moving quickly. Tonight he had to pass the best friend test and Emma was a harsh critic. We were in the Bird in Hand pub, just around the corner from my student digs. Ed was at the bar getting in a round and Emma was giving me her opening argument. Poor Ed didn't know it yet, but this wasn't just a casual drink, as I'd sold it to him, but a litmus test that would determine whether our relationship would continue or sink into oblivion. I valued Emma's opinion perhaps even more than my own. She'd warned me against getting serious with Dan and she'd been right. The excitement and constant partying that was fun at first had quickly sunk into cocaine-fuelled arguments (him on the coke, not me) and nursing his hangovers and mood swings. His roguish good looks, laddish charm and the possibility that I could change him had kept me around far too long.

'Here you go,' said Ed, returning with three drinks and a packet of salt and vinegar crisps.

'Thanks,' Emma said warmly.

Ed smiled and sat down next to me. I reached across and put my hand on his leg. We all sat in silence for a moment and sipped our drinks.

'Ed, Kate tells me you're from Slough.'

'That's right.'

I could see the tension suddenly tighten the muscles in his face. He didn't like talking about his family. In the past few weeks I'd managed to drag a few pieces of information out of him, but it had been like pulling teeth. The general consensus seemed to be that he was embarrassed and wanted to forget where he'd come from. I just hadn't found out why.

'What's it like there?'

'Pretty awful.'

'There was that John Betjeman poem wasn't there? Something about dropping bombs on Slough. I always thought that was a bit harsh. It can't be that bad.'

'You'd be surprised,' said Ed.

Another pause in conversation. I squeezed Ed's leg under the table.

'Ow, what was that for?' said Ed, looking at me a little shocked.

'Sorry,' I said, hoping he would get the hint and ask Emma a question or say something. Another pause.

'Ed's going to start his own business,' I finally said, jumping on the ticking bomb myself.

'Oh, really, what sort?' said Emma enthusiastically. She was really trying, bless her.

Ed took a long sip of his pint before he answered.

'Not sure yet,' he said in his best Gary Barlow voice. 'Probably something online.' This wasn't going well. I felt bad for Ed because he didn't know this was an interview. He'd turned up fully expecting to already have the job in the bag. He didn't know it was still up for grabs. It wasn't his fault he was a bit quiet around people he didn't know well. I was sure if Emma got to know him, he'd open up and she'd love him. Question was, would he get the time?

'Oh, right, sounds good,' said Em.

Just then the door opened and in walked Dan, completely off his face. The signs might not have been visible to the average punter, but I knew him. We'd dated for the best part of a year and I could tell from his slightly off-kilter walk and the glazed eyes. Unfortunately, before I had the chance to do anything, he saw me and his face lit up.

'Fuck me, if it isn't Kate Jones,' said Dan, walking over and almost straight into the table.

I hadn't told Ed about Dan, mainly because I was trying to forget about him myself.

'Hello, Dan,' I said coldly.

'And the gorgeous Emma.' Dan pulled up a chair and sat down next to me. He stank of beer and cigarettes.

'And Dan the twat,' Emma said without missing a beat.

'Fair play, fair play. And who's the stiff?' He nodded at Ed.

'Ed,' said Ed, offering his hand, but Dan ignored him.

'Don't suppose you fancy buying me a pint?' Dan asked. 'For old times' sake?'

'Just leave it, Dan, eh.'

'What? Don't you want to drink with your old—?'

'I said, leave it,' I half-shouted, and felt Ed stiffen up. My face was burning. I was mortified.

'Old what?' said Ed, suddenly looking across at me.

'It's nothing,' I said coyly.

I wanted the ground to open and swallow me up whole. I was embarrassed, guilty and I didn't want Ed to know anything about me and Dan.

'Oh, fuck me, she didn't mention me, did she?'

'No she didn't,' said Ed.

'We dated. For a year. Only broke up a couple of months ago. Apparently, she couldn't handle the drink . . .'

'And the drugs. Don't forget the drugs, Dan,' I snapped.

'At least it wasn't the sex, eh. That was fucking mental, wasn't it, Kate, eh?'

I went red. Very red and felt a heady mixture of loathing and resentment towards Dan. Why did he always have to ruin everything? Ed was probably going to do a runner as fast as he could after this and who could blame him? I hadn't had sex with Ed because I wanted to take things slowly, make sure before I committed myself, and there was Dan making out I was some sort of voracious sex addict.

'I think it's time you left,' said Ed suddenly.

'Oh, the fucking stiff's not dead after all,' said Dan, standing up. Despite being off his tits, Dan was still big. A lot bigger than Ed.

'Come on, mate. Just go and let us have a quiet drink,' said Ed calmly.

I felt the blood rushing through my body. Excitement, fear and a sudden affection for Ed. I didn't care that he was more Gary Barlow than Robbie. Dan was a dick and the last boyfriend I would have that would treat me like shit. Ed wouldn't ever treat me like that. He was decent, honest and not afraid to stand up for me.

'And what you going to do about it if I don't?' said Dan, a smarmy grin on his annoying face.

'Just leave it will you and go!' I shouted, standing up quickly.

'Oh you can fuck off too,' said Dan. 'You fucking bitch!'

I don't know what happened, but the next minute and Ed had punched Dan and Dan was lying on the floor, blood dribbling from his mouth.

'No one talks to my girlfriend like that. I don't want to see you around here ever again, understand?' Ed said, standing over him as the barman came rushing over. I'd never seen that side of Ed before. The Ed I knew was composed and rational. He never so much as looked angry or even slightly annoyed and here he was punching out my ex, a good four inches taller and three stone heavier. There was obviously a lot more to Ed than I'd originally thought.

Dan looked at Ed with a blank expression before the barman escorted him to the door and kicked him out.

'You all right?' Ed asked.

'I am now,' I replied.

'Our hero,' said Emma, with a smile and a wink. I knew from that moment on that he had her approval.

As Orla and I walked towards the pub, I thought about all the moments from my past and all the times with Ed. It wasn't that he'd punched Dan, but what it represented. I knew from that day on that I loved him. He kept me safe and made me feel something I hadn't felt with anyone else before: content. With men like Dan I had been trying to fill a gap. The hole left by my useless father. With Ed, I didn't feel like that. Ed wasn't a daddy stand-in. Ed was a proper boyfriend, a man who made up for all the losses I'd felt since I was a kid. In one swoop he'd made me complete.

The problem I had now was trying to work out if he still made me feel that way. I knew why I loved him, knew what he meant to me, but the only thing I didn't know was whether it was still enough.

'Beer o'clock?' said Orla, standing outside a pub.

'One last time,' I said and we disappeared inside.

## ED

'I just don't know what to do,' I said. 'For the first time in my life, I feel like I have no idea what I'm doing.'

'And what are you doing?' said Jack, opposite me.

We were at a pub in Notting Hill. I'd taken the tube up just to get out of the house. I was going crazy on my own with nothing to do all day. It had been a few weeks since I'd been unceremoniously fired and if the truth be told, I hadn't done much of anything except watch daytime television and feel sorry for myself. It was a vicious circle. It was only a matter of time before I started drinking heavily.

'Not much. I can't seem to get up the energy to find a job and plus I won't be able to get another job in the City. As soon as the truth comes out about why I was fired . . .'

'Even though it wasn't true?'

'It doesn't matter. I was fired because of a sexual complaint. Do you think I have any chance of getting a reference from Whitman that doesn't state, 'Oh, and by the way, he molested my niece.'

Jack chuckled and, maybe for the first time in weeks, I laughed too.

'Ed Hornsby, niece molester. It has a nice ring to it.'

'Yeah, right before Ed Hornsby, inmate number four-seventy-one, Wormwood Scrubs,' I said and we laughed. 'Another?' I asked, shaking my empty pint glass.

'I'd love one, but I'd better get these. You're unemployed, remember?'

Jack smiled and then walked off towards the bar to get in another round. It felt good to be out again, enjoying myself and having a laugh. It had been an awful few weeks. Between breaking up with Kate and losing my job, my life had gone from the heady heights of happiness to the depths of despair. I hadn't told Jack about me and Kate yet, probably for the same reason it had taken me weeks to pluck up the courage to come out for a drink. I was embarrassed.

'There you go, mate.' Jack put our pints on the table and sat down.

'Cheers.'

'I was just thinking,' said Jack. 'Now you're unemployed and have all that money, why don't you go and meet Kate? The only reason you didn't go in the first place was because of work, but that's gone now.'

Jack was partially right. Work wasn't the only reason I didn't go, but definitely the main one. I'd thought about it and if Kate and I weren't on a break, maybe I would have met her in Australia. I couldn't though. It was time to tell Jack everything.

'I can't.'

'Why not? Most people would jump at the chance. A few months travelling around Australia and then what, Fiji and Peru? Better than sitting at home bored on your own.'

'But I'm not most people and Kate and I sort of broke up.'

'What?!' Jack said incredulously, almost choking on his beer.

'Let me have a cigarette and I'll come back and explain everything.'

'But you don't smoke?'

'I do now,' I said and went outside to join the huddled mass of smokers.

*     *     *

'You'll amount to nothing with that attitude,' Dad said, looking at me with *that* face, his eyes burning with rage. He was never the sort of dad who hit us, but he didn't have to. His face said everything you needed to know.

'And what would you know about success?' I yelled back.

'What's that supposed to mean?'

My heart was beating like a crazy drum in my chest and my mind was racing at a million miles an hour. I was only eighteen and I'd never stood up to Dad like that before. Only it wasn't standing up. Not really. Dad hadn't done anything wrong except not live up to my expectations. He hadn't been the success I wanted him to be, but I was too angry, too afraid and too embarrassed to give in and admit that I was in the wrong.

'You know what it means,' I said spitefully. 'Just look at you.'

'What's wrong with me?'

I knew I shouldn't say it. It was hurtful and mean, but I wanted to hurt him. I wanted to punish him for his mistakes, the mistakes that had hurt me, hurt our family and made me want to get as far away from Slough as possible. I hated his average life with its pathetic routines and mundane traditions. I hated the way he spoke in that working-class accent, mispronouncing words and dropping letters like all the other wasters at the pub. I didn't care about them though. I wanted my dad to be different. I wanted my father to care more, have some respect and to be above getting pissed every Saturday with welders, mechanics and factory workers down the local. Why didn't he want more?

'You're a fucking failure, Dad. You have a shit job that pays shit money. You piss about with blokes at the pub when you should have, could have, been doing something else. You're an embarrassment to me and the whole family,' I spat out, every word hitting him below the belt and knocking the stuffing out of him. I could see the pain in his eyes. I could see the look of disbelief and then a tear escape and fall down his cheek. It was time to turn the final screw. 'I can't wait to get away from you, away from this shithole of a house. I'm going to university. I'm going to get a proper job so I can take care of my family in the way you couldn't.'

Dad stood and stared at me. He wiped the tear away from his face. I don't think he could believe what I was saying. Neither of us could. We stood there for a moment and I was shaking with nervous energy and fear. I didn't know what he was going to do. Was he going to hit me? He had every right. I'd shouted at him and told him what I thought of his life. He was fifty years old and in my eyes had wasted all fifty of them. After what seemed like an age, he finally said, quietly and coldly, 'If that's what you really think, son, then you can get out of my house.'

And I did.

'So when did you start smoking?' said Jack, back at the table.

'Oh, a while ago. It's a long story.'

'So you were saying about you and Kate?'

'We're technically on a break. She kissed a bloke in Thailand. I slept with Georgie and every time we spoke on the phone it just seemed like we were further apart.'

'You're done?'

'Not done. Just on a break. I told her we'd see what happens when she gets back. It seemed easier than trying to keep it all together while she was away.'

'Mate, I'm so sorry. That on top of work and everything else. It's no wonder you're smoking.'

'Amazed I'm not an alcoholic too,' I said with a smile. Jack laughed.

'I guess the only thing I'm not sure about all of this is why? Why did you sleep with Georgie in the first place? It seems so unlike you.'

'I've been asking myself the same question.'

'And?'

'Apart from the obvious ones like she was young, gorgeous and had the sort of body you only generally see in magazines . . .'

'Apart from that.'

'I think it was sort of payback to Kate for leaving. Fuck, that sounds bad, doesn't it? You leave and follow your dreams and I'll sleep with the first girl who shows me a bit of interest.'

'No, I mean, yes, it does sound a bit shit, but it's not that simple, is it?'

'Probably not. It's just . . .' I started and then began searching my head for the right words. Then the argument I had with Dad suddenly replayed in my mind. Was that the same? Dad hadn't been what I thought he should be and neither had Kate. I'd punished them both because they hadn't done what I wanted. What did that make me? 'I didn't think she'd leave me, is the simple answer. I thought that once I'd said no, she'd forget about it and move on, but then she didn't. I haven't even told Kate this, but a part of me wanted to go with her. I thought about it and almost changed my mind, but . . .'

'Why didn't you?'

'Probably for the same reason I've been sitting at home for the past few weeks. Because I was afraid. Afraid that leaving would ruin my career and we'd be poor and end up living back in Slough.'

'But that wouldn't have happened.'

'It's different for you, Emma and Kate. You all grew up in nice middle-class families. You didn't grow up wondering where the next meal was coming from. Wondering why you couldn't have the same toys as everyone else. We were poor. Really poor, and leaving a well-paid job to go travelling was too big of a gamble.'

'Did you tell Kate any of this?'

'I couldn't.'

'Why not? She'd understand.'

Kate had given me plenty of chances to talk about it. She'd asked me over and over again why I wouldn't go and every time I'd given the same generic answer. Because I just can't. Because of work. Because I didn't really want to travel. I'd never given her the real answer, the truthful answer, that I was too scared to take the risk, to pack everything up and go travelling because I was terrified of ending up like my father.

'I don't know, mate. I guess I thought I was doing her a favour. In my crazy mind I've always wanted her and our future kids to be proud of me. Proud I could give them whatever they wanted because I was a success. I didn't want to jeopardise that.'

'I understand. It's the same for me. I need to be a successful writer as much for Em and my mum as for me. I need it to work because I want them to be proud of me. I want to be a success like my old man was for me.'

'I guess that's the difference between us,' I said and took a sip of my pint.

'What's that?'

'You want to make your dad proud because you want him to see you've achieved what he already had, and I need to be a success so I don't become what my dad was to me.'

'Was your dad a bad dad though?'

'What do you mean?'

'Was he a good dad, but a failure in life, or was he bad at both?'

'I guess that's my problem, isn't it? I could never distinguish between them.'

'And now?'

'I don't know anymore.'.

'Sounds like you need another pint,' said Jack.

'Definitely.' I smiled. 'But this one's on me. I may be unemployed, but I still have my dignity.'

'And who do you think you got that from?' said Jack, and as I wandered off towards the bar I knew exactly who he meant.

# KATE

'You coming?' said Bryan, attempting to sound seductive.

'Just give me a second.'

I was standing in just my underwear.

'I don't bite, Kate.'

Bryan was in his hostel dorm bed. The room was empty except us. The other six people who shared the room were downstairs at the bar and they could be back at any moment, drunkenly falling through the door and stopping us in our tracks. A part of me was desperately wishing they would so I didn't have to go through with this. Not that Bryan was forcing me or making me do anything I didn't want to. If I wanted out I just had to leave. Say the safe word, not that we had one, but 'Stop. Put your penis away Bryan,' would probably be enough.

'I thought you wanted this,' said Bryan from under the single, depressingly unromantic, slightly stained sheet of his bed. A single sock lay over the metal headboard above his head.

'I do. I did. It's just . . .'

The truth was I didn't know what I wanted. Downstairs, when Bryan and I were knocking back the drinks, flirting and then kissing in dark corners, it felt all right. I felt all right. It wasn't the gap-year experience I'd imagined. In fact, it was a million miles from what I'd thought about before I left. But when Bryan grabbed my hand and led me upstairs, I didn't stop him. I knew what was happening and didn't have a feeling either way about it. It was almost as if I was watching myself doing it, but couldn't affect the outcome in any way.

Bryan reached out and held my hand.

'We don't have to if you don't want to.'

'No, it's OK,' I said, slipping out of my underwear and into bed next to Bryan.

He smelt of a mixture of Hugo Boss, cigarettes and lager. I heard voices in the hallway, giggles and the steady bass of the music from the bar. A light from the street angled towards us. Bryan positioned himself on top of me and through the darkness I could just make out his smile, and then he leaned down and began kissing me.

His tongue felt strange and he pushed too hard and a couple of times we hit teeth. He ran his hands over my body, but they were dry and felt alien. Unlike Jez, who had little excess fat and no body hair, Bryan had rolls of extra skin around his waist and slightly flabby man boobs. His chest was hairy and when I reached around I felt hair on his back too. Ed wasn't in the best shape, but I'd grown with him. When we first met he was more like Jez and I was probably a lot slimmer too. I knew I was. At twenty-one I had been slim, smooth and my skin was taut against my body, before age and bad eating habits had shifted everything south. Ed wasn't as hairless as Jez, but he took care of himself and I loved his body despite its failings and he loved mine despite its flaws. I had feelings for Jez, he meant something, but Bryan didn't have a great body and I barely knew him. Bryan was just a shag.

I'd only had two one-night stands before. Once when I was in Newquay at the age of seventeen and then another during the first week of university. Both were a total disaster and I regretted them almost as soon as they were over. I loved having sex with Ed, but shagging a complete stranger I didn't even really fancy while pissed out of my brain meant nothing to me. It was pointless and as Bryan started making his move, his slightly awkward hand grabbing and probing between my thighs, I knew I couldn't go ahead with it. I didn't want it. I didn't want nervous and slightly sweaty Bryan on top of me, desperately trying to find something that felt a bit like a clitoris, which he'd probably rub for five seconds before trying to shove his penis inside me.

'Stop, I'm sorry, I can't do this,' I said, quickly pushing him off me.

'What's the matter?'

'Nothing, it's not you Bryan, it's . . . it's me. This isn't what I want. I didn't come travelling to do this.'

'OK, calm down.'

'No I won't,' I half-shouted. Suddenly all the pent-up anger and resentment, the undefinable disgust I felt towards myself about Ed came screaming out of me. Bryan was in the wrong place at the wrong time. 'I came travelling to experience wonderful things, to live, to find out who I was and what I wanted to do with the rest of my life. I didn't come away to shag boys like you while pissed up in the hostel. This is fucking awful . . .' I said my final word before the tears came. Oh yes, the great swathes of tears. The waterworks.

'You all right?' said Bryan, sitting up and grappling with a T-shirt.

'No Bryan, I don't think I am,' I said.

Bryan reached across and put a hand on my shoulder.

'It's weird travelling. We all have highs and lows. Probably just a bit of a low, eh.'

I sniffed and felt more tears waiting to erupt. I needed to get out of that room and be alone. I grabbed my pile of clothes from the floor and began putting them on quickly.

'Don't go, Kate. Come to bed, have another drink, see what happens.'

'I'm not going to fucking sleep with you, Bryan!' I yelled.

'Jesus, I didn't know you were fucking mental,' he said, getting up and slipping his jeans on. 'See you later, nutter.'

The next moment Bryan was gone, leaving me alone in the room. As soon as the door was closed, I broke down again, the tears coming and coming without an end in sight and all I could think about was Ed.

'Love you,' said Ed.

It was the first time he'd said it out loud. We'd only been together for a couple of months and it was early for such declarations, but I knew we both felt it. I loved him too. Every sinewy fibre of my body knew it and I wanted to shout it from the rooftops and put up fliers around London next to adverts for lost cats and escort services. It was still a gamble so early on though. The L word. I'd only ever told one boy before and regretted it ever since. I had loved Dan briefly, but just saying it seemed to change things and our relationship spiralled downhill quickly afterwards. It was different with Ed though. I'd known I was in love with him probably from about the third or fourth week of our relationship, but I didn't know what to do with it. As much as I thought he felt the same, I couldn't know for sure. I didn't want to ruin what we had by jumping the gun. It was all right when men jumped the gun, it was acceptable, but if a girl did it she risked everything.

We were walking down by the Thames and it was the perfect day. We were just out of university, there was the first inkling of summer sunshine and our lives stretched out before us, doors flung wide open and all the rest of it. We were in love and nothing else mattered. I should have been the happiest girl in the world, but something was stopping me. The same thing that had always stopped me. The emotional brake that kept me back, staring into the distance and wondering if I'd ever catch up. My father. Fuck him, I thought, but I knew it wasn't that easy.

'Love you too,' I said back, but I couldn't help feeling that shade of inevitable pain that lay somewhere over the horizon. The thing was, I don't think I even knew it myself. I didn't realise just how terrified I was of being loved and loving someone because it meant they could leave me too. Ed suddenly had the same power over me that my father did. The power to hurt me. 'Just promise me one thing.'

'Anything,' said Ed with an expression of pure, unadulterated happiness.

'Promise me you'll never hurt me.'

His face changed like a flipping coin. Heads you win, tails you lose. His face was definitely tails. He knew bits and pieces about my father but not the whole sordid affair. The embarrassment I kept hidden in a small shoe box at the bottom of my wardrobe. The old photos of me and Dad: one of me when I was about five, sitting on Dad's motorbike, grinning ear-to-ear with gaps in my teeth. And a few birthday cards – they abruptly stopped after my fourteenth birthday. And the letter. The one-page scrawl that explained everything and nothing about why he had to leave. He'd always love me, it said; he'd always be my dad, always be there for me if I needed him, and everything that, as it happened, didn't turn out to be true after all.

'I promise I'll never hurt you,' said Ed, flickering sunshine dappling his gorgeous face, and I believed him. I honestly did.

When I left to go travelling, what I hadn't considered or even thought about was that it was me who was leaving. I was running away from our relationship. I was the one who'd hurt Ed. Me. The one who left a perfectly good relationship because they wanted to follow their dreams. I'd told myself over and over again that what I was doing was different. I was trying to save our relationship, make us both happy, but lying in that bed with Bryan, it had hit me. I'd run away. I'd done the one thing I promised myself I'd never do. The nightmare my father had left behind: the broken family, the distraught wife and bewildered child, I knew it wasn't the same, I had managed to save us from that, but I had hurt Ed and made what we had something a bit less.

After the tears had subsided, I walked down the corridor to the bathroom and threw some cold water on my face. I needed to call someone. Someone who'd understand and be able to help and the only person I could think of was Emma. I walked back to my room and dialled her number.

# EMMA

The first thing I heard was tears.

'Kate?'

'Sorry . . .' whimpered Kate down the line.

'Are you OK?'

She obviously wasn't OK, but I needed to know if it was just tears, tears and something bad, or tears and something life-changing.

'I'm . . .' she sniffed. 'It's just. Oh God, Em, I'm so lost.'

'Just calm down,' I said, trying to sound as composed and resolute as I could.

It was early afternoon. Jack was at work and I was having a lie down in front of the telly. I'd been feeling tired all week and luckily I had nothing to do and so I just sat, watched daytime television, read magazines and waited for Jack to come home. It was boring, but honestly, I didn't feel like doing much else. So when the phone rang and I saw it was Kate, I was deliriously happy, until I heard her voice. I was expecting a girlie chin-wag, not a girlie mess.

'Sorry,' said Kate, taking a deep breath and then starting again. 'How are you?'

'I'm fine, but let's talk about you. What's going on?'

'I really fucked up, Em. I don't know what I'm doing here. I just almost slept with some bloke I don't even fancy. I don't know what's happening with Ed and I keep thinking about Jez in Thailand. I'm just . . .' she stopped for a moment. In the background I heard giggling girls. 'I don't know what I'm doing here anymore.'

'You're a bit drunk by the sound of it. I thought you were having a great time. I know it's been hard with Ed, but I thought you were having the time of your life.'

'I was. I am. It's just . . .' She stopped again.

'Just what, Kate?'

She started crying.

'I don't want to be like Dad, Em. I don't want to do what he did to me to Ed. He deserves better.'

'Is that what you think? You think that what you're doing is somehow similar to what he did to you?'

'Isn't it?'

'No. God, no. It's completely different in every possible way. What he did was awful and horrible on every level. He abandoned a family. A wife and his little girl. Not only that but he stopped coming to see you. What you're doing is nothing like that. You're living your dream.'

'But at what expense, Em?'

'At none, hopefully. Listen, you gave Ed the chance to come with you and he said no, so you're doing it on your own. You needed to do this before you could settle down. Before you could be what Ed needed you to be. You're trying to save your relationship, not tear it apart.'

'And that's what I thought too.'

'So what's suddenly changed? Why's it different now?'

'Because I'm not doing what I thought I'd be doing. Coming away was supposed to be this great cathartic experience. I was meant to be seeing the sights, doing things I'd only dreamt about, and I have in bits, but now I feel like I'm just getting drunk and almost having one-night stands with blokes I don't even fancy and I don't know why.'

'If you aren't happy then change,' I said, using the same words she'd thrown at me more than once.

One thing I'd always admired and loved about Kate was her positive attitude. Despite her setbacks in life and awful father, she had always been the first one to step outside of the box. When she first told me about going travelling we were at sixth form. I suppose, like most teenagers, I'd thought about it too, but it wasn't something I simply had to do. If the truth be told, I was too scared. Even the idea of going with Kate scared me to death, but she couldn't wait to get away. I was happier at home with my creature comforts. Kate's motto had always been: if you aren't happy then change, which is why when she left to travel the world alone, I was more proud of her than ever. This Kate on the phone wasn't the same Kate. She sounded scared.

'I don't know if it's that easy though.'

'What do you mean, not easy? You're travelling the world on your own. The only person you have to think about is you. You can do whatever you want, whenever you want. You have complete freedom.'

'But maybe that's the problem.'

'What?'

'I have so much freedom, I don't know what to do with it and I've lost all perspective about what I'm supposed to be doing.'

'Then let me remind you,' I said. 'Hold on a minute.'

I put the phone down and got up. I walked into our bedroom, got down on my knees and pulled out a box from under the bed. It was an old shoebox containing emails Kate had written me over the years. I only printed off the really meaningful ones so I wouldn't forget to read them from time to time. I quickly flicked through the now slightly tatty pieces of paper until I found the one I was looking for.

'Kate?'

'Still here.'

'You've probably forgotten this, but this is an email you wrote to me when I was at uni in Bristol. I was thinking of dropping out because I was homesick and, anyway, let me read it to you.'

Dearest Em,

You'll never guess who called me the other day. Go on, guess. OK fine, your mum. I know, crazy. I don't think she's ever called me, but she said she's worried about you. She said you're thinking of leaving uni and going home. I told her it was nonsense because Emma would never give up acting. I said that to her.

Anyway, if you are thinking about it – even though I know you never would – but if you are, I want to tell you something. People only ever get scared when they're doing something amazing. Fear is just excitement caused by adrenalin, so if you're scared then you're just excited and that means you're doing the right thing. I get scared all the time, about so many things. Being in London without my best friend. The thought of finishing university. The thought of not finishing university. What I'm going to do after and with whom. Life is scary, Emma, but that's good. I think the only thing you should really be scared about is the day you stop being scared.

Call me when you get this and we can have a chat. I was going to call and tell you this, but I always think things seem more powerful when they're written down, don't you? I love you and miss you.

Your best friend forever, Kate.

PS I snogged a bloke last night who looked just like Damon Albarn!

I stopped reading and let it sink in. I heard sobs down the line, but eventually, after a few moments, Kate spoke.

'It's not fair, you know.'

'What?'

'Using my own words against me,' said Kate with a giggle. She sniffed up more tears.

'But they're true, aren't they? You're just scared. Just like me at uni. You're having a bad day. So, you either pack your bags and come home, and I know you aren't going to do that, or you wake up tomorrow and have the trip you always planned.'

'Thank you,' said Kate.

'What for?'

'For being you, and for keeping really old and cheesy emails,' she said and we both laughed.

'You're welcome, and, oh, Kate?'

'What?'

'I'm terrified about getting married to Jack. Absolutely shitting myself.'

'Then he must be the one.'

'Yeah, I guess so.'

may

## JACK

The day Dad died I was told to wait in the car. We'd just got home from shopping. Mum and I went inside the house and that's when we found him slumped on the sofa. I didn't see much. Barely a second elapsed before Mum's hand grabbed me on the shoulder and pulled me away. She shouted at me to wait in the car and so I did. I was too afraid to get out and so I sat there, not knowing if my father was alive or dead. I sat and cried as time seemed to stand still until eventually I heard the distant sound of sirens.

The ambulance screeched into our gravel driveway and two medics got out and ran towards the house. I sat frozen, barely able to look at them, praying over and over again in the hope that God would hear me. I begged, pleaded and made countless deals. I would do anything to keep Dad alive. I'd go to church every weekend. I'd give more to charity. I'd become a priest, anything, just don't let him die. Eventually Mum came out, her expression still and unyielding, the answer to my prayers drawn across her face. Dad was gone and all the deals in the world wouldn't bring him back.

We pulled up outside Mum's house in Guildford and I took a deep lungful of air. I reached across and held Emma's hand and gave it a gentle squeeze.

'Ready?'

'Ready,' replied Emma with an excited smile.

We were going to tell Mum about the baby. Butterflies had been circling my stomach all morning in excitement. This would mean the world to her. She was going to be a grand-mother and there was nothing in the world that would make her happier. I'd been thinking about Dad a lot since we'd found out; this new life had a small bit of his DNA. It almost felt like he was coming back.

We stood waiting on the doorstep before a Mum-shaped object became visible through the small coloured window in the door. She moved a lot slower than she used to, but even-tually the door opened and there she was with a huge smile on her face.

'Emma, Jack, what are you doing here? Quick, come in, come in,' she said, standing to one side and gesturing furi-ously. She always seemed to be in a rush to usher us in, as if it was either freezing cold or she was terrified the neighbours might get a peek inside. She had a furtive glance outside before she closed the door and then relaxed. She gave us a both a quick peck on the cheek before she moved us swiftly into the living room. 'Good timing, the kettle just boiled. I'll make us some tea.'

'Lovely,' said Emma.

'Thanks, Mum,' I said and we sat down on the sofa.

A few minutes later, Mum returned with three cups of tea and a small plate of biscuits.

'What brings you two over on a Saturday? Shouldn't you be at work, Jack?'

'We have some news. Good news.'

'Great news,' said Emma.

Mum's face lit up and I could already see the thoughts starting to explode like fireworks behind her eyes. I was sure she already knew what it might be, but she didn't want to say it. She probably didn't even want to think it, just in case it wasn't. However, just before I said the actual words, I placed my hand onto Emma's belly and then she knew. She let all the fireworks off at once.

'You're pregnant?!'

'We are,' I said and Mum immediately started crying.

'We?' said Emma with a smile. 'The last time I checked, Jack, it was only me who had to carry the baby for nine months.'

The next few minutes were a blur of tears, hugs and squeals, before we settled down and starting drinking our tea.

'I can't tell you how excited I am,' Mum said.

'Us too.'

'But what about the film, dear?' said Mum, suddenly looking at Emma. I looked at her too, trying to see any small fragments of doubt or regret reflected in her eyes. I didn't see any, but Emma was a good actress. I was starting to worry that perhaps she was in denial and would wake up one day full of regret. How could she not feel a small amount of bitterness?

'Done, for now at least. I couldn't exactly play the leading role in a romantic comedy with a huge pregnant belly. It would've been a bit unbelievable. Still, it was one film, there'll be others.'

'Of course there will,' said Mum, with that look of hers. She put her hand on Emma's knee and smiled. It was the same smile she always gave me when I was growing up, warm and comforting.

Mum's house had a certain smell: sweet like soft gooey fudge with floral high notes and an undercurrent of something savoury and old-fashioned. Her house smelt like a proper grandma's house. She even had a bowl of sweets on the coffee table and only the proper grandma ones like humbugs and Liquorice Allsorts.

Emma and Mum were in the kitchen, nattering about all things baby related, while I was in my old room lying on the bed and staring up at the Artex ceiling. I could hear them downstairs laughing and going on and it made me smile. I was so happy. The idea of a little baby crawling, running and playing in this house was a little odd to say the least, it seemed impossible, but it made me feel something I'd never felt before. I felt a connection to something bigger and more meaningful. It was as if before Emma and I were just floating around aimlessly, but with a baby we had roots and we were tied to something. I realised on my bed, in my old room, that what we were tied to was our families. Having a child meant we were extending the family cord and suddenly we weren't the last ones, flailing about without a care in the world, we had added to it. The family line had grown and it gave me incredible pleasure and a humbling feeling of responsibility.

'Ready?' said Emma, poking her head around the door.

We'd done the easy part telling Mum, but now we had to do the not-so-easy bit and tell Emma's parents. Emma's mum and dad have never liked me. I think they saw me as Emma's walk on the wild side, a youthful experiment like smoking marijuana. I was her brief dalliance with the dark side, before she'd jolly well grow up and settle down with someone who had a proper job. Only now we were going to have a baby. I'd impregnated their family tree, with its nod to aristocracy and a wink to centuries of upper-class lineage, and tainted it with my Australian blood, the blood of criminals. I'd gatecrashed their party and used the wrong cutlery, eaten all of the hors d'oeuvre and got pissed on the expensive wine. Now I had to tell them I'd also knocked up their only child.

We said goodbye to a still-beaming Mum and got back in the car. I looked across at Emma and rested a hand on her belly.

'I love you so much, Em.'

'I love you too.'

'Just promise me one thing.'

'What's that?' said Emma, starting the engine.

'That whatever happens at your parents' house, you'll still marry me.'

Emma laughed, leaned across and kissed me.

'Silly Jack,' she said. 'Of course I'll still marry you.'

What she didn't see was the emotional tumour growing inside of me. The worry that her Mum was right and I wasn't good enough for her daughter made me want to run away and hide. My biggest fear though was that it was just a matter of time before Emma realised the same thing.

## EMMA

I was terrified to tell Mum and Dad we were pregnant. Not so much Dad because he wouldn't be that bothered. Nothing seemed to bother him much these days. I think I could become a burlesque dancer and he wouldn't bat an eyelid. He was too busy with his garden, playing golf and pretending he wasn't drunk at ten o'clock in the morning. Mum, on the other hand, seemed to be getting infinitely more resentful, snobbish and pompous every time I saw her. With age comes wisdom, at least it should, but in my parents' small Oxfordshire parish age seemed to bring an ever-increasing degree of snootiness and small-mindedness. The streets near the village green were lined with fierce-faced women in wax jackets ready to run you over in their large 4 × 4's should you pronounce anything with an Estuary accent. My mother, unfortunately, was the head girl in that school of self-proclaimed prefects of little England.

I'd been dealing with her my whole life. From ballet and gymkhanas to my choice of secondary school and university, I was used to going to battle with her. It was as much a part of my childhood as worrying about the size of my breasts and whether Paul Clayton fancied me or not. My fights with her became something of a daily chore, from which neither of us emerged any the better. She wasn't a very motherly mother and even when I got my first period she didn't explain anything or give me a hug. Instead she gave me a box of tampons and told me to read the instructions carefully. I loved her, of course, and her constant pushing and cajoling had given me an inner strength that had come in handy in the acting world. Jack, on the other hand, had been brought up in a soft, nurturing environment. He couldn't deal with the harsh, cold wind that swept constantly around our house and I was worried that today it might blow him away.

'Ready?' I said in the car.

'Not really.'

We were sitting in my Mini Cooper on the large gravel driveway of my parents' home that set it back a good thirty feet from the road. The house, a four-bedroom character cottage with creeping ivy and rustic charm, was worth well over a million now and had been passed down from Dad's family to ours. Around the back was a large garden that led to a small meadow and a crop of trees. It really was idyllic; the perfect place to grow up. If only I'd had the perfect family to go along with it.

'It will be fine. Mum will rant and rave for a bit. Dad will disappear down the garden with a bottle of whisky and then we'll go home.'

'Sounds fun,' said Jack with a gorgeous little smile. I squeezed his hand and we got out.

Mum was in the kitchen when we walked in. I could see Dad in the garden pretending to weed; the small cap of a bottle was poking out of his wax jacket pocket.

'Emma, darling,' said Mum loudly with a huge smile. 'Jack,' she said with a much frostier tone.

'Hello,' said Jack, attempting to kiss her on the cheek, but before he was half-way leaned in, she had turned and switched the kettle on.

'I'll make tea. Jack, please fetch in Emma's father from the garden.'

'Right,' said Jack and snuck off gingerly.

'Do you always have to be so cold with him?' I said as soon as Jack was out of earshot.

'I don't know what you mean, darling,' said Mum, needlessly rearranging some flowers in a vase. Everything in Mum's house was spotless. I think it was part of the reason why Dad spent so much time outside, because he was too afraid of making a mess inside – in more ways than one.

'Yes you do,' I said, sitting down at the breakfast bar. 'We're getting married soon and I'd really like it if you were completely on board with the whole thing.'

'Oh, I'm on board dear. One hundred per cent on board,' she said, but as usual the words were tied together with a little ribbon of superciliousness. 'Anyway, enough about Jack, how's the film going? How's Rhys? As good-looking in real life as on film? Must be tempting. I mentioned the film in the village newsletter. Any chance of an exclusive interview? Perhaps Rhys too? You could bring him for brunch. I could make those little baked eggs.'

'Let's wait for Dad.'

'Sounds very serious, darling.'

'It is,' I said, which made her eyes lock onto mine with a glare.

It was the same glare she gave me the day Paul Clayton emerged from my bedroom looking flushed and with his shirt half undone. Only then I was fifteen and under her roof. Now I was an adult and about to be married and have a baby. Technically still under her roof, but for how much longer we would soon find out.

Ten minutes later Jack walked back in, Dad padding behind him like a naughty Labrador, looking at Mum with big sorry eyes and me with love. Slightly pissed love, of course.

'Emma,' said Dad, staggering towards me and engulfing me in his large but now slightly podgy frame.

'Hello, Dad.'

'Derek, please, straighten yourself up,' said Mum severely, looking at Dad. Dad tucked in his shirt and flicked his hair away from his eyes.

'Must keep the wife happy,' Dad said to Jack with a smile, a mischievous glint in his bloodshot eyes. He always enjoyed winding her up and to a certain extent she accepted it, but eventually she would snap. I spent most of my childhood learning how to distinguish the early-warning signs that she was on the verge. Dad, despite his ever-growing reliance on alcohol to make it through the day, always knew when to stop jabbing and back away to his corner.

'Emma and Jack have news,' Mum announced loudly. She instinctively poured a cup of dark black coffee and handed it to Dad, who, without question, took it and had a sip. 'About the film.'

I looked across at Jack and he appeared nervous. He came across and stood next to me and I put my arm around his waist: a united front.

'I'm pregnant,' I said, the words falling out and into the room. Jack's Mum had greeted the news with a heady mixture of excitement and tears, but it seemed to have the opposite effect on my mother. Her face was an amalgam of confusion, shock and horror. Dad started to break into a smile, but before the corners of his mouth could fully extend, Mum snapped.

'What do you mean pregnant?'

'We're having a baby,' I replied, feeling Jack's grip tighten around my waist.

'But what about the film?'

'I had to pull out. They've replaced me with someone else.'

'I don't believe it,' said Mum, her voice getting higher and louder. Jack's grip tightened again. 'You've spent your whole life working towards that film and you've thrown it away. I don't know what to say.'

'You could say congratulations,' I said.

'Congratulations that you've ruined your life? Oh well done, darling, bravo.'

'Now wait a minute,' said Jack, stepping into the ring.

'This is going to be priceless. And what do you have to say for yourself?'

'You're going to be a grandparent, Helen. That doesn't mean anything to you?'

'If my only daughter hadn't ruined her career in the process. It's just so irresponsible, both of you. So irresponsible.'

'Well we're very happy,' I said, feeling a wave of tears begin to swell up behind my eyes.

'And how happy will you be when the baby is crying at two in the morning? When your nipples are dry and cracked? When your career is down the drain and you haven't got two pennies to rub together? How happy are you going to be then?'

'We'll be fine,' said Jack. 'I'm going to take care of them.'

I looked at Jack and in that moment I couldn't have loved him more. He was honest, sincere and he would do anything for me. I loved him dearly, but I also knew Mum was right and that hurt more than everything else put together.

'You?' Mum looked at Jack like you might look at a piece of dog shit on the pavement. 'And how are you going to take care of them, exactly?'

'Steady on,' said Dad, but Mum shot him down like a Spitfire taking out a much larger and slower German bomber.

'Don't worry about us; we'll be fine,' spat out Jack. His determination and fighting spirit made me so proud. 'Come on, Em, we don't have to listen to this.' Jack grabbed my hand and started leading me towards the front door and freedom. Only it wasn't really freedom because we needed Mum and Dad and she knew it. Jack knew it too, but just couldn't admit it.

As soon as both car doors were closed, I burst into tears. I'd been holding myself together, but outside I let it all go. Jack put his arm around me and held me close.

'Don't let her get to you, love; she isn't worth it.'

Jack held onto me for all of his worth, but the truth was it did matter. I wasn't crying because she'd upset me. I was crying because I wanted the best for our baby. I didn't want them growing up in the gutter, while both parents scrimped and saved trying to give them a decent life. They wouldn't have the chance to go to the best schools, live in a nice house and go on European holidays. I wanted that for them more than anything in the world and I was crying because no matter what Jack said, what Jack wanted, when it came to the crunch, Mum was right. I'd be back there asking for her help. Jack could do poor, he could do just getting by, but I couldn't and, even if I could, I knew our baby shouldn't.

**To: Kate Jones**
**From: Emma Fogle**
**Subject: Re: Oz**

K,

I hope you're OK now after our chat and you're enjoying your-self again. Just remember this is a once-in-a-lifetime trip. You have the rest of your life to worry about men, careers and all the rest of it. This is about you. Enjoy every moment and don't regret a single thing.

So we told my parents about the baby (their grandchild) and what do you think Mother said? Of course she went completely ballistic and said we were irresponsible and that we'd basically ruined our lives. No mention of happiness or congratulations. I wasn't expecting anything else though, to be honest. I feel awful for Jack because he just wants to take care of us financially, but he can't. I wish he could so we could give Mother the two fingers, but unfortunately we need their money. God, I really wish we didn't. Nothing would make me happier than to be independent of them.

I'm so tired at the moment. I haven't gained much weight because I've had some fairly heavy morning sickness, but I'm doing fine. I just wish I wasn't so tired all the time. I really need to find some work to help financially, but that involves getting off the sofa. Sorry, I'm having a moan day and you're not here physically, so all I have is email. I also need to start organising the wedding, but again, too tired and Jack is always at work, taking on more shifts to help save some money, and I don't want to ask Mother unless I really have to.

Anyway, enough bitching. I will do something productive today. I promise. Miss you BFF.

Love Em X

## KATE

'It's mental though, innit?' said Mental Mike.

'To be fair though, Mike, you think everything's mental,' I said. Hence the nickname.

'It is though, innit.'

'Possibly,' I said.

I was sitting with Mental Mike, twenty-one and from Essex, Mhairi and Jamie from Edinburgh, both mid-twenties, and Tom and Tash from Denmark, who were in their early thirties. We were on a small Fijian island which was about as near to paradise as I could imagine. It was night time and we were sitting at a table overlooking the beautiful beach. A million stars littered the sky, barely any space between them, and I could hear the gentle sound of music from the bar and the occasional dog barking from the nearby bures where the hostel workers lived.

The island was small enough that you could walk around it in a couple of hours, which I did with Mhairi and Jamie on my second day. The hostel was right on the beach and consisted of a dormitory with about fifteen simple beds, a common eating area, where they served breakfast, lunch and dinner, and a bure where we showered. It was back-to-basics living and I loved it. We only had power for certain hours and the days revolved around meal times and getting together during the evening for a drink. There were kayaks to rent and they offered tours of other islands, but most days were spent relaxing, playing cards and talking. A day on the island felt like a week in the real world.

'It depends what you mean by mental,' said Tom in his steady Danish English. I'd only been on the island for four days and I was in love with Tom and Tash. They were so gorgeous: tall, athletic, with model looks and the nicest personalities of anyone I'd ever met. Most British backpackers I met seemed to be travelling to get pissed and have a laugh, but Tom and Tash were different. They were, in many respects, the Ed and me I wished Ed and me were. Interesting, cultural, relaxed and effortlessly in love. Back in Denmark Tom was a graphic designer and Tash played violin in an orchestra. They were taking one last year off before they settled down, got married and had kids.

'You know, crazy, innit,' continued Mental Mike, taking a sip of his Fiji Bitter. 'You know, people just get up, go to work for eight, nine hours a day, come home, watch TV, go to the pub, eat a kebab, go to bed and then do it all again the next day. Mental.'

'That does sound a bit mental,' said Tom with a smile. Tash had her hand on his leg and was gently rubbing it backwards and forwards. 'But life doesn't have to be that way. It doesn't have to be this way either. We can't travel all the time and we can't work all the time either.'

'Balance,' said Tash, finishing his sentence for him. 'Life is all about balance.'

I'd seen Tash down on the beach first thing in the morning doing her yoga. Her beautiful, graceful body, arching slowly and purposefully into a new position, where she'd stay before flowing effortlessly into another. It was one of the most beautiful things I'd ever seen. I'd already asked her if she could teach me a few moves, hoping to keep a piece of her for the rest of my trip and maybe my life. I wanted to be more like her.

'She's right,' said Mhairi in her lovely Scottish accent. 'I used to work long hours, was always stressed out, but then I stopped because I realised I couldn't keep doing it. I'm only twenty-five for God's sake, not forty-five.'

'And what did you do?' I said.

I was in awe of Mhairi too. She seemed a lot like me. Down-to-earth and searching for that impossible dream of being happy, but she was actually making it happen. She also had her Ed by her side. Jamie, a fellow Scot, who was really funny, had gorgeous eyes and was always quick with the compliments. Mhairi and Jamie had a bit of the hippie in them, but in the best possible way.

'I was working in sales, but I hated it and so I started a small business. It isn't much. I make jewellery and knitwear, scarves and the like. It's doing all right. My sister's taking care of it while we're away.'

'That's fantastic,' I said, taking a drag on my cigarette.

'Yeah it is. Just working for me. Being who I want to be, instead of some office drone, always being told what to do all day. I make less money but I'm happy.'

'Yeah, that's exactly it, innit,' said Mental Mike. 'It's mental people don't all think like that. Who gives a shit about money, yeah? It's happiness what counts. It's doing what you want, when you want. Sticking two fingers up to the man, yeah.' Mike gave two fingers to some imagined man in the sky to prove his point.

'And what about you, Kate?' said Jamie, suddenly looking across at me. He was peeling the label off his beer bottle. 'What did you do in the real world?'

I giggled for no reason and then lit up a cigarette.

'Public relations. I hated it. Well, I didn't at first, but like you said, Mhairi, I became something I wasn't. I knew if I didn't stop, get away while the going was good, I'd end up at forty, depressed, and still with no idea what I wanted to do with my life.'

'Good for you' said Jamie, lighting up his own cigarette. 'Once I've got a few more years in the kitchen, I'm going to open my own little café in Edinburgh. Organic, fresh, cool little bohemian place, coffee in the morning, lunches and so on.'

'Sounds magical,' I said, falling in love with his dream as much as he was.

'Mhairi can sell her stuff, make a little hippie commune in Scotland where we can eat well, live well and be happy.'

'Can I come too?' I said, only half-joking.

'You'd be more than welcome,' said Mhairi with a smile, reaching across and putting her hand on mine and then giving it a squeeze.

'But don't you think though, like, people just need to chill the fuck out, yeah, and everything will be all right?' said Mental Mike, seemingly having a conversation with himself. We all agreed that, yeah, people did need to chill the fuck out, before Mike went to get us all another drink.

I looked around the table while he was gone. Mhairi and Jamie and Tom and Tash, two beautiful, wonderful couples, but unlike in Thailand and Australia when I'd wished Ed was with me, I didn't anymore. I knew this was about me as an individual. I needed to find my path and then worry about Ed and me. Talking to Emma when I had my meltdown in Melbourne made me realise I needed to embrace my trip. I needed to stop making everything about Ed and start making everything about me. I was what I needed to work on and when I'd figured that out, maybe, just maybe, I could sort out my feelings for Ed too.

'How did you know what you wanted to do?' I said to Mhairi. 'After you decided to quit the rat race, how did you decide to start your own business?'

'I don't know really. I always liked making things, but I'd

never considered it could be my job, you know. I started small, made a few things and before I knew it, people couldn't get enough. It was then I decided to quit my job and make a go of it. I suppose it's about having the guts to follow your dreams. Know what you want and go after it.'

'Right,' I said.

'And having a boyfriend who'll give you that gentle push,' said Jamie with a smile, jabbing Mhairi playfully in the side.

'And that too,' said Mhairi, smiling. 'So what about you? What do you want to be when you grow up?' she said, looking at me expectantly.

'Just something . . . different,' I replied.

It was the beginning of the second week and Mhairi, Tash and I were heading across the island to Sunset Beach. We'd heard it was incredible and so we'd decided to make a day of it. The boys were heading back to the mainland to help pick up supplies and probably have a few beers and some real food in the process. My time on the island had been idyllic to say the least, but after nearly ten days of the same generally meatless food, I was craving a big, juicy burger.

It was another perfect day as we ambled around the rocks that led to the secluded little bay. We took our towels, laid them out and sat down. We were completely and wonderfully alone. In front of me was mile after mile of clear blue ocean, which eventually met and merged into a cloudless cerulean sky. All I could hear was the gentle lapping of waves on the beach and that was it. And there, looking out at the world and feeling smaller than I ever had, I finally thought of an answer to Mhairi's question.

I did want something else, something meaningful, and after talking with Mhairi about it the other night, it came to me. During my late teens and even at university, I'd thought about teaching. It had value and meaning and it would be a challenge. I'd decided against it because I was too afraid. Afraid the pupils would eat me alive, afraid that in front of thirty eager little teenagers, I would freeze and be a failure. I wasn't afraid anymore though. I had travelled the world and if I could do that, I could do anything. I wanted Mhairi's happiness, her confidence and her outlook on life. I just needed the guts to follow my dreams.

'Teaching,' I blurted out, breaking the silence.

'Sorry?' said Mhairi.

'The other night you asked me what I wanted to be when I grow up. I want to be a teacher. An English teacher, actually, at sixth form.'

It felt good to say it out loud for the first time. It made it seem real. I chose sixth form because it was such an important time in my own life. Those two years helped define and shape so much of the rest of my life and I wanted to go back and help shape more lives. I wanted to teach, but I also wanted to give back and share the lessons I had learnt from losing my father, getting hit by the car, falling into the wrong career and travelling. I felt like I could be a positive influence on teenagers' lives.

Mhairi smiled at me.

'That's brilliant. I think you'll be an amazing teacher.'

'I hope so,' I said.

'You don't need to hope,' said Tash. 'You will be.'

And with those three words I looked out towards the horizon at the hundreds of miles of ocean and felt the warm breeze on my face. I smiled because at last I knew what I was going to do. It would mean going back to university, but I was ready for the challenge. I had a couple of months left of travelling and I was going to enjoy them. No more worrying about Ed and thinking about things I couldn't control. I was done being afraid.

To: Emma Fogle
From: Kate Jones
Subject: Bula!

Em,

Just a quick email as I don't have much time. I'm back in Nadi, which is the main town on mainland Fiji. I'm about to head off to the airport to get my flight to Peru (via New Zealand). I just had the most amazing two weeks of my life. I was on a desert island with the best people. It really gave me time to think and reflect and I'm so happy (again). They having something here called Fiji time. What's amazing is that when you arrive Fiji time just seems like this excuse for being lazy and getting nothing done, but the longer you're here, you realise it's actually a way of life. It's more than just an expression, it's a philosophy on how to live and I must say I rather like it. Hopefully I can bring a bit of Fiji time with me back to London!

Thank you so much for the talk you gave me in Melbourne. You were totally right. I was wallowing and not being myself, but thanks to you and Fiji, I'm back! I can't wait to get back to see you again. You're probably going to be massive! For the first time in our lives you might be bigger than me! I can't wait to see that. I've also made a decision about my career, but we can talk about that when I get back. I hope everything is going well and you aren't so tired still. I can't wait to see you as a yummy mummy, you're going to be A-mazing! South America awaits . . .

Love K x

# ED

Dad was a drinker. He wasn't an alcoholic, but he definitely liked a drop of the hard stuff, or as he called it, the good stuff. He was an old-fashioned, hard-as-nails bloke. He had the kind of body, even at sixty, where you could see the layers of hard muscle that sat on him like a medal of honour. He'd never done anything but manual work his whole life and it showed. When I was a young boy he worked on building sites and then when I was a bit older for the council, fixing roads. His hands were dry and cracked and his body had scars from work accidents and drunken late-night fights.

Dad grew up in a different era. Most Saturdays I'd be sent to the pub at the end of our street to get him home for tea. I used to love getting a fleeting look at his world, his life outside the house that didn't involve me. The pub was filled with cigarette smoke and the vinegary smell of alcohol on a deep red carpet. Men in trousers and shirts played darts and pool, talking loudly about things I didn't understand. Men I saw during the week with families, off early to work or coming home late with barely a word to say, in that pub would lift me up and sit me on the bar, shout loudly, sing songs and tell jokes. Then there was my dad. His beery breath and wet kisses on my eight-year-old skin were forever locked in my mind.

Today was different though. When I walked in, Dad was sitting alone in the corner like a relic from a different age trying to go unnoticed. He was slumped over a pint of something flat and brown, while around him young kids in baseball caps, tracksuit bottoms and trainers talked loudly over pints of fizzy lager. As soon as he saw me his face lit up. I smiled back and walked over. Dad had always been a handsome man, but he was starting to look his age. His salt-and-pepper hair was now just salt and his strong face was starting to wane and look tired. The lines that had once given him character now made him look haggard.

'All right, son.'

'Hi, Dad, another?'

Dad looked down at his pint, as if he was actually trying to decide. We both knew the answer. 'I'll get a menu as well,' I said and walked over to the bar.

I'd come to tell Dad about my recent unemployment, but, standing at the bar and looking over at him, I wasn't sure I could. He'd always been so proud of me. Every time I went back home to see him and Mum, he'd take me out and parade me around like a trophy. 'This is my son, works in the City he does, earns a fortune, don't you son?' The phrase preceded me into every room.

'Here you go,' I said, sitting down and pushing a menu across the table towards him.

'I never eat here. Too expensive. Not worth the money. Decent chippy over the road. Half the price.'

'Just get something, my treat,' I said and he smiled a proud fatherly smile.

'I'll get it next time.'

'OK, Dad, next time.'

He never did, of course, but I didn't mind. I liked the fact I could take care of my old man. My brother, Joe, was off up the country, the last I heard still unemployed and living with some girl, and my sister, Becky, was in Southampton with a couple of kids and a useless husband. I was the successful one, the one who'd really made something of himself and I didn't want to disappoint him.

'What's new?'

'Not much, working too hard,' I lied.

'That's my boy,' said Dad with a sparkle in his eyes.

Dad had always worked hard, up at the crack of dawn and out the door before the bird farts, he always said. He'd been working since he was fourteen and he still worked now. Only now, at sixty, his body couldn't keep up and so he was a site manager. The fact was, he couldn't do the graft work anymore and so, like a once-great racehorse, he was put out to pasture. He'd retire in a few years, get his pension and that would be it. He didn't have much to look forward to. 'Earn it while you can, son, and then retire. Buy a place in Spain; get out of this shit-hole.' He looked around the pub where he'd spent probably as much time as anywhere else in his life. 'How's Kate? Still off gallivanting around the globe like the Queen of Sheba?'

'She's in Fiji at the moment.' Or so said the brief text I'd received the day before.

'Fiji, eh, and where's that again?'

'South Pacific.'

'Cannibalism down there. Gotta be careful. You should tell her. They'll eat her soon as look at her.'

'I'll let her know, Dad. Listen, there's something I need to tell you,' I said as the barmaid brought over our food. I waited for her to leave before I continued. 'It's Kate, it's me. We're sort of on a break.'

Dad looked at me like I'd just asked him to recite the times tables.

'What does that mean?'

'It means we're taking a break from each other while she's away.'

He still looked mystified.

'You've broken up?'

'No, not broken up, taking a break.'

'What's the difference?'

'Well, we haven't broken up exactly, but we're free to see other people while she's away, I suppose.' Dad looked even more confused. 'We're still a couple, but we just need a break to figure a few things out.'

'What sort of things?'

'It's complicated.'

'You kids today, honestly, you always think everything's so complicated. What's so complicated about love, son, let me ask you that? You either love each other or you don't. You're either together or you're not.'

Dad was of the generation that got married for life, for better or worse and they stuck at it come hell or high water. Through thick and thin, my parents had been married for forty years. They'd had rough times, like all couples, but the idea of them getting divorced or even taking a break never came into the equation. They were old-fashioned in so many ways, and we often scoff at that these days, but they had something right. They knew how to stay in love. Today we run around having affairs and one-night stands at the drop of a hat, but not my mum and dad. It just wasn't part of their vocabulary.

'Then I guess we're not.'

'And why? What happened?'

'I cheated on her with someone from work,' I said very matter-of-factly. Dad's face dropped. He looked disappointed. Actually it was worse than that, he looked heartbroken. 'And she kissed someone in Thailand.'

'Jesus.'

'And now we're on a break,' I said, suddenly getting a bit choked up. I didn't cry. I couldn't. I held it all in. The way I always had with Dad. 'But I'm sure we'll figure things out when she gets back.'

'And what if you don't?'

'I guess we'll deal with that if it happens.'

'Let's hope, eh,' said Dad before he suddenly got up. 'I need a fag. Back in a minute.'

I watched him through the glass of the door for a moment. My father, big, strong and stuck in his ways. As soon as I was eighteen, I couldn't wait to leave and head off to university. I thought mixing with people from middle-class backgrounds and expensive boarding schools would somehow rub off on me and for a while it did. Working in the City, excelling among a group of Oxbridge recruits and out-performing all of them had given me false hope. If there was one thing I'd learnt from the Georgie incident, it was that I'd never be one of them and, also, I didn't want to be. I would always be a working-class lad from Slough and more like my dad than I'd ever previously cared to admit.

While he was outside, puffing hard on his cigarette, I decided that I had to tell him about my job. He deserved to know the truth and it was time I stopped second-guessing his every response.

Dad came wandering back in and sat down. He began eating again without another word. I took a sip of my pint.

'And there's something else,' I said slowly before I put a mouthful of steak and kidney pie into my mouth.

'What?'

I slowly finished my mouthful of pie before I told him. 'I lost my job.'

I waited for his reaction. I was expecting fireworks. I was expecting incredulous disbelief. What I wasn't expecting was straightforward sympathy and optimism.

'I'm sorry, son, but these things happen. You'll find something else,' he said with a comforting smile. 'With your brains, you'll be all right.'

This from the man who walked me from pub table to pub table explaining to all and sundry what I did for a living and that I earned so much I paid for them to have a holiday abroad. 'Ten whole days in Spain. We didn't pay for a thing.' I didn't understand. I had built up the conversation in my head so much, put so much thought into it and expected a certain reaction. I was sort of pissed off.

'That's all you have to say?'

'What do you mean?'

'I got fired, Dad. I'm unemployed.'

'You'll bounce back.'

'But what if I don't? What if I fuck up and end up . . .' I stopped myself, but Dad knew what I meant. I could tell from the look on his face.

'Don't worry, son, you won't end up like me.'

'I didn't mean that.'

'It's all right. I get it.'

'Dad, honestly, I wasn't talking about you.'

I looked at him and a wave of guilt rushed through me. He didn't say it — he didn't have to — he looked defeated. He looked old and full of regret.

'You don't think I wished things had been different when you were growing up? That I'd earned more money? You don't think I wanted to give you kids everything?'

I could see the hurt in his eyes.

'Then why didn't you try harder?'

'There isn't a day goes by I don't look back and wish I'd done more. You were right, son, the day we had that fight. Right before you left for university. I didn't do enough for you, for your mum, for me. I failed at being a father.'

'You didn't fail, Dad. You did so much for us. We didn't have much money, but there wasn't anything you wouldn't do for us.'

'It wasn't enough though, was it? Be truthful, son, you resented me. You left for university and we didn't see you for six months. Your mum was beside herself. I know I let you down but don't think for one moment that you're going to end up like me. You're nothing like me. You're clever, smart. No matter what happens, you'll never be like me.'

'That's where you're wrong, Dad,' I said, looking across at him. 'And the more I think about it, the more I realise just how like you I am. I may have gone to university and worked in the City, but look at us, sitting here in your old pub, having a pint. I'm more comfortable here than I am in some poncy bar in London. I used to think I wanted all that because I thought it would make me happy, but I was wrong. Yeah, we could have used more money growing up, but we weren't unhappy were we? We spent time together and, looking back, we had loads of good times.'

'Yeah, we did,' said Dad with a wistful smile.

'I'm sorry if I made you feel like you weren't good enough.'

'Thanks, son. You have no idea what it means to hear you say that.'

Dad and I drank all afternoon before we went home and saw Mum. We actually had fun. We talked about this and that, laughed, smoked and when it was eventually time to head back to London, he gave me a hug, a proper father and son hug, and then a beery kiss on my cheek.

'Love you, son,' he said.

'Love you too, Dad,' I said for the first time in a very long time.

## JACK

It had been one of those days. It was a Friday and we were busy all day with tourists from every corner of the globe. From the moment I'd opened the door at seven and turned off the alarm, nothing had gone right. Since our night together, Therese had left and gone travelling. I'd hired two new staff members, both unreliable and completely useless. Another girl had called in sick and Tom, my assistant manager, was in Spain for the week. For a whole twelve-hour shift, it was just me and two other staff members. I knew then it was going to be hell.

Of course with staff members falling faster than soldiers at the Somme, we had one of our busiest days in history. Hour after hour we fought them off, serving coffee and pastries, but they kept coming and coming. Wave after wave of Americans demanding their caffeine fix, interspersed with undercurrents of Japanese and European tourists looking and pointing at items on the menu. I didn't even have time for lunch and so as the afternoon wore on, I became tired and irate. At just after four o'clock, when it felt like the day was never going to end, my phone buzzed frantically in my pocket. I looked down expecting Emma, but it was an unknown number.

'I'm taking fifteen,' I said to Laura, who gave me a painful smile in return.

She'd only been working with us for a few weeks and I wouldn't normally have left her alone, but what choice did I have?

'Hello?' I said, while walking out back, grabbing a pre-made sandwich on the way.

'Mr Chapman?' a female voice said. I didn't recognise her and so assumed it was one of those annoying cold-calling companies trying to sell me something I didn't need.

'Yes?'

'Hi, my name's Abby Fischer and I'm with the Gladstone Company,' she said. She sounded young, maybe early twenties. She had a sweet voice, quite posh and slightly uncertain. I was searching for the name in my head. The Gladstone Company. It sounded familiar, but I couldn't place it.

'The Gladstone Company?'

'I'm so sorry. Perhaps you're more familiar with The Morris Gladstone Literary Agency? You sent us the first chapters of your novel, *One Day Soon*?'

As soon as I heard the words 'literary agency' I froze. My heart skipped and jumped a few beats like a scratched record before it settled down and I regained some sort of rhythm.

'Oh, right, yes, sorry.'

'No problem. I'm Morris Gladstone's assistant. He really loved your book and he'd like to set up an appointment for you to come in. Can you make Monday at four?'

'Yes, yes, of course, I'll be there. Monday at four.'

'We have your email. I'll send over the details.'

'Thank you so much, I can't wait.'

'Have a great weekend.'

'Yes, yes, you too,' I said and then she was gone.

I was alone in the small office, completely shocked, bewildered and smiling ridiculously. I'd waited so many years for that call. I tried to keep my head together and not get carried away, but it was impossible. It didn't mean I was suddenly going to be an international bestselling author and that all of my problems and financial worries were going to disappear, but it was a start. It was something. I was about to call Emma with the good news when Laura poked her head around the corner looking worried and said she needed me, 'like, right away'.

I left work at seven o'clock and popped into the off-licence on the way home. I grabbed a few beers and a couple of non-alcoholic ones for Emma to celebrate, and then stopped in the Thai restaurant around the corner and got a takeaway. I couldn't wait to see Emma and tell her the good news. I couldn't help but daydream about the life we were going to have. A beautiful wife, a baby and the job of my dreams. I couldn't have been any happier. Everything was finally falling into place.

I opened the front door and walked in. Usually I'd see Emma watching television in the lounge, or in the kitchen cooking, but I didn't. Our flat wasn't huge and so it meant she would either be in the bathroom or the bedroom.

'Honey, I'm home,' I said in a syrupy American accent. 'I have the best news.'

I walked into the bedroom and that was when I saw her. Emma was in bed, sitting up and looking at me in horror. She'd been crying, her face was puffy and red; I'd never seen her looking like that before. My heart sank when I looked down at the bed. Moving out from her body was a red stain like wine, which had soaked the sheets and duvet. It stretched out towards the bottom of the bed like river tributaries. As soon as I saw it, I dropped the bags I was carrying.

'Fuck.'

'I'm so sorry,' muttered Emma, bursting into tears.

The next fifteen minutes were a blur. I called for an ambulance and when they asked what the emergency was I didn't know what to say.

'It's my wife, the baby,' was all I could muster. 'Please come quickly.'

I couldn't say anymore and I didn't know what to say because I knew what had happened. It was obvious. Emma knew what had happened too; her face said everything. I lay on the bed next to her and held her until the ambulance came, the sound of the sirens reminding me of the day Dad died. Only it wasn't my father this time, but my unborn baby that had leaked out and onto our bed.

Emma was asleep in the cold white bed and I was sitting on the chair next to her. She looked pale and so innocent; I watched the gentle rhythm of her breathing as her chest went slowly up and then down. It was past midnight and the nurse said I should leave and come back in the morning. Emma was tired and needed her sleep and I couldn't do anything, but I couldn't leave her. If she woke up, I wanted mine to be the first face she saw. If she needed a glass of water, I wanted to get it for her. We'd lost our baby only a few hours before and Emma, asleep or not, needed me in the same way I needed her.

I knew the next few weeks and months were going to be a nightmare. We were getting married soon and it was supposed to be the happiest day of our lives, and maybe it still would be, but at that moment I was numb. It was the strangest feeling I'd ever had. After Emma had fallen asleep, I'd finally let myself grieve for our lost child. I didn't want to cry in front of her, she'd cried enough and needed me to be strong, but once her eyes were closed and the gentle hum of snoring escaped her lips, I let go.

It wasn't as though I knew our baby yet or properly loved them, but I knew the idea of them and loved them for what they were going to be. I remembered back to the ultrasound and hearing the soft thump of their heartbeat and something inside of me cracked. I felt some primeval instinct that overtook everything else, and I wanted to protect the baby and protect Emma. There was nothing I could have done about it, I knew that, but a part of me still felt like I'd failed them.

The morning came early with the shrill rattling of morning rounds, mumbling voices and the smell of institutional food being cooked.

'Morning, love,' I said to Emma, leaning across and kissing her on the forehead.

She gave me a smile, but it was sad and numb. Eventually, the doctor came around and said she was fine to go home. Her body was healed, but her mind and her heart would take a lot longer.

When we got home, I had her sit on the sofa with a cup of tea while I made up the bed. I threw the old sheets and duvet away. I didn't want the reminder of our lost child with us anymore and so I put on new bedding. Emma went back to bed for a few hours while I sat in the lounge and called Mum.

'I was just thinking about you,' said Mum when she answered. I didn't say anything and instead broke into tears. I thought I was going to be strong. I thought I could handle it and that I'd cried enough already, but just hearing Mum's voice, I broke down again. 'Jack, what is it?'

'It's the baby, Mum; we lost the baby.'

Mum didn't cry, miss a beat or dally in her own loss for a moment. There was always something so hardened about people of her generation. Life didn't seem as precious to them as it did to us.

'Oh, Jack, I'm so sorry, but miscarriages happen for a reason. Trust me, it will be OK. Just be there for Emma, take care of her and if you need me, for anything, call me and I'll be there in a flash.'

'Thanks, Mum. Love you.'

'Love you too, Jack. You're a strong boy. Be strong for Emma, she's going to need you.'

I lay down next to Emma and we slept for a few hours. We had lunch in relative silence and then watched TV, but something had changed that we'd never get back. Maybe in time we would try for a baby again, but having lost something so important and so wonderful, it truly felt like a piece of us was lost forever. During dinner, as Emma nibbled disinterestedly on some cheese on toast, I told her my news.

'I got a call from a literary agent yesterday. I have a meeting with them on Monday.'

'Oh, Jack that's wonderful,' said Emma, her smile disintegrating quickly into floods and floods of tears.

june

## KATE

I met Rebecca at university. Rebecca was the sort of person who'd done everything. She was the same age as me, but while at eighteen I'd done nothing spectacular with my life, she'd seen the Great Wall of China, the Great Barrier Reef, gone on an African safari, skied in Switzerland and sailed across the Channel. There was almost nothing she hadn't done. Her bucket list must have been awfully short. However, of all the conversations we had, I best remember the one about Machu Picchu. It was the one place she said I simply had to go and ever since it had sat proudly at the top of my must-do list.

I arrived in Cusco and was getting ready for the four-day hike I'd been dreaming about for years. I'd even planned it so the day I finally saw the ruins of Machu Picchu was my birthday. Up until last November, I'd always imagined I would turn thirty in a pub somewhere in London, surrounded by close friends, getting drunk on expensive cocktails and making a fool of myself in a club until the wee hours of the morning. I hadn't considered in my wildest dreams that I'd turn thirty at an ancient Inca ruin in Peru.

The journey to Machu Picchu began in a pub, where I was due to meet the rest of my group. There were ten of us so far. Two Canadians with the mandatory flags all over their outfits, an American also called Kate, a beautiful Swede called Irma, three Irish sisters, two young boys from Leeds who looked just out of school and made me feel very old, and then there was me.

'Just waiting on one more,' said our tour guide, a Frenchman named Claude. We had a local guide, but he didn't speak much English and so the tour company also gave us Claude. Claude was thirty-five and one of those travellers who'd seemingly started travelling at the age of ten and never stopped. He had a tired, weathered look about him, as though he hadn't slept in years. His skin was like leather and he had the look of Indiana Jones at the end of a film. I didn't know if that was a good indication of what was to come or not.

We sat around waiting for the last member of our group to arrive. Eventually, the door of the pub opened and someone walked in wearing a multicoloured poncho. They looked as if they'd been lost in South America for the last six months. Either that or they'd just got off the plane and bought their whole outfit at the airport gift shop. But as they got nearer to our table, there was something about the walk, the way they moved and their hair; I had a moment of déjà vu. I knew them. I was certain of it. The long hair and traditional knitted hat covered most of their face, but when he took it off and flicked the hair away from his eyes, my heart burst out of my chest in excitement.

'Jez!' I screamed.

'Kate, fucking hell!' said Jez, walking towards me with a huge grin and then wrapping his arms around me. 'What are the chances?'

What were the chances? A hundred to one? A thousand to one? I was utterly blown away. I hadn't seen Jez in months, not since our awkward goodbye at the bus station in Thailand. It felt strange, almost surreal, that we were together again. I could only equate him with my time in Thailand, but a lot of weeks and miles had been notched up since then. I'd changed and I was sure he had too. That's the thing about travelling, a few months on the road was more like a few years back in the real world. It felt like a lifetime ago that I'd stepped off the plane into the oppressive heat of Bangkok and been rescued by the dashing young man with the smooth toffee skin and brilliant blue eyes.

We spent an hour with the rest of our group before Claude told us to get an early night because we'd be leaving at an ungodly hour in the morning. The rest of our group went back to their hostels, while Jez and I stayed for a drink. We had a lot to catch up on.

'Is it really you?' I said, giving him a playful pinch on the arm.

'I still can't believe it. I remember you telling me you were coming here but I had no idea when.'

'And what are you doing here so soon? I thought you'd still be in Australia or New Zealand bonking lots of young girls.'

'Do people bonk nowadays?' said Jez, making me fall into hysterics. 'I think that was in the eighties, maybe the nineties, but people haven't been bonking for a while. Shagging, doing the beast with two backs and a funny-looking middle, but not bonking . . .'

'OK, I get it.'

'It's really good to see you again,' said Jez and he smiled his electric smile.

I felt the tension that still lingered between us, like honey clinging to the lip of a jar, stretched out, unable to let go. I'd thought about him a lot since I left Thailand and wondered whether I'd made the right decision. Jez and I had clicked on so many levels. Was it destiny we had met again?

'You too,' I said. 'But we'd better get off to bed. Early start and all that.'

'Righto, Miss Jones. Don't want to do anything reckless, do we?' said Jez and I blushed wildly.

I was already worried about a repeat performance with Jez. Not that I needed to feel guilty this time, because Ed and I were on a break. I could do what I liked and if there hadn't been feelings involved, if it had been just a laissez-faire bonk or whatever the kids called it, I probably would've let myself. The thing was though, I'd sort of promised myself that the last part of my trip was going to be about me. No more worrying about men. No agonising about Ed, my father or Jez.

'Where are you staying?' I said, trying to keep the conversation as mundane as possible.

'Little place around the corner. The Flying Dog?'

'The Flying Dog, seriously?'

'What?'

'That's where I'm staying,' I said and my heart, already squeezed tightly in my chest, began to feel like it was being suctioned through my body and into my lower intestines.

'What a coincidence,' said Jez.

'Indeed.'

'Fancy a nightcap back at the hostel?' Jez stood up.

'Maybe a small one,' I said, trying to keep my emotions in check.

Outside it was cold and I was desperate to get back to our hostel.

'Just one thing.'

'And what's that,' I said, turning to face him; the yellow lights of the city gave his face an ethereal glow.

'How are things with you and Ed?'

'It's . . .' I said and then paused, trying to find the right adjective. 'Complicated.'

'That's all I needed to know.'

'And why's that?'

We were just starting to stroll along the cobbled street, the far-away noise of celebrations filtering into my ears, when he reached down and held my hand softly in his. I could have pulled it away but I didn't. I liked how it felt.

My alarm clock woke me up with a jolt. It was the first time in months I had to actually get up. Most mornings came when they came, but it was time to start the trek to Machu Picchu. I looked across at the alarm clock and the faint numbers barely visible through my slightly blurry morning vision. Was it really five-thirty a.m.? It was almost impossible to imagine it was the same time I used to wake up every weekday in London. Up at five-thirty, shower, spend half an hour straightening hair and applying make-up, have breakfast, drink a large black coffee before I left the house at seven to be at work before eight. Outside it was pitch black and my bed was warm. The nights in Cusco were cold due to the altitude and so I had sheets and blankets galore. Although the real reason I was so warm was the body next to me.

'Morning, gorgeous,' said Jez, reaching across an arm and pulling me close to him. 'What time is it?'

'Do you really want to know?'

'Probably not. It's still dark so I'll just go with too bloody early.'

'That's close enough. I'd better take a shower,' I said and was about to get up when Jez pulled me over and on top of him. Through the darkness of the room he looked me in the eyes and then kissed me.

'You know this time I'm not going to let you go so easily.'

'We'll see. Four days hiking through the mountains and you might be bored of me,' I said with a self-conscious little smile.

'I don't think I could ever get bored of you, Kate.'

'I give you two days,' I said wriggling free and skipping off towards the shower room.

When I thought about Jez in the real world I knew it couldn't work. He was twenty-two and I was almost thirty. It might not matter in Thailand and Peru, but it would when we got home. I'd be the crusty old girlfriend with the toy-boy boyfriend. He probably didn't think it mattered but it did. Then, of course, there was Ed. I loved Ed, but I'd cheated on him and he'd cheated on me. Would we be able to get over that? As I stood in the shower, I thought about Jez and I smiled. He made me smile, and that was something that had been missing from my relationship with Ed for some time.

Jez and I met up with the rest of our group at seven o'clock for the beginning of our four-day trek. It was still dark when we set off on the bus for Habra Malaga, where we'd pick up the bikes for the first section of the trek. All I had for breakfast was a dark cup of coffee, a bread roll and an old Mars bar I had in my backpack.

It was still freezing and so we had to wear lots of layers and Jez was in his funny hat and poncho. I looked at him and thought of Ed. Ed would never be seen dead in an outfit like that. We were once invited to a fancy dress party for Halloween and I went as a slightly sluttier version of Little Red Riding Hood; Ed was supposed to be the Big Bad Wolf, but he couldn't do it. I even went to the trouble of hiring the outfit and he said it made him look like a complete knob. I explained it was Halloween and that everyone would look like a knob, but he wouldn't go through with it. Jez was wearing a multi-coloured Peruvian chullo hat and a poncho that had more colours than a paint fight at a playschool along with long hair, two weeks' worth of facial hair and baggy purple hippy trousers. Ed would discount him as a hippy traveller layabout, a waste of space. But I didn't think that at all. Jez was kind, warm, funny and intelligent and he made me happy. At that moment, he was exactly what I needed in my life. We still hadn't had sex though and I wasn't sure I could. We went to bed together the night before and kissed, but that was it. He'd asked, but I said I couldn't. It still seemed wrong somehow. I also knew how much he liked me and I didn't want to muddy the waters more than they already were. Keep things simple, I told myself over and over again as we lay in bed fighting the sexual urges that seemed almost too strong to fend off.

I decided that morning, during the four-hour bus ride, that I wanted to give him a chance. I had to see if Jez could be more than he already was. I guess what I needed to know was if he was worth giving up Ed for. If he could be my everything.

## ED

I couldn't face the prospect of job hunting and worrying about how I was going to pay the mortgage once my savings ran out. Also, after my chat with Dad, I'd been thinking about what I really wanted to do with the rest of my life. So, on a bright Tuesday I went into central London. While the rest of the world was working, putting meaningless numbers in Excel boxes and plotting charts, I was idling about on Oxford Street, skulking about by the Thames at Embankment, going for a stroll past Buckingham Palace and then stopping for lunch at a pub in Covent Garden.

I sat at a table by myself and watched the world go by. Men in suits came and sat, talking loudly about their days, while tourists popped in for a quick pint before continuing on their way. Everyone, it seemed, had somewhere to go except me. I wasn't a tourist or a worker. I was an inbetweener and suddenly I wanted to escape. I needed to get away and that was when I thought of Pete.

Pete Wilson was one of my housemates at university and from the moment I met him, I was in awe. He wasn't extraordinary, he wasn't the most handsome, the most intelligent or even the funniest person I knew at university, but he was the only one who knew with an absolute certainty what sort of life they wanted. While everyone else was still shaping and forming themselves into the doughy balls of their twenties, he was fully formed and incredibly happy at nineteen. Pete moved into our house in the second year and

I spent two years with him learning what it meant to be truly happy.

I'd spent the last ten years trying to work out his secret and replicate his confidence, but it couldn't be done because that sort of happiness can only be achieved when you know what it is you want. It was something that had taken me far too long to realise. No matter how much money I had, no matter how successful I was, I still wouldn't have what he had – contentment. The only way I could have that was to find my passion and maybe the only person who could help me was Pete.

I found his number in my phone and dialled.

'Ed bloody Hornsby,' said Pete. 'How are you?'

'I've been better. I need to come and see you.'

'Is everything all right?'

'It's a long story. What are you doing tonight?'

'Not much, but you do realise I live in Nottingham. It's a bit far for a quick pint.'

'I'll be there by five. Can you pick me up from the station?'

'No problem. I'll see you then.'

I went home, threw some clothes in a duffel bag and left.

Pete was standing on the platform waiting for me. I hadn't seen him in over a year, when he'd been in London for work and we'd had a few pints. As I got off the train and onto the platform, I realised that apart from the occasional trip to see my parents, this was the first time I'd left London in six months. Pete was packing a few extra married pounds these days and sporting a goatee beard.

'Ed Hornsby, you old dog,' said Pete, greeting me with a firm handshake.

'Pete Wilson, looking very well,' I said, patting him on his belly.

'Downside of having a wife who can cook.'

'Home cooking a downside? I can't remember the last time I had a decent home-cooked meal.'

'Kate doesn't feed you?'

'Not since she left for her trip, and even before that I worked such long hours, I usually just grabbed something on the go. The life of working in the City. Not anymore though.'

'You left your job? I thought you were a lifer.'

'It's a long story, but I left, was pushed. Either way I'm done with it.'

'And that's why you're here?'

'Partly.'

'Sounds like you could use a pint.'

'I'd absolutely love one.'

'We have to pop back to the house first and see Nat. I told her you were staying. She made up the spare room and is making something for dinner. Lasagne, I think.'

'Thanks mate, really.'

'It's nothing.'

Pete and Natalie lived in a three-bedroom semi-detached in a quiet little village just outside of Nottingham. It was beautiful. There was even a little village green and a quaint, picturesque old country church next to it. Their house was huge in comparison to our place in Wandsworth, and probably only a quarter of the price. The inside was open-plan with a living room opening into a larger dining area and modern kitchen. There were lots of photos on the walls of family and friends and the year Pete and Natalie went travelling. It had a real family feel to it and felt lived in. It was the picture of happiness.

I hadn't seen Natalie since their wedding three years before, but she hadn't changed and greeted me with a huge hug. She always reminded me of a farmer's wife: big, busty and full of life. She was lovely and suited Pete perfectly.

'It's so nice to see you. We really don't see enough of you and Kate.'

'I'm sorry, it's so hard with work and life and . . .'

'Save the excuses,' she said, cutting in. 'And get your laughing gear around this.' She passed me a pint of beer with a warm smile. She was from Yorkshire and had a wonderfully broad accent.

Looking around, Pete had exactly what he'd always wanted and it started me thinking about my own life. I'd tried to overcompensate for my childhood. I thought I needed so much because I came from so little, but I was wrong. Pete and Natalie didn't have as much financially, but they spent time together, enjoyed life and seemed content. I wanted that with Kate. I thought I needed the magazine house, the coffee table life and the picture-perfect wife, but the reality was that it didn't really exist. Pete and Natalie's house was messy, uncoordinated and they had fishing trophies over the fireplace. In contrast, Kate and I had created a beautiful space full of whimsical, trendy and modern design, but it had no humanity because we were never in it. It wasn't really us, but more a reflection of who we thought we should be. Maybe it was a part of the reason why Kate left, because I hadn't given her a good enough reason to stay.

We had an amazing meal of lasagne, garlic bread and salad, while I explained about Kate going away and like everyone else in the world they couldn't understand why I hadn't gone too.

'Oh my God, Ed, it's the best thing ever, why didn't you go?' said Natalie.

'Because I was afraid. Afraid of losing my job, which I've lost anyway, but you're right, I should've gone.'

'It's not too late,' said Natalie.

'What do you mean?'

'Go meet her, surprise her.'

'I can't,' I said, more in hope than with any real conviction. 'I thought about it, but decided to stay here and get things sorted out for when she gets back. I need to figure me out.'

'If it were me, I'd be on that plane faster than a cat up a drainpipe.'

'And what about me?' said Pete with a wry grin. 'You'd leave me to fend for myself?'

'I'd never leave you,' said Natalie, leaning across and kissing him.

They were still so in love and in some ways reminded me of what my parents had. It was solid, real and sort of old-fashioned, but it worked. Maybe it was the only way it ever really worked.

'Behave,' said Natalie with a smile.

'Don't worry, I'll have him back by midnight,' I said, zipping up my jacket to keep out the cold. The early promise of sunshine had been replaced with a bitter cold.

'You'll be lucky. The Swann's usually closed by eleven, sometimes ten-thirty,' said Pete.

'You're joking.'

'You're not in London now, mate. It's a Tuesday night; we'll probably be the only ones in there.'

Pete wasn't wrong. The Swann was dead. It was a traditional, old-fashioned country pub – my dad would have loved it, the old red carpet, walls full of photos of the countryside and farmer knick-knacks. The barmaid, a buxom lady in her late fifties, was reading a magazine and there was one other customer, a wizened old man and his dog, who was asleep on the floor next to him. Pete got in a couple of pints and we sat down at an old wooden table next to a roaring fire.

'What's going on?' said Pete straight away, not even waiting for me to open the packet of prawn cocktail crisps that sat between us.

'I'm lost mate and I was sort of hoping you could help me.'

'I'm all ears,' said Pete and I told him everything.

'I want to know how you knew what you wanted. From the day I met you, you always had everything sorted out. You always knew what you wanted and it amazed me, still does.'

Pete looked at me for a moment. I don't think he knew what to say.

'The answer is, I don't know. It wasn't like I woke up one day at fourteen and said, I'm going to be an environmental scientist.'

'But you did though, didn't you? Admit it.'

'Maybe I wasn't fourteen exactly,' he said with a smile. 'Perhaps fifteen, but the point is I don't know why I knew, I just did. All I will say is that you always seemed to be rushing towards something. You could never really relax. It was always about work, about getting ahead. I don't know, mate. It's hard to put my finger on. I always knew I wanted a certain lifestyle. A bit more relaxed, chilled out and I wanted a job that involved the environment and that inspired me.'

'But I don't know what kind of life I want. Being here right now, I want what you have, but when I get back to London, I'll probably want that too.'

'You just need to figure out what's important to you. Do you want money? Do you want more time to spend with Kate? Do you want to live in London or somewhere else? The important thing, the thing you really need to think about, is what makes you happy, because that's all that really matters.'

Pete and I had a few more beers and we talked about everything. The good old days, the future and his and Natalie's current attempts to have a baby, which had so far been fruitless. However, all I could think about was his last question. What made me happy? It was a question I'd been asking myself my whole life and I'd never found a satisfactory answer. I thought I was happy in banking, but looking back, was I? I hated the hours and the continual pressure. I loved the money and I loved that I was good at it, but did it make me happy? Ultimately it didn't and so I was left with a gaping chasm that I needed to fill with something.

As I lay in their spare room that night, thinking over my life, I did decide something. I decided I was going to be happy. It sounded trivial and feckless because I still didn't know what it was I wanted, but I think it would come with time. What was important was I finally realised my happiness wasn't tied to my career so much as the other way around. My career should come from my happiness. I closed my eyes and thought of Kate, the one thing I knew made me happy, before I fell into a deep and happy sleep.

## JACK

I couldn't help but feel guilty as I sat on the tube and headed towards Holborn for my meeting with Morris Gladstone. I'd left Emma at home by herself and I knew she needed me. I felt bad because I should have been thinking about her and the baby, but I wasn't. I was thinking about becoming a writer with an agent. I felt like an awful human being, but I'd waited so long for this opportunity and it could change our lives.

I felt a surge of optimism as I stood in front of the Morris Gladstone Literary Agency. It was a lovely old whitewashed building with an immense wooden door that looked very grandiose. I was already feeling a bit nervous about the whole experience and the large door didn't really help. I was terrified Morris Gladstone was going to quiz me about what I read and current authors I wouldn't have heard of and I was going to be tossed out as a pretender, an unknowledgeable, talentless fraud.

I pushed on the door and it actually opened with considerable ease. I walked into a stunningly bright and modern reception area that was completely unexpected after the traditional exterior. It was incredibly white with lots of natural light and wood and there were vases of beautiful flowers that added splashes of colour. There was a woman on reception who gave me a smile as I walked in.

'Can I help you?'

'I have a four o'clock with Morris Gladstone,' I said uncertainly.

I was convinced there had been some kind of mix up, the assistant was probably new at her job and had me confused with someone else.

'Jack Chapman, pleased to meet you. I'm Sylvia. Let me take that manuscript from you. Can I get you a coffee or tea?'

'Coffee please,' I said, handing her the full manuscript they'd requested I bring along, the three hundred pages of loosely tied-together ramblings that held my future.

'Please take a seat,' she said and then sauntered off to get my coffee.

I sat down on a remarkably soft chocolate-brown leather sofa and looked around. The walls were adorned with framed book covers, which did very little to ease my already frayed nerves. I just wanted to write novels. I didn't belong among the covers I saw staring back at me; books that had been written by proper published authors. A part of me wanted to get up and run away as fast as I could, but I knew I couldn't. I needed to remain calm and composed and try to think positively. The trouble was that because I'd worked at a shitty coffee shop for years and had faced rejection after rejection, I'd started to doubt my ability. The old me who knew exactly what he wanted and where he belonged had long since left the building.

'Here you go,' said Sylvia, handing me a cup of coffee and then a small tray of milk and sugar. 'He shouldn't be much longer.'

'Thank you,' I said, and added milk and a couple of sugars to my coffee. There was also a small biscuit on the tray, which I took and ate quickly. My stomach was an acid bath of sickness.

'I loved it,' said Sylvia from her desk.

'Sorry?'

'The chapters you wrote, I loved them. We get a lot of manuscripts through here and I get to read a few. I read yours over the weekend and it blew me away. So funny and simply gorgeous.'

'Oh, thank you,' I said, trying to filter through my variety of facial expressions until I found one that looked vaguely like confident. I wanted to believe that what I'd written was as wonderful as she'd said, but it was difficult.

I sat and waited, drinking my coffee and trying not to think about Emma being at home by herself. When I left she was sitting in bed watching television with a blank expression on her face. She was heartbroken and this whole thing had affected her far more than even I had expected. I was afraid to talk about it in case I opened the floodgates, but I didn't want to ignore it either. I honestly didn't know what to do. I was hurting too, but I knew it was different. Men don't really become parents until the baby is born, while women are mothers as soon as they become pregnant.

'Jack Chapman?' a booming voice said.

I looked up and a man was standing in front of me. He was short with a bird's nest of unruly grey hair that sat upon a squat face. He was wearing a tweed suit and holding out a podgy hand with a smile.

'Oh, hello, hi,' I said, getting up quickly and shaking his hand.

For a short scruffy man he had a particularly fearsome handshake.

'Morris Gladstone, very excited to meet you,' he said in the same sonorous voice. 'Come through, come through.' He gestured for me to follow him. We walked down a short corridor decorated with more framed book covers and photos of writers before we turned into a small office. Morris asked me to take a seat while he sat opposite, across a desk piled high with manuscripts. 'Sorry about the mess; one of the perils of the job I'm afraid.'

'Oh, no problem,' I said, having a quick look around the room.

It was small but packed to the rafters with books and manuscripts. It had the feel and smell of an educational institution and reminded me of my old English lecturer's office. I felt instantly at home. Morris obviously wasn't the most orderly person in the world, but I rather liked that about him.

'Jack, tell me a bit about yourself.'

I'd done my best to be ready for this meeting, but I suddenly felt very ill prepared. I had no idea what to say about myself. I felt like the most boring, nondescript person in the world.

'I'm twenty-nine, almost thirty. Getting married this year to my lovely fiancée Emma. I'm originally from Australia; I moved here with my mother when I was fifteen. I live in a tiny flat in Notting Hill and I currently work at To Bean or Not to Bean on the Southbank . . .'

'Oh, God, not that awful Shakespearean-themed place around the corner from The Globe?'

'Unfortunately, yes.'

'My condolences.'

'I have to do something to pay the rent.'

''Tis true, Jack, 'tis true. And how about the book. Where did it come from? Where was the inspiration?'

It was difficult, at first, talking about the book and especially to a stranger. I hadn't ever been one to really talk in-depth about my writing. It was something personal and I always found it hard to verbalise. However, with Morris looking at me intently, I started talking and before I knew it, floods of words were pouring out of me. I was telling him things I didn't even realise myself. The book was essentially a love story, but it had darker moments, profound moments and I didn't really realise until then just how much the death of my father had contributed to it.

'You do realise I never do this. I always read the entire manuscript of any novel before I meet with an author, but your opening chapters were incredible, Jack, utterly absorbing. I read so much drivel, absolute tosh and some of it I even take on, so when I read something like this that truly excites me, I'm not one to mess about. I had to meet you in person and I'm glad I did. I'll need to read the rest of the book, but I want you, Jack. I want to sign you now, today, before somebody else does. Are you with me?'

I was literally, utterly and comprehensively bewildered. He wanted me to sign there and then. I was going to have an agent. A proper literary agent. For a moment a small game of competitiveness broke out in my brain and I thought foolishly that maybe I should wait, see what other options appeared, but the game was soon abandoned. I didn't care what else was offered and who else was offering it. Morris had rung me and he loved my work and I really, truly liked him. It was the opportunity I'd been waiting for since I was fourteen.

'Too bloody right I am,' I said, a smile breaking over my face.

'You aren't going to regret this,' said Morris and we shook hands.

The air outside felt much lighter when I left the office. I realised quickly it wasn't the air that was lighter, but that the pressure on my shoulders seemed to be gone. I wasn't being naïve. I knew that just because I had a literary agent, it didn't mean I would suddenly become a rich and successful writer, but it gave me hope. Before, I had nothing but a dream, but now I had someone else who believed in it. I wanted to call Emma and tell her but I was afraid. I didn't want to seem like

I was belittling her feelings about the baby or that I didn't care. I didn't know how to tell her without seeming like a callous idiot. Unsure what to do, but still on a high after the meeting, I saw a pub across the street and went for a quick drink alone to celebrate and to bask in the glow of my success.

I got a pint and sat by the window. I watched people walk past: office workers, shop assistants. The whole of London moved like a giant ant farm, everyone set on their specific role and going about their business with a blinkered determination. I'd always known I didn't want that. I didn't want to spend my days in air-conditioned office blocks doing something I didn't love just to pay for a life I couldn't afford. I'd always wanted to do something different and that something had always been writing. It was my passion and if I made it, if I actually got published and did well enough, then I'd never have to work another day in a meaningless job again. That thought made me smile and I was so happy a few tears leaked out and slid down my face.

## EMMA

I met Paul when I was sixteen. I was in my last year of school and Paul was nineteen and studying at St Martin's college in London. I thought he was literally the coolest bloke in the world. He was studying photography and was one of those incredibly urbane, intelligent, sophisticated boys with the looks to match. He was tall, dark and handsome and had the most wonderful deep, sultry eyes. I was head over heels in love.

My parents, of course, weren't enamoured of the idea of me having a nineteen-year-old boyfriend who lived in London. I used to have to sneak out to see him when he was home for the weekend and I'd occasionally get into London via some tenuous excuse. Mum would always grill me before I left and made me promise I wasn't going to see Paul. I lied, of course. I was sixteen and in love and what did my mother know about the delicate feelings of young love? I wrote him mawkish poems and it was, for six months, the greatest love story the world had ever known. I felt like Juliet and Paul was my Romeo.

I was a virgin when I met Paul and it took a few months but eventually we had sex and it seemed to make everything more intense and passionate between us. I tried to get away more often and he would come home more frequently at weekends. His parents lived just around the corner from mine, so it was easy to sneak out after bedtime or for Paul to sneak in. My parents were getting increasingly suspicious though and so we had to be careful, but the element of risk just seemed to heighten our desire for each other.

It was the summer holidays just before I was about to start sixth form and Paul was back for a few weeks. I hadn't gone on the pill because I didn't want Mum to find out and so we just used condoms and occasionally not even that. We were young, foolish and the thought of getting pregnant hadn't crossed our minds. Surely it couldn't happen to us?

My period was late. Paul was convinced it was nothing and I couldn't tell Mum. Eventually, one afternoon I plucked up the courage to get a test. I sat alone in the bathroom and waited for the little plastic stick to tell me if I'd been a silly young girl or not. I sat, prayed and waited. I crossed my fingers as hard as I could and closed my eyes so tightly it hurt. I wanted time to stop so I wouldn't have to find out what deep down I already knew. I was pregnant.

I don't know how long I cried for, but it felt like forever. I would have to tell Paul and, worse, I'd have to tell my parents. They'd be so ashamed and embarrassed. I had big plans. I wanted to be an actress and I couldn't do that with a baby. Paul was still at university and had no money. I knew what I had to do.

'I'm making an appointment at the doctors,' said Mum with a stoic face. She didn't flinch, she didn't shout, she didn't do anything except what she knew had to be done. 'You can't have a baby at your age; it will ruin everything. You're having an abortion and that's it. And not a word to your father.'

Mum and I went in one sunny day in early August. It was all very practical and cold. We sat in the waiting room and Mum read a magazine; I wanted to cry, but I couldn't because I was afraid that if I started, I wouldn't be able to stop.

We left a short while later, the baby gone, and it was never spoken about again. We went on holiday to Corfu a week later and when we came back I went to sixth form. It was funny because it happened so quickly and because Mum took care of everything, I managed to almost wipe it from my memory. It was the one moment in my life when I truly needed and loved my mother. Maybe our reasoning for the abortion was different, maybe the way we handled it wasn't the same, but without her, I don't know what I would have done.

I'd thought about the abortion sporadically over the years, but when I felt the sickness rise up inside of me and the warm bloody trickle down the inside of my leg, and then the pain deep within me, it was all I could think about. Maybe it was karma, I thought. You couldn't just go around getting abortions when it suited you and think it wasn't going to come back and repay the debt one day. I don't know if I believed that or not, whether cosmic karma even existed, but I couldn't help but think it was some sort of payback. The hardest part though, and the bit that kept me awake, was not sharing it with Jack. I didn't want him to know what I'd done at sixteen and maybe it was irrational, maybe it was stupid and wrong, but I didn't want him to blame me too.

I was in the bath when Jack walked in. It was a Sunday night. It had been a marginally better day than the one before, but there was still a huge hole in my life I didn't know how we were ever going to fill. I was trying to be happy and support-ive about Jack's meeting with the literary agent, and I was really excited for him, but I couldn't summon the strength to show it.

'All right, love,' said Jack, sitting on the toilet next to me. I'd filled the bath with hot water and lots of soothing bubbles.

My body still ached and I wanted to lie there and not think about anything. 'How would you feel about a little ceremony for the baby? It wouldn't have to be much, just a few words. I thought we could plant something.'

Jack looked at me with those gorgeous eyes and for the first time since it happened, I had the realisation that he was hurting too. I'd been so wrapped up in my own pain, I hadn't even thought about him.

'I'd like that.'

Jack reached out a hand and held mine.

'I thought we could do it at Kensington Gardens. Maybe we could walk down in the morning.'

'Thank you.'

'For what?'

'For being you. I wouldn't have got through this on my own.'

'You're stronger than you think, Em,' said Jack, but he didn't know. He didn't know how weak I was inside. He didn't know about the other baby that Mum and I had gotten rid of. Jack was a good person. He believed I was this pure, wholesome girl, but he didn't know this one truth, and I felt awful.

It was a chilly morning and a cool white fog lay across Kensington Gardens like a blanket of marshmallows as Jack and I walked hand-in-hand to say goodbye to our baby. Jack had bought a little potted shrub and we were going to plant it and say a few words. I hadn't slept much the night before, trying to think what I was going to say. It felt like an impossible task. How could I say goodbye to someone I never knew but loved so much? I also wondered what Jack was thinking. Did he feel the same as me? Was he as distraught? So heartbroken? I knew Jack and he was so full of love and compassion, but how could he truly feel the same sense of loss? Jack would never know how I felt about our baby and I could never properly tell him.

We walked around until we found a nice, quiet spot beneath a clump of trees. It was slightly shaded and seemed like the perfect place. Jack had a trowel and dug a small hole. I lowered in the shrub and then Jack filled in the dirt around it. It was only a symbolic gesture, but I couldn't help but feel a tug on my heart, as though we were actually burying my baby. Jack got up and we both stood there looking down at the shrub.

'Do you want to say something?' said Jack, holding my hand.

I'd been thinking all morning about what to say. Words, as usual, didn't feel like enough to convey what I felt inside.

'You didn't know us. We didn't know you yet, but we loved you so much. We'd already thought about all the things we were going to do together, all the places we were going to go and how much we were going to love you. You may not have lived for very long but you changed us forever. Sleep tight little one,' I said and then fell against Jack, the tears coming again. Jack held me tightly until I'd regained some composure and then he spoke.

'When Emma told me she was pregnant, I was shocked. I hadn't thought about having a baby yet; it was always something for the future. Something for one day. But as soon as she told me, I was ready. I wanted you more than I've wanted anything else my whole life. I didn't know if you were a boy or a girl, but I loved you unconditionally and knew I would for the rest of my life. You were taken before I had the chance to meet you, but you'll always be in my heart. Always be my baby.'

Jack spoke quietly and compassionately and I loved him more and more with every word. I wasn't sure how much he felt the loss until I heard his voice, wavering on the brink of tears. Jack and I stood together staring down at the plant for maybe thirty minutes. From the moment I found out I was pregnant, my whole body had felt such a huge rush of love, I knew then that I wanted a baby more than anything else in the world.

As I stood there with Jack, I realised something. I still wanted to be a mother and I wanted Jack to be a dad. I wanted us to try again. I wanted a baby.

**To: Kate Jones**
**From: Emma Fogle**
**Subject: Re: Bula!**

K,

I don't really know how to begin this. I lost the baby, Kate. I'm just completely numb with pain and shock and I don't know what to do with myself. Sorry it's taken me so long to write to you, but I didn't know what to say. I still don't, actually. When it happened, I knew I was losing my baby. I could feel it deep inside me. It sounds crazy, but I felt them die and I haven't been able to shake that feeling since.

Jack's been wonderful and before I forget to mention it, he's got an agent. They contacted him and offered to represent him. It couldn't have come at a better time. I have my fingers crossed for him because he deserves it. And I'm useless at the moment. I can barely get out of bed in the morning.

I'm sorry I'm telling you the news like this. I was going to call but I would have just cried for an hour and I didn't want to do that to you. By the time you get back, I hope it won't be quite as raw and painful as it is now. I've never felt anything like it. I was so excited to be a mummy, but now I just feel lost. I can't even think about acting. All I want is to be pregnant again. I loved waking up every day knowing that a baby was growing inside me. It gave my life a whole new perspective and I miss it so much.

I'm going to ask Jack if we can try again. I know this baby wasn't planned, but it changed me. It made me realise what I need to be happy. I want that feeling again. I don't expect anyone to understand, but being pregnant I felt for the first time a complete sense of calm. It's like there was always a hole in my life and being pregnant filled it up.

I hope you're having fun in South America and I can't wait to see you soon.

Love Em X

## KATE

'I wanted to be amazing,' I said to Jez, my voice almost breathless. The hike was becoming harder and harder the higher we got and the air became thinner with every footstep. It didn't seem to bother Jez, but it really got to me and gave me a constant headache. Luckily, the pleasure and pure awe I felt just being there made it bearable. 'That sounds so silly now. "I wanted to be amazing." Doesn't everyone?'

'You'd be surprised,' said Jez with a smile.

'I don't know, it just sounds so juvenile. I'm going to be thirty in two days and I had this ridiculous idea I needed to feel amazing again, but that isn't real life, is it? Real life's getting up for work, paying bills, shopping, laundry. That's real life. This is just . . .'

'Just what?' said Jez, looking at me for a moment. 'This isn't real? We aren't real?'

'Of course we are, but one day we're going to have to go home and face reality.'

'And we can't keep this up, is that what you're saying? You and I can only work when we're thousands of miles from home without the day-to-day of real life. Doing laundry or popping to Tesco for a pint of milk is going to ruin what we have?'

It seemed to be the sword of Damocles that constantly hung over us. Everything had felt so right in Thailand and again in Peru, but my time travelling was almost up – and then what? How would it feel back home in England? How would I feel when I saw Ed again? Jez and I were on holiday and it was fun and romantic, but we were in a bubble and neither of us really knew what was going to happen when the bubble burst.

'That's not what I'm saying.' I tried to be reassuring, reaching down and holding his hand. 'I'm saying that eventually this is going to end and real life's going to resume, but right now, I just want to enjoy this. Live only in the moment.'

'That's fine by me,' said Jez with a lovely smile, squeezing my hand.

'And it was a lot more than just wanting to feel amazing again.'

'What else was it?' said Jez as we trudged slowly up the hillside.

'It was about getting back something I'd lost. Something I used to have. I don't know. I've made a lot of bad decisions over the last few years and it had nothing to do with Ed. It was me and they didn't necessarily feel like bad decisions at the time, but looking back they were. I think coming away was a way to start over. Push the reset button.'

'And?'

'And life doesn't work like that, does it? As much as I want to be twenty-one again, I'm not. I can't feel the same way I used to. We can't go backwards, only forwards, and that old me is long gone, but I think I've found something else. A new me.'

'And isn't that what travelling's really about? Discovering bits of ourselves we didn't know existed.'

'Between the drinking, lying on beaches and incredible experiences like this, yes, that's exactly what it's about.'

'And what did you discover?'

Jez looked at me with a salacious grin, but I wasn't going to give him that piece of me yet. What I'd learnt and become on that trip needed more time to formulate and grow.

'That's a conversation for another day,' I said, looking up the long path ahead, steep, rocky and full of overgrown plants that blocked our way.

It was day two of our hike and another long but wonderful one. The mountainous scenery was breathtakingly beautiful and being with Jez made the whole experience unforgettable. After meeting up again it was like we'd never been apart. After Machu Picchu, I only had a few more days left in Peru before I flew to Los Angeles for the last few weeks of my trip. Seven nights in LA, a week going to see the Grand Canyon, Las Vegas and San Francisco, and then it was back to England; back to Ed and time to face the music. Six months had gone so quickly and it was almost time to make a decision about Jez. Neither of us had said much about it, both of us too afraid to contemplate the inevitable. Our paths, which had crossed so serendipitously, would soon be veering off in different directions yet again and I couldn't help but wonder if there would be another chapter to our story.

Then there was Ed. Where did I stand with Ed? I honestly didn't know. Would he even be at the airport when I got back? We owned the house together and so, whatever happened, it wasn't going to be an easy plaster to rip off. Our lives were intertwined so intricately that pulling them apart would take time and considerable effort. I didn't even know if I wanted to break it apart, because I still loved him. I couldn't forget the happier times because there had been so many, and just thinking about those made me question everything I felt for Jez.

At the end of our second day we had time at Cocalmayo medicinal hot springs near Santa Teresa. They were beautiful and surrounded on all sides by lush, green mountains. After hiking for eight hours, taking our shoes and socks off felt beyond wonderful and then slipping into a bikini and into the hot springs was heaven. I sat in there with Jez, looking around at the extraordinary view, a beer in my hand, and I felt like so lucky. It was exactly why I'd gone travelling in the first place.

'A penny for your thoughts?' said Jez, poking a finger at my forehead like a pretend gun.

'I was just thinking how incredible this is and how I couldn't ever regret travelling because of moments like this.'

'I was thinking the same thing.'

'Oh, really.'

'Well, not exactly the same. I've never for one moment regretted coming away or thought about anything but enjoying myself. And Richard, of course. I was just thinking how perfect this was though, being here with you, seeing Machu Picchu. I couldn't be any happier.'

'Any happier?'

'If you were officially my girlfriend that might make me a smidgen happier.'

'You know it isn't that simple, right?'

'I know,' said Jez, disappointed.

'I don't know what's going to happen with Ed when I get back. I don't know what's going to happen with me.'

'It's OK, Kate, I understand,' said Jez and then he kissed me. 'Just promise me one thing.' I had a sudden case of déjà vu. 'Promise me you'll consider me. Promise you'll at least give us a shot.'

This part of the trip was supposed to be about me. I needed to figure out my problems. I couldn't promise Jez anything any more than I could promise Ed. At that moment, I just needed to be me. I thought about my time in Fiji with Mhairi and Tash. I thought about Orla and Bryan. I thought about everything. Ed, my father and the mess I was going home too. I was the last person to be promising anything to anyone.

'I can't make any promises,' I said with a smile. 'Sorry.'

The warm water of the spa fizzed around our bodies and we sat in there for maybe an hour before we got out, our skin shrivelled up like prunes. We had the evening ahead of us. A night of drinking, talking, playing cards and relaxing before another early night. The six a.m. starts were killing us. Just one more day of hiking and then the following morning we'd be at Machu Picchu and I'd be thirty years old. It was hard to imagine. Thirty, it seemed so old.

It was pitch black as Jez and I stood with the rest of our group outside the gates of Machu Picchu. It was just before six o'clock and we'd made it – we were just waiting to go in and see the sunrise over the ancient ruins. It was freezing cold and Jez had on his full Incan outfit, but I wasn't laughing: I was wearing as many layers as I could fit on and it wasn't keeping me quite so warm. The sheer number of stars was incredible but the moon was the real star of the show, shining brighter and bigger than I'd ever seen it before.

Before I left England, this was the one thing I couldn't wait to experience. It was also my birthday. My big Three-O. I'd already received a text from Emma and one from Mum, but nothing from Ed. We hadn't spoken at all since our conversation in Australia and he hadn't replied to my last couple of texts.

'Happy birthday,' said Jez as they finally opened the gates; the sun peeked around a mountain and we started the walk in. I smiled and held his hand.

There are no words to describe the beauty of Machu Picchu at sunrise. Jez and I found a small patch of grass and sat and watched as the sun rose over the mountains and bathed Machu Picchu in light. We kept warm under a blanket, holding hands, and it felt like the end of my trip in many ways. I still had a couple more days in Peru and then America, but at that moment I realised I'd achieved everything I had set out to do.

'Why are you crying?' said Jez, wiping a tear from my cheek.

'I don't know,' I said, the tears still coming. 'Because it's so beautiful.'

'It is,' said Jez. 'The most beautiful thing I've ever seen.'

**To: Emma Fogle**
**From: Kate Jones**
**Subject: Re: Bula!**

Em,

I'm so sorry. I can't even begin to imagine the pain of losing a baby. I just can't believe it and I feel numb too. I wish I was there to help you through this. I'll be back soon. I don't know what to say. I already bought the baby a present from Peru. I'll still bring it home for you. It's just unbelievable that it could happen to you and so far in. I always thought once you got past the first few months you'd be all right. I realise this must be the hardest thing you've ever had to go through and nothing I say is going to help, but just know I'm here for you. Always.

It feels a bit insensitive to go on about what I've been doing, but then again maybe reading this might help take your mind off it for a minute or two, so here's my update. I just got back from Machu Picchu and celebrating my thirtieth birthday. Machu Picchu was even more impressive and even more incredible than I could ever describe. The hike itself was difficult, which was part of the experience and made it even more memorable. There is one interesting piece of news. You'll never guess who's here . . . Jez!

I won't bore you with the details, but suffice to say it's complicated. I will try and give you a call when I get to Los Angeles. Things are a bit more rustic in Peru. I'm leaving tomorrow and time to say goodbye to Jez again.

I love you so much, Em, and it might be impossible to think about now, but one day you're going to be a wonderful mother. I just know it.

Love K x

## ED

There was something I'd never told Kate about the day we met.

I met her during the last month of university. We were both studying at Middlesex University in north London. I was studying business and finance and she was studying English literature. We were at different campuses, which would explain why we hadn't met during the previous three years.

It was a slightly damp afternoon and I was in the union bar waiting for a girl. Not Kate, but a girl I'd slept with the previous night. I didn't have many one-night stands at university, but the previous evening I'd gone out with some friends and met a girl. We were drunk and I ended up back at her place in Palmers Green. I didn't remember much in the harsh light of morning, but we agreed to meet for a drink later on in the union.

As a student, I wasn't the sort you'd generally see loitering around the union bar in the middle of the day. There were plenty of those: the usual crowd of mature students and bohemian types who always seemed to be hanging out and rolling their annoying little cigarettes. I wasn't really interested in the student life and, to be honest, I couldn't wait to leave, get a job and earn some money. I was sick and tired of being poor. Unlike a lot of other students I knew, I wasn't given handouts from my parents and had to pay for everything myself. On that day, as the bar was filling up, I sat and waited for my one-night stand to show up. We were supposed to meet at three o'clock, but by four I realised she probably wasn't coming. By five I had given up all hope and was about to leave when I noticed a girl walking my way. She was really pretty and unlike the rest of the afternoon drinkers, she was dressed smartly and had the most gorgeously intoxicating smile.

'Do you have the time?'

I looked down at my watch. 'Just past five.'

'Thanks.' She was about to walk away, but I knew I had to stop her.

'Wait,' I said quickly, standing up as if I was about to make a huge announcement. I, of course, had no idea what I was going to say, but she was looking at me expectantly.

'Yes?'

'I was just wondering, now you know the time, if you had time for a quick drink?'

I hadn't asked many girls out before. There had been girls, but they were usually friends of friends and so it happened organically. But with Kate, I'd had to actually put myself out there, put myself in the shop window and it was terrifying. Luckily, after a brief moment when the whole world seemed to lose all shape and form, she said yes.

'So, is this your thing?' she said when I sat down with a couple of drinks.

'Thing?'

'You know, you hang around the union trying to pick up unsuspecting girls without watches.'

'Oh yeah, definitely my thing.'

'Good job, it worked,' she said, and I was in love.

She had dark hair that was tied back neatly in a ponytail, the greenest eyes, a slightly pointy nose that was littered with freckles and a wide slim mouth that glistened with red lipstick.

She had the fairest lily-white skin and a tall, slim body with the most incredible long legs.

'Are you waiting for someone?' I asked, desperate to keep the conversation going.

'No, well, yes, sort of, but it doesn't matter. I'm free.'

'Me too.'

Meeting Kate was like finally finding the missing piece of a jigsaw puzzle. For years I'd often wondered how I would know when I met the right person, if that person even existed, but from the moment she sat down, we just clicked. We were ending each other's sentences before the first drinks were finished.

'Where do you think you'll be in ten years' time?' I said, pushing the conversational boat out.

'Wow, ten years, I'll be thirty-one. Shit that's old. Let me see. I want to be doing something that makes me happy, something I'm passionate about, not just a job, you know,' she said, tilting her head slightly. 'Something that makes a difference. I'll probably be living in London or somewhere near. I don't care really. I'd like to live near the coast one day because I've never done that. Maybe Brighton. I'd have been travelling for a year and be with the perfect man who loved me unconditionally, just as I was. And what about you, Ed? Where will you be ten years from now?'

I looked at her and I thought for a moment. I didn't really have a grand plan except to do well. I'd spent so many years knowing what I didn't want that I hadn't really figured out what I did want. I knew then though that what I wanted was her. If I had Kate then I would be OK.

'I'll be married to you,' I said, and I knew it was a gamble. I knew it was risky, but she didn't get up and leave. She didn't freak out and instead she smiled. A warm, happy smile.

'That's quite a statement. And how are you going to support me?'

'By then I'll have my own business.'

'Oh, really.'

'Really.'

'Here's to ten years from now,' she said, raising her glass in the air.

'Ten years.'

Just then a Snow Patrol song, 'Chocolate', came on.

'Oh God, I love this song,' said Kate.

'Me too,' I said and I smiled.

'What?'

'Nothing,' I said, but I already knew we had our song.

On the train home from Nottingham I was thinking about the day I first met Kate because it suddenly dawned on me that we were almost at ten years. Ten years since we'd met and ten years since we'd mapped out our future. Everything seemed so certain then, so easy and open. Our lives stretched out before us and we were eager, full of hope and wonder. Nothing seemed impossible and I was so certain Kate and I would get married and live happily ever after. Happy endings seemed so easy back then, but somehow, over the last nine years, we'd messed it all up. I'd never told Kate I was there to meet another girl, but it wasn't because I thought she'd be mad or because I was embarrassed, but because I believed I was really there to meet her.

Being unemployed and having time to actually sit back and take stock, it was so much easier to see where it had all gone wrong. I was sitting in our lounge looking around at the house we had created. It was beautiful, but it meant nothing without Kate. Kate was the spark that made it all possible and worthwhile. Without her it was just a room and that's where I'd gone wrong. I'd lost sight of why I was doing what I was doing.

I wanted in that moment to go back, start again from the day I met Kate and get it right. I wanted us to have all of those things we'd said back then. That was when the plan came to me. It wasn't by any means foolproof and it could backfire, but I had to give it a go. I wanted what we'd dreamed about at twenty-one and it was possible. I couldn't go back in time, but I could change the future and hope and pray that Kate came along with me because without her nothing else mattered.

I went upstairs and rifled through some old boxes we'd been storing in the spare room. They were boxes of child-hood memories and things we hadn't found a place for yet. I rummaged around until I found the box I was looking for. I hadn't been inside it for a couple of years and it was packed full of memories and memorabilia. I'd wanted to chuck it away when we moved in, but Kate insisted we keep it and I finally understood why. I looked through the box until I found what I was looking for. I took out some old clothes and laid them on the spare bed. I smiled because I hadn't seen them in years and I didn't even know if they'd still fit me. I quickly tried them on and amazingly they did. I looked in the mirror and it was like going back in time. It was the exact outfit I was wearing the day I met Kate. I smiled because I finally knew what I wanted. I finally knew what would make me happy.

## EMMA

There had been days when I hadn't just questioned whether I liked my mother, but whether I even loved her. She'd been a cold, hard, taciturn woman for most of my life and I'd become used to it. It was just her. My father was hardly home, always working so we could have the best of everything. I saw other parents who would cover their children in kisses and cuddles and I always wondered why I never got that. It wasn't that she didn't love me, but that she couldn't show it. From the day I was born she was preparing me for the real world. Maybe it was the honourable thing, the dignified way to raise a baby, but so many times in my life I would have swapped it all for a simple hug and a kiss.

I drove to Oxford on my own. Since Jack's fantastic news, he'd been so busy between working at To Bean or Not to Bean and going backwards and forwards with his literary agent on changes for the book. I was so happy for him because he'd wanted it for such a long time and he deserved it. I'd never seen him so happy and so energised, but as much as I wanted to jump on his bandwagon of bliss, I was still thinking about the baby. Our baby. I was sure Jack was too and it wasn't as if he was being insensitive about it, but he seemed to have moved on, while I just couldn't.

It was a Thursday afternoon. Dad was off playing golf and I wanted to see Mum alone because I needed to talk to someone other than Jack. When I walked in Mum was in the living room waiting for me. I hadn't told her about the baby yet or

Jack's news, but as soon as she saw me her face changed and she stood up.

'What's the matter, darling?' She'd barely finished her sentence before I was in tears. They seemed to come so easily and so strongly I could barely control them. I fell towards Mum and she hugged me. It was slightly uncomfortable, as it always was with her, as though I had a handle-with-care sticker on me and she didn't quite know where to put her hands or how hard to squeeze. 'Sit down, darling, and I'll get you a stiff drink. Oh, wait, the baby,' she said, but as soon as she did, she seemed to realise.

'I lost the baby, Mum.'

'Then you'll definitely need that drink,' she said and walked off towards the drinks cabinet. She returned with two large gin and tonics. 'Here you go, darling.' She handed me my drink and I took a sip. It was strong, but I didn't care.

'Thanks,' I said, and took a longer sip.

'What happened?'

'Everything was fine, it seemed fine anyway, but then Jack was at work and I started feeling sick. At first I thought it was just the pregnancy, but soon I started to realise it was something serious. I probably should have called for an ambulance straight away, but I didn't. I knew I was losing the baby and it sounds crazy, but I wanted to be alone with them before they were gone.'

Mum didn't do well with tears at the best of times. Her traditional English stiffness made me stronger and harder because we didn't cry in our family. I'd never seen Mum cry, not even at her mother's funeral. 'Tears are just biology, darling,' she told me afterwards. 'The physical act of sadness, but just because you don't cry, it doesn't mean you aren't sad inside.' However, the usually stoic, heavily made-up face of my mother, for once, showed a crack.

'Listen, darling. There's something I've never told you before, never told anyone for that matter, not even your father. I was twenty-one. Your father and I had only been married for a few months. He was still at university and we lived in this little flat in Chiswick. Lovely little place and we were so happy there. I had a part-time job at a local doctor's surgery . . .'

'You worked?'

'Five years, darling, until I had you and then I stopped. I enjoyed it. It gave me a sense of independence and your father was busy with studying and I had a few girlfriends. We had only been married a couple of months when I fell pregnant. I didn't even tell your father because I wasn't sure. I was late and so after a few weeks I asked a doctor at the surgery to give me a test and it was positive. I can't tell you how happy I was. Your father was away for a few days on a course, somewhere up north, and before he came back the baby was gone. It wasn't meant to be. I was distraught. It felt like my whole world had suddenly crashed around me, so I know what it's like,' said Mum with a comforting smile. 'But it gets better.'

'God, Mum.'

'It's fine because then we had you and that made everything all right.'

'But do you still think about the baby you lost? Don't you ever wonder what might have been?'

'Of course, all of the time, but what's done is done. I often say a prayer for them at church. It's all we can do, darling.'

'A part of me feels like I'm being punished for what happened with Paul.'

'Absolute nonsense,' said Mum, suddenly sterner, and her old stoic face returned with a vengeance. 'Tosh and you know it. You did what you had to do back then and this had nothing to do with that.'

'It's just, I can't help but think it's some sort of payback.'

'Emma Fogle, you look at me and don't forget this. You don't deserve to lose a baby. No one does and if there's one thing I'm certain of, it's that you didn't lose that child because of any kind of karma nonsense. It happens. It's a sad part of life but it happens. We grieve and then we move on. I did and you will too. You and Jack will try again and you'll have another baby.'

'I hope so,' I said, fighting back the tears.

'You will,' said Mum and she reached across and put a hand on mine. 'You will, darling.'

It was a strange feeling, being emotionally connected with my mother. We'd never shared anything quite so personal before and I suddenly felt a warmth for her.

'I know you probably think of me as this cold-hearted ogre, but all I have ever wanted is for you to be happy.'

'I know.'

'I love you so much, Emma; we both do.'

'And what about Jack?' I said, throwing a spanner in the works. 'Do you love him too?'

For a moment she looked like she didn't know what to say.

'Jack's lovely, but you know I've had my reservations about him. We're just worried he isn't good enough for you, that's all.'

'And what if I told you he's just been signed by a major literary agent?'

'He has, really?'

'Yes, the Morris Gladstone Literary Agency in Holborn. His novel was so good the agent didn't even wait to read the whole book before he signed him up. Does that change things?'

'Of course I'm pleased for him, for you both. I just want what's best for you, that's all, darling. One day you'll understand,' she said and got up. 'Another drink?'

It was still early and I'd planned on driving back to London later that afternoon, but I was enjoying spending time with Mum, probably for the first time in my life. Maybe I was starting to understand her better, understand our relationship better and maybe I was beginning to understand myself better too.

'One for the road,' I said and Mum smiled.

'We do love you so much,' said Mum as she was getting up. 'Even your useless father. He only worked so hard so you could have the best of everything.'

'And what about now?'

'What do you mean?'

'Now he's retired and he's still never at home. What's his excuse now?'

'Now,' she said, with a slightly sad laugh. 'I think he just wants to get away from me.'

'You don't mean that,' I said, but I had the awful feeling she did.

'Emma, your father and I have a certain kind of marriage. We did love each other very much once, but now it's more about companionship, support, the fear of change. We're settled and I can't complain. I have this lovely house and your father has his hobbies. I wouldn't change it for the world.'

'But don't you miss the passion, the closeness?'

Mum and I had never had a conversation like that before. Maybe it was the alcohol, maybe it was that I was finally grown up, but I suddenly felt like I could talk to her in a way I never had before. Mum returned with two hefty gin and tonics and then sat down again.

'Sometimes, yes, of course.'

'Then why don't you do something about it?'

'Like what, darling?' I couldn't believe what I was about to say and especially to my mother. 'Nothing inappropriate, I hope?'

'All I was going to suggest is that it's never too late for a bit of fun. Make an effort, put on some sexy underwear and you never know what might happen.'

'Oh, Emma, really,' said Mum, but she had a sparkle in her eyes.

Maybe I'd just resurrected my parents' sex life; I didn't really want to think about it, but I wanted them to be happy and we all need a bit of love now and again. Even my cold-hearted, gin-swilling mother.

To: Kate Jones
From: Emma Fogle
Subject: Re: Bula!

K,

I can't believe you're going to be home in a week! The last six months seems to have gone by so fast and so much has changed. It feels like we've all grown up a lot. I'm doing better today and it's sort of thanks to my mother. I know, it seems impossible. I went home to see her, tell her about the baby, and she was wonderful. We actually talked and bonded like we never have before and I even gave her advice on sex! I know, disgusting, but in a way it was sort of cathartic. For the both of us, I think. She'll probably be back to her usual, horrible old self next time I see her, but it was nice for one day to think of her as just my mother.

Jack and I had a ceremony for the baby. We planted a little shrub in Kensington Gardens and we both said a few words. If anything good has come out of this, it's that I feel closer and more in love with Jack than ever before. I know we'll try again and I hope next time things will be different. Hopefully you'll be there too.

I really can't wait to see you. Sorry we can't be there for you at the airport, but we'll see you as soon as we can. Pre-warning, I'm going to cry a-lot! Have a safe flight home.

For the last time,

Love Em X

## KATE

'It's just something I've been thinking about,' I said.

'That your life is essentially over?'

'I didn't mean that at all. I just meant that we need to have something to look forward to. We can't stop trying otherwise what's the point?'

It was the last conversation I'd have with Jez. I was about to get on a plane for Los Angeles and he had a few more days in Peru before he headed to Argentina. We were at a small café in Cusco drinking coffee. I'd just told him my thoughts on travelling. One of the reasons why I came travelling was because I was worried all the good times were behind me. It's the trouble with getting older: we have far less to look forward to. People are always looking back on their school days, their sixth form days or their university years and saying they were the best times of their life, but surely that can't be right. I finished university at twenty-one – was that it? Were my best years really behind me?

'That's why you're going back to university, to relive the old days?'

'No, the exact opposite, actually. I want to make new days, better days, and it's fine to look back nostalgically, but shouldn't we always be trying to make life better and more exciting? I don't want to be one of those sad, middle-aged people who regret not doing things. I don't want to end up bored, with four kids and a husband I no longer have sex with and wishing I was eighteen again. Wishing I'd done everything different.'

I stopped speaking and Jez was looking at me.

'Can I say something?'

'Depends what it is.'

'It's good, hopefully.'

'OK,' I said and felt nervousness ripple down my spine.

'I think I'm falling in love with you, Kate. Am in love with you, actually. I know this is a bit soon and you're about to get on a plane to Los Angeles, but I wanted you to know. I love you.'

I didn't know what to say. A part of me wanted to reciprocate and tell him I loved him too, but the truth was, I didn't know. I didn't want to raise his hopes or make him think something that wasn't true. I could love him, I knew that much, but it was too soon and, more importantly, I still loved Ed. The more I thought about it, the more I realised how much of what I was doing was because of my father. If I chose Jez and left Ed, I would still be running. I didn't know how to explain that to him, but as he looked at me with his gorgeous face and beautiful blue eyes, I knew I couldn't choose him. I couldn't keep running. I couldn't be like my father.

'Jez, look . . .' I started, but I could see the sadness fill his eyes.

'Kate, it's OK, you don't have to explain. I understand.'

'I don't think you do, Jez. I'm not choosing Ed either. The truth is I don't know what I want. I know I don't want to go back to my old life. I want to start over. I need to work on me, make me happy and right now I don't know who that involves.'

'It just definitely doesn't involve me?'

'You'll find someone much better than me, Jez. Someone who loves you more than anything in the world.'

'She just won't be you,' he said, showering me in guilt.

'No, she won't – she'll be better. Look, Jez, I like you a lot. More than a lot, actually, and I want you to be happy, I do, but I don't think that'll happen with me.'

'But how can you be sure?' he said, his voice suddenly louder and full of emotion.

'I can't. You of all people should know that. We can't be sure of anything in life; we just have to follow our hearts and hope the choices we make are the best ones.'

'And your heart's telling you I'm not the one?'

'Not exactly,' I said. 'But right now, at this moment, I can't be what you need. I just can't.' I started to cry. Slow, steady tears slid down my face. Jez reached across and wiped them away. I reached up and held his hand for a moment. 'I'm sorry.'

'It's OK,' said Jez, finally with a smile. A wilted, forlorn smile, but a smile nonetheless. 'You were worth the shot.'

'Oh, thanks,' I said, playfully sniffling up tears, trying to lighten the mood.

'You know what I mean.'

'I do.'

We sat in silence for a few minutes, sipping our coffees and taking in our surroundings. Cusco was beautiful and I didn't want to leave. The idea that I would be in Los Angeles soon filled me with dread. I'd left Jez once before and it was even harder the second time around.

'You know, Richard would have been so proud of you.'

'Why do you say that?'

'Because you found the perfect way to remember him and say goodbye and I feel so proud, so honoured to have been part of it.'

Jez looked down for a moment. He was trying to hold back his own tears now, but I saw one drop and fall somewhere beneath the table. I reached across and held his hand. He squeezed it and then looked up at me, the sun suddenly catching the side of his face and making me squint.

'He would have loved you,' said Jez with a smile.

'I think I would have loved him too,' I said.

We drank our coffees and walked around a small market, waiting for my departure time.

Eventually I left. We kissed and cried at the airport, and then I was on a plane heading towards Los Angeles.

As the plane took off and I looked out of the window at the ground below, it felt almost unreal that I'd been there with Jez and we'd hiked to Machu Picchu together. It was something that continually baffled me about travelling. Everything I did and every experience I had was so much in the moment that almost as soon as it was over, it felt like it hadn't happened at all.

My time in America turned out to be nothing more than a decompression chamber for my return to England. I didn't have the energy or enthusiasm to do much and I couldn't really be bothered to meet anyone new. I met a couple of girls who were just starting out on their trip and I envied them. They still had South America, the Cook Islands, New Zealand, Australia, Thailand, Vietnam and India left to do over the next twelve months, while I was almost done. My trip was almost complete and already I was starting to feel slightly depressed. I felt in between everything. In between travelling, in between life and in between relationships; Los Angeles was my purgatory.

As the plane took off, I looked out of the window at Los Angeles disappearing into the distance, the brown tint of smog lying over the city and the clearer mountains beyond. Next to me was a woman probably in her sixties, and next to her was a businessman who had his laptop on as soon as the plane was ten feet off the ground. I couldn't imagine being like that. What made people want to work so hard and so aggressively when they could travel, relax and enjoy life? Sadly, it reminded me of Ed. I could already imagine him at the arrivals gate in a suit with a bunch of overly expensive flowers, hoping to continue just where we'd left off. He'd have me back to work in a week and it would be like the last six months had never happened.

'Some people, eh,' said the woman next to me, nodding towards the suit.

'I know, right.'

'Can't turn off their phones and laptops for two seconds just in case they miss an email.'

'It's pretty sad.'

'It is, dear, not like you though, eh. Been travelling have we?'

She had a sweet northern voice, maybe from Manchester or Bolton.

'How can you tell?'

'No offence, dear, but you don't look like you've been on a two-week holiday.'

I wasn't quite sure what she meant, but then I had a flash-back to the airport. I'd popped into the toilets to freshen up before the flight and when I looked in the mirror, I barely recognised the face that stared back at me.

When I'd left England six months before I was kitted out with all new travelling clothes: pretty summer dresses, sandals, cut-off jeans, T-shirts and lots of bikinis. Now I was dressed in a T-shirt I'd bought in Thailand. It was orange and had the words, 'Phuket, I'd rather be in Thailand!' on the front in purple. I had on an assortment of necklaces. One from a market in Bangkok, one from Byron Bay and two that I'd got in Cusco. My hair, once cut religiously every month in London, straightened and moisturised, was now longer, wilder and unkempt. My face, devoid of make-up, but much darker due to six months of sunshine, looked older somehow. Around my wrists I had a jumble of different bracelets I'd picked up along the way and I was wearing baggy purple hippy trousers I'd got in Cusco – a present from Jez. The nice old lady hadn't had to guess I'd been travelling because it was emblazoned across every square inch of my being.

'None taken and yes, I'm on my way back home.'

'My daughter went travelling in her twenties, said it was the best thing she ever did. You kids are so lucky nowadays. I would love to have gone travelling.'

'You're travelling now. Making up for lost time?'

'Something like that,' she said and then the air hostess came around with drinks and snacks. Before long the woman next to me was asleep, the suit was still staring intently at his laptop and I started watching a film.

The rest of the flight was a mixture of fitful sleep, attempting but failing to read, watching bits of films and eating the meals that all seemed to merge into one. Eventually though, as the sun came bursting through the small cabin windows, we were almost home. I couldn't believe that six months had come and gone so quickly. I didn't know what to expect when I got off the plane. I didn't know if Ed would be there, where I would go if he wasn't and what I was going to do next. Travelling was supposed to be something I got out of my system before I settled down, but instead it had thrown up more questions than it had answered. As I prepared to get off the plane, I turned to say goodbye to the woman next to me.

'Safe travels.'

'Oh, you too, love. I hope you have someone special waiting for you.'

I smiled back, but the truth was I didn't know. I didn't know if he was there or if he was even special anymore.

After the anxious wait at the luggage carrousel for my backpack, I finally made my way through customs and then I walked into the arrivals area. For some reason whenever I walked through arrivals, I always felt a bit like a celebrity: everyone looking at me, hordes of unfamiliar faces and all I was doing was trying to find my special face, the one who was there just for me.

I walked through and the sunlight from behind the gathered crowd hit me. Somewhere in the distance I could hear the Snow Patrol song 'Chocolate' and I smiled; a flood of memories came back in a second. Our song. The song that had been playing the day I met Ed in the student union. My heart was beating wildly in my chest as I kept walking, looking and not knowing. Then, just as I was giving up hope, I saw him. I stopped dead in my tracks because there, about ten feet in front of me, was Ed and he looked different. Very different.

I didn't know what to do. Should I run to him or should I not? What was I going to say? The only thing I knew was that he looked better. Younger. Like the Ed I used to know. It wasn't until he started walking towards me that I realised the music was coming from Ed. He was carrying an iPod with speakers. The Snow Patrol song got louder as Ed walked towards me, until eventually, when he was right in front of me, the last line rang out.

'Our song,' is all I could say.

'I've missed you,' said Ed with a dizzy smile.

'Missed you too,' I said, looking at him quizzically. 'What's with the circa-two-thousand-and-four outfit?'

'I'll explain that later. Fancy a drink?'

'I'd love one.'

'I hoped you'd say that,' said Ed, picking up my backpack with a smile.

**To: Emma Fogle**
**From: Kate Jones**
**Subject: I made it!**

Em,

I'm writing this at the airport in LA. I'm about to get on the plane and come home. It's so strange to think that in thirteen hours I'll be landing back in London. It's even stranger to think that my trip is over. I don't feel ready for it to be done yet. I want to come back to see everyone, especially you, of course, but I'm so worried about Ed and what I'm going to do next. I guess Ed was right in one respect, it is really hard going back because it feels like I've changed so much, done so many things, but I'm going back to the same old London.

I wanted to write you a last email because I want to remember how I felt. I want you to know how I feel right now because I'm sure at some point in the future I'm going to need you to remind me.

I realised something while I was away. Life is short and we can't spend years and years of it being unhappy because we're afraid to change. There's nothing scarier than travelling the world on your own, arriving in new towns, in new hostels and not knowing a single soul. It's terrifying, but exhilarating at the same time. Life before wasn't exciting or exhilarating, it was dull and I don't want to go back to that. I'm not saying I don't want Ed, but I don't want our old life. Our old life was shit. Not the bits with you in, obviously, but the bit with me, Ed, our house and jobs.

I'm going to travel more. I'm going to teach English at sixth form and be a positive influence on teenagers' lives. I'm not going to accept second best and being fairly happy. I'm going to strive to be as happy as I can be. I'm going to be fearless.

I don't know what the future holds. I don't know if Ed is going to be at the airport when I get back or not, but, whatever happens, I will always be your best friend, Em. Writing these emails and thinking about you and us for the past six months, I've come to realise that you are the love of my life. Forget the men; when it comes to it, I can always rely on you. I'll see you soon. Off to take my last flight. My future awaits . . .

For the last time,

Love K x

## ED

I was ten years old when Dad first took me into London. We grew up in Slough, which was only a short train ride away, but for some reason we never went into the big city. Dad didn't like it much; too big, too loud, too many people, too expensive, was his litany. London was practically a dirty word in our house.

I didn't realise then, of course, but it was because he didn't like to see what he was missing out on. He lived in a dingy part of a satellite town that clung onto the coat-tails of London; he didn't need reminding he hadn't quite made it in life. I, on the other hand, loved it. London was everything I was missing in Slough.

Dad and I had an argument the day he took me to London. I wanted a Happy Meal, but he'd brought along a packed lunch Mum had made. I saw other kids eating out with their parents and I wanted the same. I stomped, shouted and screamed like a right little brat until Dad dragged me away. He was probably angry, embarrassed, and I remember being furious with him. Why couldn't I have what all the other kids had? Why was I forced to eat a jam sandwich and a packet of crisps when the other kids had burgers and fries? I look back now and wince because I realise that my parents just couldn't afford it. They would have given me the world if they could, but they just didn't have the money. What I didn't know then, and what it's taken me years to appreciate is that although we didn't have much money, they gave me all of their time and every ounce of their love, which was far more important than any Happy Meal.

I looked into the mirror in the dingy old toilets of the pub Kate and I were in and smiled. I suppose the biggest thing I'd learnt had been that I needed Kate. Nothing more, nothing less, just Kate, and if I had her then everything else would fall into place. Everything I wanted in life was sitting just a few feet behind a door. I dried my hands, had one last look in the mirror, took a deep breath and then opened the door.

Kate looked different. She still looked beautiful, but not how I remember. Obviously the longer hair, the hippy trousers and her skin being sun-kissed olive instead of pale white made a difference, but it was more than that. She had changed too.

'How was it?' I said, sitting down and taking a sip of my pint.

'It was incredible, Ed. Really, really incredible. I did things I never thought I'd do and met so many amazing people. But more importantly what's happened to you? What's with the outfit, the week of stubble and the long hair? What happened to old Ed?'

'Old Ed got fired.'

'What?!' said Kate incredulously. 'You mean you don't work at the bank anymore?'

'Nope.'

'You're no longer a wanker banker?'

'No longer a wanker full stop, I hope.'

'I, for one, think that's fantastic news.'

'I'm glad you said that.'

'Why?'

'Listen, Kate, a lot has happened since you left, with me, with us and it feels impossible to tell you about everything, but something's changed in me. I can feel it. You were right before by the way. I was lost in my job, but now . . .'

'You've seen the light?'

'Something like that. Let me start at the beginning.'

'I'm sitting comfortably,' said Kate with a smile, adjusting herself in her seat.

'Then I'll begin.'

I told her everything. I told her all about Georgie, which was difficult but good to get off my chest. I told her about losing my job and how Hugh had made me realise that no matter how hard I worked, I would never be one of them. I explained how I went to see my dad and discovered I was more like him than I'd realised and that maybe I'd spent too long chasing the wrong dream. I explained all about going to see Pete in Nottingham and how it had affected me. I told her how I'd thought back to when we first met at university and I realised that all I really needed, had ever needed, was her.

'I guess what I'm really saying is that I love you, Kate, and if you'll have me, I'd like to spend the rest of my life trying to make you as happy as we imagined back then. I'm not asking you to marry me, but just imagine a life together.' Kate looked at me for a moment and I don't think she knew what to say. I'd told her a lot. I was still coming to terms with everything myself and so I couldn't expect her to jump on the band-wagon straight away. 'And I understand a lot has changed. You've changed and probably have plans of your own. I don't need an answer right now, take all the time you need. I know we can't go back and change what's happened, but maybe we can start again.'

'But I'm not sure we want the same things anymore, Ed,' she replied and I felt a knot in my chest; I caught my breath for a moment. 'You've changed and I'm happy about that, I really am, but I don't want you to be something you're not just for me. One thing I realised while I was away is that we have to be true to ourselves. I wasn't happy before because I was living your dream, your version of life and I don't want you to be unhappy because you're living mine.'

I think my biggest problem was I was always looking forward and never appreciating the present. I was forever pushing for something intangible and far away, trying to better myself, better us, but in the clamour I forgot about the now. It was like Kate and I had been doing the three-legged race, but instead of working together in harmony, I was dragging her along with me, more worried about the win than enjoying being tied to the love of my life.

'I was wrong in November, Kate. When you asked me to come travelling with you I should have come. I was scared. Scared of change, of leaving my job, of wandering off into the unknown and not knowing what was going to happen when I got back . . .'

'But it was my dream, not yours.'

'But don't you see, it doesn't matter because the only dream I have is you. I've been thinking a lot about the future and I do want to start my own business like I always planned. I want to be the me I was at twenty-one. I want to follow his dreams because he was right. But right now, before I can do that, I need to fix things with you. So I don't care what we do next or where we go. If you want to jump on a plane to Azerbaijan, then book me a ticket too. If you want to start a small organic farm in north Wales, then buy me some welling-ton boots.'

'And whatever I do, you'll come with me?'

'I'm all in. You're the love of my life, Kate. I'd follow you anywhere. For a start, I'm unemployed, I have nothing else to do,' I said and she laughed. 'I just want to be with you.'

'I'm going to be a sixth form teacher,' she said suddenly.

'That's great. You'll be a fantastic teacher.'

'You think so?'

'You're intelligent, funny and kind and you love telling people what to do, you'll be a knockout.'

'It means going back to university, but I won't be able to get in this year. I've almost a whole year to wait so I was thinking about teaching English abroad.'

'Right . . .'

'What's that face?'

'What face?'

'That face with the wrinkled forehead. See, the idea of going abroad terrifies you.'

'It does, of course it does, but what terrifies me more is losing you again.'

'You'll come with me?' said Kate, looking at me with those beautiful eyes. 'Wherever I end up?'

'I'd follow you to the ends of the earth.'

'But what about when we get back? What then?'

'Then,' I said, reaching across and holding her hand. 'We'll see what happens. Maybe a year off is just what we both need. It will give me time to figure out what sort of business I want to run and you some time too. This is what we both need, Kate.

I looked across at her and she smiled.

'Love you,' she said.

'Love you too,' I replied.

july

## JACK

We were in The Goat in Boots pub on the Fulham Road waiting for Ed and Kate. It was a Friday afternoon and it would be the first time we'd seen Kate since she'd left us six months earlier. Emma was excited to have her best friend back and I was too. It had been heart-wrenching losing the baby and I knew it would help Emma to have Kate around again. As much as Emma loved me and as much as I wanted to help and comfort her, I realised I could only do so much. Kate could fill in where I couldn't.

I was waiting to hear back from Morris Gladstone because he'd submitted my novel to a selection of publishers and we were waiting on offers. I was beyond nervous. It was the moment I'd been working towards since I was fourteen and despite all of the words of encouragement from Morris, I was fully expecting him to come back and tell me it was drivel after all. I'd been kidding myself the past month that I was going to be published. Visions of grandeur seemed to constantly cloud my mind: book signings, an award or two, a number-one bestseller and maybe a film. Morris was probably having a midlife crisis, was going barmy or was just plain wrong and I'd be found out as the talentless hack I was. I'd work at To Bean or Not to Bean for the rest of my worthless life. I'd retire at sixty-five and they'd give me a Shakespeare mug for all my years of service.

'Oh my God!' screamed Emma suddenly.

'Oh my God!' came an equally high-pitched squeal from across the pub.

I looked across and Kate and Ed had just walked in. Emma was immediately up and running across the pub. It was the happiest I'd seen her in a long time and it made me smile.

'Agh!' screamed Kate.

'Agh!' screamed Emma and they grabbed each other and did a girlie jig that involved them holding each other and going around in circles and bouncing up and down. Some of the other punters were looking across at them, while Ed and I just stood and watched.

'Hello, mate,' said Ed calmly.

'All right,' I replied, while the girls' squealing volume eventually died down and instead they just resorted to saying, 'Oh my God' over and over again. And then they started crying.

'I'll get the drinks,' I said.

'I'll give you a hand,' said Ed, while the weeping girls staggered off together towards our table.

I hadn't seen Ed since our last big chat and I was desperate to ask him how things were going with Kate. It can't have been easy seeing her again and I assumed they were still together and everything was all right. Ed looked different too. He looked younger somehow and instead of his usual outfit of polo shirt and smart jeans, he was wearing a white T-shirt with a Fiji Bitter logo and casual jeans. He also had a few days stubble and his hair was longer. Something was definitely going on.

'Nice T-shirt,' I said.

'Oh, yeah, Kate got it for me.'

'And how's things with you two?'

Ed looked at me and smiled.

'Never better,' he said before his face dropped into a frown. 'Listen, Kate told me all about the baby. I'm so sorry, mate; I can't imagine how difficult it must be.'

'Oh, right, thanks. It's been tough, but we're getting through it together,' I said, smiling, but inside the knots of pain began to pull at my heart. Ed and I stood together for a moment, neither of us really sure what to say next. Ed gave me a pat on the shoulder and a solid smile. 'So, what's next for you and Kate?'

'We have a bit of an announcement, actually, but I'll wait until we're all together for that,' said Ed conspiratorially. 'Let's get the drinks in first.'

'Sounds like a plan.'

It was a mixture of the surreal and wonderful to all be together again. It had felt like such a long time, but with Kate back in the group it worked. We'd been missing a side to our square, but now she was back, it was just like old times again.

Back at the table Kate was going through the highlights of her trip with Emma, who sat laughing, smiling and nodding and looking completely enthralled. I knew inside she was still distraught about the baby, but she didn't show it.

Emma had always amazed me. From the moment we met at that karaoke night in Camden, I'd always been in such awe of her inner strength and determination.

I was drunk because it was karaoke and I could only sing in front of people with at least five pints in me. Emma was in the crowd with a couple of actor friends and I was supposed to be singing 'Angels' by Robbie Williams. However, as soon as the music started playing I realised it wasn't 'Angels' at all, but 'I Got You Babe' by Sonny and Cher – a couple's duet. I stood up there like a lemon for the first few bars without a clue what to do next, while my friends were in hysterics in the crowd. It was embarrassing to say the least and just as I was about to walk off stage and return to my group, tail between my legs, someone appeared next to me, grabbed the other microphone and started singing. It was Emma.

I was in love with her by the second verse. She always claimed she did it because she was an actress and wanted to hog the limelight, but I always thought she did it because she saw something in me. Either way we never looked back after that night and haven't since.

'We have some news,' said Kate when we were all caught up and there was a small break in conversation. Ed and Kate looked at one another and then smiled. 'We're moving to Japan to teach English for the next year.'

As soon as Kate said it my eyes drifted across to Emma. She had that look she gets just before she's about to burst into tears. She was desperately trying to hold it in, but she couldn't.

'What's the matter?' said Kate straight away, putting an arm around her shoulder.

'It's OK,' said Emma through snotty tears. 'I'm OK.' She wasn't though. I knew her and she wasn't OK. Emma had always been so strong; through every acting disappointment and argument with her mother, but when it came to losing her baby, she'd fallen apart. 'I'm just sad you're leaving again.'

'I'm sorry, Em,' said Kate. 'You can always come and visit.'

'We'd love to,' I said, reaching across and putting my hand on Emma's leg and giving it a gentle squeeze.

'Are you going to be here for our wedding?' said Emma, sniffing up tears.

'I wouldn't miss it for the world and anyway, I'm a brides-maid remember,' said Kate. 'I'm sort of a big deal.'

We spent the next few hours drinking, talking and enjoying each other's company again. Kate told us all about life as a backpacker and Ed gave us the rundown on his new life on the dole. It was strange to think of Ed as anything but a City boy because that's all I'd ever known. He definitely seemed happier though and more relaxed. Instead of checking his phone every few minutes for texts or popping outside to take a quick phone call, he was involved in the conversation, making jokes and behaving very un-Ed-like. But it was better. He was a better version of himself and it was all because of Kate.

I think that when it comes down to it, that's what real love is. It makes us a better version of ourselves. Emma definitely made me better than I was on my own. Every part of me that didn't work, every bit that brought me down, she fixed and made better. We all have our faults, but isn't that the meaning of life? To find the one person who has all the answers to your questions and all the solutions to your problems. I think that's why losing the baby was so hard on Emma, because she finally realised what she needed to complete her. She needed a baby and for a moment she thought she had it. We both did.

As the afternoon wore on, I became more and more frantic with worry. I was sure Morris wasn't going to call or, if he did, it was going to be bad news. It had to be. Emma, Ed and Kate tried to keep my spirits raised and kept me lubricated and fed. It was almost six o'clock when my phone finally rang. It was sitting in the middle of the table surrounded by empty crisp packets and half-finished drinks. We all stopped talking and just stared at it. I'd been waiting all day, but once it came, I didn't know what to do. I was frozen.

'Pick it up!' everyone shouted in unison.

'Hello,' I mumbled.

My tongue felt very large in my mouth and I stood up, expecting the worst.

'Jack, it's Morris.'

'Right.'

Kate, Emma and Ed were all standing up too, looking at me with excited but nervous faces, crossing their fingers in a show of unity.

'It's good news, Jack. We've had a fantastic response from several of the publishers we sent the book to already. The auction started this morning and we've received a two-book deal with an advance of eighty thousand pounds, which I wholeheartedly encourage you to accept. Give me your decision on Monday. You're going to be a published author, Jack, and trust me you're going to be huge. Lots of work still to be done, but we can go over that next week. For the time being though, I'd have a few drinks if I were you.'

Morris stopped talking and it was as if the whole world stopped with him. I didn't know what to say. My whole life seemed to be squeezed into a moment. I felt like I'd won the lottery and in many ways I had. My dreams had finally come true.

'You OK, Jack?' said Morris when I hadn't said anything for thirty seconds.

'Yes, sorry, a bit lost. I don't know what to say.'

'Then don't say anything. I'll see you on Monday. Enjoy your weekend.'

'I will, bye,' I said and then he was gone.

'Well?' everyone shouted at me.

I looked around at my friends and an overwhelming feeling of happiness, elation and relief washed over me.

'They offered me a two-book deal, a huge advance, plus royalties,' I said, looking at Emma, tears suddenly awash in my eyes. 'I'm going to be a writer.'

Emma was crying, Kate was crying, Ed was patting me on the back and tears were streaming down my face. I had made it and suddenly I thought of my father. It was like I could feel him in me and I knew he was proud. I had everything I'd ever wanted.

Just at that moment, as if to make it even more profound, the Oasis classic 'Rock 'n' Roll Star' started pouring out of the speakers. I was there with my soon-to-be wife and our two best friends, huddled together in happiness singing along in the middle of the pub.

It wasn't that I was or would ever be a rock 'n' roll star, but for that glorious moment, I certainly felt like one.

## EMMA

The first time I fell in love I was eight years old. I saw the
video to a Jason Donovan song and I instantly fell in love
with him. In the video Jason was walking over a mountain,
his gorgeous blond hair blowing in the wind and he was
playing guitar and singing and suddenly I knew what I
wanted more than anything in the world. I wanted to live on
that mountain with Jason Donovan and at eight I really
thought it might come true. Of course, when it didn't pan
out, I was bitterly disappointed, but by then I'd also grown
up a bit and realised it probably wasn't a realistic target
anyway. Jason was a lot older than me and he probably
didn't really spend his time up mountains singing love
songs.

Paul was my second love and that didn't end well either. It
wasn't until I met Jack that I found love again. Jack. My
wonderful Jack, who seemed the perfect combination of
Jason Donovan and Paul: an Australian artist with devastat-
ing good looks and blond hair.

Then there was my fourth love, my latest love, and the one
that would end before it had really begun. Our baby. It might
sound a bit silly because it wasn't yet a fully formed life, but
I already loved our little baby so much. I'd known so many
different sorts of love during my life, from the celebrity crush,
the adolescent first boyfriend to Jack, my soulmate, but none
of them felt the same as being a mother. It was a different
love altogether that grew as the baby grew inside of me: a

pure, aching desire that was more biological than anything else. Then it was gone.

It was a Thursday two weeks before our wedding and I was at home with my feet curled up on the sofa, a glass of red wine hanging limply from my fingers and Kate opposite me. Jack and Ed were at the pub and so we finally had the chance for a proper girlie catch up. Since she'd got back from her trip, we hadn't had the time, but finally it was just us.

'How're you doing now?' said Kate, taking a sip of wine.

'OK, I suppose. I don't cry every minute of every day anymore, but it still makes me sad.'

'Of course, Em, you lost a baby. Anyone would be sad in your boat.'

'And I suppose that's it, isn't it? With Jason Donovan I grew up, with Paul we broke up, and I still have Jack, but with the baby it was taken from me. No warning, no time to say goodbye and it hurt. Really hurt.'

'You're allowed to grieve. Just because it wasn't born, it doesn't mean you didn't lose a baby, a whole life. It doesn't mean you didn't love it. And what about Jack? How's he dealing with it?'

'He's been so busy with the book. I know he's hurting too, but he can lose himself in work.'

'Not getting back to work yourself?'

'Not at the moment. To tell you the truth, I've sort of lost my passion for it. All I really want at the moment is to get pregnant again.'

'Have you and Jack been, you know, trying?'

I'd told Jack about my decision to try for another baby. I think he was a bit shocked at first because he'd assumed I would try and get back on the horse and start auditioning again. However, once the dust had settled, he agreed and said he couldn't wait to be a father. I think losing his dad had left a hole in his life and what better way to fix it than to become a father himself.

'It's early days,' I said with a grin and Kate yelled excitedly. 'Anyway, enough about me. I want all the juicy details from your trip. All the goss about Jez and leave nothing out.'

Kate gave me a coy smile.

'He was wonderful, Em, truly gorgeous, and he had this way about him that made me so happy. You know we met in Bangkok; he saved me at the airport when I was all alone and it grew from there. We spent ten days on Koh Phangan, and we only had one bed in our cottage by the beach.'

'Which you didn't have sex in, right?'

'It's sort of funny but because we were so close and we got on so well, it made sex seem less important. I suppose because in my head I had already cheated on Ed, I didn't need to actually do the act. Plus, I didn't want to lead Jez on. I didn't want him to like me any more than he already did.'

'And then what happened in Peru? You never said.'

'I was getting ready to go to Machu Picchu and he just turned up out of the blue. It was magic, Em, better than Thailand, actually. God, it sounds silly now sitting here with you, but it was so in the moment, you know. He told me he loved me.'

'Shit, what did you say?'

'I didn't know what to say, but I sort of knew then that we couldn't be together. I felt awful and I really liked him, but it wouldn't have worked out. He was twenty-two, just starting out, and I already had a few miles on the clock. It was fine when we were travelling, but back home I knew it wouldn't have been the same. Then there was Ed.'

'The man you still love, right?'

'I never stopped loving him, Em. It's hard to explain, but it wasn't about love, it was about something else. He'd changed and our goals were different. He wanted to stay in London, work twelve hours a day and I didn't. When I was coming back on the plane, I honestly didn't know if we'd make it or not. I'd already decided I wanted to teach abroad and I didn't think he'd come with me, but as soon as I saw him, I just knew.'

'How?'

'Because he'd changed, and not just the clothes and the haircut, but something inside of him. It was as if a great weight had been lifted off his shoulders and he was the same boy I met at university. If he'd been the same old Ed who worked sixty hours a week and acted as though we were already middle-aged, I don't think it would have worked.'

'Good job, Ed, then, I suppose.'

'It was a close call.'

A close call. Those words started me thinking. Wasn't everything in life just a close call when we really thought about it? Getting pregnant when I was sixteen. What if I'd had the baby instead of getting the abortion? What if I hadn't got pregnant and carried on with the film? Moments make us and moments break us and most of them are too close to call.

'Do you think you and Ed will be OK?'

Kate took a sip of wine and then looked at me.

'We've broken up, been apart for six months, we've both cheated and now we're back together again and heading off to Japan. How am I supposed to know if we'll make it? I think people who say they know what the future holds, that they'll be together forever, are lying to themselves. I hope we'll make it. I hope we'll be together forever and live happily ever after, but the truth is, I just don't know. Today it couldn't be any better, but tomorrow is a new day.'

'Don't you think that's a bit cynical?'

'Not cynical, just realistic. When I was travelling, I learnt so much about relationships and myself. If it wasn't for Ed, I'd probably have given Jez a go, but it was more than that. I think I realised the number of opportunities we have in life and really, despite our best intentions, anything is possible.'

'I'm sure Jack and I are going to go the distance,' I said, and we would. That much I knew. I think with our career choices, Jack and I hadn't always known what was going to happen, but with each other we had. Kate and I had been friends for so many years and shared so much in common, but perhaps our one glaring difference, our one defining mismatching quality, was she would always be searching for something, while I was happy to be settled. Jack and I would last because we didn't know any other way. Kate and Ed would probably make it too, but Kate would never allow herself the luxury of admitting it.

Just at that moment I heard the key in the lock and then Ed and Jack came stumbling and laughing into our flat. Jack was holding a bottle of champagne and immediately leaned down and gave me a kiss.

'Good news,' said Jack, beaming.

Out of the corner of my eye, I saw Ed fall down in the chair next to Kate and give her a kiss too.

'Oh God, what have you two drunken fools done?' I said.

'I just got us a house,' said Jack with a huge smile on his half-pissed face.

'What do you mean?' I said.

'You two need a bigger place and we're moving to Japan,' said Ed and it suddenly dawned on me what they'd done. 'So you can have our place while we're away.'

'Seriously?' I said.

'Seriously,' said Jack. 'What do you think? We'll have to pay their mortgage, but it will give us the space we need if we're going to, you know, try for a baby.'

I looked across at Kate, who seemed as shocked as me about all of this.

'What do you think?' I said to her.

'I think it's an absolutely perfect idea,' said Kate.

'A toast?' said Jack, holding the bottle of champagne in the air.

'Definitely.' I gave Jack a big kiss. My Jack. Jack the author and my soon-to-be husband and the love of my life, without a shadow of a doubt.

'To happy endings,' said Jack once we all had a glass of champagne in our hands.

'Happy endings,' we all said together.

## KATE

'Kate, I need you now!' came a shout from the other room. It was Emma and she sounded in a panic. So far the morning had gone smoothly enough. We'd had breakfast in the hotel restaurant, had our manicures and pedicures, my hair was finished and Emma was supposed to be getting hers done while I did my make-up.

'Coming,' I shouted back.

I walked into the bedroom expecting to find some sort of chaos. I thought there'd be tears and recriminations or, at the very least, Emma and her mum going at it. Maybe the photographer had called in sick or the caterers had double-booked. From the high-pitched tension in her voice, it must have been something awful. However, when I walked in, Emma was standing in front of me in her dress looking absolutely incredible.

'What do you think?' she said with a radiant smile.

'You look absolutely beautiful, Em.'

'Thanks,' said Emma and then we both started to cry.

Maybe it was the occasion, the fact we were both so tired from being up most of the night, that we were hung-over, or maybe we were being sentimental, but we hugged and wept for maybe five minutes.

I don't have lots of childhood memories. I'm not one of those annoying people who say they can remember breast-feeding or their first tentative steps, but one of the clearest memories I have is the day I met Emma. We were five and it was the first day of school. The playground was a scary place. A football-pitch-sized expanse of concrete completely and utterly jam-packed with kids in brand-new school uniforms. I didn't have any friends and so I stood there on the precipice of tears when suddenly there was a tap on my shoulder. I turned around and standing there was a little girl with curly blonde hair and huge green eyes.

'Will you be my friend?' she said.

'I'm Kate,' I said calmly, but inside I was jumping with joy that I wasn't alone. I had a friend.

We held hands and walked around the playground together, safe in the knowledge that whatever happened during the first day of school, it would be OK because we weren't alone. This continued and we were soon the very best of friends. We stayed that way from primary school, through middle school and when Emma's mum tried to get her to attend a private secondary school Emma refused and we went to the same comprehensive. It wasn't until university, when she'd gone to Bristol and me London, that we were finally separated, but even then we were on the phone every week. Emma and Kate. Kate and Emma. Best friends forever.

'Good luck,' I said when we finally parted.

'You too,' said Emma, sniffing up tears.

'OK that's enough,' said Emma's mum, suddenly stepping in. 'There will be time for all of that soppiness later. Emma, darling, we need to take photos and Kate dear, I think you need to get back in the bathroom and finish your make-up.'

Emma and I smiled at one another and did as we were told, but not because we were fourteen anymore and terrified of Emma's mum. We did it because we'd said our goodbyes. We would always be best friends, we would always find time for each other and maybe at some point in our lives, we'd be on the same trajectory again, but for the time being we knew we had reached the end of an era. The two little girls who'd become friends so easily were all grown up and finally ready to let go of each other's hands.

The church bells rang out through the village. It was a clear, brilliant day in the small Oxfordshire parish where Emma and Jack were going to be married. The beautiful old Norman church, with an entrance surrounded by trees that swayed gently on the faint breeze, was surrounded by close-cut grass and old lichen-covered gravestones. Everyone was already inside when we arrived in the Rolls Royce. I was in the back with Emma and her father, who was taking quick sips from the flask he kept in his jacket pocket.

'Give me a sip,' said Emma. Her father handed her the flask and she took a nip. 'Jesus Christ, Dad, what's in here, rocket fuel?'

'Just a little something I concocted in the shed,' replied her father with a wry smile. 'Mum's the word, eh.'

Emma, her dad and I got out and walked towards the church. The bells were loud and crisp as we approached the huge entrance. The vicar, a bumbling man in his late sixties, was standing at the door and gave us a pensive smile as we approached.

'Perfect timing, Emma. Ready?'

'As I'll ever be,' she said and then the vicar disappeared inside and the organ started with the opening bars of 'I Was Glad'. It was time.

Jack and Ed stood at the front of the church in their grey morning suits looking as dapper as I had ever seen them. They were smiling and there were tears in Jack's eyes. We walked down the aisle and all I could see was Ed looking at me. My Ed, whom I loved dearly and could have lost, had it not been for both of our infidelities. It was funny because most people would assume that cheating would break us up, not keep us together. The thing was though, we were stronger because of it. We had both been unfaithful, but, in a way, it had made us both realise just how much we loved each other.

I think it's easy to love someone if you aren't tested, if you don't question your happiness or step outside of your comfort zone and really think about what you want. I knew that Ed and I were more in love than ever. I also knew that life wasn't as straightforward as a wedding. It wasn't just a simple 'I do' and that was it. It required work, commitment and it needed us to keep trying every single day, because if we stopped and took it for granted, it could slip away from us. I guess what I realised as we walked slowly down the aisle, smiling faces watching us as we made our way towards our futures, was that there was no such thing as a happy ending. An ending was never happy because it was the end, and endings by their very nature are bittersweet at best. True happiness was in new beginnings, clean slates and the promise of a better future.

A few hours later the disco was in full swing. People were on the dance floor making all sorts of shapes, while Ed and I were sitting together at a table. Jack and Emma were circling the room, talking to old friends and long-lost relatives and looking happier than I'd ever seen them.

'Do you think this will be us one day?' said Ed, looking at me.

'If you play your cards right,' I said and then leaned in and gave him a kiss.

'And how will I know when I have a winning hand?'

'You won't,' I said and then I smiled. 'That's the thing about cards, Ed. It's a gamble.'

At that moment the music suddenly stopped, the room was bathed in silence and everyone looked towards the DJ. Only the DJ wasn't there. In his place was Emma, and she was holding a guitar.

'Do you know what's she doing?' Ed whispered to me.

'No idea.'

The next moment she had a microphone handed to her.

'Ladies and gentlemen, I'd like to take this opportunity to thank you all for coming. I'd also like to invite Jack over,' said Emma with a smile. Jack, who looked as baffled as everyone else, walked over and stood next to Emma. 'Some of you probably know how Jack and I met, but for those of you who don't, it happened like this. I was at a karaoke bar in Camden with some friends. I hadn't really wanted to go, but they dragged me along. I wasn't feeling the best and I didn't want to sing, but then something happened. This poor lost, drunk soul was up on stage, staring at the crowd like a rabbit in the headlights, while 'I Got You Babe' started. I took one look at the gorgeous but desperate man on stage and something inside of me just melted. I fell in love with Jack that night and haven't looked back since. So, Jack, darling, if you're up to it, I thought we could relive that night one more time,' said Emma with a smile. 'You in?'

'Do I have any choice?' said Jack, which caused the room to erupt in chants of, 'Jack! Jack, Jack!'

'Ready?' said Emma and then she started playing the guitar.

Emma started singing confidently, her beautiful voice ringing out around the room, before Jack joined in, slightly off-key, but trying his hardest. It was a wonderful sight and I'd never seen them look so happy.

As Emma and Jack continued, with Jack getting more

confident and singing slightly better, I nestled into Ed. We sat together, cuddled up, and in that moment I knew I had made the right decision. Ed looked at me and we kissed. Ed and I were going to be OK. I didn't know for sure because we can never be one hundred per cent sure about anything in life, but what I did know and what made me feel the happiest I'd ever felt, was at that moment I didn't want to be anywhere else. I didn't want to be twenty-one again. I didn't want to be in Thailand or Australia. I didn't want to be with anybody else, anywhere else, and surely that's all we can ever hope for. I think if happy endings are possible, this was the closest I'd ever get.

## ACKNOWLEDGEMENTS

As I didn't dedicate this book to her, I'd like to start by thanking my wonderful wife for literally everything. I tell her all the time, but I don't know if she really believes me. Without you I wouldn't be doing this. You make this possible, me possible and every day better than the last. I love you.

A HUGE hug and a kiss to my children, Charlotte and Jack, who are just too cute and perfect and who put up with me having to 'do some work' when they want to play a game or dance around the living room. You both inspire me so much.

The biggest thank you has to go to Harriet. Without you I wouldn't be doing any of this. You're the best editor, support and friend a writer could wish for. I have loved working with you and you've made this book infinitely better. Thank you.

Poppy, for being a brilliant publicist and a lovely girl who knows where to find fabulous cakes.

I'd also love to thank everyone else at Hodder: the designer who has done a wonderful job with the covers, the rights team who continue to get the word out there one country at a time, and all the other lovely people who have done so much. I'm sure I owe you all a drink.

To Ariella, my fabulous agent, thank you for giving me a shot. I won't let you down.

A whopping thank you to Fleur and Kath, two lovely women who read and helped me with early versions of *Happy Endings*. I hope you like the finished book.

To my usual crew of best friends and family. You know who you are. I love you all.

Lastly, a massive thank you to everyone who bought, read and reviewed *This Thirtysomething Life*. I received so many lovely emails and tweets, and it sounds a bit clichéd – though it is actually true – but if you didn't buy my book, I couldn't do this for a living. So thank you. Until next time. Cheers X

Read on for an extract of Jon Rance's hilarious, heart-warming bestselling novel,

# this
# thirty
# some
# thing
# life

This is a love story about what happens after we've fallen in love, when we've swapped frolicking in the bed for cigarettes in the shed and *Match of the Day* for Mothercare. Brutally honest and laugh-out-loud funny, this is a diary about one man's bumbling journey on the road to adulthood.

HODDER

# january

## SUNDAY, January 1st, 2.00 p.m.
New Year's Day

In the kitchen. Emily upstairs. Cloudy overhead. I think it might rain.

Less than a day into the bright sparkly new year and already I'm in the dog house with Emily. What have I done wrong? Your guess is as good as mine. All I know is that she's acting very strangely and she's definitely in a strop about something. I heard the toilet flush about fifteen minutes ago, but otherwise silence. I'm afraid to go up there.

Possible reasons why she might be mad at me:

1. I may have done something awful last night which has yet to filter back into my consciousness. Was I that drunk? Possibly. I did throw up in the front garden, use the bath as a toilet and I somehow managed to fall asleep with my trousers on backwards. All bad signs.

2. She might be annoyed I haven't cleaned out the shed yet. She's been asking me to do it for months, but based on her current stroppiness, this feels like something much worse.

3. Period? She does get very hormonal when Aunt Flo comes for her monthly visit. Must check the period calendar.

4. Could she still be mad at me vis-à-vis buying the classic Star Wars figures on eBay? Emily doesn't understand that they're a family investment. She just thinks I bought some old toys off the internet. I tried to explain that I could take them on the *Antiques Roadshow*, but she said, 'I don't care

3

about the fucking *Antiques Roadshow*, Harry. You spent five hundred quid on figurines!'

5. Some completely irrational Emily thing like the time she didn't talk to me for three days and called me a, 'useless, immature, emotionally redundant fuckwit, who wouldn't understand the meaning of romance if it kicked me in the testicles'. Admittedly, I forgot our wedding anniversary, but still, I think she went a bit over the top. Yes, she'd spent a good deal of time making that photo album, the mix CD of our favourite songs and the six-course meal, but did she need to take out that ad in the local paper and offer me in exchange for a better model? The worst part was she didn't get a single bloody reply.

**4.00 p.m.**
Emily still upstairs and presumably still pissed off. Will she ever come down? Am I brave enough to go up? It's the first day of January and already this year's looking as depressing and gloomy as a Charles Dickens novel. I feel like I'm living in an actual Bleak House.

**4.40 p.m.**
I'm going over the top. Actually, dearest diary, I'm going upstairs, but running towards a barrage of German artillery doesn't feel like a bad alternative compared to facing Emily when she has the hump. I already checked the period calendar to see if she is premenstrual (negative) and I made her a cup of tea. As Mum always says, 'Start the New Year as you mean to go on.' Based on the first twelve hours, it's going to be a difficult one.

**5.30 p.m.**
Having a cigarette by the back door. Emily upstairs getting ready. It just started to rain.

I went upstairs with my PG Tips peace offering and she was in bed reading a book. I placed the tea on her nightstand and said lovingly, 'There you go, Em, a nice cup of tea.' She didn't say anything and continued reading her book in a cheerless silence. Not wanting to take this lying down, I did. 'I'm sorry.' I didn't know what for, but best to apologise anyway. Whatever I'd done wrong, she was making it perfectly clear it was going to take a lot more than tea and apologies to get back in her good books.

Eventually, when the cold shoulder had become bloody frosty, she slammed her book shut, rolled over and fixed me with a Himalayan stare. Her deep, dark Irish eyes gave me a look that said, 'This is bloody serious, Harry, and don't even think about making one of your stupid, asinine jokes. This is major, big-picture stuff and you'd better bloody well pay attention.'

'I want to have a baby, Harry.'

'But, Em, we've already talked about this.'

Twice last year she brought up the subject and both times it ended with the same result. I'm not ready. I don't know why exactly, but I'm not ready to give up what we have. Maybe I'm being selfish, but I love our life the way it is. I love the fact that if we wanted to we could spend the weekend in Dublin, Dubrovnik or Düsseldorf. Admittedly, we haven't done much mini-breaking over the last few years, and I have no real desire to spend any amount of time in Düsseldorf, but it's nice to have the option.

Unfortunately, Emily didn't care about weekend mini-breaks. She'd had enough of her career. She used to love her job, but now it weighed her down and she was ready for a change. She was ready to start a family and be probably what she always dreamt of being, a mummy.

'Well, I want to talk about it again. I want a family. I'm ready.'

'But . . .'

'But what? Give me one good reason why we can't.'

The truth is I didn't have one good reason. I didn't have any number of reasons, good or otherwise. Is being selfish a good enough reason? Probably not. Is being afraid to grow up a decent argument for not having kids? Definitely not. What about inexplicable fear? I should probably have told her how much I loved her and explained I definitely wanted a family one day, because I do. I want to have kids, do things like the 'school run', possibly buy a people carrier and wear slippers around the house. I want all of that, but not yet. I couldn't confess any of this to Emily though and so I said the first thing that came to mind.

'Because what about our trip to Italy? We said we'd definitely do that before we had kids.'

'And we can, Harry. We can go in the next couple of months, I promise. Please just say you'll think about it. It's important.'

I took the easy way out and agreed to think about it. This led to a cuddle and a kiss. Women are so sneaky. Men are so weak. Why does starting a family scare me so much? Why when everyone around us is making babies with all the ease and excitement of the von Trapp family am I putting it off for a fantasy holiday once mentioned over a drunken Valentine's meal? I fear I might be on the verge of some sort of early mid-life crisis.

And to rub salt in an already gaping wound, we're having dinner tonight at Steve and Fiona's in Worcester Park. Not only do they have three kids, but also the audacity (or stupidity) to give them all names beginning with the letter J (Jane, Joseph and James). How mental is that?

## MONDAY, January 2nd, 9.00 a.m.
Bank holiday

On the sofa. Eating a bacon sandwich. Emily still asleep. Cloudy.

What a truly awful night. Steve and Fiona are expecting another baby. A fourth J to add to their jumble of Js. When are they going to stop? They told us over the guacamole dip. There must be something in the water (or perhaps the guacamole dip) in Worcester Park.

We have known Steve and Fiona since university and they used to be our regular going out partners. They used to be normal until about seven years ago when they announced they were pregnant. At first it wasn't too bad, I was even mildly happy for them, but gradually, as they added to their collection of Js, rumblings of change began to sweep across our relationship. Steve and Fiona couldn't go out anymore so we always had to go to their house for dinner, which would usually end before eight o'clock with both Steve and Fiona asleep on the sofa. Twice we threw a blanket over them and sneaked out. They also (very quickly it seemed to me) became walking clichés of exactly the type of people who have kids. They went from a snazzy four-door Audi to a boxy people carrier. They both gained enough weight that they were only physically attractive to each other. They started dressing as though clothes were merely canvasses for their children's vomit and the last time we went to their house for dinner, Steve said to me (and I'm not making this up), 'Daddy has to go pee pee on the potty wotty!' It was the last straw. Baby talk had crossed the line.

Of course, their announcement led to the inevitable questions about when we were going to start trying for a baby.

7

Cue glares of disappointment and despondency from Emily. I was prepared for this, but what followed completely threw me. Steve and I popped out to the garden for a cigarette. Actually, I popped out for a cigarette while Steve came to remember what it was like to smoke (Fiona made him quit when they had their first J). I was finally relieved to get some peace and quiet when Steve said, while inhaling my second-hand smoke:

'So, Harry old boy, what's the problemo?'

'Excuse me?'

'Why don't you want to have kids? Kids are brilliant!'

They had pulled Steve in too. It was a bloody conspiracy. He was one of them. A woman in man's clothing!

'I'm not ready yet, that's all.'

'I wasn't either, but now I'm having number four and I couldn't be any happier. They change your life, they really do.'

'So does going bald and I'm not ready for that either!' I exclaimed and went back indoors.

The rest of the night was a complete and utter disaster. Hint upon bloody hint about having kids. At every opportunity they would pass me one of their Js to play with in the hope I'd suddenly see the error of my ways and proclaim, 'I'm ready to have a family!'

Why does every parent in the world think you can't be happy until you have kids? I don't ring them up at eleven o'clock every Sunday morning when I've had a glorious lie-in to gloat. I don't text them every time I'm at the pub having a few pints, while they're at home changing nappies and I don't brag about how much sex we have, knowing they probably haven't done it for months. Parents are like the bloody Jehovah's Witnesses of your thirties: hounding you to succumb to the almighty power of parenthood. Back. The. Fuck. Off!

**10.30 a.m.**
New neighbours next door. I had a quick peek out of the window when they were moving in and it's a terrible thing to even think, I know, but they had the whiff of terrorists about them. Mrs Crawley from number four (head of the neighbourhood watch committee) was immediately outside in her front garden having a good old nose. No doubt she'll call an emergency meeting. Unfortunately, I'm on the committee.

Off to Canary Wharf to meet best mate Ben for lunch. Hopefully this will cheer me up.

**3.00 p.m.**
In the kitchen. Watching a squirrel run around the garden. Feeling a wee bit tipsy after lunch with Ben. (Why do I always start using Scottish vernacular when I'm drunk?)

It was great to spend an hour with someone who didn't only want to talk about the power of procreation. We talked about football, the good old days and his latest adventure to Peru. We smoked, drank and I had a very nice lunch before Ben had to get back to work. Although, before he headed off, I told him about the baby conversation I'd had with Emily and he said, 'It's perfectly natural, mate. You've been married for what, six years now? She's in her thirties. It was bound to happen eventually. If you're not ready to be a father, you need to figure out why and soon because, trust me, when it comes to babies, women get very impatient. Bloke at work, Rupert Strang, only been married for five minutes and he just got divorced. His wife wanted a baby and he didn't. Admittedly, the devil was also screwing his assistant, but still, you get my point.'

I did.

I'm watching a squirrel run around the garden and I'm

wondering if I'm being a bit unreasonable. Maybe Ben's right. It is a natural progression and we aren't getting any younger. Should I give Emily a child whether I'm ready or not? Will I ever be ready? Sometimes I think it would be easier to be a squirrel because all he has to worry about is his nuts. Perhaps we aren't that dissimilar after all.

## TUESDAY, January 3rd, 10.00 a.m.

In the study. Listening to The Beatles. Emily at work. Blustery showers on their way from the north (according to the BBC weatherman).

Last night when Emily got home from work, I made her a sumptuous dinner of citrus-seared tuna with crispy noodles, herbs and chilli (thanks Jamie Oliver). She seemed impressed. I opened a bottle of Italian red and attempted to have a proper conversation about starting a family. I was open, honest and everything she claims I'm not. I told her about my lunch with Ben and watching the squirrel, which to be honest, seemed to confuse her, but she listened intently and when I'd finished she said very calmly, 'Harry, don't freak out, but I'm pregnant!'

'What? I . . . err . . . don't understand, Em . . . how?'

'About three weeks ago. We both had our work Christmas parties.'

'Not ringing any bells.'

'I came home drunk. You were eating a lamb kebab.'

'Oh, right, yeah, the lamb shish . . .'

'That's what jogged your memory? Anyway, I forgot to take my pill that morning and we were a little lax with the condom.'

'Shit.'

'I took the pregnancy test on Saturday and it was positive.'

'Are you sure though because pregnancy tests are notoriously hard to read? Blue lines, pink lines, single lines, double lines, who can really tell?'

'It said pregnant, in words.'

'Oh.'

'I'm definitely pregnant, Harry. You're going to be a father.'

There is nothing in the world that can really prepare you for those words. You're going to be a father. You, Harry Spencer, aged thirty-two, will soon be responsible for a little baby being. My whole life flashed before my eyes and I even surprised myself because no sooner had the words left her mouth than I started to cry. I wasn't expecting that and I don't think Emily was either. The tricky part though is I'm not entirely sure what sort of tears they were. It's hard to categorise because I was certainly happy, but I was also scared, terrified and my mouth suddenly got very dry. However, after the initial shock had slowly downgraded to just surprise, I had a question.

'But if you were pregnant all along, why were you asking me if I wanted to be a dad? Why the whole guilty baby parade at Steve and Fiona's? Why didn't you tell me straight away? I'm confused, Em.' For the record I still am.

'Because I knew it would be a big deal and I thought if maybe I could get you used to the idea first . . . I'm sorry, Harry, but you know what you're like.' (Yes, brilliant.) 'Are you happy about this?'

She had asked the question. It had to be asked I suppose and to be honest, I was. I didn't think I'd be quite so delirious about it, but the reality was very different than the nightmare in my head. Maybe I was ready to be a father after all. I looked at her and smiled.

'Of course I'm happy about it, Em. We're having a baby.'

We kissed, hugged, she cried, I stopped, until gradually the horror of the situation slipped into my mind. I'm going to be a father forever. What if I fuck it up? What if I'm an awful dad? What if I don't love them as much as I'm supposed to? What if . . . I could go on, but while Emily was snuggled firmly into my neck, her tears of joy trickling slowly down my shirt, I couldn't let go of the fear. It took me three attempts to pass my driving test and I studied hard for that, but this didn't come with a learner's manual and I only had one chance to get it right.

'Are you going to be ready?' Emily said or something along those lines because I'd slipped into a man-coma. Emily was talking (her lips were moving anyway), but I was locked inside my own little world, until she suddenly brought me back with a click of her fingers.

'Harry, are you listening to me?'

'Sorry, I was thinking.'

'I know this is a lot to digest, but it's not the time to have a mid-life crisis.'

'Who's having a mid-life crisis? I'm not having a mid-life crisis.'

'Because the last thing I need at the moment is you losing touch with reality. You're going to be ready aren't you, Harry?'

Am I going to be ready? Obviously not. Am I having a premature mid-life crisis? Quite possibly. I didn't know what to say. Unfortunately, while I was thinking about it, I slipped into another man-coma and before I knew what was happening, Emily was clicking her fingers again.

'Harry, Harry . . .'

'Yes, sorry?'

'I said I'm going to need you for this. I can't do this on my own.'

'I know and I'm going to be here for you every step of the way.'

'Promise?'

'Promise.'

**1.00 p.m.**

Still awaiting the blustery showers from the north. Eating a packet of prawn cocktail crisps. Squirrel outside taunting me with his carefree happiness. Pain in my side.

In an attempt to delay the onset of middle-aged spread and prepare myself physically for the rigours of fatherhood, I attempted to do some sit-ups and almost fainted. I've had a sharp pain in my side ever since. I looked up the pain in my side and it could be anything from a stitch, kidney tumour, shingles, to an impending heart attack! Fantastic. I tried working out and it could lead to an early death.

I also made a list of pros and cons about having a baby:

PROS

1. Babies are cute and generally considered to be a good thing.
2. It will make my mother the happiest mother in the whole world.
3. It will make Emily the happiest wife in the whole world.
4. It might even make me happy.
5. We will have someone to take care of us when we're old and miserable.
6. I will have someone to mould in my own image.
7. It might be fun.
8. I'm not getting any younger.

CONS

1. They're expensive.
2. Changing nappies.

3. Lack of sleep.
4. It would severely hamper our freedom.
5. No more weekend lie-ins.
6. What if it destroys our sex life?
7. What if it destroys our marriage?
8. I don't feel anywhere near ready.
9. I'm too young.
10. At the moment we have a good life. We have two steady jobs and a nice house in a good part of London. Am I ready to put all of that in jeopardy for a baby?
11. Lastly (and most importantly I think) every couple we know with kids are the most boring people on the face of the planet. All they ever want to talk about is their bloody kids, e.g. 'Last week Angus did his first banana-shaped poo, it was too adorable.' Am I ready to become that dull? Am I ready to openly discuss poo with my nearest and dearest?

The cons won 11–8. Not a good sign. Bugger.

**9.00 p.m.**
Emily in bed. Still no sign of the mysterious blustery showers from the north. Having a last cigarette of the day by the back door. Side throbbing.

Strange banging noises coming from next door. Maybe they're making a bomb! What should you do when you think your new neighbours might be potential terrorists? I'm tempted to do nothing, but what if they are terrorists and they blow up the Houses of Parliament? I'll always be the bloke who could have stopped them, but didn't. My ugly mug will be on the front pages of every newspaper in the country: 'HISTORY TEACHER IN BOMB PLOT BUNGLE!' I can already see the disappointment on my parents' faces.

Do you wish this wasn't the end?

Join us at www.hodder.co.uk, or follow us on
Twitter @hodderbooks to be a part of our community
of people who love the very best in books and reading.

Whether you want to discover more about a book
or an author, watch trailers and interviews, have the
chance to win early limited editions, or simply browse
our expert readers' selection of the very best books,
we think you'll find what you're looking for.

And if you don't,
that's the place to tell us what's missing.

We love what we do, and we'd love you to be part of it.

www.hodder.co.uk

 @hodderbooks

 HodderBooks

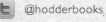 HodderBooks